TRUE
LOVE
AND OTHER
IMPOSSIBLE
ODDS

CHRISTINA LI

True Love

AND OTHER

IMPOSSIBLE

ODDS

Quill Tree Books
An Imprint of HarperCollinsPublishers

To all forms of love

ONE

"YOU'RE SUPPOSED TO just *take* personality quizzes," my roommate Ava says from across the room. "Not take them apart from the inside out."

I look up from where I'm sitting on my bed, tucked under a blanket. The uQuiz link that Ava sent in our roommate group chat is pulled up on my computer. "How does picking your favorite color tell you what city you're supposed to live in?"

"It just works," Ava says. She's sprawled on the blue beanbag that takes up half our college dorm room. "You don't question it. You trust the process. I took the quiz and it told me I was going to be living in New York. It pretty much manifested my future."

"Oh, wait!" my roommate Ruhi says from her desk, looking up from annotating her reading. "That's what I got, too."

"Really? It's decided," Ava says, in a bright voice. "We'll be living in New York after college. I'll be a Broadway actress working three odd jobs on the side, and you'll be a high-powered journalist working for the *New York Times*."

Ruhi laughs. "Ava, we don't even know what we're eating for dinner tonight."

"Mark it on that color-coded calendar of yours," Ava says. "We'll make it happen."

Ruhi glances over. "Please tell us you're joining us in New York."

I click through to the quiz. "Ah. Nope. This gave me Seattle."

"Aw," Ava says. "The quiz separated us. I no longer believe in it."

"But how *does* it decide?" I click back to look at my options. "It literally asked for my favorite color and Hozier quote. I mean, is there an algorithm? How are the questions weighted?" I scroll up. "Or this one. 'Tell us your breakfast order and we'll pair you up with your ideal Disney prince soul mate.'"

Ava emerges from the beanbag. "I have to take this." She reaches for her computer and searches for the quiz. I lean over and watch her click through the options. *Eggs Benedict. Orange juice.*

"Oooh, Flynn Rider," Ava says. "I'll take it. Anything's better than my current prospects."

Ruhi closes her textbook. "The apps not doing it for you?"

"Ugh," Ava says, sinking back into the beanbag. "Don't remind me of the cursed Leighton dating scene."

I look up. "You went on a date?"

"*Did* I." She shrugs out of her fluffy white cardigan and puts her curly shoulder-length red hair in a bun. Her energy constantly reminds me of Hana. My heart cinches at that thought. "It was last Saturday when you were home. We met at Coffee House. His messages were, I don't know, decent? But then he shows up, like, twenty minutes late, and he tells me about how his congressman dad sucks and how he wants to pursue indie filmmaking. Then his friends come through and his voice goes five pitches lower and he basically ignores me the rest of the time."

I grimace.

"Next date that goes south," Ruhi says. "Text us and we'll crash it. I'll prep a contingency plan."

"There won't be another date." Ava clutches her palms emphatically over her chest as if she's making some kind of fervent vow. "I'm swearing off dates forever. I'm just dating myself at this point. Me, a mug of shitty Barefoot wine, some microwavable mozzarella sticks, and *Love, Rosie* on Friday nights."

"*Love, Rosie?*" Ruhi says firmly, with her authoritative, high school debate champion voice. She crosses the room in long strides and takes Ava's hands in hers. "That's masochism, and we refuse to let it happen. At least let us watch it together."

"It's just—" Ava sighs. "I thought it would be easier? People always tell us that college is the best time to date someone because you're surrounded by so many people your age. Yet I can't find anyone to even cuddle and watch Halloween movies with. I wish it was as easy as taking a quiz." She glances over at me. "Anyway. What did you get?"

3

I click through the last question. "Huh. Hercules."

"A god," Ava says in admiration. "Powerful."

I look up. "What about you, Ruhi?"

She taps through on her phone. "*Ooooh*. Li Shang."

"Ruhi wins," Ava says. "Arjun's got competition."

Ruhi suppresses a small smile that comes up every time we mention her boyfriend. She tucks her long dark hair behind her ears. "Oh, no competition. I would take Li Shang any day. Arjun would understand."

I glance at all three of our screens, scrutinizing the options. Ava and I had both picked pancakes but differed on the beverages. Ruhi had opted for a simpler breakfast of fruit and a bagel. There's a pattern here. I just have to crack it.

Aha.

"We'll be your Halloween dates," Ruhi says to Ava. "Us and our imaginary Disney princes. You can pick the movie."

"This sounds amazing," Ava says. "This weekend?"

Ruhi looks over. "Stay the weekend for once? We'll have movie night, and we might even take a trip to the pumpkin patch."

My roommate looks so hopeful. I smile and shake my head, swallowing a knot in my throat. "I've got to go home. You two have fun, though."

After weeks of practice, it isn't that hard to say anymore. Even if the pumpkin patch does sound lovely.

"Oh." Ruhi's shoulders sink, but she doesn't seem surprised. "Well, we'll miss you."

"I'll be back Sunday." I check my phone. "Shit. I have to go to class. I'm late." I grab my coat and pause at the doorway. "I think it's a simple tally."

My roommates look up.

"Each option corresponds to a different result," I say. "And then at the end you simply tally up whichever result got picked the most." I point at my screen. "Bacon goes with Hercules. Orange juice, Flynn Rider."

"And *voilà*," Ava says, spreading her palms out. "Soul mates."

"If only it were that easy." I pull on my boots and run out the door.

The seats of my lecture are surprisingly full when I slip in five minutes late. It's close to midterms, and students are actually showing up to class instead of just scrolling through the lesson slides and frantically cramming their textbook while hungover in bed. I've shown up to every class.

I'd worked to get in. Game Theory and Market Design is an upper-level mathematics elective class with intro-class prerequisites. Freshmen like me aren't supposed to take it, but I'd wanted to graduate in three years and, through an appeal and the careful coaxing of the registrar's office, I'd gotten it. I'd heard good things about the professor, too. Professor Rand is the mathematics department head, and he's been teaching at Leighton for the past twenty-one years. Word is that a recommendation from him could all but guarantee a coveted summer math research position with a professor in the department. Which is what I want.

It's interesting. We've talked about all sorts of strategy games: about zero-sum games that give one person what they want at the expense of the other person's total loss, or about probability and payout. We talk about psychology and political negotiations. The professor's animated and gestures wildly with his hands. He teaches old-school, too, which means he covers the blackboard with nearly unreadable chalky text and half the work is to decipher it for our notes. On the board today is scrawled *Market Design and Matching Algorithms*.

"We have cooperative and noncooperative games." Professor Rand runs his fingers through his wispy blond hair and crosses his arms. The shoulder pads of his suit jacket peak up. "Games that can be achieved by forming coalitions, and games that can be achieved by simple strategy alone. Like we'd mentioned last time, mathematicians and economists always thought that those two things were separate. But as it turns out, they came together to form the basis of market design." He pauses. "And markets form the basis of a lot of the matching systems out there."

My phone lights up with a notification. Hana's posted a photo. Without thinking, I click on the notification. It's a picture of Hana sitting on the beach, huddled close with two friends, their cheeks glowing from the golden light. She has her same goofy upturned smile, her hoodie pulled tight around her face.

I click out of it quickly and push my phone away.

"Markets are all around us," Professor Rand continues once he reaches the end of the lecture slides. "Even systems that we think aren't markets are, in fact, just a system of supply and demand. What are some examples that you found in the reading?"

People look around at each other, clearly not having done said reading. I have, but I rarely talk in class, to the point where I'm slightly worried about my participation grade. Someone in the front row thankfully raises their hand. "Matching doctors to residencies?"

"Yes, exactly," Professor Rand says. "What else?"

There is a prolonged silence. I swallow and speak up. "By matching organ donors to receptors?"

"Precisely." Professor Rand nods at me. "These are systems that can be complex but, with the correct bipartite matching algorithm, can save lives and place people with their perfect matches. Can I hear some other potential uses for a matching algorithm?"

The class is quiet. There's the crinkle of a granola bar wrapper under a table.

Professor Rand crosses his arms. "What about marriages?"

Someone in the class snickers.

"It's not that ridiculous, actually," he says. "There was a study in the 1960s that applied the stability of matching to marriages. Within a group of men and women each person ranked their preferences for their ideal match. It was said that between couples, the matches would reach a stable state if no one had anything to gain by altering the matching. For example, someone might not get their first preference because their first preference has someone else they'd more prefer. But eventually, the matches achieve a stable equilibrium, and everyone is happy." He straightens up and almost seems to look right at me. "This is hypothetical, of course. People don't get married through an econ experiment. But it's quite a straightforward example of what a stable-state matching system can look like."

I think of the soul mate quiz my roommates and I were taking earlier. And now there's a marriage matching algorithm. Today seems to have a theme.

Professor Rand sets down the nub of chalk and straightens up. "All right. Take-home midterm is in two weeks, and I hope you and your project groups all start thinking about your final projects this semester on a proposed original application of a game theory or market design concept to a real-life scenario. They're not due for a while, but I want to know what you're working on by the next two weeks or so, so get brainstorming. If anyone has any questions, my office hours are on Wednesday mornings at ten or by appointment." He collects his lecture notes and shrugs on his coat and scarf. "Enjoy your weekend, everyone."

I look around for the two seniors in the class who are supposed to be my project group mates, but one is rushing out the door and the other is long gone. I sigh and quickly send them a Google Calendar invite for this weekend. I double-check my schedule to make sure that I still have the time right with my next meeting. I pull up a picture of the campus map, even though it's October and I basically know my way around at this point. Campus consists of essentially five buildings and a scattering of dorms. One more thing today, and then I'm on my way home.

As I walk past the admin office to the campus library, double-triple-checking my application on my phone, tires screech around me, and I jump, narrowly missing a sideways bike collision.

The cyclist pushes his unruly hair out of his eyes as he leaps off. He's wearing leg warmers and a thick jacket over shorts. I realize, surprisingly, that I recognize him as someone who's in my math class—Set Theory, maybe?—but I can't place a name. "Sorry," he says, breathlessly, barely meeting my eyes. "Didn't see you there. Are you good?"

"Oh, um." I straighten up. "Yeah, I'm okay."

"I really should have stopped sooner." He pauses, glancing down. "Here, after you."

I cross the street, and when I look back, he's gone. I turn back toward the library, a tall Gothic structure with a gray brick facade. It's kind of old-school and beautiful, actually. I enter the front doors and approach the reference desk. There's a text from Ava in my chat with her and Ruhi. Safe trip home! We'll miss you this weekend.

The same text she sends every weekend.

I put my phone away as someone across the atrium says, "Grace Tang?"

I sit in a stuffy back room behind the reference desk. Carts of old books surround us. The librarian who's interviewing me is this small elderly white woman with short gray hair and a beige

9

cardigan. *Roberta*, her name tag says. She peers down through her square purple glasses. "So, dear. Your previous working experience is . . . at a local recreation center. Is that right?"

"Yes," I say. "I worked for a year." I put on a hopeful smile. I don't even know if I qualify to work in a library, seeing as the last book I really read was during senior year of high school. In truth, I'd wanted to get some kind of a research position, but then I realized that no one really took on first-semester freshmen for that. Then an email for a part-time student job at the library emerged from the chaos of the dorm email list.

"Got it," she says, putting down my résumé. She purses her lips, with a look that I can't decipher. "Hold on a second, let me just respond to this email real quick." She types slowly, with her index finger. I glance up at the ceiling tiles. The heater rattles with drafts of recycled air.

Roberta looks over at me, and then at the résumé. "You're good with Tuesday and Thursday afternoons? One to six?"

I nod in relief. I'd gotten it.

She offers me a smile. "Well, I'll have you start next week, then. Training shouldn't take long. I can explain the cataloging system and get you squared away. The other student employees learned in no time."

"Perfect. Thank you so much, Roberta."

I get up. She hands me my résumé. "You're from Woodward High?"

I nod. "Yeah. I'm local."

"Must be nice for the parents," Roberta says.

The résumé wrinkles in my hands. My voice only snags a bit as I answer. "Yeah. It is."

"You have a good weekend, Grace." She gives me a sweet smile.

"You, too." I head back out into the library atrium. I pull my car keys out of my backpack, and then my phone. I text my dad, switching to the Mandarin keyboard.

快回到家了。

Home soon. On my way.

I zip my coat up and head out into the gathering cold.

TWO

DRIVING HOME FROM campus has become second nature. I venture out past the main quad with the tall, arched buildings. I pass the wrought-iron gate that they paraded us through the week of orientation, pointing out the pine insignia to each of us, the letters inscribed *Leighton College*. "Just wait until tulips come in the spring," I hear the tour guides say all the time. That's what this small liberal arts school tucked away in northern Vermont is known for. Tulip season, and also apparently its renowned English and creative writing program. A group of famous alum graduated in the '80s in what Ruhi once mentioned as "Leighton's shroomy artistic renaissance" and went in circles collecting book awards and cultivating generational indie movie fame.

When I first went through those gates during orientation, we were surrounded by thick, humid greenery that has since slowly receded into dappled gold and red. At last now, I turn onto the main road, which turns into a four-lane road, which merges onto the highway that takes me home. I switch on my headlights.

The radio plays some old James Bay song. It's strange to listen to music in this car that used to be my mom's. Ma always preferred silence because she said that distractions would lead to car accidents. On a second thought, I reach over and wind the knob down.

By now, I've gone home enough times that I know this drive will take, on average, twenty-nine minutes. I have memorized the exit numbers on the highway and the location of the shin-deep pothole, about a third of the way home. As I pass the foliage that lines the road, burnt orange folding into rust, I wonder if I can still name all the trees I used to with my dad. We'd made it a game on road trips. Eastern white pine. Norway spruce. Green ash. The Mandarin names surface with the English ones. 松树。I'd memorized them in my head in a list, looking for the leaves that I could discern as we passed by in a blur. "You're better at this than my graduate students," he'd tell me when I was little. My mom would sigh and ask why he chose to come all the way to this country for his geobiology PhD when trees and soil were everywhere. I pass some more forestry and try to scrounge up the Mandarin names, until I give up and take my exit.

As I drive, I feel myself morphing back into my high school self. I sit straighter. I spot a marker-made homecoming banner flapping on the corner of the town hall. Hana and I used to drive around that corner all the time coming home from school. Not that Hana and I went to homecoming, anyway. We bought pints of ice cream from the local grocery store and went to her house and watched movies while we speculated on which kids would host the after-parties and which of those kids would get busted. Homecoming seems like both yesterday and lifetimes ago. I pass the church that my mother used to go to, and I am fully home.

I pull up to my driveway. I sling my backpack over my shoulder and text Ba with my free hand. Before I even knock, the door opens.

"Xiǎoyàn," he says, his nickname for me. 小燕。 Little swallow, like the bird. My full name is 唐燕。 "Did you drive safe?"

"当然了," I say. *Of course.*

"Remember to come to a full stop at those stop signs."

And suddenly I am sixteen again, practicing driving with my father clenching the handle of the passenger side. "Yes, Ba," I said. "I know."

He nods and adjusts his thin-framed professor glasses and smooths his graying hair. "I made dinner. Beef noodles."

I follow him to the table, where there are full bowls of beef noodle soup and a bowl of cucumber slices soaked in sugar and vinegar and a bit of sesame oil, one of my favorite snacks from when I was a kid. Those were Ba's specialty. The noodles were Ma's. I take a tentative sip. The beef soup is tepid, the spices overwhelming to the point where I almost cough. I eat a piece of cucumber, hearing the crisp crunch, the sweetness biting into

14

the acid tang of the vinegar. "It's good."

His eyes light up. We sit at the table in silence. After a week of overhearing FIFA screaming matches through the wall at three in the morning from the frat-like boys next door and listening to Ava's spot-on celebrity impressions and Ruhi's late-night phone calls to her older sister, the lack of background noise is unnerving. A fine layer of dust settles on our words. I fiddle with my chopsticks.

He leans forward and clears his throat. "How is school?"

I crunch into my bite of cucumber. "Good," I say. "Finally got a job."

Ba raises an eyebrow. "Someone let you do research?"

I shake my head. The sugar sours into vinegar on my tongue. "I got a job at the library."

"Okay." He pauses. "How are classes?"

"Set Theory's okay. I'm working on some homework tonight. And studying for a Game Theory take-home midterm."

"This is the professor that can get you a summer research position, right?"

"Yep. Or recommend me for one, at least."

He doesn't press further. My dad was never the one who read up on my courses' syllabi or the one who drove me to my math competitions. He just nods. "Good," he says. "乖。That's what I like to hear. She'd be proud of you. That's why I want you home on the weekends. So you can eat nutritious meals and get a good night's sleep. Not party like those wild college students."

I could almost hear my mother through those words. *Get*

15

enough sleep. Don't be sneaking out or talking to people late at night like those other kids from your school do. Otherwise you're going to get wrinkles and get into trouble. Do you want that?

I glance down at the watery broth. "Yeah, of course."

Let him think he's taking care of me.

We retreat back into silence, punctuated by a few slurps. He reaches over and picks up the TV remote. I relax my shoulders. There is a Chinese rom-com playing. As the characters run in slow motion through the rain to dramatic music, I quietly finish my bowl of noodles.

After dinner, he migrates to the couch. I sit on the other end and pull up the assignments on my computer. I work on the first problem. Ba laughs at something funny the actors are saying to each other.

When the credits roll on the episode, I look up. "Ba?"

He tilts his chin absentmindedly toward me.

"How are you feeling these days?"

He doesn't meet my eyes. "Don't worry about me."

"Are you getting out of the house? Taking walks?"

My dad doesn't answer. And suddenly I'm watching my dad watch television but neither of us are paying attention to the screen. I pick my words carefully. "Have you been thinking about seeing someone? To talk to yet?"

He turns toward me. "Xiǎoyàn."

I stop.

"I know some people from the university. I'm filling my time just fine." He nods to the corner of the living room, where a digital piano appeared three weeks ago, something Ba rescued from one of his colleagues who was giving it away, along with a pile of weathered piano books. I hear him practicing it sometimes, very slowly. But the piano isn't a person to talk to. Playing it is, in fact, the most solitary thing someone can do.

"Besides," he says, "I should be taking care of you."

I turn back to my homework. Under the lamplight, I stare at the question and try to visualize how the rotational symmetries would unfold. I lean back with a sigh. I text the math group chat that formed at the beginning of the year, where we helped each other brainstorm answers. I then realize that I'm probably exposing myself as a loser because, really, who would be working on a Set Theory problem set on a Friday night?

I don't realize how much time has passed until I hear soft snoring on the couch. My father's chin tips forward, his head nodding into his chest, his hands folded together. I go into his bedroom. I take a blanket from the edge of the bed. I carry the blanket to the living room and carefully drape it over him, trying not to wake him. His snores rumble through his chest. I grab the remote and turn the volume down.

I look around. I stack the bills carefully on the counter. There's another stack of his own college students' problem sets to grade. A red pen lies on top, uncapped. I cap it and go to my own room. Just then, my phone buzzes. A text from Ruhi appears, with a mirror picture of her and Ava. Ruhi's dressed in a tight leather jacket that her wavy black hair crests over, with perfect gold-tinted eye shadow that brings out her dark eyes.

Ava's wearing a cropped crochet sweater top, baggy jeans, and heeled boots, which marginally reduces the height difference between them both. I text back with three heart emojis. My loves 😊 So cute.

I turn my phone facedown. I'll be asleep when the drunk *I love you* texts will pour in, the *fuck we impulse bought a dozen doughnuts* messages. The pang in my chest never eases up when I see those texts. It's not that I miss parties that much—I'd gone to one at the beginning of the year and had beer sloshed onto my chest and practically had to catch someone falling from a table. But I miss my roommates. I miss hearing their voices overlap over one another. I immediately feel guilty for that thought. I want to be here. Ba wants me to be here.

I wonder what Hana's doing this weekend.

In another world, I might be out there with her. Or I'm a state away at MIT. In that other world my mother is here instead of me. I turn back to my homework and mute my texts.

I always leave Sunday mornings. We bundle up and go on a walk after breakfast down the road and through the nearby park. The sunlight cuts through the red-gold trees and touches the tops of our heads. Church bells ring. Our shoes crunch over the leaves.

My father points at one of the trees. "Eastern white pine," I say automatically. Trees that grow through the winter. He nods and folds his hands back in his pockets.

After lunch, I pack up my backpack.

"Come back next weekend?" he asks.

"Of course." He nods in relief. "Don't worry, Ba."

And then I'm back in my car. My phone buzzes, and I see that someone has finally responded to my inane Friday-night homework question.

Jamie Anton: Check out page 35 of the Monday notes, it's all there.

I lean back. I peek closer at his profile picture and realize that this was the guy that almost ran me over with a bike on Friday. And yet now he's saving my ass. I type, thanks, I appreciate it.

I turn the radio on and turn onto the road. I pass the homecoming banner again. At the light, I impulsively take a left and head for the town center. I pull up to the small ice-cream shop on the corner, and I head in. I walk up to the register. I used to get iced lemonades in the summer here with Hana. The kid up front looks no older than a sophomore. His hat's too big on him. "Fifteen percent homecoming weekend discount for students," he says, hand outstretched for a school ID.

I shake my head and smile. "Just graduated. I want a cookie dough single cone, please."

He scoops up a hefty ball and lopsidedly lands it on the cone. I eat every single bite in my car until there is nothing but the tip of the cone with the melted ice cream inside. I tilt it back, feeling the cone crunch between my teeth. And then I turn the car back onto the road. Two lanes become four, and the road merges into the highway. My shoulders relax, my stomach contracting around my cold ice cream. High School Grace once again morphs back into College Grace. I take the exit and drive back toward the place where I can pretend like I'm not coming from a home that doesn't really feel like home anymore. Where I can pretend like I could be the person I was before I lost my mother and fucked up the one friendship I cared about.

The thing is, I actually didn't mean to come home that first weekend of college. It was still summer and humid and sticky. I'd woken up to the sunlight drifting through the windows. My randomly assigned roommates were asleep in their beds. Ruhi had pulled her blankets tight around her, her hair falling out of its bun. Ava had kicked off all her blankets and hugged all her pillows to her. Our three fans whirred valiantly to little use. We still worried about how loud we could play our music and how to take up space around each other in this one-room triple. We'd just spent our first Saturday night together going to a party, and I'd woken up feeling hollow and smelling like beer. I'd thought about texting Hana. I thought about asking her how California was. I thought about calling her to tell her sorry for not responding to her texts. I thought about telling her how much I missed her.

But I didn't do any of that.

I pulled my phone to me. It was 10:07. I had been away from home for a week, and it was Sunday again. The church

20

bells would be ringing near my house. And in that space of a moment, I missed her so much I curled up with a sharp, specific ache.

And Ba—

He was home alone. He'd been home alone for a week.

Before I knew it, I grabbed my car keys. I shrugged on my backpack and walked past the beanbag and out into the hallway. Too late, I remembered that Ava had drunkenly suggested brunch this morning. *I'll go with them next week.*

This was back when I hadn't applied and gotten a campus parking permit yet, back when my car was parked at the outskirts of the student apartments off campus. It took a twenty-minute walk. I started the car and blasted the AC. I had texted Ba, coming home.

I plugged my address into my phone GPS. I drove onto roads that I would eventually know by heart, and then merged onto the highway.

There were still vestiges of summer, in the part of August when things seem still and unmoving. But I knew it would only be weeks before the leaves became golden. The air would cool by the next two weeks, and then sharply drop. This all I knew.

Soon I saw the sign for my town, and it was as if I'd never left. I drove past the town square with its post office and its sandwich place that Hana and I always went to for lunch. I drove past the rec center, where I used to work. The ice-cream shop that had been around for decades. Past the church.

And then I pulled into my driveway.

Ba opened the door before I could. He stared at me. "Xiǎoyàn," he said, alarmed. Fine wrinkles traced down and sank around his cheekbones. "Did something happen?"

I shook my head. "I just—" I paused. "I wanted to come home for lunch. Is that okay?"

He relaxed. "Oh." He brightened. "Of course. Here, let me make you food."

He heated up soupy somen noodles on the stove and chopped up mushrooms and cucumbers. I sat at the table, sweat crawling down my neck.

"You seem thinner," Ba said. "Are they feeding you enough in those dining halls?"

"Yeah," I said. "I'm eating okay."

He looked doubtful. I drank the soup and looked around. The papers were stacked high. It felt familiar to be back home. College still felt a little too overwhelming and strange.

"How are your classes?"

"Good," I said. "Set Theory and Linear Algebra are okay. And Game Theory is going well, too."

Ba nodded. "And how are your roommates?"

I relaxed, and for the first time, there was a small warmth in me. "They're really nice."

Ba nodded. "What about a job?"

"Looking for one," I said. I'd reached out to professors with the hope of doing paid research. Maybe some data analysis. I could even clean datasets. None of them were responding to me.

"What else have you been doing?"

22

I told him orientation stories. I told him about the big mascot bear that showed us around campus and chased everyone. I told him about the activities fair and how people would unicycle around campus. When the stories ran out, we ate in silence.

I sat around the house. I organized the papers and bills until the light was golden and it was late afternoon. I got up to leave.

And as I headed out the door, Ba leaned out. "Are you coming back next weekend?"

I looked up.

"The school isn't feeding you enough. I can cook you nutritious things at home."

His eyes were hopeful.

How could I not?

I nodded. "Okay, yeah. I'll be back."

And so it was. One week turned into two, turned into every. Every Friday I returned home. Because I knew, even if he didn't admit it, that he needed me to.

THREE

COLLEGE GRACE, IT seems, is running fifteen minutes late for her four p.m. group project meeting.

I wedge into a space on the outskirts of the campus parking lot and swing my backpack over my shoulder. I half walk, half run past the admin buildings and past the fountain until I come to the library doors. I check my phone. It's 4:19. I'll be twenty minutes late.

I take the stairs of my future place of employment by two. By the time I open the door to the study room on the third floor, I'm out of breath. The two seniors that I was paired with stop talking and glance up. The guy—whose name I'm blanking out on—grins. "Freshman, late to her own meeting?"

The girl takes a swig of her extra-tall coffee. Her short blond hair's half-pulled back by a claw clip. "Danny, stop giving her shit."

"Kidding," Danny says. He has an easy smile that goes with

his floppy brown hair. "For real, though, thanks for making this meeting happen. Caroline and I wouldn't have gotten around to this until, like, a week before it's due."

"Or if we were on Danny's timeline, two hours before class while frantically emailing the TA asking for some kind of extension."

"I'm two for two on those," Danny says, pushing the sleeves of his hoodie up. "My group projects always pull together. Somehow."

Caroline rolls her eyes. "Danny's really prioritizing his senioritis."

"Everyone's feeling it," Danny says. "Unless you're Caroline, whose idea of letting loose senior year is being the president of three clubs while taking an engineering class for fun."

I don't say anything. I just give a small smile. They seem like they know each other well, and here I am, a freshman that got haphazardly inserted because their third friend dropped the class and I knew no one else. I pull up our Google Doc for our ideas, and the cursor blinks at me from the blank page.

"So," I say. "Any thoughts?"

Caroline takes another sip of coffee. She taps her foot impatiently. "The prof wants us to come up with a proposal for a real-life application of any game theory or market design theory. Honestly, I wish he'd just made us write an individual paper or something."

"And it has to be semi-original," Danny says, scratching his head.

"Maybe we should do something around market design,"

Caroline says. "Friday's lecture was pretty cool."

"We can't write about the examples that we talked about in class. Like residency matching or something."

We sit around in silence.

"Or school choice," Caroline says, taking the claw clip and shaking out her hair. "That was also mentioned in class."

A pause.

"I feel like we should do something that people could participate in. We could do, like, an algorithm that matches study partners?"

"That's boring," Caroline says.

"Really?"

"Would *you* want to take a survey that matches you up with study partners?"

"Moot point." Danny shrugs. "I'm bad at studying. I thought you'd be into it, though."

Caroline taps her digital pen to her chin. "I like this whole matching-people-up-to-each-other, though. You're onto something. We could maybe match up people to potential friends?"

I look up.

"Hmm." Danny leans forward, his elbows on his knees. "That could work. So what would that look like?"

Matches.

"The stable match algorithm," I blurt out.

Both heads swivel toward me.

Caroline raises an eyebrow. "That *marriage* match algorithm? Like. For friends?"

"For friends," I say slowly. "Or . . . it could still be for love."

The light fixtures hum above us. The seniors look blankly at me.

The idea's already piecing itself together in my head, and my words knot together on my tongue while I try to chase it. "It would still be an original idea. Well. It'd be like an original twist. The marriage example was just a simple ranked preference, right? But what are the components that feed into the preference? So why not make it a survey? And for college dating instead? It'll be like a—BuzzFeed quiz for your romantic match. For college dating. Let's say you fill it out based on your personality and values and everything you care about, and the algorithm pairs you up with someone who has those same values. It's who you're most compatible with, I guess? Like—" I pause, and say softly, "Like the person you're most likely to fall in love with."

I am now incredibly aware of the fact that my group project members are staring at me. What am I doing, waxing poetic about love to two seniors I've barely interacted with?

The lights continue to hum, and I clear my throat. "Never mind. Just . . . yeah, never mind." I stare at the blank Google Doc, my cheeks burning.

"A BuzzFeed quiz for actual love," Caroline says. "That's fucking brilliant."

"Agree." Danny turns to Caroline. "I told you we needed the freshman."

"Hold on." Caroline leans forward. "I do like this. But

we're . . . going to make this? Not just write about this idea in a proposal?"

"We can." I shrug. "It would be fun."

"Going above and beyond will get us a good grade," Caroline says. "But aren't we just inventing something like a dating app?"

"It's . . . similar," I say slowly, parsing it out in my head. "But dating apps only find you good matches at best, and even then, that's debatable." I think of the time I spent hours on the blue Spiegel 302 beanbag as Ava's swiper in crime, flicking through the endless profiles. "This does the filtering for you. This one finds you your most *ideal* match on campus. Or in your grade, I guess, if we want to look at a more specific dating pool."

"You know," Danny says, "there was, like, a study in one of my Behavioral Econ classes that talked about people having a decision paradox in dating apps. If people get overwhelmed with too many choices, they can't pick one, let alone pick the right one."

"So this gets rid of that issue. One: You know you have a perfect match out there. Two: It's someone on campus and in your grade, so you'll know who they are for sure." Caroline straightens up. "Okay. Okay! We're onto something."

"I personally would take this quiz in a heartbeat," Danny says.

"Danny just wants to get laid."

"For science, of course."

"A noble cause."

"Come on, tell me you wouldn't take this."

"I would," Caroline says. "Purely out of curiosity." She

pauses. "The senior class board always does this thing where they list their crushes, and if people end up on each other's list of crushes, the school sets up a date for them. It'd be like that, but a lot more organized."

"Exactly. A whole-school thing."

I lean forward. "You think we can get people in the school in on it?"

"For sure," Danny says. "I'd get all my friends to take it. And my club lacrosse team. And whoever else I can convince." He tilts his head. "And Caroline can make all her clubs take it."

I nod. "I would get my roommates to take it." Well, roommate. Ruhi was very much spoken for. But Ava would be up for it. Probably.

"Okay, so we have the people," Danny says. "And the algorithm."

"We would have to revise the premise of the stable match algorithm a lot," Caroline says. "Like expand the parameters to make it a whole survey-based preference system. Also, it's very hetero."

"True," I say. "We should definitely expand it to include all dating preferences. And make sure we come up with the most important questions on preferences and values. Like views on politics, relationships . . ."

"Religion," Caroline says.

"Future plans," Danny adds.

"Finances."

"Ambition."

"Sexuality."

"Cultural background."

"And how willing people are to date people with *different* preferences," I said. "And different views."

"Oh, absolutely," Caroline says. "I think we need to get a wide range of questions on these values and traits. And romantic preferences, too. We'll get this down to an exact science."

"We have to figure out the matches that are good for each person, and then see who has matching preferences, and whether either person is the most stable match for each other, or if one of them could be better off with another," I say. "A lot of conditional statements."

"We can do it," Caroline asserts. "How about this. I'll take a first pass and get a preliminary Python script up and running by tomorrow to make the matches." She looks up at me. "Some machine learning, nothing I haven't done before. And then we can just refine and iterate."

"And I'll help talk it up," Danny says. "I'll get as many people as I can manage to take it."

We glance at each other around the table.

"Well." Danny puts his hands on the table. "Sounds like we're matchmaking for a math class."

I laugh at the sheer absurdity of it. "Yeah. I guess we are."

"You're inventing a romance equation," Ava says.

"Sort of?" I say, setting my backpack down. "It's more of like. An algorithm?"

"Hold on." Ruhi picks up haphazardly scattered textbooks from the floor and stacks them neatly, and then sits down next to them. "Walk me through this. You're going to find people's *ideal* matches? Like, the loves of their lives?"

"How's that going to work?" Ava asks. "We're nineteen-year-olds with seventy-percent-formed frontal lobes. We're trying to find dates that we can even *stand* for two hours."

Ruhi pulls the blanket tighter around her. "The campus selection *is* kinda questionable."

"Yeah. Not everyone can have a high school sweetheart that adores them," Ava says. She turns to me. "We're at this party on Friday, right? Two shots in and she's FaceTiming Arjun in the corner."

"Hey!"

"It was *wholesome*." Ava smiles. "At least you weren't getting shit-faced at Rage Cage like the rest of us."

Ruhi leans back, pushing her hair behind her shoulder, and then turns to squint at a small nook between the beanbag and the wall. She extracts a crinkled pack. "Ava, how did your Hot Cheetos get here?"

Ava's expression lights up. "Oh, my Cheetos!" She opens her arms, and Ruhi throws the bag at her. She cradles it to her chest.

"You know that shelves exist, right?" Ruhi teases. "To store things?"

"I wanted to put them somewhere where I knew I could come back to. And I did."

Ruhi laughs. I've lost their attention. Slowly, I sink into the chair, about to pull out my computer and return to my work.

Ava turns back to me. "Wait, tell us more about this ideal-love-match thing."

I look up. "Right. So remember when we talked about which Disney princes would be our perfect matches?"

"Ah, yes," Ruhi says. "The Disney Prince Soul Mate debacle."

"Right. For our final project we have to propose a real-life application of one of the concepts from game theory or market design. And we'd just learned about the stable match algorithm. Like, this Nobel Prize–winning theory that says that in a perfectly designed market, everything reaches a stable state. And I kept thinking about that BuzzFeed-quiz-for-dating concept we were talking about earlier. So everyone keeps looking for the people they'd be compatible to date, but it's always hard to filter out who the good matches are."

"Decision paralysis," Ruhi says. "Which leads to dating fatigue. I was listening to someone talk about this on a podcast the other day, actually."

"Right. Exactly. And then I just thought, what if people were paired up with their theoretically perfect match on campus? Or in their year, really, so it's more likely they already know them? Like, we'd ask a series of questions to get their outlook on life and their opinions and everything, and we'd use this algorithm that sorted the preferences and then matched people up who had similar beliefs?" I fiddle with the straps of my backpack. "In conclusion, we're, like, creating people's matches. But we're making it so you're matched to the one ideal person on campus, or in your year, who you're most compatible with."

I pause.

Ava's mouth hangs open. "Grace, your brain is literally *so* big. You leave this campus for two days and come back with this genius project."

"While we're simply losing brain cells by slapping the wine bag at Tuttle House," Ruhi says. "We truly do need better things to do with our Friday nights."

I look at Ruhi incredulously. "*You* drank from the wine bag?"

"Oh, absolutely," Ava says, glancing over at the mirror and adjusting her earrings. "After she got off the call, we moved from shots to wine. Wine-drunk Ruhi is incredibly fun to hang out with. She had us up dancing on tops of tables."

Ruhi shrugs. "Which, I admit in retrospect, is not the safest thing to do."

I stare at Ruhi and try to picture it. This is Ruhi, who wakes up early to plan her day. Ruhi, who takes the maximum number of classes possible and joins in the occasional intramural volleyball game and makes a methodical to-do list on her whiteboard that she hangs over her desk and dutifully crosses tasks out on. Ruhi and Ava share a grin, and my stomach flips. What *am* I missing out on during the weekends?

Ruhi turns to me. "So who's taking this survey?"

"Well, it's open to the whole campus," I say. "But I'd need people to take it. I know you're spoken for, Ruhi. But, Ava—"

"I'll take it," she says. "My romantic life is so dire. *Please* let an algorithm save it." She stands up and says in her improv-show voice. "Match me up, my love. I'm ready."

The Match-Up. That potential name dawns on me. "So true. But as a disclaimer, if enough people don't participate, there's a very real possibility that five people across campus will take this survey and you could fully get matched with, like, one of my project partners. Who I'm pretty sure is a lacrosse bro."

"If it's meant to be," Ava says. "We'll elope to Coffee House. We'll cater some Papa John's and call it a day. As long as he likes Papa John's. If not, this relationship is doomed from the start."

"I can officiate," Ruhi adds, completely seriously. "I think you can get certified on the internet."

"Okay," I laugh. "No one's saying anything about *marriage.*"

"We're planning ahead," Ava says. She clasps her hands together. "I'm so excited for this."

"The question is," Ruhi says, turning to me and fixing me with her dark brown eyes, "are *you* taking your quiz, Grace?"

Ava turns to me.

I pause. "Should I?"

"What do you *mean*, should you?" Ava's brown eyes are wide. "Of *course* you have to. It's your own algorithm!"

"You *have* been wondering who your perfect type is," Ruhi says. "Ava and I know ours. Ava loves emotionally unavailable guys with cute puppy-like expressions—"

"Hey!" Ava's cheeks turn bright pink. "Deeply true and entirely unfair. Ruhi likes preppy nice boys who wear salmon-colored shorts. Preferably, a childhood friend turned debate partner who harbors feelings for years before confessing right before senior-year homecoming."

Ruhi grins. "Touché," she says. "But what about you, Grace?"

I exhale. "I don't know. I guess I should find out."

Ava claps. "You're taking the quiz with me! Our double matrimony is gonna be *sick*." She glances at her phone. "Oh, shoot. It's almost four, and I have to be at improv practice." She jumps up and pulls on a large sweater over her turtleneck.

"And I have to go attend a staff writer meeting," Ruhi says. She taps at her smartwatch. "When is the survey coming out again?"

"Probably in, like, a week? We're still coding it up."

"I'll take it first thing," Ava calls out as she leaves.

And Ruhi dips out too and then I have the room to myself.

I sigh and lean back on the beanbag. I reach over and turn the fairy lights on so the room is cast in a soft glow. I pull up the Google Doc.

What is my type?

It's not the first time I've been asked this. The first time was when I was lying on Hana's floor, my stomach bursting from stuffing myself with Chips Ahoy!, with glitter on our eyelids from when she tried to practice applying makeup on me while telling me in detail about how she'd made out with Kristen Levy after her theater practice the other day. "I've never heard *you* talk about your crushes," Hana said. "Who *do* you like, anyway?"

I'd closed my eyes then. "No clue and no point. As if my mom would let me go on a single date, ever."

Rumors always swept their way through school. Who kissed whom at a weekend party. Who had broken up with whom in the parking lot behind the gym. But they never involved me. My name never passed through the hallways. Love was as abstract as set theory.

"Don't get a boyfriend," Ma had always said. "He's only going to distract you from school. Once you get into MIT, you can find a smart boy."

"But you're still allowed to have crushes," Hana said. She sat up. "Okay, out of everyone at Woodward. Who would you be most into?"

I opened my eyes and sat up, and glitter drifted to my lap. I shrugged and scoured the yearbook in my mind. "I don't know. Isaac Richards?"

"The dude in English class? The one who we always ran into when we skied?"

"Yeah?" I said. "He's nice. Has a cute smile." I'd also caught a glimpse of him during our soccer unit, when he lifted up the bottom of his shirt to wipe the sweat off his forehead and I saw a band of tanned lean muscle, for just a moment. But I didn't want to talk about that. Even if my mom wasn't here listening. I'd always felt sort of weird when Hana talked about her crush on Kristen around me. They were never officially a thing. I felt like Kristen was always stringing her along. But every time I said anything about not liking her, Hana said that I was just taking it too seriously.

"Nice and cute smile," Hana said. "You're not giving me much to work with."

36

"What do you want, an essay?"

"Could help," Hana said. She laughed. "Don't look so flustered. I was only wondering."

I settled back on the floor, the back of my neck on scratchy carpet. "Maybe love's not for me."

"All right, you cynic," Hana laughed, flopping down right next to me. "We'll figure it out for you eventually."

"Eventually," I said before I closed my eyes.

My only data point so far on true love, really, was my parents, who met at a karaoke bar in the nineties. It sounds almost fictitiously romantic for the two stoic individuals who raised me. But once they did tell the story. Ba's friends had convinced him to stop working on classwork on a weekend night and go out instead. One of Ma's friends had just broken off a relationship, and so she was the one who dragged her group of friends to that bar.

"My friends and I walked into that karaoke place," my dad would narrate, years later, in our Honda Civic while we were on one of our road trips. Ba did all the driving because Ma wanted to travel but she was scared of flying and also of driving long distances. So he drove us up to Maine, down to Virginia and the Smoky Mountains, and once, all the way down to Florida. "And your ma was singing on the small stage. Wah, she got the attention of every single person in that room. You were singing—"

Ma laughed. "我愿意."

"Right," my dad said. "And there she was, this beautiful woman, singing high notes with the brightest voice I had ever heard."

"Of course I could sing," Ma scoffed, even though she'd started to smile. "I hadn't gone to music school all for nothing."

I'd turned to my mom from the back seat. "And what did you think of Ba?"

My mom feigned indifference. "He was all right. I didn't notice him much at first."

"And yet she fell in love with me," my dad said, meeting my eyes in the rearview. "Not bad for your lǎo ba."

"Aiyah." But my mom was smiling as she said it. She didn't stop me from asking more questions and didn't stop Ba from telling the rest of the story. Ma asked the crowd if anyone wanted to do a duet, and his friends dared him to go up and ask. They sang "Goodbye Kiss" together and my dad got embarrassed and flustered halfway through but at the end everyone clapped for them. By the end of the night, he worked up the courage to ask her out to dinner.

"And then what?" I'd ask.

"And then she turned me down," Ba said, laughing.

"I wanted to set you up with my friend instead! She was the heartbroken one. I made you ask my friend to dinner, but then she didn't want to go. So I went to save some face. And because I went to that dinner, I came all the long way to this country so your ba could do his doctorate." Ma shook her head. "Can you imagine?"

Sometimes Ma did sound a little resentful when she talked about coming here. It was clear then and now that all my dad's dreams were out here and none of my mom's were. But maybe her dreams had fallen apart long ago. When they met she was working as a voice teacher and wanted to be a famous singer, after all. I wondered if she could have been. In another world, she could have been on center stages, draped in chiffon, and serenading a crowd that knew her name, instead of working late hours at a department store thirty minutes away.

But most times it was so clear that she was meant to go to dinner with my dad and fall in love with him, because out of all odds they ended up being good for each other in ways that I did not even see until now, until I'd felt and continue to feel, unrelentingly, the acute, gaping loss of her. Ba was soft-spoken, and Ma's voice filled the house. She liked making all the decisions on her whim, and he let her: the fruits to buy at the grocery store, the decorations in our house, the summer classes she wanted me to take. Ba liked to disappear into his work. He stayed in his study poring over a data set instead of joining us at dinner. He delayed things until Ma got mad at him. But when he showed up, he really did. When she wanted a new car, he spent weeks researching every aspect across brands. Every year on her birthday and their anniversary, he got her peonies. And after Ma received a formal diagnosis of non-Hodgkin's lymphoma during my eighth-grade year, Ba requested his first tenure-permitted sabbatical so he could go with her to every single one of her appointments and filled pages with notes, which he digitized in English and Mandarin.

That first time her cancer went into remission, we took a road trip down to Panama City Beach in Florida. As we passed the highway signs, Ba slotted in a CD. The car speakers came to life with fervent piano notes and the intro drum. My mother sat up. She was weak and motion sick and had lost weight and she was wearing three layers of sweaters and a hat. But she sang the first words, quietly and steadily, her notes sure. My dad joined in with his rich tenor, the first time I'd heard him sing. I listened to their voices rise toward the chorus. They glanced at each other, for the briefest moment. I caught that light, miraculous force that had brought them together in that karaoke bar. They sang that song on the highway, drifting in between states and on nondescript roads, and I watched their love story unfold in front of me all over again.

FOUR

I SHOW UP at the library a half hour before my shift at one starts, as communicated over email. Roberta teaches me how to check books in and out of the system and points me to the general locations of the library collections. She also gives me a whole lecture on how to access and request books from other nearby colleges. I look over the map. Our reference desk is in the corner, right near the entrance. First floor is printers and university archives, second is nonfiction, and third is fiction. I know there are students that practically live in the library, but I've actually rarely been here except to convene in study rooms for group projects. Ava likes to frequent Coffee House, Ruhi the attic lounge of the *Daily Leighton*, and, well, I get our room. And my home.

Roberta goes into the back room and tells me to retrieve a couple of documents she sent to the printer. I swing the gate out to exit the desk just as someone comes up to it.

The gate collides with what sounds like kneecaps. I find myself face-to-face with a tall Asian girl I've never seen around campus. She has her backpack slung over her shoulder, steel rings glinting on her fingers.

"Oh, I— Oh my God, I'm so sorry."

I'm fixed with a pointed stare. And then she pushes past me and shrugs off her oversized jean jacket. She pulls a bright yellow book out of her worn tote bag as Roberta emerges from the back. "Here's your book. Thanks for letting me borrow it."

"Oooh," Roberta clasps her hands. "Tell me all your thoughts. Did you like it?" Just then she glances over at me. "By the way, this is Grace, the new student library assistant. Grace, this is Julia."

Julia looks over her shoulder, her long hair falling like a curtain, revealing a triple cartilage piercing. She turns slightly. I'm not short, but she makes me feel like it. Her gray platform boots aren't helping. Within a blink she seems to have scrutinized me. "Cool," she says. She gets herself situated behind the desk. I go retrieve the forms from the printer, my cheeks burning. By the time I come back, she and Roberta are chatting. Julia's even cracked a smile. It's clear that Roberta is fond of my coworker. Then Roberta disappears, and it's just the two of us. She retrieves books from the drop-off cart and starts checking them in.

I glance over at Julia. "I'm so sorry," I offer again. "You okay?"

She shrugs. "All good."

"So," I try to say. "Are you . . . a senior?"

She doesn't look up from scanning. "Freshman."

I brighten. "Oh, I'm a freshman, too. Sorry for assuming. I guess I've just never seen you on campus, so."

"There's a lot of people."

"Right," I say. "Maybe you know Ava Lange or Ruhi Agrawal?"

Her hands pause over the book. She presses her lips together as her eyes narrow. "Look, I'd love to play the name game all day, but I do need to reshelve these."

She loads a hefty stack onto the cart and pushes the cart toward the elevator. I fall silent. It's like she's trying to get out of talking to me. Suddenly it's like the first week of classes after orientation week and I'm there, trying to introduce myself to people who all met over the weekend.

People come and go. Julia and I say nothing to each other for the rest of the work shift, or after. I don't have time to talk, anyway. I have a meeting with my project group to get to.

Two weeks, a midterm, four slow library shifts in which I scan and sort and reshelve books and help students find obscure textbooks, and several brainstorming sessions after we come up with the idea for the Match-Up, my project group stays up late Tuesday night in Caroline's room and schedules the survey to send out at nine the following morning. The entire Wednesday morning, I try not to think about it. What if no one answers? What if I make a fool of myself on all the campus mailing lists? Not that people don't do that regularly—anonymous satire

43

publications circulate each week, each more ridiculous than the next. And there was the one time someone started a reply-all fight in the Spiegel dorm mailing list about whether someone stole his box of Nature Valley bars. At best, maybe fifty people would participate in the survey. At worst—well, maybe they'd mistake it as a joke mailing, we'd redo our econ project, and we'd just all forget about it and make up something new.

I stop by Coffee House on my way home from class to pick up a drink for Ava. I wrap myself tightly in my too-thin flannel jacket, cursing myself for forgetting how much the temperatures drop in late October. I'm a bad local.

I walk up to the counter and search the stickered drinks for a maple cookie butter latte.

I glance around as I wait for Ava's drink, stewing on my interactions with Julia. She has not warmed even a little bit. She mostly talks with Roberta about books they read, or she fiddles with her rings, or she's peeking at her phone under the desk, or she's out and about reshelving things. Basically, doing anything but talking to me. I remember that not everyone's like my roommates. I realize, once again, how lucky I am to not have roommates who froze me out.

I glance at the students lounging on the couches. Coffee House is everyone's favorite place to work, with its unlimited hot coffee deal on Wednesday afternoons. It's too small to fit half a liberal arts college. People cram in on the plush couches and crowd together on the wood-paneled tables. I glance at the open laptop screens and see a fantasy football chart pulled up on one, a Bath & Body Works candle sale on another, and a Microsoft Word doc open and one solitary title line with the blinking cursor on the third.

Ava's drink finally comes out. Out of the corner of my eye I see a flash of short blond hair. Caroline's picking up a towering cup of iced coffee.

"Grace!"

I jump and turn. Caroline and I had run into each other in the dining hall before, but we'd nodded in acknowledgment and walked past each other. Now she's briskly walking toward me, clutching her massive cup and trying to juggle her wallet and car keys in the same hand, her heeled boots clicking as she expertly navigates the crowd. I give a tentative wave. "Hey?"

"Five *hundred*," she says.

"Five what?"

"As in, the Match-Up has five *fucking* hundred responses already."

I almost drop Ava's drink.

"I know. Right?" She looks past me to the couches. "Hold on. I think I see Danny, actually." She gestures wildly, her car keys jangling in her hand. He glances up, his eyebrows knit in confusion, and slowly comes over. "What's going on?"

"Calling an impromptu group meeting," Caroline says. "Table. There."

We settle down around an impossibly small circular table, our knees touching.

"So." Caroline extracts her laptop from her backpack. "The

Match-Up has over five hundred responses so far."

Danny's jaw practically unhinges itself. "No *way*? For real? Is there a glitch?"

"Of course not. I coded it myself." Caroline places the laptop between us. She refreshes the page, and the spreadsheet expands by even more rows. "Five hundred and twenty-six now. All unique names and responses. You were the second response, Danny."

"That's . . . so many?" I say, my heart racing. Our email made it around the school. "A fifth of our school has taken it just since this morning."

"Let's *go*." Danny pumps his fist in the air and leans back with a wide grin. "I told you guys I'd get people to take it. See? I get things done in group projects."

"Oh, you did well. Too well." Caroline grins. She stares at the spreadsheet, her fingers hovering over the cursor.

"Hold up," Danny says. "Look. Someone's taking it right now."

I glance over. One of the Bath & Body Works shoppers had now shifted into another tab. I see the familiar white-and-green background of our survey.

Under the table, I twist my scarf into a tight ball, feeling faint. A *fifth* of campus knows about this. More, probably. "This is . . . a lot of people. Do you think we should, like, pull this, or cap it at a certain amount of survey responses, or—"

"Are you joking? This is the best thing *ever*. If anything, the more people that take it, the better our matching pool is." Caroline is beaming. "This is it. We started a campus-wide *thing*."

"And it's only the first day," Danny says. "This one's taking off for sure."

"Incredible," Caroline says, shaking her head in giddy disbelief. She glances over. "Grace. You good?"

I clear my throat. "Yes. Yeah. I just . . . had no idea it would be *this* popular." I stand, a little bit dizzy from the magnitude of the response. I need to tell my roommates about this, I think. Also I'm still holding Ava's drink, which is cooling as we speak.

Caroline reaches over. "And *you* came up with this as a freshman. And it's brilliant. Kudos to you."

I let out a small affirmative sound.

We disperse, and I emerge into the sunlight, clutching Ava's drink to my chest.

We thought we were going to struggle to get people to participate. And now we were matching up a good fifth of our student body. More. This survey wouldn't close for another week. This could be a runaway success, we'd get a good grade, *and* I could secure a recommendation for the summer research program.

I reach Spiegel and take the elevator to the third floor. Ava's not here, so I put the drink on her table. Her table is messy, stationery packaging and receipts everywhere. She's got pictures strung up around her desk with clothespins, pictures of her with her friends at national parks and on mountains and piled in someone's backyard. She's got family photos with her parents and twin little brothers from what looks like beach and camping trips. Ruhi has a ton of pictures with her friends and family, too: pictures of her dressed in uniform at the private day school she went to in Texas, pictures of her dressed up with her sister in bright colors at weddings, photos from her travels and speech and debate tournaments. My wall is bare. I didn't even know people decorated their walls in college. I ordered in a nondescript geometric tapestry the second week.

I settle onto my bed and pull the fluffy gray blanket around me and fidget. After a while, I click on the survey that was sent to our dorm email list. Our group had pored over the questions to include for so long that I could recite them in my sleep.

Maybe there's a reason so many people are taking this. Maybe this is something actually, truly *real*. And now that people are taking it, hundreds of people, even, these thirty questions might actually pair me up with the person I'm meant to meet.

And for the first time, the nerves in the pit of my stomach jangle in excitement.

Please, tell me who to fall in love with.

I take a deep breath and start the quiz.

Have you ever wondered about finding your perfect match on campus? The one who shares all your values, understands you on a deeper level, and is the one you're most compatible with?

Well, you're in luck, lovebirds! November is quickly approaching, bringing comfy sweaters, holidays, and . . . the perfect time to cozy up to a new boo. In case you're looking for someone in time for cuffing season and cute hot chocolate dates at Coffee House, we invite you to fill out the Match-Up, based on a Nobel Prize–winning algorithm! Answer these thirty questions in our survey and our algorithm just might introduce you to your perfect match on campus, who shares your values and your outlook . . . and could be the potential future love of your life.

The news of the Match-Up spreads faster than the news of free Krispy Kreme at freshman orientation. By noon the next day, we have just under eight hundred responses. And by the next day we have over fifteen hundred.

"My entire improv team took it," Ava says, sprawling on the beanbag, her bright red hair fanned out around her. "It's going in one of our shows. The comedic possibilities are endless."

I turn from my chair, curling my knees to my chest. "It's been three days. And we've got way over *half the school*."

Ava shrugs. "Everyone wants to be in on it."

"The editorial team spent *our* meeting taking it the day it came out," Ruhi says from her spot at her desk. She takes off her wireless earbuds and turns to face us. "Speaking of. The news desk will probably reach out to you guys in the next couple days for an interview."

I sit straight up. "What?"

"Grace will be front-page *Daily Leighton* news?" Ava turns to me, her eyes wide. "I love living with a celebrity."

"I *may* or may not have suggested the story to them." Ruhi

grins. "I mean, they were going to run a story anyway. It's a fascinating concept. Also, I did peek at the questions. For research. It was very well thought out. Very thorough."

"Oh, there were so many questions!" Ava says. "I didn't know so many things could go into whether you'd be a good match for someone or not."

"Like how much you valued verbal affirmations," Ruhi said. "Or whether you valued ambition over collaboration."

"Or how *physically adventurous* you like to be," Ava says, her eyebrows raised.

I blush. "*That* was a Caroline-suggested question."

"Valid," Ruhi says, matter-of-fact. "Sexual chemistry can be important between couples. Anyway. How does an interview tonight sound?"

That night, all three of us and Ruhi gather in the library study room, Ruhi recording on her phone. I go home for the weekend. On Tuesday, I check my texts in Set Theory class and come across a flood of messages in the project group chat.

Caroline: holy shit!! look at us in campus news
Danny: sweet
Caroline: !!!!
Caroline: love the article. Op-ed is :/ though. like tf???

I pause.

Me: op-ed???? weren't we in the news section

No answer.

I glance up at the clock. Class ends in two minutes, but I'm already packing my bag. The moment the professor starts erasing the whiteboard, I spring to my feet and run out the door and down the stairs. I look for one of the newspaper stands I swear I've seen before, but now I can't find them in this building. Ruhi would have a copy, though. I half run across the campus, passing the blocky gray class buildings, the fountain that has dried out since the summer, and take the stairs by two in Spiegel until I reached the third floor.

I open the door, seeing both Ava and Ruhi leaning over something.

Ruhi's the first to make eye contact. Her words rush out. "I'm so sorry. I had no idea the opinions section would publish this or I would have told you about it, I swear—"

I set my backpack down. "Is it . . . bad?"

Ava frowns. "It's . . . eh?"

I reach down and gingerly pick up the newspaper.

Calculating the Odds of Love: Unpacking the Match-Up, the front News column is titled.

I flip to the opinions section.

Why I'm Skeptical of that Survey that's Going Around Campus

And under it, in smaller letters:

How could a math equation ever determine love?

I blur past the words. I can't read them right now: it's a block of text and I don't want to. I set the newspaper down. I search farther down the article until my gaze lands on a name.

By Julia Zhang

I put down the article on Ruhi's table.

"Wait," I say. I pick the paper back up. "Can you look up who the author is?"

"Oh, Julia? Yeah, she writes for our arts and opinions section." Ruhi types in her phone and swivels it around to show me a picture.

Long dark hair and eyes. Triple cartilage piercing.

I look into the unsmiling face of my new coworker.

FIVE

RUHI'S STILL TRYING to reassure me about the newspaper when I leave for the ski team informational meeting.

"You're fine. Promise." Her voice is calm. "They publish weird shit in the op-ed section all the time. The other day someone legitimately wrote a long article about why everything bagels are overhyped, and it made it past the opinions desk."

"It's just—" I wrap my jacket around me. I already feel strange about it getting so much attention so quickly. Now it's getting bad press in the student newspaper, which goes out across the entire campus? *Professor Rand is going to read it*, I think in a panic. *He's going to be convinced that the algorithm doesn't work. Any chance I have at the summer research position just disappeared on the fifth page of the* Daily Leighton. "Before the matches come out, even? Like, at least look at it and try to disprove something about it, not tear it to shreds before it even launches."

"Well, I personally think that this is a great idea and this Julia person clearly has too much time on her hands," Ava says from the beanbag, where she's eating a granola bar and scrolling through her phone. "She's just a hater."

"It's solid, Grace," Ruhi says. "You showed us all your diagrams."

I lean against the wall. "*And* she's my coworker, too. At the library."

Ruhi raises an eyebrow. "Does she know your group made it?"

"I mean," I say, "no. But she does now." I glance at the paper and then push it out of view. I pick up my backpack. "Okay. Well. I have to go to the ski team meeting."

"See, you're being a brilliant, accomplished student athlete with a project based on a Nobel Prize–winning algorithm." Ava polishes off her granola bar. "And that Julia person is still a hater nobody in the opinions section."

I laugh. "I'm not a student athlete. It's not, like, NCAA or something. It's a club sport. I probably won't even compete." But now a new set of anxiety kicks around the back of my mind. I know that Julia and I didn't get off to the friendliest start, but what if it's more than that? What if my coworker actually hates me?

I sling my backpack over my shoulder and head out toward the center of campus and try to shake the thoughts from my head.

Ski team was something I signed up for on a whim at the activities fair the second day of orientation, when my roommates and I had wandered out. Ava had immediately gravitated toward the improv team table. Ruhi was chatting with the editor-in-chief at the *Daily Leighton* booth. The ski team table was in the middle of the two. I'd stood there awkwardly, waiting for my roommates to come back to me. But Ava had started talking movies with the improv team and Ruhi had joyfully recognized someone she went to a high school summer newspaper program with. I checked my phone and surreptitiously went to Hana's social media. I scrolled it for a bit. The latest picture she'd posted was three days ago, where she was standing in a wet suit at the beach, hoisting a surfboard next to her, blinking against the sun. trading mountains for the sea, she'd commented in her caption.

I'd stuffed my phone in my pocket. If she were here, she might have gone for ski team with no hesitation. She and her parents were the ones who got me into skiing. In the winters leading up to high school, we'd spent weekends up on the slopes together, feeling the wind rush on our cheeks and seep into our teeth. Yet she had left this all behind. She'd wanted to leave all this more than anything.

Look at you, I'd thought. *You can't do a single thing without Hana, can you?*

I'd glanced ahead of me and made eye contact with the person at the ski team table. My roommates were still talking. I'd marched ahead and put my email down. And then I forgot all about it until an email popped up this past Monday.

Now I make my way to the second landing of Coffee House,

where there's a conference room. It's a Tuesday night, too, which is open mic night and so I hear the sounds of a guitar as I head up the stairs.

The room's packed. People mill about in the front with green windbreakers that say *LEIGHTON SKI TEAM* on it. They seem like the people who would backpack through the mountains for the summer. I sit in the corner and grab a pamphlet and wait for the informational meeting to start.

"All right," says a tall girl who wears a big Patagonia sweatshirt. Her long brown hair's gathered up in a ponytail, and she has a low, husky voice. "Let's get started."

Just then the door creaks open, and I see those gray platform boots first.

Julia walks in, her arms crossed, and after a moment, she gets to the one empty seat in the room. Which is next to me.

Our eyes meet, and then spring away.

Have I *summoned* her? Why is she everywhere? What even are the odds of this?

"Welcome to the informational meeting for the ski team!" the girl up front says. "I'm Nicole Hofner. I'm your co-captain along with Johnny Callahan, who isn't here because he's taking a midterm. We're really excited for a great season ahead of us."

A bright PowerPoint slide flashes on the screen. There are pictures of people crammed in at restaurant booths, on snowy slopes, grinning from ear to ear under their ski helmets. "We have an incredible schedule lined up for all of you this year. And you don't just get a ski team—you get a whole family that you'll get to travel with, hang out with on the weekends, and host *legendary* chocolate fountain parties with."

People at the front laugh.

Family. I glance at the pictures with people with their arms huddled, and at another picture where the team members hug each other while someone proudly raises the trophy, cheeks red and eyes shining, rimmed with the red circles of the ski mask.

I glance at Julia. She's spinning one of her rings absentmindedly around her finger.

"Not only do we know how to have a good time, we know how to win," Nicole continues. "We've won back-to-back invitationals in the last five years, and we have every intention of keeping that streak this season. But we also welcome—encourage, even—people who've never competed to give it a shot. Above all, we want to be a team where people send and have fun." She gestures to the table to the right, which is lined with trophies and medals. "The team is as high commitment as you want. Some just like going to practice. Some compete every weekend during season. Choose what works for you."

She clicks forward a few slides, ending on a picture with the team on the slope, their arms raised in a cheer.

"Cool," Nicole says, clapping her hands together. "We're passing along a sign-up sheet, if you're interested in joining the team. Some members are up here if anyone wants to ask questions or chat, and reach out to me if you have any questions after today. And feel free to grab some doughnut holes."

Everyone slowly disperses, gravitating toward the doughnut

holes. The sign-up sheet gets passed to me. I flip to the tentative calendar. Practices are on Wednesdays, from three to six. I can make that. I glance at the January weekends, which are filled with tournaments and invitationals. It doesn't matter. I just won't compete for the season. I can still go home. Even if competing does sound nice.

But will this get in the way of my studies? I'll definitely have less time for classwork, that's for sure. I can't have my grades go down because I'm having *fun*.

I pause, my pen hesitating over the sheet.

"Hey." I hear Julia's impatient voice behind me. "You done? Can I have the sheet?"

My fingers clench around the pen. I straighten up and look her in the eye. "Just a second." And then I lean over and take a full minute to spell out the nine letters of my full name, and a longer minute more to write down my email. *Grace Tang. gracextang@leighton.edu.*

I set the pen down more forcefully than I intend to. Then I head out.

"Put on a thicker jacket," Ba says. "It's going to be chilly."

I switch to one of my puffy jackets as we set out for our Sunday-afternoon walk, a mile and a half down the road. I tuck my hands in my pockets and brace myself against the chill. We're silent, hearing our footsteps crunch over the leaves on our usual path.

"You seem tense, Xiǎoyàn," Ba says. "Everything okay?"

"I'm okay." I relax my shoulders. At the survey's close on Friday at 11:59, 1,802 people had completed the Match-Up. All weekend, I'd stayed up in my room, frantically looking over the code and preparing matches. I put together the matches for juniors and seniors, and Caroline did sophomores and freshmen, so we had no chance of putting together our own matches. Danny's sending out the emails through a prewritten code. It has to be as perfect and quantifiably sound as it can.

"Are you not doing well in your classes?"

I exhale through my teeth. "I'm doing fine, Ba," I say. "I got a standard deviation above the median on both my Set Theory and Linear Algebra midterms. It's just a group project that I'm working on."

My father nods. We continue our walk. I haven't brought up ski team all weekend, and I should. It seems so routine that I'd just come home every weekend. But can he stand me missing one? More than one?

I'm composing something to say in my head when we hear the church bells.

Ba stills and looks toward the direction of the church.

It's the end of service. I know that, even without checking the phone for the time. I used to go every Sunday morning for more than half of my life. I know how immovable Ba is toward religion; he says the only higher power he will ever believe in is science. So it surprises me now that he starts walking in that direction.

The doors are open. People are filing out, down the steps,

hugging their coats around them. I see the familiar faces of Ma's old church acquaintances and duck my head down, averting myself from their gaze. They don't come approach me; they know better to. The last time I attended a service was February of last year. Ma's acquaintances took care of us after the funeral in their own ways. They sent us blankets and cards and left meals on our doorsteps, meals that congealed in the fridge because we got tired of eating pasta bakes. The cards said that they were praying for us and hoped I would come back to church soon. I had texted back each one of them, as politely as I could, that I would not be coming back to church. I couldn't bring myself to. I'd prayed for every bit of divine intervention, just like I had the first time Mom was diagnosed in eighth grade, when Hana squeezed my hand tight in service as we both prayed for her. I'd leaned against hospital bathroom doors and bargained with God endlessly. In the end, He still let my mom die, and after that, God was not the same to me anymore.

And yet now Ba is here, looking toward the open door, and then back at me.

I wonder what he's going to do.

I follow Ba up the steps. He stops short at the door, peering in at the pews and at the Bibles that lined the side, and then at the altar and the church organ. He looks down at the floor, and then up again at the stained-glass windows.

I know every bit of this church. I know which pew is coming loose. I know the stairs that lead to the back room, where the youth group is held every Wednesday evening. I know exactly how sound carries, how if you're in the back corner and whisper you can hear it all the way at the front. I'd written my college essays on church choir harmonies, how certain patterns of notes were perceived by our senses. How I saw mathematical patterns everywhere: in the stained glass of the church windows, in the geometric symmetry of this space. I remember going to Sunday school and eating cold pizza with Hana. I remember my mother bowing her head during the prayers, knuckles locked tight, fervently praying for something I still didn't know. I bowed my head and I tried to pray like she did. Like it came naturally to me.

Ba does not go much farther in. He looks in with a kind of fragile and curious wonder.

After a long moment, he says, "Let's go."

I follow him.

"I come here sometimes," he says quietly when we walk home. "I don't know why."

He practices piano that afternoon. I pack my backpack. And when it's time to leave, I hug my father extra hard.

"Bye, Ba," I say. "See you next week."

My mom found the church in a fog.

Or at least that's how she described it to me. Shortly after arriving to Vermont, while she was taking business classes at the local community college and Ba was working around the clock doing his postdoc and lecturing night classes at the university, she entered this strange period of her life where she

61

couldn't quite sleep, where time blurred together, where some strange, immobile sense of fear took over her and she didn't know what to do during the day.

It wasn't like she could leave the house and just bike down the street like she used to be able to back in Hangzhou. The roads were wide and the signs didn't make sense. She missed home.

"Why didn't you go back?"

"Well, your ba was here. And my class was here. I had to finish it." And I understood her. To go back was to give up, in a sense. To have conceded failure. She would never do that. "So I made do. I walked."

She started going on walks, first circling the hallways around their apartment at the time, and then in the park trails behind the building. "It was during winter, too," she said. "I had to watch out for hidden ice. And I was walking on this Sunday morning, down this path I hadn't gone down before, and then"—her eyes lit up—"I heard bells."

This part she loved talking about. She never said very many words about the fog, about the strange, dazed months that led up to this point. For her, the beginning was the moment she heard the bells.

"And it was a church," Ma said. "It was Sunday service and the choir was singing. It was so bright, Xiǎoyàn." *Little swallow bird.*

"And the doors were open. So I walked in, and listened to them sing, and then left. So I started going Sundays. I went to

62

church. I'd been wanting a child for a long time at that point. So I prayed for you, and God gave me you, and everything became clear again."

There was the church, and then there was me. Ma went every Sunday and she sat in the last pew. She bought the Mandarin-English version of the Bible and moved up to the third pew. She joined the choir. She bent her head fervently in prayer, in a silence all her own, and the fog went away and she never spoke of it again, and so she was saved.

And I grew up in stuffy Sunday school rooms, wondering if God could hear me while I talked and whether he would judge me for wondering if he was there. Ba didn't believe in any of that stuff. I wanted to. I wanted it to be proven to me. I asked God all kinds of questions in my head. I don't know what I was expecting, maybe for some disembodied voice to come to me. *I'll believe in you if you say something*, I always thought. Maybe I was a bad believer for thinking that. But Ma believed because the church had saved her, over and over. She finally belonged somewhere. She would volunteer at events. She would sing in the choir, her soaring voice beaming out above them all, the voice that could have made her a famous singer. All these years and the most sure I felt of God was when I heard her sing.

SIX

"I HEAR THE results are out tonight?" Ruhi says. "Asking for a friend."

I glance up. She's wrapped up in a microfleece UT Austin blanket and a bunch of sweaters. Our heater rattles in the background. "No, really. The friend is the *Daily Leighton*. Although I also am personally curious as a third-party observer."

"I, too, am asking for a friend, actually," Ava says as she comes in and drops her backpack.

I look toward the computer. "Danny's releasing the results tonight. He's the one who's sending out the emails with all the matches." All nine hundred or so of them, automated through another one of Caroline's Python scripts. One thousand eight hundred and two responses make up more than two-thirds of the campus. A statistic that still truly bewilders me. And everywhere people are talking about it. Ruhi says I'm all over Leighton YikYak, whatever that means.

"Just think, we might be responsible for the love lives of more than half this campus," Caroline said offhandedly just last week, when we all hung out at the library until it closed, testing the code and making sure that the matches were running. That we had taken all the parameters and edge cases into consideration. She sounded like she was joking, but I'd been thinking about that ever since. With a pool this big and this many people invested in the results, we had to make it perfect.

Maybe not truly perfect. The tricky thing is that the algorithm couldn't match up everyone; based on the sign-up pool, fifty-two girls who'd identified as heterosexual were left without a match. Caroline's solution for that problem, as we'd thought of last night, was just to match them with each other as friendship matches. But otherwise, everyone had a romantic match.

Ava leans forward, her chin resting on the back of her chair. "Do you already know who my match is? Or who *your* match is?"

"Nope."

"Not even *yours?*"

"I did juniors and seniors. There were so many names in there when I was running the thing that I barely caught any one match in particular. Danny has the final list, and we agreed to all wait until the email for our reveals as well."

"Oh, so a *true* surprise for everyone involved."

Ruhi goes back to reading a PDF on her tablet for an assignment while Ava lies on the beanbag and takes out a textbook. Our email pings with a notification. I start. Ruhi scrambles for her phone. "False alarm. Someone is asking our entire dorm email list if they've seen their single missing Chewbacca sock in the dryer."

"That sock has certainly disappeared," Ava says morosely. "Good luck getting that back." She stretches. "The anticipation is *killing* me. I haven't been more hyped up since Maisie Peters tour tickets dropped. Oh my God, I hope my match is worth it. I hope he's not a weirdo."

"He won't be," Ruhi says. "It's Grace's algorithm."

But what if I do mess this up? I glance at my roommate. This is one of my best friends in college so far. What if I match her up with someone that she dislikes? Someone who rejects her? Or someone who's toxic or manipulative? A wave of anxiety curls over me. I needed more time for this, I think. I should have looked at every single name on the list. I should have—

Our email notifications ping again. Ruhi sits up. "It's out."

Ava launches herself from the beanbag. I grab my phone, and there it is, the email, with a pixelated heart emoji.

Your Match-Up Results . . .

Outside our door, I hear a whoop, followed by shouts and laughter. The hall bursts into the cacophony of thirty college freshmen buzzing with their assigned matches.

I hear a small shriek from across the room. Ava stares at her phone, her jaw open.

"Oh my *fucking* God," she says, her eyes trained on her phone.

My heart races. I look up from my email at Ava, my fingers trembling. What if—

"I got matched up with someone on my improv team!"

Ava does a lap around the room, holding her phone out and jumping up and down, her hand covering a grin. "Cameron Chang. What are the odds?" She doubles over, laughing. "Oh, Grace, I never should have doubted you."

I relax in relief. Ava adores her improv team. At least my algorithm had matched her up to someone that she knew. I haven't messed up.

"Bryce is FaceTiming me right now." She picks up. "You saw my text? Yes, I'm *literally* sending this to the group chat right now. They're going to lose their minds over this. Who'd you get matched to?" She pauses. "Oooh, Elena Cruz? I think I know her. Oh! I think I briefly met her during some kind of orientation thing."

"Grace," Ruhi says, nodding at my phone. "*Hello?*"

I jolt back. My thumb is still hovering over the email.

Ava sits up. "*Wait*, Grace!" She turns to the phone. "Bryce, I'm calling you back in five. My roommate is about to figure out the love of her life right now." She taps out of the call and leans toward me. "Well?"

"Okay, hold on."

My heart races.

And—

I click on the email.

Your match is Jamie Anton.

I look up.

"Jamie," I say. "It's Jamie Anton."

Jamie. The guy who I ran into, *quite literally*, just a few weeks ago.

The entire freshman dorm complex barely gets any sleep that night, judging by the ongoing chatter in the hallways. Hours after the initial matches release, everyone's still crowding around each other, exchanging names and looking people up on social media. We observe the din and retreat back into our room. "You *have* to look him up," Ava says toward me, one headphone in, having jumped back onto her FaceTime with Bryce Santoso. They met in improv rehearsal the first month of school and have been inseparable friends since. "Or at least follow his Insta or something."

"*Or.* Radical thought," Ruhi jumps in. "Try LinkedIn."

I look up. "The *job* site?"

"People actually keep their profiles updated on there. You find out a surprising amount of information."

I search for Jamie on Instagram. His profile comes up, a grainy picture of him in what I assume is a soccer uniform. He's on private, and I can see that he has two posts. Ava turns back to her phone. "She already requested to follow you? Follow her back! Wait, hold on, help me with Cameron. Should I, like, text him? Or do you think I should wait until practice to talk to him instead?" She pauses. "I mean, I'd definitely try out a date. But do you think he would?" She sits up. "I'm *screaming*. Someone just asked in the group chat if we could include a fake wedding in our upcoming show. And he just liked the message!" She paces around the room, brushing her bangs out of her forehead.

Meanwhile, Ruhi's laughing from her desk. "The *Daily Leighton* Slack is going *off* right now. One of the staff writers just got matched up to his ex, and now we're all debating with him on whether he should text them or not." She claps a hand over her mouth. "Oh, and the two news editors got paired up. They *hate* each other."

"Really?" I lean in. "Well, they must be compatible in some way."

"Oh, yeah, they're the same person. They always argue about some obscure grammar rules." Ruhi glances at me. "Grace, this algorithm is gold." She scrolls her phone. "And the meme page is having a field day." She laughs. "This is all anyone's ever going to be talking about. Even Arjun is begging me for updates."

"Okay, my ADHD can't handle all these conversations at once. I'll see you tomorrow." Ava gets off her FaceTime with Bryce and comes over to peer at Ruhi's group chat. Ruhi reaches out to ruffle her wavy hair. "So? Who's Improv Boy?"

Ava glances at us with her wide brown eyes. "Oh, just this guy. He's sweet. I've never . . . thought about dating anyone from the improv team, though? I mean, we're just kind of clowning around all the time. I've seen this guy's Dr. Doofenshmirtz impression, but I've never, like, had a serious conversation with him, you know? But Bryce told me I should try out a date." She shrugs. "So I will. I'm going in with zero expectations. It'll be chill."

"Cameron's in one of my friends' study groups," Ruhi says. "I heard he's great. Always shares his notes with people. I support it."

Ruhi knows everyone on campus, I swear.

"An endorsement." Ava glances at me. "And how's *Jamie*?"

My internet search is sparse. The search term *Jamie Anton* turns up a lot of white guys. I think I come across a picture of him holding up some kind of trophy—competition math? Quiz bowl? I scroll down a little farther. It seems like a local news feature from Massachusetts. "He seems nice? I mean, I can't really tell." I shrug. "To be fair, I have no online presence, either."

"True," Ava says. "I could not find you on the internet. *I* had to make you an Instagram profile."

Ava's the one who always updates her social media with pretty pictures and posts in her stories, whether it's studying at Coffee House or capturing the way the light filters through the leaves. She, Ruhi, and I have a DM group chat, although Ava's the only one who sends us funny stuff and bugs us to check it.

I wonder if Jamie's opened his email. I think of the message he sent to me in the Set Theory group chat. His shy grin.

"He seems cute, though," Ruhi says. "He does club soccer. You do ski team. An athletic couple." She points over my shoulder. "Ooh, a follower request."

I glance down, seeing a notification pop up.

Jamie Anton has requested to follow you.

Ava crowds against my other shoulder, right against my ear, and cups my phone. "Grace! Accept it!"

"Okay, ow, calm down," I say, leaning away. I tap the screen twice. "Cool. Done."

"Message him!" Ava says. She's now moving clothes across the room into her laundry hamper. "Ask him out!"

I glance up. "Ava, we've been mutuals for three seconds."

"Maybe wait a day, and see if he messages you, and if he doesn't, *then* message him for coffee," Ruhi adds.

"A day?"

"You guys have to meet eventually."

"But we have," I say.

"*What?*" Ava bellows from her laundry hamper.

"He's . . . in my Set Theory class?"

Ruhi nearly drops my phone. "We've been talking about this guy for literally half an hour, and *now* you choose to bring up the fact that you two are in the same class?"

"Dude," Ava says. "The stars are all aligning for you."

"And the numbers are, too," Ruhi says. "This Nobel Prize–winning algorithm *specifically* matched you up with this athletic math nerd."

"If you don't walk up to him tomorrow in Set Theory and ask him out on a date to Coffee House, the spirit of Alfred Nobel will be personally heartbroken on your behalf."

"But I've never—" I pause. "I've never asked someone out before."

"Well, neither have I," Ava says. "But if I'm asking the guy from my improv team on a date, then you're asking the guy from your math class on a date, too."

Ruhi smiles. "If anything, it's for the algorithm. And you're a diligent mathematician."

"You're right." Numbers don't fail. Maybe this is it; the

algorithm pulling, from the hundreds of people in our grade, the two people that are just right for us.

The campus chatter doesn't die down throughout the week, not even when I go home for the weekend. Caroline texts our project group chat, albeit with some seemingly drunken typos, about seeing pairs of people she's never spotted together during her four years hanging out at Senior Bar Night.

I don't tell Ba about the algorithm, mostly because it feels strange to bring it out of the context of campus, and because once I tell him I'm setting everyone on campus up, he'll probably ask me follow-up questions about who I'm setting myself up with, and I don't quite want to answer. I've never talked about dating, not with either of my parents before. So I eat dinner and clear the dishes and listen to Ba practice a minuet on the electric piano while I lie on my bed and watch Ruhi provide our roommate group chat with live updates about the editors who got matched to each other.

> **Ruhi:** they wouldn't stop arguing about formatting in our editorial meeting
> **Ruhi:** and this girl eliza told them they bickered like a married couple would lmfaoooo
> **Ava:** eliza sees the vision
> **Me:** exactly
> **Ruhi:** talking about typesets is just English major flirting
> **Ava:** i was gonna say

Ava: also btw Cameron asked me on a date

Me: !!!!! When?

Ava: Tuesday afternoon. Coffee house! Ofc

Ruhi: Grace are you down to also coincidentally have a
   date on Tuesday afternoon at Coffee House

Ruhi: kidding

Me: Lmao I have work then

Ava: if u guys observe my date from afar I will be moving
   out of Spiegel 302

Ava: and taking all my party lights with me

I come back to campus on Sunday morning. The next day, I see so many people on dates at Coffee House that they actually run out of tables and chairs for people to sit at. Even Professor Rand mentions it during lecture, with an approving nod toward our direction. "I go home for the weekend and I hear that half the campus is apparently paired up, thanks to one of our group projects," he says. Caroline practically beams with the praise; Danny fist-bumps the both of us. My heart jumps. Professor Rand has noticed our project, which means he'll remember me when I apply for the summer research program.

I clock in for my shift at the library on Tuesday afternoon, after being glued to my phone for updates. I hurriedly turn my phone on silent and put on my tag. I only make eye contact with Julia once when we both enter the library, and I can almost *see* the words in the op-ed. I don't talk to her.

The Match-Up *does* get mentioned halfway through our

shift. It's Roberta who brings it up. "What's this online match-making thing that everybody's been talking about? It came up in the morning from one of the other students."

Julia glances my way, briefly. If she didn't know I created the Match-Up before, she definitely does now. Is her expression . . . amusement? Judgment? "It was just a survey," she says. "People on campus take it and apparently it finds your perfect match."

The tone in which she says *perfect match* makes me grit my teeth.

"Oh?" Roberta perks up. "Well. Did you take it?"

Julia shrugs. "Nope."

"Someone in your life already?"

Julia shakes her head and smiles a bit at her. "Just wasn't feeling it."

The library manager turns to me. "Did you, Grace?"

I peel my stare away. "Yeah. I did."

"*Oh.*" Roberta clasps her wrinkled hands together, and her blue eyes crinkle around the corners. "And who was the lucky match?"

I brighten. "A guy from my math class, actually."

She is even more intrigued. "That's *so* wonderful." She turns to Julia. "I mean, come *on. This* sounds like it could be a rom-com plot, doesn't it? It's like those books we read."

Julia shrugs, marginally. "I guess," she says, in a blasé, tone-less voice. She turns away. Her cheeks are slightly pink.

Someone comes up to the desk to ask Roberta a question about the archives. She leads them away. I fully stare at Julia.

She catches me. "*What?*"

I could ask her so many questions. But the first one that flies out is "You read *romance* books?"

Julia swivels in her chair to me. "And? What if I do?"

"I don't know. Didn't see that one coming."

"What?" She gives me a sardonic smile. "That I'm literate? I'm an English major."

"No, that . . . I don't know. I wouldn't have thought of you as someone who likes rom-coms, that's all." I glance at her, at her black jean jacket, at her distressed jeans that are cuffed around her gray boots. She looks like someone who'd read thrillers. The kind they sell at airports.

"Are you really judging me for my reading preferences?"

"Well, you judged *me* for my algorithm. Pretty publicly, I'd like to add."

She shifts. "I didn't know *you* made the survey when I wrote the op-ed, okay?"

"So you don't have a problem with me; you just take issue with my project. Which is quite ironic for someone who likes romance."

"Yeah, because I think it's ridiculous. I literally thought that email was satire."

Anger curdles in my chest.

"Sorry," Julia says. "I didn't know you cared about this so much. Maybe I shouldn't say that to your face."

She doesn't look remotely sorry. "No, I'm glad you did. Tell me, what's ridiculous about it?"

She shrugs. "Like I said already—"

"Don't MLA cite your op-ed. Tell me to my face."

Julia narrows her eyes. "Fine. The entire premise of pairing people up out of numbers? Thinking you can predict love as if it's some kind of experiment? There's no way you can ever make love into an equation."

"But you didn't even try it."

"I don't have to. I know it doesn't work. My friends all took it, and let me just tell you, it made all kinds of wrong pairs."

"How do you know?"

"I just know. They're not right for each other."

"That seems like your opinion."

"Well, maybe my opinion is better than your dumbass equation that you think can pair the whole campus up and have them miraculously start dating."

I concede. "Fine. Maybe *you* might not think that this equation can put together every couple, but—"

"Oh, it's not just that," Julia says. "I would be surprised if any equation at all can put together *any* couple. How is it going to force them to fall in love?"

"It doesn't force—*anyone*," I say. "You get set up with the person who is most compatible with you, and in theory, the more compatible you are with a person, the statistically higher chance you have at love."

"You really think you can calculate the odds of—what, *love*?"

"Yeah," I say, tilting my chin up to meet her eyes. "I can."

"Okay, *genius*," she says, in a tone of voice that clearly implies that I'm delusional. She swivels back, which seems to signal the end of the conversation. Roberta returns and chirps to Julia about a dessert recipe she recently tried, and Julia shows Roberta pictures of these key lime pies she made over the summer. "I'm trying to nail a brownie recipe in the dorm kitchenettes," she says. "But those tiny ovens are abysmal."

"They're from the seventies, that's why," Roberta laughs. "They haven't changed in decades."

Then they talk about this British baking show. Roberta tries to bring me into the conversation, but I have no idea what show they're talking about and have no baked goods stories to offer them. I end up checking books out for students and tuning both of my coworkers out.

SEVEN

I FUME ON my way home. None of my roommates are back; Ava has improv practice Tuesday nights, and Ruhi has her production meeting. I stew on the beanbag for a while before I get up and go over to Ruhi's desk. The newspaper from the other day is still there. I've only skimmed a few lines of the op-ed before. But now I sit down and read the full thing, snagging on certain sections.

Love is a spontaneous expression, something that sparks at the most random and unpredictable of circumstances. As I hear about the Match-Up algorithm, I'm baffled at the thought of an equation that claims to have the power of predicting someone's "ideal" match who they are destined to fall in love with.

In a sense, the algorithm can lull someone into the false sense of security; if an algorithm tells you who your ideal match is, then surely it should be correct, right? But can an algorithm account for every single factor—especially those that are inexplicable? And haven't there been so many stories that have explored the premise of a person whose romantic match has been determined for them, only to be proven wrong at the end? If someone is compatible with you, does that equate to love?

It's not as easy as that.

True love is something that hasn't been—and shouldn't ever be—reduced down to any kind of mathematical or scientific analysis, especially one thought of by a bunch of college students. Can an equation predict love?

The chances of that, I think, are pretty close to impossible.

I finish reading the op-ed article and lean back, letting the large beanbag swallow me up. As if Julia can make any sweeping claims about love, I think. Isn't she a college student, too? We're operating from the same plane of maturity. Who made her the expert on this?

Maybe the algorithm isn't going to have a 100 percent success rate. But we spent *hours* on this thing. I think of me and Caroline and Danny crowded into a library room, pushing our laptops against Caroline's cold brew cans. We had so meticulously crafted the thirty questions around each potential factor of compatibility. How optimistic someone was. How ambitious. What their political beliefs were. What values were important to them. We'd debated how much each factor should be weighted, and how the weights were determined. The survey takers themselves had the ability to select which questions mattered the most to them. And if someone is compatible with you, doesn't it mean that so many important things—their values, the things that matter to them—are aligned with yours? And wouldn't that make it easier to fall in love?

And if the algorithm leads to at least *some* people falling in love, then wouldn't it be a net positive?

I would be surprised if any equation at all can put together any *couple.*

Julia's words clatter through my head. What if she's right? What if no one falls in love—and, in turn, the project is a failure? How could I have hinged a class project for the head of the math department—and my future grade and potential faculty recommendation—on something this personal?

Just then, my phone dings with a notification in our roommate group chat:

Ava: dlfkjsdlfkjsdlkjlsj I have officially gone on a first date that i did not hate
Me: tell us!!!
Ava: grabbing food and then will be back after improv practice
Ruhi: back at 9:30 I WANT A FULL UNPACK

I smile a bit and send a bunch of celebration emojis. I place the op-ed down on Ruhi's desk, Julia's picture smirking up at me.

Take that.

I can prove her wrong and I will.

"It was actually really nice," Ava says from her lofted bed, curled up next to her textbook. She is allergic to desks, I swear. "We got coffee and talked until improv practice. The conversation wasn't painful for once."

I lean forward. "What'd you guys talk about?"

"A lot of things, really. Classes, people we know. He showed me pictures of his family's cats. He has a big family just like me. And he's from California, too. Near San Jose."

"Ooooh," Ruhi says. Her phone buzzes. It's a text from her boyfriend, based on how she reacts. She glows. She responds and swivels back around in her chair. "And will there be a second date?"

"Yeah. I'm going to trivia night with a couple of his dorm friends, I think. He lives in Saunders."

"Already meeting the friends," Ruhi says, with a discreet smile. "That's promising."

"We'll see," Ava says. "But enough about me. Grace, when are *you* going on your date with your hot math nerd?"

"Working on it," I say, turning back to my online textbook. Ava's eyes are lit up with her smile, and I feel a flicker of warmth in my chest. *This can work out.* And if this works out for Ava, maybe it can work out for me, too.

But *he* hasn't reached out to me yet. What if he doesn't want to? What if this is doomed to fail?

I have to try. If anything, I have to see it through for the algorithm I created.

I show up to Set Theory early the next day. We usually sit on opposite sides of the lecture room. I open the doors and glance at the rows of seats. He's there, on the right side of the lecture hall, at the very edge of the back row, as he always is.

The professor approaches the lectern. I go for the right side of the lecture hall. I get to the back row and am trying to consider which seat to pick before the professor starts talking, and I chicken out and sit all the way at the end of his row. But he raises his head, and then our eyes meet, and his flicker in recognition.

My pencil clatters to the floor. Startled, I pick it up and turn my attention to the lecture.

I can barely focus. Today's lecture is on the continuum hypothesis, something I skimmed through in the textbook when I was home this past weekend. Familiar terms float in and out, but mostly I just copy down what the professor scrawls on the squeaky blackboard and hope to make some sense of it later. My phone buzzes in my lap with notifications; I sneak a peek down.

Ava: hello I need to know everything about your math class rn ru hitting this boy up

I laugh. Since I'm up in the back row for once and hidden from the professor's line of sight, I send back a quick message, typing with one hand.

Me: currently sitting in the same row as him for lecture 😊

Ava: . . . that is not my definition of hitting someone up

Ava: talk to himmmmm

Me: did I mention there was a lecture going on

I flip my phone facedown and try to continue note taking, but all my mind keeps thinking of is the Match-Up. Now that the results are out, how are we going to gauge how well it's worked? Should we run statistics? Or conduct a follow-up survey? We have to analyze this data, right?

My mind continues to drift until I hear rustling and see the professor packing up his stuff. Class is over, I realize, and I've just been sitting here, staring off into the ether. I glance down at the end of the row and realize that Jamie's gone before I realize that the person approaching me is *him*.

I hurriedly snap my notebook shut and stuff it in my backpack. I unhinge and drop down the lecture seat table and scramble to my feet. My shoe catches onto the edge of the chair, and I almost wipe out, in the math lecture hall, right in front of him.

"Grace?"

It feels so strangely surreal, hearing him say my name. "Hi. That's me."

"I remember you from the Set Theory group chat. I was wondering if I'd run into you today." He shifts from foot to foot, his warm brown eyes coming up to meet mine.

"Well, good thing there's no bike."

His cheeks flood pink. I wonder if I've gone too far, but he laughs, a soft exhale. "Oh. Yeah. Sorry about that. Can't believe I almost ran over my most compatible match on campus."

"No harm, no foul," I say lightly.

"I *have* since gotten my brake pads fixed."

"Good to hear."

It's just us in the lecture hall now. *What now?* What would my roommates do? I can practically hear Ava in all caps over text, shouting at me to ask him out. I mean, that's what I'm supposed to do next, right? But now I'm in front of him, and I open my mouth and the words don't come out, and now the silence has gone on too long between us.

"Um," I say when he says, "So—"

We both stop short.

He nods at me. "You go first."

"Oh. I was just. Coffee?" I pause, my cheeks getting red. I clear my throat. "As in, would you want to get some sometime? With me?"

My words come out a jumbled mess, but I've done it.

I glance up at Jamie, who gives me a tentative smile. "I was going to ask the same. Coffee sounds perfect."

"Coffee House? Friday afternoon?"

"Great." He hands his phone out to me. I put my number in, my heart fluttering, and hand it back to him.

"Cool. See you then," he says, with a small, tentative smile, and my chest flutters, real and true.

Success.

* * *

The energy is different when Caroline and Danny and I meet up for our project tonight. I'm usually the first person in that study room in the library, but when I climb the three flights of stairs and open the door, I find Caroline, typing furiously on the computer. She sees me and stands up.

"Holy *shit*," she says.

"I know."

"Like, we knew it could be big. But *still*. It didn't hit me until I saw, like, five *hundred* people on a date at Coffee House. It's more packed than finals season."

Danny comes in on time, even, shrugging off his lacrosse jersey. We gather around the table and unpack our results.

"So," Caroline says. "I've been hearing that a lot of matches have been talking."

"Can confirm." Danny nods, grinning. "I definitely saw friends getting together on Senior Night."

"Oooh, who?" Caroline tilts toward him.

"Chloe Lin and Javi Marrero, for one."

"This makes a lot of sense, actually."

"My roommate went on a date with her match," I say. "And my other roommate says that two of the editors at the *Daily* have been talking."

Caroline nods vigorously. "Okay, let's get this all down. I'm opening up a Google Doc."

"Wait," I say. "Who did *you* guys get matched to?"

Caroline nods at Danny, and a look passes between the two of them.

"Liv Harris," Danny says with a bit of a smile. "She's pretty chill. We were in the same hall freshman year."

Caroline raises a perfectly drawn eyebrow. "He's omitting the fact that he had a *massive* crush on her freshman year."

I turn to him. "Really?"

"Yeah. We were talking a bit. Nothing much happened."

"Right, because your definition of 'talking' was to say 'What's up' to her at parties and then run away."

"Hey."

She shrugs. "Just saying, I was in that same hall. I saw it all happen."

Danny sighs and glances at me. "Never work on group projects with people who know your embarrassing freshman-year stories. You'll regret it."

"But you don't." Caroline is smug. "I save your ass every semester and you know it."

I feel like I'm watching a tennis match happen. I jump in. "But this is *perfect*. I mean, the algorithm works, right? It's like this is meant to happen. With Liv." This is all coming together; I feel excitement hum in my chest. I turn to Caroline. "What about you?"

Now Danny gives Caroline a look. She shrugs. "Got matched to some guy with a girlfriend. It's fine."

Wait. "*What?* How do you know?"

"Because I know everyone in our grade, and I know they're dating and when I asked him he said they both took it as a joke?"

I'm momentarily speechless. "A joke? That's what they

thought of this? You're—" I spread my palms out. "You're *not* supposed to take it if you've already found your person."

"It's not my idea of a Friday-date activity, that's for sure," Danny quips. "People are weird."

But Caroline just shrugs stiffly, as if she's brushing off some minor inconvenience. "Maybe they thought it was funny. It's fine, you guys. I'll live."

"Right, but . . ." That throws a wrench in everything. "I mean, that means that the girlfriend got matched to someone else, right? That person who was most likely single and looking for someone. Which means that the algorithm failed *two* people. Then . . ." My head starts to spin. "The stable match algorithm falls apart, because it's literally predicated on the fact that everyone's *looking for someone.*"

There's a pause.

"But it doesn't have to work every time to prove its efficacy, right?" Caroline says. "Grace, there's no way."

I let my shoulders drop. I guess so. "In an ideal world, it should."

"Yeah, but it's a college campus," Danny says. "People flake. And get busy. We don't make the soundest decisions a hundred percent of the time."

Caroline nods. "Just because there's a hitch doesn't mean the whole thing collapses."

They have a point. Maybe I did have some dim sense that people might not even have gotten around to meeting their matches. Sure, I hadn't considered that people would take the survey as a joke, knowing that they'd never be interested in the person on the other end. But maybe the algorithm isn't completely invalid. "So. What we're saying here is that if we can prove that most of our matches work, then we can still claim some kind of effectiveness with the algorithm?"

"Or even *some*," Caroline says. "And it seems like we have plenty right now. Off the top of my head I can think of ten pairs of matches that are talking. I mean, there's also you and Liv, and . . ." She turns to me. "How's it going with *your* match, Grace? I swear I can picture his name. John?"

"Jamie Anton. It's good. We're going on a date later this week."

"See? I'd call this a success, even from that. And think of how many other matches on campus that we're not aware of right now. What do you think?"

Caroline's logic does placate me a bit. But the more I think about it, the more other worries slot in. Should we have filtered for that kind of circumstance? Specified that it was only for people who were single and serious about love? But even if we had solved for that problem, were there other unknowns that could have knocked our algorithm off-balance?

If we did this again, maybe next year, we'd just put a disclaimer or something. A box to check that the survey taker is, in fact, serious about this. My mind's leaping ahead; I'm already starting to think about the next iteration.

"Grace?" Caroline taps me with her digital pen. "I said, we're doing great right now."

I snap back. "Yeah." I think of what Julia said. *I would be surprised if any equation at all can put together* any *couple.* But this hasn't gone off the tracks; that's just an outlier. An exception. I try to approach this logically. "So out of our sample size of three, we have two successful matches."

"If Danny ever gets the guts to text her," Caroline says with a sly smile.

"Bruh. I'm working on it."

"Two *tentative* successful matches," I say. Will things work out with Jamie? I push down that uncertainty and charge forward with my assumption. "That's already a sixty-seven percent success rate. Again, with an extremely small sample size, but I feel like we're onto something here." I pause. I cross over to the other side of the study room, where I pick up a dry-erase marker that's seemingly on its last leg of life. "We can analyze how well the matches work out through follow-up surveys. Like, maybe send a preliminary survey in November to see who's gone on at least one date with their match. Then, in December, we send a survey to those who've gone on at least one date to see who's continued to go on dates with their match. And then in January we send out one last follow-up to see how things have turned out. And through those, we can analyze to see what percentages of matches were successful. And then, well, we calculate the odds that this algorithm really finds true love."

I turn to face my other group members.

"I feel like . . . this is too *numbers*-y."

I frown at Danny. "This is an algorithm. Of course it has numbers."

"But how are we supposed to define success?"

"If people are in love. We can add a question in. Yes or no."

"Right, but I feel like it feels weird to ask a question in a survey like, 'Oh, hey, by the way, have you said 'I love you' yet? If not, your entire relationship is a sham.'"

"Fine, maybe we can just ask whether they're still exclusively dating. That can serve as a proxy variable for love."

Danny still looks skeptical.

Caroline jumps in. "Danny's right. I do think it has to be more nuanced than that. What if we introduce, like, a qualitative component to this as well? So we can feature a few stories of people who'd like to share how the Match-Up has influenced their dating lives. We can open up a form and invite people to submit their stories, and share that along with our data. And share that in storybook form. With their participatory consent, of course."

Danny leans forward. "Okay, I like *that* idea. Qualitative and quantitative."

Caroline nods. "Since it's October already, we can present our preliminary findings in our December final paper and presentation, and then, if we're cool with going on into the next semester, we can conduct the three-month follow-up based on those intermediary survey results and circle back to see if the couples have truly lasted." She looks around. "What do you think?"

I lift my chin. "Yeah. I want to continue this."

"I can't believe I'm saying this for a class, but I actually want to see this one through, too." Danny's eyes brighten and he snaps his fingers. "Oh. The three-month follow-up lands around mid-January, so we can release a report to coincide with Valentine's Day."

Caroline excitedly jabs the air with her digital pen. "*Yes.* Brilliant." She looks around. "Okay, team. I think we have a plan."

EIGHT

LIKE BASICALLY EVERYONE else, I meet Jamie at Coffee House. He's standing around, staring intently at his phone, before taking a peek up in front of him. When he sees me approach, he brightens. "Hey."

"Hi," I say. I stand in front of him for a moment, not sure of what to do. How do people do first dates? I've never done one. Should I have gone for a hug? "Um. I'll go order something."

"Oh, I got you," he says. "What's the drink of choice?"

"Earl Grey latte, thanks."

I watch him order and gather my coat up in my arms. I search through the crowd, trying to find a free table. It's futile. Instead I try to think of things to say. What do you talk about on a date? In a panic, I realize I should have prepared a list of questions. Or possible conversation topics.

Jamie comes back holding our cups. I take mine and hold it with two hands, savoring the warmth. "I was looking for a table," I say. "But there don't seem to be any around for now."

"Just wait until, like, one thirty-five," Jamie says. "It usually clears out when people go to their afternoon class."

I look at him. "Really?"

"Take it from someone who basically lives at Coffee House. I'd say there's a fifty percent chance something opens up in the next five minutes."

Sure enough, as he takes a sip of his coffee, a person in the corner stands. They hurriedly shove their laptop into their backpack and head out, scooping up their skateboard on the way.

Jamie glances at me, an eyebrow raised. "See?"

"Impressive," I say as we walk over. I set my coat on the back of the chair and sit.

"Thanks. That's how I show off on all my first dates."

I pause, my cup halfway to my lips.

"I'm kidding. I haven't been on a first date here yet. And I don't think my Coffee House stats calculations would really impress anyone."

"I *am* a math major," I say.

"True." Jamie smiles. "I guess there was a reason we were matched up, after all."

I wrap my fingers around the cup, feeling the warmth radiate through the sleeve.

"I was telling my family about it over FaceTime this weekend," Jamie says. "They were *super* intrigued. They didn't believe me until I forwarded them the email."

I look up. "Really?"

"Yeah, my family's full of nerds. My sister's doing a PhD in astrophysics. My parents met in a library. Here, actually."

"They met at the Leighton library?"

"Yep." Jamie laughs. "They got an absolute kick out of hearing about this."

"Oh, yeah, but—you tell your family these things?"

"I tell them everything," he says, shrugging. "They're always asking me for updates from college. I'm the youngest, so they're kind of both a little bored right now." He glances at me. "What about you? How are your parents taking it?"

I swallow. *There it is.* Something closes up in me. My throat gets tight, like it did on move-in day, when Ruhi's parents shook my dad's hand and asked if my mom was working or something. I lower my voice. "I, uh. Don't know how my mom feels. She died earlier this year."

I look up. Jamie has frozen still, like he doesn't quite know what to do. "Oh," he says, and it sounds like an exhale. "I'm really sorry, Grace. I didn't mean to be insensitive about it."

"No, it's . . ." I search for what to say. How much to say. Instead I hurry to fill the space with words. "My dad's okay. We're pretty close. I live half an hour from home, so I see him every weekend."

"That's really nice of you," Jamie says gently. I look up, and he meets my eyes. "I'm glad you're close with him."

My fingers trace the stained wooden table. I force a smile and take a sip of my latte. "So," I say, "what do you like to do, when you're not calculating the probability of open tables at Coffee House?"

He relaxes. And then we're talking. *Really* talking. He tells me about soccer, something he's played since he was little. "I didn't want to give it up after high school," he says. "So I picked up club soccer here."

"Big soccer guy?"

"Oh, yeah," he says. "I even used to think I wanted to grow up into some kind of sports statistician. Although, who am I kidding? I still kind of do."

"You do love your probabilities."

"Probabilities, odds, anything. I feel like it's cool to put some kind of definition on uncertainty. Sorry, I'm just going on one of my tangents."

I lean forward. *Definition on uncertainty.* And there, in that moment, it's like he's reached into my mind. "No, wait. Tell me more."

I don't know how much time passes; all I know is that it's dark and our cups are cold when I finally pull out my phone to check. It's almost six. I need to grab my stuff and go home soon. I look up to meet Jamie's eyes. "Have to go?" he asks with a small smile.

"Yeah, I just . . . My roommates and I have a standing dinner at six every Friday."

"That's cute," Jamie says. "I should get going, too. I have practice at six thirty. Besides, that person on the couch has been eyeing our table for a while."

"We can walk back," I say. "Do you live in Spiegel?"

"Saunders. But I'll walk you back."

We bundle up in our coats and leave our table. I don't even need to turn back to know that someone's already claimed it. Our shoes crunch over the leaves as we pass the science buildings, and then the cluster of small liberal arts buildings. Over the rooftop of the campus chapel far away, the sun is setting, vivid with color. The trees are sparsely dotted with bright gold and red, and there are more leaves off branches than on. Right before we get to Spiegel, I accidentally kick over a branch and almost trip, before Jamie steadies me.

My cheeks warm. "Thanks."

"Just making up for the bike thing." He smiles.

I laugh. "Don't worry," I say. "We're pretty even now."

I realize I'm holding on to his arm still. I don't move away. Neither does he.

I glance up at him. He peers down at his feet, and then at me. We're close. I know what this means; it's the moment *before*.

And yet I don't say anything.

"If I asked to kiss you," Jamie says, his voice soft, "what are the odds you say yes?"

I relax, almost in relief. "Pretty good odds," I say, and then I reach up. His lips press against mine, softly, for a moment, and we're kissing. It's my second time kissing a boy, and it feels natural and lovely. The wind picks up around us. We break apart, and my cheeks are warm.

"See you, Grace," he says with a small smile.

I slip into my dorm building and lean against the wall, curling the memory of the kiss in me like a secret.

My mom was the first person who knew I wanted to be a mathematician, even before I did. My first-grade teachers thought I had trouble paying attention in class and called her in for a parent-teacher conference. In reality I was bored and had finished half the workbook and had jumped ahead to multiplication when the teachers were still explaining subtraction.

She came home mad. She told my dad. He found it kind of funny. "You're my daughter," Ma said. "You can't embarrass yourself like that in front of teachers. That embarrasses me."

But her anger only lasted a day or so. That weekend, she went to the local Target and brought home a third-grade workbook. She told me when I got through it, she'd take me out to get as much ice cream as I wanted. I finished it in three days, and we went out to get ice cream at the shop in the center of town. I got a huge peanut butter chocolate chip cone. Our stomachs both ended up hurting on the way home because Ma didn't take dairy very well and I had never eaten that much ice cream.

The next thing she did was schedule a meeting with my teacher and ask for me to be put in the gifted math program. When the teacher said that that wasn't possible, that I had to take a bunch of IQ tests first and that those tests got offered only once before each school year, my mom took it all the way up to the principal. She alone went to those meetings with a whole prewritten speech in English. Ba was laboring over research papers around the clock to get on the tenure track. A week later, I went into the school on a weekend to take those tests. I was alone, surrounded by the sea of desks, the projector humming, and worked through a bunch of weird problems about shapes. And by the following week, I would leave my class for an hour each day to sit in a spare, empty classroom with three other kids.

In second grade, I drew a self-portrait in crayon and said I wanted to be a famous mathematician. Ma hung that up on the fridge. From that point, she also fiercely latched on to that idea. Though I didn't know it then the trajectory of my life was being mapped out. I think she had it in her head that I truly would be famous somehow, that people would know my name and that I would get a Wikipedia page or something. During weekends in middle school, she signed me up for competitions. Summers were spent taking online math classes. Ones that I could actually sit through because they weren't just practice problems; they were puzzles and took me all day to think through them. Ma printed out biographies of women who won famous math awards. "She won the Fields Medal," Ma said, gesturing at the article with a spoon while she ate her oatmeal in the morning. "Look at what she does. Hy-per-bolic geometry. You know that?"

I shook my head. "Not yet," I said. *But I will.*

At the beginning of high school, after Ma had gone through vicious rounds of chemo for lymphoma and come out of it, weak but cancer-free, SAT books miraculously appeared on the kitchen table. It became an unspoken agreement between the two of us that MIT was the dream school. It slipped between conversations at the dinner table, and soon ifs became whens. It would only be a state away. "I'll come visit you on the week-ends," she'd say.

"Ma," I said, "I don't think parents visit their kids every weekend at college."

"Well, how else am I going to make sure you eat healthy?"

While I considered the mildly terrifying aspect of my mother pulling up to a frat party with a pot of jujube soup, Ba raised an eyebrow. "You're talking about this as if she's already gotten in?"

"She will." Ma jutted her chin at me. She barely ate at din-ner; she still felt queasy but her voice was strong. "It's perfect for you. Right?"

I nodded and ate a mouthful of rice. "当然了。Of course."

In her mind, it was all so very clear. She prayed for it every weekend and prepared me for it. Ma was healthy again, with a new steely determination. The odds were cautiously, tenuously on our side. Of course I would go. It was only a state away, close enough to her. This was our dream now, hers and mine. Of course I wanted to make it come true.

Summer after Junior Year

HANA CAME IN ten minutes before my shift at the Woodward Recreation Center was over at four. She peeled her hair back from her forehead into a ponytail and lingered around the front desk.

"Hey," I said, glancing up. It was a slow day indoors. Everyone was at the outside pool instead. My coworker Miles and I were trying to see if we could make Bic pens into the pen cup.

"Hi there." Miles straightened up, his blue shirt draped over his lanky shoulders. "How can I help you?"

"Here to book the basketball court, please," Hana said. She's five feet tall with her platform New Balances. She reached out her hand, and I handed her a pen. She tossed it lightly, and it clattered into the pen cup. She tilted her head. *See?*

"Oh?"

"I'm fucking with you." She grinned. "I'm just waiting for Grace to get off her shift."

"Gotcha." Miles leaned back and twirled the pen in his hand, drumming it lightly against the desk. He has gelled sandy-colored hair and freckles across his nose. "What are you guys up to after this?"

"Going on a romantic walk in the woods."

"A hike," I clarified, rolling my eyes. If anything, Hana probably wanted to unpack with me the trials and tribulations of her heartache. Her semi-girlfriend and first love Kristen broke up with her last weekend, the day before Hana's week-long family camping trip. I'd woken up to at least fifteen texts all with a timestamp of 2:30–2:35 the following morning. We'd been texting all through last week, as much as spotty Maine backwoods cell service would let us, which wasn't much.

"Neat."

"What are you up to after this?" Hana nodded at Miles with a casual familiarity that I didn't have, not even after two months of working next to this kid. I mean, we all went to school together. He was in our grade. I wondered if they knew each other—theater and band were adjacent worlds, neither of which I was remotely familiar with. But maybe Hana was also just better at talking to people than I was.

"Setting up in the Village Green."

"Oh, right," I said. "For summer-band Fridays, right?"

He nodded. "Come through. If you don't have better Friday plans."

Hana texted as Miles and I clocked out. She and I headed out from the crisp, air-conditioned rec center and waded into the humid heat. I peeled out of my blue collared shirt and stuffed it into my drawstring bag, shaking my hair out of my ponytail. Hana blasted her car air conditioner in her Jeep Wrangler, which swallowed her up. I hauled in my backpack, and Hana glanced at it skeptically. "We're studying for the SAT on this hike?"

"My mom thinks we're at the library."

Her expression cleared. "Oh." She turned back. After seven years she was used to this, skirting around my mom's rules just a bit. Hana circled the ice cream shop twice, and I wondered if I lied to my mother for Hana to circle the block forever until she finally decided to go in and get a frozen lemonade. I peeled out a five and asked Hana to get me one.

And then Hana drove onto the main four-lane road, and then toward the highway. She turned up some indie pop shuffle playlist. There was a quiet strum of guitar, a soft ethereal voice, and Hana quickly changed songs. "Fuck, not MUNA."

"I liked that song!"

"They're on my Kristen playlist."

"*Oh*." She was waiting for me to ask, so I did. "What happened?"

Hana heaved a sigh. She changed lanes toward the exit and glanced behind her. "Well, what it came down to was that she's going to college in a few weeks. That's all. It was an amicable split. Just rough."

"Ah." I leaned back. Even I could see that coming. Logically speaking, a relationship was never easier to maintain over a distance than it was in a shared hometown.

"I'm fine now, I think."

"You seemed pretty cut up about it in your texts from the backwoods."

"Yeah, that first day was *awful*," Hana said. "But, you know, I got space. Had my *Walden Pond* nature offline moment. Bruised a toenail hiking and watched the stars and all. Had a whole talk with Dad about girls, which is hilarious, because this man could not even say the word *lesbian* at one point in time. I think I'm okay now. Just no MUNA." She took a long sip of her iced lemonade. We pulled into a gravelly parking lot, in a vaguely marked spot shielded by the overhanging branches of a tree. She looked at me frankly. "I really fell for her."

"Oh, I know. I barely saw you after the musical."

"Sorry," Hana said. "But yeah. I don't know if she felt the same. The breakup was, like . . . super efficient. But then I'm the one who makes a whole heartbreak playlist."

I glanced her way. "You just have a lot of love to give."

"Speaking of," Hana said. "Ready for our romantic stroll?"

I rolled my eyes. "Don't rebound with your straight best friend."

We made our way down the small rocky trail, brushing aside ferns and small branches. I kicked aside little rocks on the path and looked around me. Deep green surrounded us, with dappled light coming in between the leaves. We walked in silence. About a mile or so in, I heard the soft rustle of water and we arrived at a small pond. We found rocks with level surfaces to sit on and sipped on our frozen lemonades and listened to the sound of crickets and cicadas. People liked to come smoke here, but usually later in the day. I still caught onto the remnants of something weedy. Despite us being in shade, the air was hot and muggy and sweat pooled between my shoulder blades. The frozen lemonade was cool and tart and delightful. Hana hugged her knees. "*We're* the seniors this year," she said. "I still can't really wrap my head around it."

"Yeah," I said. I shrugged. "Maybe I'll finally go to a football game or something."

"Don't bother," Hana said. "They're boring and our team sucks. There's gotta be something else on your senior-year bucket list."

I settled my cheek on my knees. "Get into college."

"What else?"

"Can't really think of anything else."

"Oh, right, because you're not allowed to have fun until the moment you step into college."

"That's kind of the deal." At least, college felt like the time when anything remarkable was truly allowed to begin. Other people went to high school parties and on weekend trips and hung out in the parking lot of the sandwich shop after school. I studied at home. At best, I slept over at Hana's house and heard all about it. Lately Ma had been making up reasons for me not to go. I knew the true reason; Ma didn't think Hana was a good influence.

"I'm getting you into a party this year." Hana straightened

up. "There's one this Friday. You should come. Tell your mom you're sleeping over at my place. Or whatever."

I shook my head. "I'm working on my college essays this weekend."

"It's *August*. MIT applications aren't even due for a few months."

"Yeah, but it's MIT."

"You're going to be eighteen soon. No one can legally make you write your college apps."

"Yeah, but it's my mom."

"You're going to be thirty and she's still going to make you do math problems and go to church."

There was an edge to her voice, and I didn't blame her. After Hana came out junior year and her family stopped going to church, my mom slowly froze them out. Our moms went from hanging out every Sunday and holidays to barely texting. I made it clear that I thought my mom was being ridiculous about it, but Hana still wasn't obligated to think kindly of her. "You know," I said, skimming my fingers through the water's surface, "she did say she was going to bring me soup every weekend."

"Jeez," Hana said. She examines me with a gentle scrutiny that only seven years of friendship could allow. "Is MIT really your dream, Grace?"

She put emphasis on *your* and not on *MIT*. I answered, "As much as Wellesley is yours."

Hana looked out at the water. "I think I actually want to go to California instead."

I glance at her. "California?" It was a drastic change from Wellesley, a school on the outskirts of Boston. I couldn't even solidify the images that came to mind: billboards and movies and flashes of music videos set on beaches.

"Yeah, I've been looking into schools over there. USC in particular. I don't know. I know it's a cliché. But I keep looking at pictures of those coastlines you can just drive up and—I want that. To move to somewhere entirely different. I feel like here I'm like a piece of paper that keeps getting folded up into smaller pieces until I can't be folded up anymore."

"You can't wait to get out of here," I said.

Hana nodded. I looked out over at the water. It felt surreal, the thought of Hana existing on the other side of the country. "That's wild. We won't be near each other."

Hana tilted her head. She said, "What if we both went out to California?"

I looked at her.

"I mean, there's Caltech, right? Super mathy. They pretty much feed into Nobel Prizes. Or there's UCLA."

I shrugged. "Maybe."

"Applying can't hurt. Do it. Then we both get to be out there. I can't imagine life without you, really."

I laughed. "Says the person who barely replied to my texts for half the summer."

"I'm just a shitty texter. But I mean it."

She did. Hana and I did our own thing at school. We each did different extracurriculars and hung out with different

106

people here and there, but we always floated back to each other, meeting up for open lunch sometimes, or hanging out on the weekends. We were each other's oldest friendships. I didn't have to see her every day to know her faceted history, her chameleonlike changes. She wanted to leave so badly and no one saw it more than I did.

"Maybe," I said again, noncommittally.

We hiked back in the late-afternoon light. The humidity drenched my back in sweat. The iced lemonade melted into a lukewarm, sticky syrup. Hana drove away and pulled onto the highway. The window was open, and there was green all around us. A breeze streamed through my shoulder-length hair. Sufjan Stevens played on the aux, and I watched how the light fell on my best friend's sunglasses, her button nose, her pursed lips. We didn't talk about California for a while. But for a moment I let myself think about us, like this, driving along the coastline. About flying out west. About being in motion.

I met Hana Mari Takamura in fifth grade when she and her family came into Sunday church service. I remember she and two other kids followed her parents into the pews. She stared at me the whole time, because it was easy to spot the only other Asian people in church. The congregation welcomed them, and after, when everyone had greeted them and clasped their hands, my mother approached her family after service and invited them to our house for dumplings.

Hana's name sounded light, like the chime of bells.

Takamura and Tang were right next to each other, so we stood in lines and got seated with each other. The next week, our moms sat together in church, so we did, too. When they stood around talking in the parking lot after service in the summers, Hana and I sat on the edges of the sidewalk and made bracelets out of the small daisies that bloomed in the cracks. We hung out at recess. Hana's parents made her sandwiches and gave her carrot sticks and cut-up strawberries on the side. She gave me the strawberries because she didn't like them. After school, I'd go over to her house, where her parents let us watch movies and TV shows in the living room. My family didn't have cable. Ba liked watching historical Chinese dramas at home. Hana's family was Japanese, but they didn't have Japanese TV shows. They were second generation, Hana told me. She didn't know how to speak it, except for a few words that she'd say to her grandma. But I liked the shows she watched better anyway.

We saw each other six days a week, at school and at church. We sat in youth group together, learning a type of Morse code with our blinks so we could send messages to each other. In the wintertime, her family took me skiing. Ma always warned me to be careful. The mountains had ice. One slip could break my back. I stayed on the easy green runs before Hana made me come with her on blue squares, and then on black diamonds, finally. She'd always go down first and I'd go after her, clutching my poles tightly to me, following her pink helmet. And Hana and I went to church together for years. But during our sophomore year our pastor at the time came out as gay and the majority of our church leadership voted him out, Ma among those votes. And after that Hana became super disillusioned and resentful. The winter break of sophomore year she told me she might like girls, too. She came out officially during junior year. And then, eventually, she and her family left the church altogether.

But I still saw her at school, at lunch, during weekends. To be honest I didn't even really remember a time before Hana. We'd come this far together, and a part of me couldn't imagine a future without her. So maybe that was why her dream became mine, too. In the end, California burrowed into my consciousness, an errant thought sprouting into daydreams. I sat in AP English, and when we did our *Twelfth Night* readings, I zoned out and looked up pictures of the Caltech campus instead of taking my notes. On the bus ride to the community college's multivariable calc classes, I put in headphones and with my cell data I Google Maps'd my way around the beach and picked out the coffee shops I'd do my homework in on the weekends. The ocean was there, a serene 2D spread of blue on my small screen.

The more I thought about California, the easier lying to my mother became. I lugged my unopened SAT textbooks around in Hana's car as we went on hikes and long drives and talked with the windows down and milkshakes in the cupholders. Once, I lied about having to make up a work shift on Sunday morning so I wouldn't have to go to church and we went to the matinee instead. On weekends, I sat in my room with the door closed. I looked at the questions for the MIT application and suddenly Boston was too close. I clicked to the next windows, where two applications stood: Caltech and UCLA.

I brought it up just once, with my parents, at the dinner table. Ba put down his bowl and gave me a long look. My mother's expression was frozen. "*Why* California?"

"They have good math programs," I said.

She placed her chopsticks on top of her bowl, and they rattled sharply. "Not better than MIT."

"But what if I don't get into MIT?"

"What are you saying, Xiǎoyàn? You're my daughter. You're getting into MIT." Her tongue clicked in disapproval. "And doubting yourself like this won't get you anywhere. It's wasting the time you could be spending on writing your essays."

"I'm just saying I should have safety schools."

"You do. You have the University of Vermont. Your ba's university. And colleges like Leighton and Middlebury. Not in *California*." Ma leaned forward. "Where did this thought even come from?"

"I—"

"Is Hana applying there?"

"That has nothing to do with it," I lied, but Ma's sharp eyes were on me. I was a terrible liar.

"I knew it. She's not a good example for you. Do I have to keep telling you this?"

I gritted my teeth. Always, it came back to this. As if Ma wasn't the one that cut the Takamuras out from her life despite the kindness they showed us; as if she wasn't the one who turned her back on Hana.

"*I* want to go to California," I said.

"Grace," Ba said. "What's the reason?"

"Do you want to be thousands of miles away? All the way across the country, alone, by yourself?" Her voice rose. "Do you want to be far from us? We raised you, and you become so *selfish* as to leave us?"

"No!" I blurted out.

"Why would you do that to your family?" Ma looked at Ba. "Can you believe her?"

"MIT is your dream," Ba said. "I don't understand."

My mom's lips pressed together. "If Hana wants to leave her family behind and go all the way to California, that's her own *choice*. She makes her own decisions. You make yours." She jabbed her chopsticks at the refrigerator, where my drawing from second grade hung up. "But you wanted this. It's your dream. I didn't spend all my hours doing overtime and driving you to competitions for you to throw it all away." My mother slammed her chopsticks down and lifted the back of her hand to her neck, as if me bringing up this topic made her feverish with anger.

It's your *dream*, I wanted to shout. The rice formed into glue in my mouth. For a moment, I fantasized about standing on the chair and letting my voice rise. *I am carrying the weight of your dream, do you know that? All because you couldn't achieve yours.* But I couldn't. Not like other kids could. Not like they could in the movies, in those high school movies that Hana and I watched in her room, the movies where the kids went on road trips and had their first kisses and stomped from their parents when they stood in their way.

So I retreated into stony, iron-willed silence. I couldn't stop, but I could simply say nothing. "Okay," I said flatly instead. *And . . . scene*, I thought in my head. It was an inevitability that this conversation would go the way I thought it would.

That night, I reached to close the tabs on my laptop. I hesitated, and then opened up a Google Doc and pasted in each of the prompts. I put on my headphones and started typing.

I typed those essays quickly within the span of two weeks in early October. I didn't want to race against deadlines. I wanted to slip those applications through, almost as if they didn't exist. I decided not to apply to Caltech and opt for UCLA and UC Berkeley instead because they were on a separate application platform and wouldn't show up on the Common App. The Thursday after homecoming weekend, I worked the late shift with Miles until the rec center closed at ten. We cleaned up the remnants of a birthday party and played a game of pool. At 10:15, I stood in front of the gift card rack at the convenience store. I took a deep breath and grabbed a Visa gift card off the rack. The cashier didn't even bat an eye as she rang me up. I recognized her as a girl in my English class. "Have a nice day," she said, her lip ring glittering. I tucked the gift card into the front pocket of my backpack and headed home in Ma's car. That night I sat in front of my computer, the heated laptop pad whirring under my palms. I carefully copied and pasted my answers from the Google Doc into the answer boxes on the application website. I stared at the questions that blinked at me in tiny font, the same question that reminded me of what my mother had asked: *Why University of California?*

Why there of all places?

It was so clear why Hana wanted to leave. I thought of her kicking up against this place each time: marching out of church service at sixteen after the youth group leader made a speech that was subtly targeted at her. Making out with Kristen the weekend after she broke up with her boyfriend and being called a slur and a homewrecker all the same. Gathering up petitions and sitting in on school board meetings so they would take books off their banned list. Sure, it was Vermont, but above all it was still a small town. Hana stood out so clearly and this place disdained her for it.

But why did *I* want to go?

Because you can. It was a hypothetical decision tree, branching out. There was one reality where I stayed here and the decisions branched out into MIT and into any other school. The other reality where I went out west. I'd wondered about this decision tree, branching back decades. There could have been a reality where my parents never met in that karaoke bar, a world in which my dad came here and my mom stayed back in China. Would she be a famous singer then? Would she still be a mother? In that reality, would she be happier and fulfilled by her own dreams?

113

Now there was a future version of Grace that was out there, with her best friend, doing what she'd always wanted to do. This version of me walked to class under the endless sun and went to the beach on Sunday mornings. She did what she wanted, just like her parents had done all those years ago. I wanted that for myself, too. Maybe that reason was enough.

I checked over my essays for typos. I took out the gift card and scratched off the PIN.

My finger hovered over the submit button.

Do you want to be far from us? How could you be so selfish? My mom's sharp voice rang out in my head, even now. She was in the next room over. Any moment and she could come through the door and see what I was doing. This was a lie bigger than other lies.

I wouldn't tell my mother about it. Even now, I could barely acknowledge the page. This would be an errant hope. A letter in a bottle tossed out to sea. I'd never felt like I really belonged here, either. Here I would stay still. But what if I wanted to be in motion? So what if I wanted to know what it was like to finally be on my own?

All the small little lies built up in me over the months. Pressing the button now was easier than I'd thought.

When I walked into AP Psych the next day, Hana was sitting in her usual seat next to the window, with one leg propped against the edge of the desk. Her wired earbuds were in. She doodled in her notebook. I slid into the seat next to her, and she glanced at me.

"Hey."

"Hey," I said.

Hana raised an eyebrow and took out her earphone.

I smiled slightly.

"I can't tell if this is something good or bad."

"I did it." I shrugged my shoulders. "UCLA and Berkeley. I submitted them."

Hana was still for a moment. And then her face lit up with a brilliant grin, and in that instant, I knew that everything I'd done up until that point was all worth it.

"Oh my God, Grace," she whispered. "We're going to Cali."

"Well, I don't know what's going to happen. I could get rejected."

Hana shook her head. "It's going to happen," she said. She leaned in with a small, conspiratorial smile. Right before the bell rang and the period started she said, "We're getting the fuck out of here."

NINE

THINGS ALWAYS SEEM to happen on the weekends.
Parties. Hiking day trips. But I was always away during the
weekends, so I was used to feeling the twinge of jealousy when
Ava and Ruhi sent me pictures. I'd gotten used to coming back
to my room quietly. I'd see Ruhi emerge from her bed first in an
oversized crew neck, water bottle cradled in her arms. And then
Ava would climb down from her lofted bed around noon. In
the afternoons, my roommates would scramble to complete all
their assignments for Monday. They'd sit at their desks, drilled
into their work, Ava's noise-canceling headphones over her ears
and Ruhi staring at her planner or listening to another one of
her podcasts or audiobooks. I'd make cups of tea with our com-
munal kettle and double-check my answers on my homework.
We'd all go to the dining hall for dinner, and they'd catch me
up on the parties they went to over the weekend. But Halloween
falls on a Thursday this year, and according to my roommates,

there's no excuse not to get dressed up and go to a party.

"It's your *first* college party," Ruhi says that Tuesday night. "We have to go all out."

"Technically second," I say. "Remember O-week?" Half of the Leighton freshman population tried to cram into someone's suite on the first floor of Spiegel. Ruhi almost got in a fist-fight after someone spilled beer on her (and me), and Ava got crowded by a bunch of tall dudes, and we all left promptly.

"O-week parties don't count," Ruhi says. "This is a party hosted by *Daily* people, so it's trustworthy. The drinks might even be chilled."

"A classy affair," Ava pipes up. She's bundled in a blanket, laptop perched in front of her. She has a sociology essay due at 5:00 p.m., and in typical Ava fashion, she started working on it at 2:30. "Speaking of, what costumes are we wearing?"

"Oh, I didn't even think of that," Ruhi says. "But also, write your essay."

"I *am*," she grumbles. "But now I'm distracted and I want to plan group costumes."

"Don't worry," Ruhi reassures her. "We're not making exec-utive decisions without you."

At the library, Roberta decks out the reference desk in mini pumpkins and orange tinsel and shows up in a skeleton cardi-gan. I'm finding out more about her. Turns out, she went to Leighton, too, back in the '80s. "I was Leslie Aguilar's TA in her writing seminar, actually," she says. "You know, the poet."

Julia finds this fact fascinating. I do not. I wonder if Roberta, too, was a part of that hippie '80s artistic wave that Ruhi mentioned to me. I do see it.

"Were your parents supportive of you studying English?" Julia asks Roberta.

"Oh, sure," my library manager says. "My mom was my high school English teacher, actually. What about yours? Do they?"

Julia sets her mouth in a flat line. She shrugs. "Not really. I think they're secretly waiting for me to change it."

The day of Halloween comes. Professors throw out candy during lectures. That night, after dinner, Ruhi plays music from her speaker when we get ready. Ava eats an edible. Between our three closets (mostly Ruhi's), we've managed to scrounge together a Powerpuff Girls group costume. Ruhi looks stunning in an ice-blue dress and blue sparkly platform heels, which put her at well over six feet, Ava has her signature red hair up in space buns, and I have a green shirt dress and a dark green headband. We put on our coats, each take a shot of cinnamon whiskey for insulation, and set out toward the other dormitory on the other side of campus. On the way, Ava shows us pictures of her family's group costumes from the previous years.

It's ten on a Thursday night, yet there's already music thudding out of the first story. Even muffled, the bass is so loud that the windows seem to rattle. I wrap my coat tighter around me. It's one of those nights where the wind seems to cut under every last layer of clothing, and I'm relieved when we finally step into the dorm. We follow Ruhi up two floors of stairs and gingerly sidestep the boys in the hallway who are seemingly chugging beer sideways from the can for some reason, foam spraying everywhere. Ruhi rolls her eyes. "People have the most creative ways of pretending that they like beer."

We arrive at the room. Ghost cutouts line the doorframe. We filter through the tinsel curtain. Inside, fairy lights are draped everywhere, and along with the fake candles, they cast a soft glow all over the room. A purple-light speaker slowly pulses with the music, tinging the room with a soft violet. "Someone went all out with these decorations," Ava says, admiring the lights.

Ruhi brushes a low-hanging strand of lights out of the way. "*Oh*. Cider's in the corner."

There's already a crowd of people in the room. A group sits on the sofa in the corner in the back, mouthing the lyrics, someone shuffling cards in their hands. Others crowd around on the floor, playing some kind of game. Ruhi beelines us for the bucket of hard ciders in the back and hands each of us one like it's some prized possession. The glass is cold against my palm, and I take a sip. It's like those Martinelli's sparkling ciders that my mom always had out for holidays, but less sweet. It tastes brighter almost, with a slight kick to it. "This is amazing."

"Told you."

Ava brightens. "Oh! I see Bryce and Rocky. I'm gonna say hi to the improv people. Be right back." She gives both of our hands a squeeze, and then her five-foot frame disappears into the crowd.

"Ruhi!" Someone approaches us. She has blond braids and

is dressed in a Princess Peach costume, her pink eyeshadow bright against her dark skin. "Are Isa and Adrian . . . *genuinely flirting*?"

Ruhi clutches the girl's arm. "Oh my God." I peer in that direction. Through the crowd I can just barely make out two people, standing close next to the dressers, tipped toward each other. Ruhi turns to me. "Those were the editors I told you about! Oh, by the way, Ari, this is Grace, my roommate. She invented the whole algorithm in the first place."

Ari raises an eyebrow. "I've been rooting for this since last year. *Thank* you."

I smile. "It was mostly the algorithm."

Ruhi and Ari start talking about something newspaper related, something about a feature they're trying to run on this local visual artist. I glance around. The cider's burned away a bit of my self-consciousness from not really knowing anyone here, and so I wander a bit.

My phone buzzes in my pocket, and I see that Hana has posted on Instagram. Last Halloween, we were in Travis Kelly's house in the basement, getting drunk off mixed vodka drinks, and now I can't even bear to see her post. I get another cider and spot Ava in the corner, talking animatedly to her friend Bryce.

And then I spot my coworker.

Julia Zhang's sitting on the sofa near me with three other people, one of whom is still shuffling around some kind of cards. She's wearing a witchy-looking long dress with bell sleeves, her long hair draped over her shoulders. It's the first time I'm seeing black lipstick on her. Or any lipstick, really. Her eyes are lined, too, bringing out her striking features and her sharp jawline. Her eyes sweep around the crowd, and then they meet mine.

I stand still, my cider clutched in my hand. I must have stared for a bit too long because the person next to Julia calls out, "Hey, want a tarot reading?"

I glance at her. She's dressed in a black dress and a white collar, her brown hair in two braids. "A what?"

She holds up a deck. "Tarot card reading. Have you ever had one?"

I shake my head.

"Here, sit." She gestures to a chair on the other side. Julia's now transfixed on something on her phone. The girl holds the deck out to me. "Hi. I'm Tashie." She tilts toward the left, where a girl with short dark hair is dressed up in a suit, beaming at me with a drunken grin. "This is Claudia." She nods toward her right. My coworker and I lock eyes again. "And this is Julia." Tashie sets the cards down on the table. "Okay. These are cards to give you insight into what you're dealing with. Past, present, or future."

"Really?" I glance at her. "Is this stuff, like, proven?"

"Of *course* you'd ask that."

Julia looks straight at me. Claudia looks confused. Tashie glances at Julia and then back at me. "You know her?"

"She's the person who came up with the algorithm thing. And everything has to make sense with her *data* and *statistics*."

My face feels warm. But Tashie only brightens. "Oh! Really? You matched up two of our friends, actually." She nods to the corner, where two girls stand with their fingers linked together, talking over their drinks. "They're *so* cute together. We've been saying they should be together ever since O-week."

Something warms in my chest. It's sweet validation. I'm putting together people who were *meant* to be together. First Ruhi's editors, then this. I glance over at Julia. Her expression sours.

She stands. "I'm getting another drink."

I watch her walk briskly away and smile widely at Tashie. "Let's do a reading."

"Cool," she says. "How about a basic one card read? Just what's on your mind right now."

I shrug. "Sure." She fans the facedown cards out in front of me, and I carefully select one.

"Now flip it over."

I turn the card.

It's three knives, plunging into a heart.

Tashie's eyes widen.

I look up. "What does it mean?"

"Hmm," Claudia says thoughtfully. She looks up at me, her green eyes wide. "Three of swords means some kind of heartbreak. Does that feel true?"

I become still. The cold glass from the cider seeps into my palm.

"No," I say, but my words feel far away, as if I'm hearing

them from across the room. "I've never . . . had that before."

"*Any* past heartbreak?" Tashie probes. "A situation with someone you like that didn't go your way?"

I shake my head. The alcohol is starting to go to my head, I think. I feel strangely detached from myself.

"Ironic, isn't it?" someone says behind me.

I turn to face Julia.

"You guys should know that Grace doesn't do heartbreak or *feelings*," Julia says to her friends, laughing and swaying a little. "She draws up her *perfect* little diagrams and crunches her numbers and gets all her dates from an Excel spreadsheet. She's a lost cause."

My eyes smart. My cheeks grow hot.

Julia's still laughing. She climbs over my chair, drunkenly, and part of her drink sloshes onto the green dress I've borrowed from Ruhi. I flinch. Her friends are looking between the two of us. Claudia says quietly, "Dude, what?"

I stand. "Do you hate me? Or do you just like tearing into everything all the time?"

My words hang in the air. Julia's smile disappears. She meets my eyes, and for once her mouth hangs open. My heartbeat is loud in my ears.

I need to leave. I've ruined their fun.

I try to wipe off the drink that Julia spilled, but it's already soaked into the shoulder of Ruhi's dress. I don't meet her eyes. I think I'm going to cry. I push through the crowd of people. Ruhi's still with her friends, talking over the drinks table. Ava's with another crowd of people. People they *know*. I know no one else here.

I'm just going to go home.

I emerge into the hallway, which is significantly cooler. I weave through people who are talking and taking hits out of a joint, and I chug the rest of the cider, the bubbles harsh and cold against my throat. I pull out my phone and look at Hana's latest story.

It's a picture of her and her friends, dressed in glittery clothing, the lights in the background slightly blurred. I shut my phone off and shove it into my back pocket. I tear off my headband. I don't feel slightly buzzed or happy or fearless anymore. The cider churns in my stomach. I see a group of friends passing around a handle of tequila, and I remember last year's Halloween party again. And before I know it, everything floods back from that night: the spinning lights, the shots of vodka, the missed calls.

I can't be here, at this party, anymore. I slip down the stairs and step through puddles of beer. Then I'm out and I march home.

When my roommates ask where I went later that night, I tell them that I got tired. It's half the truth, anyway. My head spins and my steps are wobbly. Of course I'm a lightweight. After all, while my roommates were out building up their alcohol tolerance, I've been at home, falling asleep to the TV.

I don't look at Hana's post again. I think of the way Julia's friend looked at me when I flipped over the card. Three swords in the heart. *Have you had your heart broken?*

What constitutes a heartbreak? I've never been in love, that much I know. But can someone's heart break over a friend? That's what it feels like; a slow splintering, the feeling that the cord between me and Hana strained to the point of breaking before it was cut.

Before *I* cut it.

You were the one who stopped texting her.

It's not like I'd talk about my former best friend to strangers dressed as Addams Family characters, anyway. I haven't even told my roommates about Hana. But when my roommates come home, I do tell them about what Julia said.

"Oh, *fuck* that," Ava says, with crossfaded emphasis, dropping gummy bears into her mouth. One falls to the beanbag. She picks it up and eats it. "What is her problem? You are literally the kindest and most empathetic person."

"She's a contrarian," Ruhi says, pulling a sweater over her head. She roots under her bed and pulls out a gallon container of Goldfish. "She's like that in class, too."

"Like what?"

"*Super* blunt. Kind of standoffish. Thinks she's better than everyone." Ruhi waves her hands around. "*I* dunno. She hangs out with a bunch of people from her creative writing workshops, so I don't interact with her much. Now I'm glad I don't."

"But I have to," I say. "I work with her two days a week. I mean, maybe she's right. I haven't been in love before. Who

125

am I to say how it should work?"

"But the thing is, it *does*," Ruhi says. She makes a sweeping gesture at herself. "I've been in a whole relationship for more than a year, and I couldn't even come up with this shit. My editors started talking at Senior Bar Night last week." She gestures to us. "And you had a great date with Jamie."

"*Cutie boy Jamie*," Ava singsongs.

"Right," I say. "And Ava's hitting it off with Cameron."

"Exactly," Ava says, reaching for another handful.

"See?" Ruhi spreads her palms out. "Don't worry, Grace. You're on to something."

I glance down and hand her stained dress to her. "I'm sorry that her drink got on this."

"My dude," Ruhi says. "Do not even worry. That Forever 21 dress has been around since, like, the turn of the millennium. It's survived far worse."

I feel better.

She turns. "Okay. Just throwing this out there. Does anyone want to order Taco Bell?"

FALL OF SENIOR YEAR

"WE SHOULD DO something to celebrate," Hana said. We sat in the parking lot of the sandwich shop. Seniors got to have open lunch, a privilege that Hana and I made liberal use of, although I mostly just brought food and used it as an excuse to get off campus.

I scooped pieces of lettuce off my car seat and laughed. "What, applying to college? Everyone does that."

"Yeah, but applying to college in California." Hana nudged me. "What did Mama Tang have to say to that?"

I stared at the windshield.

"You didn't tell her?"

I glanced over. "Is that bad?"

Hana shrugged. "Oh. Shit. You've got guts, Grace. I'm proud."

The knot in my stomach tightened at Hana's snark. I shrugged. "I'm just going to see if I get in first. I'm not gonna start a whole thing with my mom just to get rejected.

And out of state is expensive."

"Yeah," Hana said. "Okay, well. There's a party Saturday night. Travis Kelly's parents are out of town. From what I heard they do those *let's go to a beach and try to remind each other we still love each other* trips that rich white parents do. Theater people are going to be there. Wanna come?"

I paused. I vaguely knew of Travis Kelly. He was the kid who always got the lead of some musical or another. I said, "I don't know."

"Come on," Hana said. She started the car. She connected her phone to the aux and turned the sound up. I glanced out the window. I hadn't been caught for it, not yet. In fact, my SAT scores had come back in fourth period and it was my highest yet. It was like the universe and God were telling me *yes, go, do what you want.* I thought of these small, rebellious acts, these tiny, imperceptible degrees of change. The reminders to myself that I could conceivably have some command over my future.

It was all so easy, wasn't it? I could just tell Ma that I was staying over at Hana's. I could show her my SAT scores and promise to be back early in the morning for church. If she was in a good mood, she wouldn't object to it.

A real live high school party. A thrill picked up in my chest.

I turned to Hana. "You're not gonna drink and drive, are you?"

"Travis lives two blocks away from my house," she said. "We can just walk."

* * *

I had dinner at Hana's house. They brought home pizzas. Her parents still liked me, even despite my mother's coldness. They asked me about school and looked relaxed drinking wine at the dinner table. Their dog came up to me and nudged my leg.

After dinner, Hana and I went up to her room and got dressed. Hana gave me a shirt, and after I tugged it on, her eyes met mine in the mirror. "What do you think?"

On instinct my hands wrapped around myself self-consciously. I was wearing her cropped Halsey concert T-shirt, except on my longer torso it was even more cropped. I tugged my high-waisted jeans up. Hana tapped her fingers along her smooth cheekbones, leaving the slightest shimmery trail. I glanced at my own reflection. I wore a subtle, dusty rose shade of lipstick. Hana blended my eye shadow. She had monolids, too. She knew what to do to make my eyes pop because she'd watched YouTube tutorials. Glitter dusted my eyelids, and highlighter brought out the soft bridge of my nose.

"Yeah," I said. "Looks good." I turned and gathered up my coat.

"Wait," Hana said. "What are you doing? The party doesn't start for another two hours."

I checked my phone. "It's already nine."

"Things don't *really* start until eleven," she said. "Let's watch a movie." She put on an illegally downloaded Marvel movie, and we curled up on the bed together to watch. I half paid attention, even though I was so backlogged on Marvel movies that I couldn't begin to decipher it, even though Hana tried explaining it all to me over countless lunches. Mostly I just laid on the bed, watching the ceiling. I'd missed getting to hang out with Hana all the time. Maybe her family would go skiing again this year and I could come with. I half expected Ma to check in, to ask me what I'd eaten for dinner, but no texts came in. "What's the move?" Hana glanced at me. "Anyone you're trying to talk to?"

I glance at her. "As if."

"What about Miles?"

"You're not shipping me with my coworker."

"He's endearing, that's all," she said. "I think he likes you."

"How do you know?"

"I just get the sense."

I laughed and shook my head. "He's probably not even coming. What about you?"

"Oh, not at all. Girls take, like, a year to get over. I'm just trying to get drunk." Her phone buzzed, twice, and she paused the movie. "Okay, Ella tells me people are finally showing up. Let's go."

By the time we bundled up and walked the two blocks under the light of the streetlamp, it had become brutally cold. Our breaths became small, condensed puffs.

"I don't hear anything," I said as we walked up to the house.

"That's because it's in the basement." She whipped out her phone. "Hold on. I'm texting her."

The door soon opened. I could hear the faint reverberating bass. Ella Mahoney glanced at Hana. "Oh, you're here."

"Yup," Hana said. "I brought Grace, if that's okay."

Ella glanced at me and raised an eyebrow. My school was small enough. People knew I was the furthest from a party on a Friday night. But she simply said, "Yeah, of course."

Coats piled up on the dining table. The rest of the house was dark, but as Ella opened the door to the basement, light streamed out, flashing and shifting from one bright color to the next. The music got louder the farther we went into the basement until it seemed like my very limbs were vibrating. The smell of beer and contradicting colognes saturated the air. Handles were lined up in front of the unlit fireplace, forming a small teetering tower. Lights were strung up all around—holiday lights, the kind that you use to decorate your front porch.

"Travis Kelly always throws the best parties," Hana muttered to me. She grabbed the Smirnoff off the table. "Shots?"

She splashed some into a cup and handed it to me. Suddenly a thrill of excitement picked up in me. I took the cup and threw it down. It stung and I exhaled fumes, coughing a little.

"Ugh, terrible," Hana said. She waved hi to some people. I toyed with my cup and glanced around. I wondered, for a half a second, if I would see my coworker here. But he was probably practicing with his band or something.

"Okay." Hana appeared at my side again. "We're playing beer pong. Their game is wrapping up." There was a small cheer, and she edged her way in. "We're playing. Grace and I are a team."

The guys on the other end raised their eyebrows.

I glanced at her. *You sure?*

"Just for shits and giggles," she said. "And it's an easy way to get drunk."

She went up for the first shot, and it bounced off the edge. The guys shook their heads. She shrugged and looked at me. I came up to the edge of the table. I thought of when I used to play with stones at the creek. I'd try to hit the stepping paths. I released the ball. It sank into a cup. The guys glanced our way.

"Well, would you look at that." Hana turned to me. "A natural."

The two guys came up next. Their balls bounced, one after another, and they swore.

Hana went up. She sank one. I took a deep breath and eyed the center cup.

It dropped in.

The guys stopped talking.

As it turned out, I was good at this. By the next round, Hana and I had the boys drinking one cup after another. "Suck it," she taunted them playfully as another shot of mine sank in. People crowded around the table to watch. They knew Hana. But for the first time, people were watching *me*.

My last shot sank in easy. The people around me cheered, and even the boys gave me an appreciative nod. Ella grabbed the Smirnoff and nodded at me and Hana to join. "You guys didn't drink enough."

Hana glanced at me. "She aced it. Can you blame us?" But she grinned and accepted the bottle. The second shot of vodka went down easy. And as time went on, the basement no longer chilled me. The room was warm and full of light, the colors from the lava lamp speaker dappling across the room. Hana started shouting the lyrics to the song at me, her hair wild and flying, the glitter dusted across her reddened cheeks, and I sang along with her.

And it felt so good.

"Slow down," Hana told me, and we collapsed in the corner of the room.

"Yeah, yeah," I said.

She glanced at me. "Your makeup is smudged. Here." She took a thumb and swiped it against my lipstick.

"Mmmm," I said. I leaned my head against her shoulder, feeling the solid warmth over her. She smelled like citrus and vanilla and beer. "Hana," I said.

"Yeah?"

"You're pretty, you know that?"

Hana laughed softly. She leaned her head on mine. "And you're drunk, you know that?"

"Not true," I said.

My phone buzzed in my pocket. I pulled it out and stared at the screen. My eyes took a while to focus, and my heart dropped. "Shit," I said. "It's my mom."

I stared at Hana in panic. She was quiet. "I can't pick up," I said. "She'll know I'm drunk."

"It's okay," Hana said. "Don't answer. You could just say that you were asleep. It's late, remember?"

I stared at the screen for a moment. "She knows I'm staying

at yours." I tucked my phone in my pocket. "She's probably checking on me." I stared at the screen. If Ma was really worried about me, she'd text me. But I stared at my messages. Nothing.

I tucked my phone away. "I'll talk to her tomorrow."

The room was getting crowded. She stood up. "Come on. Let's get some water."

We snuck upstairs, and the cool air blasted us in the face. We crept through the kitchen and ran our Solo cups under the sink. The cold water tasted deliciously sweet. Hana and I went back down. She said she wanted to dance and pulled me with her. In that moment, all I was aware of was the music and glitter dust and Hana's flushed cheeks. All I'd known was Hana pulling me to her, her whispering, "I'm so glad you're coming to California with me." I'd known a feeling in my stomach that fluttered to the beat of the bass. My heart hammered loud in my ears, and light swum around me. It was the beginning of everything. I could see the night expand into a tenuous array of possibilities.

It was all so beautiful until I ended up puking.

Hana sat beside me, and I felt the tile beneath my knees, the sour remnants of vodka and stomach acid in my throat and my cheek against the cold toilet seat of a kid I barely knew in high school.

I walked into my kitchen the next morning, changed back into my clothes, hoping I didn't reek of beer or puke. My head pounded and I took one look at my parents sitting at the kitchen table and knew something was wrong. They'd changed their minds. They could tell I went to a party. They were angry at me.

That's what I'd thought. Ma stood up and said, "Let's go to church," and her voice was brittle. Ba looked at her in disbelief, and then at me, and his expression collapsed. "But—"

"We're going."

I didn't know until after church. After Ma prayed and clutched her knuckles so hard they turned white, her expression locked up and moving rigidly, after we got back into the car, she said, "Wait a minute, Xiǎoyàn. I need to tell you something."

That was how I found out that her cancer had come back.

TEN

JAMIE HAS A club soccer tournament this weekend, so we text while he's on the bus and I'm home. We make plans to hang out and watch a movie after my work shift on Tuesday. He invites me to his roommates' Catan game night next Friday. I ask if I can bring Ava. She loves board games. At home I work on my problem sets and open up LaTeX (why someone would let a bunch of college students use a formatting software called LaTeX is beyond me) to start to type up our game theory project paper. Our final paper isn't due until mid-December and the accompanying presentation will be given in class around that time, too, but I want to at least attempt a head start.

The algorithm works. And we're going to prove it.

When I come back to campus that week, I bring my winter coats. The foliage is gone now, the trees mostly bare, the days clouded over. I get added to a ski team group chat. I see Julia introduce herself in it, and I close out.

That Tuesday at work, Roberta catches someone trying to sneak a whole dining hall chicken plate into the library. She's normally lax with coffee cups, but this is next level. I hear Julia chatting with Roberta about some books they call fluffy romance. I still can't wrap my head around the fact that the Grinch of campus dating likes reading romance. I offer to reshelve books and spend the rest of the shift carting those books around. I can feel Julia's eyes on me, but I this time I fully ignore her. If I look at her, or talk to her, then we'll have to acknowledge what happened at the Halloween party. So I don't.

It works, and I almost make it out of the library at 6:10 when I hear Julia call out.

"Hey."

I stop. Slowly, I turn to face my coworker, who's holding up a small paper bag. "What?"

"It's a doughnut. Brought one for you. You want it?"

I frown. "I, uh. Don't want your leftover doughnut?"

"It's not. I got it from Coffee House before work. Do you not like doughnuts?"

I cross my arms. "It's not the doughnuts I have a problem with." There. I said it. She winces, and for a splinter of a second, I feel a bit bad. "I don't get it. One day you're bashing my work and, well, *me*, all over campus, and the next day you're trying to . . . give me food?"

She sighs. "I don't know. I was going to . . . offer it. As a gesture of apology."

I stare at her.

"Look, I'm sorry for what I said, okay? On Halloween. My friends called me out on my shit, and they're right. It was mean."

I tilt my head. "Why do you hate the idea of the Match-Up so much? Why couldn't you have just written your op-ed and left it at that?"

"I mean, I just *generally* don't believe in the concept of predetermined romance through—" She stops short when she sees the look on my face. Her expression softens. "I also was kind of . . . talking to this girl in my friend group. But your algorithm put her with someone else."

I wrap my coat tighter around me. "Talking . . . to? Wait, as in? Romantically?"

"Yeah. I'm into girls." She gives me a deadpan look. "Did my platform boots not give it away?"

"Oh, is that . . . ?" Come to think of it, Hana had a pair of those boots, too. Maybe there is some kind of correlation? I feel a sudden jolt of curiosity. When did Julia know? When did she come out? Does everyone? Do her parents care? Are they supportive, like Hana's? "Right. So. You were in love with this girl?"

"*Not* in love." Julia shifts from foot to foot. "But, like, I feel like we were on our way to a kind of . . . casual fling?" She shrugs and pulls her jean jacket around her. "But now she's going on dates and hanging out all the time with her match. So, yeah."

She's *jealous*. That's why, I realize. "You know, *you* could have gotten matched to her. If you just took the Match-Up survey."

"Yeah, except there's, like, literally no odds of that happening.

Also, I didn't want to."

"Right. Because you don't believe in it."

"Precisely. But that doesn't mean I should have personally insulted you at a Halloween party. And if you're someone I work with and will probably see around club ski when the season starts next semester, apparently, well, I wanted to make sure things were good." She holds up the doughnut. "So, truce?"

I take the paper doughnut bag. "Sorry about stealing your girl. Kind of."

"She wasn't really my girl to begin with," Julia says. "I'll live."

"Just saying, if you'd wanted to find your perfect compatible match on campus that already has proven success . . ."

"I regret buying this doughnut already," Julia says.

My mouth is already half full. "Too late."

She smiles, a little, and it's a genuine smile, even as she shakes her head. "Okay, genius. See you Thursday."

I finish the doughnut on the way back to Spiegel. It *is* really good. She must have caught Coffee House with a fresh batch.

I'm still going to prove her wrong, of course. But a tentative truce isn't too bad, either.

That night, Jamie and I watch a sweet and expositional movie on his roommate's futon. It's about these strangers who meet on a train in Budapest and spend a subsequent day together. Jamie's really into movies. He's doing a film minor. I watch with my head tucked into his shoulder. He smells faintly of pine and clean laundry. I'm not sure what's happening for most of the movie, but I think I'm supposed to be feeling something.

At some point when they're talking on a Ferris wheel, he looks down, at me. I glance back at him, and then we're kissing, slowly. He pulls me tighter to him, shifts me onto his lap. He reaches for the edge of my shirt and whispers to me, "Is this okay with you?" I nod and kiss him again, deeper this time. "Perfectly okay," I say, and smile against his lips. It is, and it seems right, it feels like exactly what I should be doing. He's a good kisser. I wonder who else he's made out with. I think of the last boy I kissed. My thoughts flit around. I wonder if I should have taken one of the free condoms that the RAs always have by their door. He probably has some. I trace my fingers under his shirt and tug it free.

"You know, if I believe there is any kind of God, it wouldn't be in any of us," the woman in the movie says in a soft voice that's filled with wonder. "Not you, or me. But just this little space in between." It's the line that my mind snags on when Jamie finally fumbles over and closes the laptop.

And after that, things are calm again. My shifts at the library are no longer a drag. I learn how the computer cataloging system works, figure out a more efficient route to reshelve books, and help people book study rooms. Ten hours a week at twenty-two dollars an hour builds up to a steady paycheck. Ruhi gets bumped up from staff writer to desk editor, and Ava starts to think about putting together her acting portfolio.

We all go home for Thanksgiving. When we come back, the

energy is slightly different. Everyone starts to get a little busier ahead of finals. Ava brings back a care package from her family and distributes bags of hot chocolate to us. The Match-Up's follow-up surveys roll in; 73 percent of people who took the survey did, in fact, go on a first date. But anecdotally, things aren't looking great. First dates aren't turning into second ones. Coffee House has returned to its equilibrium of frantic, stressed studying students, featuring only the occasional date. Danny's dates with his match have fizzled out, despite his attempts to rekindle a connection with his freshman-year-hall crush. "I don't know," he says when Caroline prods him in class. "We just kind of became different people over the last few years. I don't know if we're the right person for each other anymore. Ya know?"

"But you *are*," I insist. "You were each other's most compatible match on campus. You shared all the same values and priorities."

"Right, that's what I *thought*." He shrugs. "I tried. We went on two dates. We just didn't . . ." He slots his fingers together. "Mesh. I can't really put it into words. I could tell she wasn't feeling it."

"Did she say that?"

"Well, she left me on read, so I think it's pretty clear. I think she's started talking to someone else, too. I thought I knew what I wanted. But I don't know. Maybe we just changed a lot since freshman year. Maybe I didn't know what I wanted then."

Caroline grimaces. "Rough, dude."

I look around. All of a sudden in our project group, we've gone from two people with successful matches to one. Sixty-seven percent chance of success to thirty-three.

"It's fine," Danny says. "All the other matches are going well, right?"

"Grace is still with hers," Caroline says quietly.

"Yeah." Jamie and I got dinner last night and watched one of the first snows descend on Leighton through the window. The dining hall had strawberry cupcakes. On our way back, we'd kissed while the snow was falling and the kiss tasted like strawberry frosting. "And my roommate Ava is still with hers." Sure, Ava has gotten a little busy lately and hasn't told me much about her and Cameron. She also hasn't replied to the December follow-up survey we sent out, the one that asked if they'd gone on several dates with their match. But they do see each other at least once a week at improv team practice. And it's only been a month, after all.

As if she's been reading my mind, Caroline says, "These are only the preliminary results. We can focus more on the theory and analyze the data at the three-month follow-up report." She pauses. "That's the plan. Sound good?"

So that's what we do. Caroline shows up in glasses and an oversized hoodie and brings a towering cup of iced coffee with her to the library and types at double speed, her fingers flying over her keyboard. "We could reenter the Ice Age and Caroline would still be ordering her iced coffees," Danny comments. In the seventy-two hours before class, we scrape together a presentation and a final paper that folds in the follow-up survey responses as something "for continued analysis." Maybe things at the three-month mark will be more definitive. We finally format and publish everything in LaTeX.

The following morning, we present the preliminary results of the Match-Up to a full house. Everyone shows up on the first day of presentations to hear us speak, including the entire Economics department faculty and even some math and psychology professors, which makes me slightly anxious. I just focus on the slides and try not to look at the growing crowd in front of me. I walk everyone through the stable matching algorithm and on our alterations. When I peek at the class, people are following along, rapt.

And then come the questions.

"I'd like to ask about the limitations of this study," someone in the back asks. He's a random Econ department grad student, I think. We've never seen him before. "Romantic love can be rather unquantifiable. There's a lot of emotion involved, for instance. Were there any similar intangible factors that could impact the predictability of love itself?"

My group members exchange looks. Caroline steps forward. "Sure, I mean, with any study, there are limitations, right? But we tried to quantify every single factor that we believe goes into love as much as we can, in order to limit the unknowns. We're happy to go over that list of thirty factors again."

Another person raises her hand. "This seems like more of

a compatibility algorithm, not necessarily a love algorithm. I think that's an important distinction to make. Who's to say that these matches actually end up in love in the long term?"

There's a silence. Even Caroline looks slightly baffled. I speak up. "Compatibility can and should lead to romance, though. Everything in the algorithm is constructed so that it makes it *easier* to be attracted to someone via their values or their qualities. We even had a statistical weighting attached, in which individuals could select the questions that were most important to them, and that weighting factored into our analysis as well. Judging from our preliminary survey results, people are happy with their matches and that's due to the compatibility."

"And the whole point of this project," Danny adds, "is to make it easier for people to find love."

The girl doesn't let up. "But what if people change over time? What if their preferences change?"

I pause. The girl narrows her eyes at me, and I recognize the look. It's the same look Julia gave me at the Halloween party. I hold my ground. "I'd say that people are pretty self-aware of their preferences. They shouldn't change much."

"And that's outside of the scope of this project," Danny interjects smoothly. "We will be conducting a three-month follow-up, so hopefully some of those questions can be resolved. There'll be a Valentine's Day report. Stay tuned."

"All right," Professor Rand says, coming to the front. "Great presentation. Very rigorous social science practice to take this project beyond this semester. I myself am very much looking forward to this follow-up. Now, is the next group ready?"

We sit back down. Caroline gives us both a thumbs-up. I smile back weakly.

I thought I'd accounted for all the questions and unknowns throughout the process of this project. But now my mind clouds with even more uncertainties. What is the longevity of a match? What will happen at the three-month follow-up? Should we have thought more about preferences? What if people have imperfect information about their romantic preferences?

It wouldn't just alter a part of this; that would fundamentally change the entire project.

And there's another question that now seeps through: We might have done okay for now, but applications to the summer math research program are due at the beginning of February. What if things take a turn for the worse? What if Professor Rand changes his mind?

ELEVEN

MY LIBRARY SHIFTS have also gotten busy at the end of the semester. Study rooms are booking up, people are frantically trying to search for obscure manuscripts on the second floor for their research papers, and the library regulars have started bringing their blankets in and camping out for finals. But during the quiet moments, it's peaceful. Afternoon sun streams in through the arched panes and creates patches of warmth. On our last shift before break, Julia and I try to strategically place ourselves in those spots. Sometimes we end up right next to each other. She turns to me. "I hear there's a party at your place tomorrow night."

"Wait. How did— Oh, right. Ruhi." I fiddle with the paper with the directions to request books from other libraries. The tape is coming loose, and I smear it back.

"Yeah. She dropped an invite in our daily Slack," Julia says.

She straightens up and raises an eyebrow. "If I'm allowed to come, that is."

"What? Of course." I laugh. "Please come. My roommates have gone all out." It's true. Ava and Ruhi have been itching to throw a party all semester, and now they have been drawing up elaborate plans all week, from ordering multicolored string lights to putting together a 109-song playlist called "All I Want for Christmas is Room 302." I've contributed by driving to the nearest grocery store to buy Jell-O mix and a baby spruce. Ruhi is raiding the *Daily Leighton* alcohol reserves. I lower my voice. "There'll be peppermint-schnapps-spiked hot chocolate. And Jell-O shots?"

Her expression lights up. "I'll come just to see Grace Tang take a Jell-O shot at a party *she's* hosting."

"What, you think all I do is hide in my textbooks and study in the math building?"

"Well, do you?" Julia asks. "I sure never see you at parties on the weekends."

"Of course not. That basement has traces of asbestos."

"Really?"

"That's what the TAs say."

"Another compelling reason not to study math, of all things," Julia says. I give her a pointed look. She has two kinds of smiles: a soft teasing smile, where her eyebrows raise a little, and a broader grin when she is genuinely happy. This seems to be the former. I've begun noticing these smaller details: the freckle under her eye, her varied earrings. Today she's wearing earrings with dangling gems that glitter like raindrops.

147

I fix up Roberta's decorations. The circulation desk is decked with pine bundles and holiday lights. There's even a teddy bear next to the baby tree that wears a handmade mini sweater and a scarf. Roberta's really into holidays. Her son's family is coming up from New York for the holidays, and she won't stop talking about it. It's very cute.

It's the end of the semester, and people are coordinating their finals schedules with their flights home. I can't believe a whole semester has passed. One-eighth of college. After our shift ends, Roberta gifts us mini bags with chocolate and a candle. "Good luck on those finals," she says. "Have a good break."

"You got any?" I ask Julia on the way out. "Finals, I mean?"

"I'm not taking a single final test this semester," she says. "But I will be going back to my dorm, steeping two bags of green tea, and writing my entire Modern Literature paper. You? How's your match theory class or whatever?"

"Gave my final presentation yesterday," I say. I shrug. "It was . . . interesting, I guess. A lot of questions."

Julia leans in. "Having second thoughts about this?"

I glance up. I can't tell if she's serious or still poking fun at me; if I can tell her about the whole questions of imperfect information and preferences. I wonder how to answer, but then I see Jamie heading toward me. "Hey," he says. "Hi, Julia."

She nods a hi at him.

"Coffee House?" I say.

He grins. "You read my mind."

Julia observes us, amused. "Never mind. I got my answer."

She turns and heads off, her boots crunching over the salt-lined sidewalk.

Jamie nudges me. "What?"

I shake my head. "Oh, nothing." I glance back at her retreating figure as we slog through the slushy paths. At Coffee House, Jamie and I snag the corner of a long table; the place is crowded, too, with printed practice exams and textbooks everywhere. Against the background buzz and whir of the coffee machines, I pore over my Linear Algebra notes while he takes a practice exam. I've had enough time to absorb the material over the past semester, having never fallen behind on lectures or homework. It's going to be different next semester with the ski team, I know. But for now I am solid. The final is only 30 percent, and my midterm scores are well over the median. So I silently confirm what I know and glance up at Jamie surreptitiously. His eyebrows knit together as he focuses. Even in the dim light, he looks good. His jaw tightens as he works through the problems, and his forearm tenses as he threads his fingers through his curls. He glances up and his eyes meet mine, and my heart kicks a slow, steady beat. "Yes?"

"Oh." I nod at the practice exam. "Nothing. Do your thing."

He raises an eyebrow and leans in. "Hard to focus when there's a cute girl staring at me."

My cheeks warm. "Sorry. I zoned out."

"No, I like it."

I laugh a little and stare at the bright screen of the computer. I wonder what the algorithm knows that I don't yet know. I wonder what it is like to be in love, and to know it. I've looked this up on the internet before. Google says that it takes someone about three to four months to say it.

It seems like an abstract concept to me. I like Jamie. Things are good as is right now. I wonder how feelings eventually develop into love. I wonder when I'll get there. I wonder what it'll be like when it happens, if it's like the sure feeling of looking at a question on a test and then the answer suddenly falls into your head, all at once, like a revelation. And even though nothing has functionally changed and the page is still blank before you, you finally know: you are in love.

It's 9 p.m. the Friday before break, and our colorful Christmas lights slowly flicker over the room. We've sweated through the morning in tense, silent lecture halls and finished all our individual finals, save for Ruhi, who got an extension on her take-home paper. We sloshed home through snow drifts and finally have gathered to set up. The room is marvelously clean, with all the papers and sticky notes and granola bar wrappers and rogue Flamin' Hot Cheeto bags stowed away. Ruhi cranes over her mirror, carefully putting finishing glittery touches on her makeup, her full lips lined in bright red and her pastel eye shadow shimmery against her smooth brown skin. Ava's fussing over the twin Nespresso machines that hum alongside the handles of cheap vodka and wine bags. "This is the hot chocolate machine that's spiked," she says, bringing us both paper cups. "Taste test, please."

I take a sip and feel the sharp peppermint punch-up. I blink. "Oh my God, Ava," Ruhi says, coughing and laughing. "What the fuck? You're trying to take us all out."

"Death by schnapps," I say.

"Too much?"

"Little bit." Ruhi goes to help Ava. I glance sidewise into the mirror. Ruhi has done my makeup, swiping glitter softly over my cheekbones and making even my monolids pop. She's an expert. I'm wearing a patterned sweater and reindeer-ear headbands that we all ordered online together. My room-mates sort out the schnapps-to-hot-chocolate ratio, and then check on the still-setting Jell-O shots in our mini fridge. Ava chews her thumbnail. "Guys, it's after nine. What if no one comes?"

"Someone's going to," I say. I check my phone. Jamie has tex-ted that he'll show up later since he's still finishing up a final. "Don't people show up late anyway?"

"I mean, in *theory*," Ava says. "But what if everyone hates us?"

"The odds of that," I say, "are near impossible. You two of all people on campus have friends."

"I mean, if no one *truly* comes," Ruhi says, leaning against the table, "then we can have *very* strong hot chocolate with a movie. And seven kinds of Jell-O."

I'm right, of course. By eleven, people are pouring in. The improv team arrives all at once and we see Ava's eyes light up. I search the crowd for Cameron, with his short black hair, but I don't see him. I nudge Ava. "Where's Cameron?"

"Oh," Ava says. "He'd had his flight scheduled for early tonight. We got lunch today."

"Aw," I say. I see her friend Bryce come in, running his fingers through his tight curls to get the snow out of it. He nods at us, and we wave. "Took you long enough," Ava laughs. She holds up a tentative thumbs-up. "Final?"

He shrugs. He's wearing a bright red holiday sweater. "Brutal. Done. Now I'm here," he succinctly summarizes. "Oh, hey, look. My Nespresso machine's all decked out."

"It's strong," I say. "Be forewarned."

"Excellent," Bryce says. He gives us a grin and winks. "It's being put to good use." He gestures to it and turns to Ava. "Want one?"

"*Please*," Ava says, following him. I see Ruhi glancing over at me carefully. Then she turns and retrieves a tray from the mini fridge. "Jell-O shots, anyone?"

The night goes on. The once still, drafty room becomes warm, coming alive as friends of friends crowd in and spill out into the hallway. The colorful lights wink softly, and I feel my thoughts loosen. Ava introduces me to all her improv friends, most of whom I've only heard of. They are loud and welcome me to take a Jell-O shot with them, and suddenly we are all tentatively friends.

Ruhi's *Daily Leighton* friends show up, and I catch the flash of Julia's earrings. Our gazes sweep past each other for a second. And suddenly, strangely, even though I'm still with Ava and her improv friends and Julia is across the room, I become very aware of her presence. She feels like an anchor, somehow, the only truly familiar face other than my roommates. I weave through people until I'm just partially enmeshed with the staff writer cohort.

"Hi," I say. "You came."

"Hey, genius," Julia says, leaning against Ruhi's desk, dressed in a plain oversized sweater that hangs off her shoulders, her arms folded around her. She raises an eyebrow, and a slow smile spreads across her cheeks; in my slightly drunk state, I can't accurately tell if it's a teasing one. She holds out something wrapped in tinfoil. "Here."

"What's this?"

"I made sugar cookies. They're probably a little burnt. Definitely, actually. I blame the dorm kitchenette."

I cradle the cookies to my chest and extract one with sprinkles. It crumbles in my mouth, buttery and sweet. She made cookies specifically for this party. "Mmm," I say contentedly.

Julia gestures at my reindeer ears. "I like the festive outfit."

"What, do I look ridiculous?"

"No, I like it. Really." She looks at herself. "I feel underdressed for the occasion, if anything."

"Take it." In a bold sweep, I take off the reindeer ears and slot them on her head. My fingertips accidentally brush against her hair and her cheekbones. "Better," I say, pretending to scrutinize her.

"Thank you," Julia says. She grins, a true one this time. "Please tell me where to get some of that hot chocolate so I can get to whatever level you're at. It seems like a fun place to be."

I make her a drink. She downs it in one go and cradles the cup in her hand. "Where's lover boy?"

My cheeks warm. I peek at my phone and squint against the suddenly bright screen. Voices rise around us. I feel light on my feet. "Finishing a final before midnight. He's coming later."

"Nice."

"That sounded sarcastic."

"I mean it. You two seem good together. Really."

I smile at this concession of hers. Ruhi pulls me into the ongoing game of king's cup. Julia goes off to talk to someone else. I come a hair's width close to breaking the chain of cards and having to drink the murky bitch cup in the center that's a combination of hot chocolate, coconut rum, hot sauce, and mango hard seltzer. Ava's friends Bryce and Rocky egg me on and cheer when I successfully pry the card away. I warm to this sudden glow of attention. I find myself getting louder. Someone's self-produced song gets played, and I add them on Spotify. Conversations weave in and out about music theory, debates about superior airlines to fly home with, and TV shows we're watching. Someone asks me offhandedly about the Match-Up, and I lean against Ava's dresser giving a whole likely unintelligible speech about the stable match algorithm while the room slightly tilts on its axis.

"You gave me a pretty good match," she says. "It's going really well." She leans in. "I'd actually been talking to someone else before," she says, nodding toward Julia. I follow her gaze.

"Really?" *Oh*. I look back at the girl in front of me. Short dark hair, freckles, hazel eyes. This must have been the girl that Julia had mentioned. "Didn't work out with Julia?"

"Yeah, I just . . ." She shrugs. "She just seemed emotionally closed off. I could never really get a read on her. She wanted to keep it casual." She shrugs. "Anyway." She holds a bottle out. "Want to take a shot with me?"

It is that easy to talk. I float around and I don't feel self-conscious. This is somehow much, much better than Halloween already, maybe because I'm drunker and because I'm in my own room. I remember names and wonder what it's like to do this every weekend, to have already narrowed your world here to two degrees of separation instead of driving back and forth from campus. *This* is what it's like to be here all the time. *It's fun.*

I feel a hand brush my shoulder, and I turn. Jamie stands there, hands tucked his jeans pockets. "Hey!" I say. "You finished! How was it?"

"Barely," he laughs, and his brown eyes are soft in the light, framed by his thick lashes. "Wrote up a bunch of paragraphs that don't quite make sense, but it's over now." He glances around. "And now I have to catch up, it seems."

I thrust my cup at him. "Welcome to our holiday party. Want some hot chocolate?"

He takes a sip. "Oh, this is really good," he says. His eyes widen. "A *lot* of peppermint."

"Oh, yes. That's the schnapps."

"No wonder everyone's in a good place right now."

"Everything's a little . . ." I take in a breath. "*Wavy.*"

He laughs.

"I'm drunk, aren't I?"

"A little. You good?"

"Oh, yes. I'm incredible."

He gently rubs my back. I turn and press a kiss to his shoulder.

Ava's eyes soften as she sees us. "You're finally here," she says. "Come on, we're starting a new round of king's cup." The circle widens with new people, and the cards get shuffled and respread around the cup in the middle. Voices get louder. I linger against Jamie, and his fingers lace around mine on the carpet, gentle. Ruhi brings in her *Daily* friends. Julia settles across from me and leans against the wall, a knee propped up, deep in conversation with one of Ava's friends, glancing across only when it's her turn. Jamie accidentally breaks the card chain and the entire group erupts, and he takes down the cup in the middle like a good sport. "It's efficient," he says, coughing a little from the hot sauce. Even Julia cracks a smile from across the circle. I glance at her and remember what the girl earlier said. *Emotionally closed off.*

The games continue. After king's cup, we play drunk Bananagrams, and Julia wins three times in a row to an increasingly irate crowd. Then we all disperse for a bit. The "All I Want for Christmas is Room 302" playlist is going strong—we must be something, like, four hours in at this point. Jamie goes to refill his drink, and I follow him. He says hi to some people I know and then turns to me. His cheeks are a little pink. "I might head home in a bit," he says.

"Really? But you weren't here for long."

"Yeah," he says. "October me thought it was good idea to book an eight-thirty train."

"Mistake," I tease him, leaning slightly against the table.

"Yeah." He glances down and then meets my eyes. "Do you, uh, want to go back to my place? You could stay over. My room-mate's out for break."

I pause. *Oh.* His blush deepens. He shakes his head. "You don't have to. I just— Yeah."

I look up at him, at his slightly parted lips, the tentative look in his eyes. "I do," I say, and I can feel the heat on my own cheeks. I think back to our movie nights, to fumbling hands and quiet whispers. But I've never stayed overnight or woken up with him in the morning. "I should stay with my roommates tonight. If that's okay."

He nods. "I get it."

He stays for one more round of Bananagrams and then heads out. At the doorway, I reach up and pull him in for a kiss. He leans into the kiss, deepening it, and a bit of warmth curls in my chest. "Text me tomorrow," I say.

"Course."

The party thins out. Most of us end up sitting on the floor around the scattered deck of cards, talking about our holiday plans.

"I'm visiting my cousins in SF," Ava says. "We always take turns hosting New Year's, and this year we're road-tripping to theirs and then playing board games and watching Christmas movies for five days straight."

"My family's going to see my grandma in Palm Beach," Bryce says. "And we're spending Christmas Eve at church and staying up late to call my family abroad."

"Same with the late calls. Where's your family from?" Ruhi asks.

"Dad's side's from Indonesia. Mom's side's from Jamaica. So. A lot of WhatsApp calls."

"I feel you," Ruhi says. "I have a lot of cousins in India. And we always call all the aunties around New Year's."

"The aunties," Bryce laughs in agreement. He turns to me. "What about you, Grace?"

I shrug. "Yeah. With family," I say lightly. Family as in Ba and me. I turn to Julia. "You?"

"Your plans all sound lovely," Julia says. "*I* will personally probably be mediating my parents' divorce at a Chinese restaurant on Christmas." She grimaces and raises her cup. "Cheers."

The room quiets. My roommates glance at each other, their smiles disappearing. "Fuck. Sorry. Just made it awkward," Julia laughs. "Anyone up for another round of king's cup?"

Soon it's three in the morning and the Solo cups outnumber the people. "Happy holidays," Julia says to me, smiling drunkenly before she follows the newspaper crowd out. I look after her. I hadn't known her parents were having issues. But then again, how would I? I really only work with her. I don't know her like that. Eventually, it's just my roommates and me. Ruhi goes out in the hallway to FaceTime Arjun, since it's still midnight in Seattle, where he is. Ava lays her head in my lap, and I stroke her hair while she snacks on stale Flamin' Hot Cheetos. Somehow, in our plastered state, nothing in the world tastes better. The 109-song playlist has finally come to an end, and we're now hearing repeats.

"God, this was fun," Ava says. She sits up and offers me a cup of water.

"I'm good." There's enough liquid sloshing around in me.

"Trust me," Ava says, looking at me intently. "You'll thank yourself tomorrow."

I dutifully sip.

"You and Jamie are the cutestfuckingcouple on this campus," Ava says, her words blending together. "You know that?"

I smile shyly at my knees. "Really?"

"Do you see the way he looks at you?"

"Sometimes I don't know if I'm doing relationships right," I admit.

"*Grace.*"

"What?"

"It's not necessarily about doing it good or right. Do you like it?"

I stare at the ceiling. "Yeah," I say to the hollow air. "I do."

"Then there we go." Ava pauses for a moment. And then she

says softly, "Sometimes I think that's all it takes."

"How are you and Cameron?"

Ava pauses for a moment. "Good. He's sweet." She peels herself from the beanbag. "I'm getting us more water."

She retrieves water from the drinking fountain. Ruhi comes back into the room at that moment, all smiley, her eyes shining. "How's Arjun?" I ask.

Ruhi smiles wearily. "Three more days." She exhales and sits on the floor, leaning against the bed and stretching out her long legs. "I'm so ready to see him. Long distance is ass."

All this time I thought things were going perfect. I guess it's harder than my roommate lets on.

"Aw," Ava says. "It'll be *so* soon. Here. Come here." She pulls Ruhi onto the beanbag, forming a cuddle pile.

"We should clean up," I say half-heartedly, glancing at the sticky tabletops and the Solo cups everywhere.

"Tomorrow morning," Ava says.

We all stare at the ceiling for a bit, our limbs intertwined.

"I can't believe first semester is already over," she says. "I only have half a year left with you guys."

"Correction," Ruhi mumbles. "Three and a half more years. Bold to assume I'm not making us live together for the rest of college."

A draft sneaks in from the window crack, but I'm so comfortable and snuggled under the blankets that I think that I may fall asleep right here, the last night of the semester, with two people who were complete strangers in August. These two people who will go back to their homes tomorrow in Texas and California. These roommates who, in spite of me being gone all the time this first semester, still do things with me. And for a moment I am overwhelmed with emotion.

"I love you guys," Ava says suddenly.

I clasp her hand. Ruhi pulls us tighter. "Love you too."

Ba and I spend the morning of Christmas Eve in the aisles of the Asian Super Store, an hour away from our house. He gathers up ground pork and leeks and dumpling wrappers for this party that he's taking us to tonight, with a colleague from his university. "She teaches multivariable," he tells me as we drive back on the snowy roads to our house. "You would like her. She has kids, too."

I get suspicious. I don't know why he's introducing her to me like that, like I should get to know her better. Is she truly just a colleague to him?

In another world, maybe I could have had her as a professor. Ba and I had talked about it, too, the possibility of me going to his university since there would be a faculty discount. But in the end, Leighton had offered me a hefty scholarship and I'd liked the campus better.

We spend all afternoon wrapping dumplings. Ba remembers how Ma made the filling. We mix the leeks, soy sauce, sesame oil, salt, and cooking wine with the pork. I seal the dumplings extra tight so they don't leak in the water. After they're all cooked and cooled, Ba wraps the platter in aluminum foil, and

161

during the entire thirty-minute drive to the party, I cradle the heated platter of dumplings in my lap.

Professor Xu's house is bright and loud. She seems to know everyone; she's assembled what I assume is the entire Chinese American community of central Vermont in her living room. All the people who are under the age of thirty are squished onto the couches, balancing our plates in our laps. The dumplings that Ba and I made are good actually. I have some vermicelli noodles and stir-fried cabbage. Most of the kids are either high school aged and crowded around something on their phones, or they're in their mid-twenties and checking their phones impatiently, responding to some work email. I sit in the corner and glance around at the gaming sets strewn around the TV and the Asian Super Store calendar on the wall. I check my roommate group chat before I spot the professor. Her graying hair is drawn back. Wire-rimmed glasses perch on her broad nose. I overhear her talking to Ba a little bit about college. She has a son who's a freshman, too. "He's always out partying," she laments.

"Grace never does that," Ba laughs. "She always comes home during the weekends instead. 非常乖. That's how her ma raised her."

Ba goes to get more food, and eventually the professor comes to find me. She sits on the couch opposite me and asks polite questions about my classes and about Leighton and tells me that it's impressive, studying mathematics. She keeps looking like she wants to say something and deciding against it. Someone

162

calls her away, and I settle back into the couch. My core feels tense. I wish I were home. I go for another helping of vermicelli noodles and overhear Professor Xu talking, quietly, in Mandarin, with one of the other women at this party. "At such a young age, too. How unfortunate. 可怜."

I know they're talking about my mom. I dump my plate in the trash and stand in one of the darkened hallways. I hate the way they're talking. *We're fine*, I want to retort back. *You don't know us.* I know I can't say that. They're trying to be helpful, just like the church ladies were when they said they'd pray for me at Ma's funeral. *Pray for what?* I'd wanted to ask. What good is it begging for grace from a higher power who let your mom die, who let her suffer through brutal rounds of chemo before letting her liver fail over a slow, agonizing week?

I don't look at them when Ba and I finally leave the party a bit after ten. Ba seems bright-eyed. He turns on the radio on the way home. Headlights beam on the highway, and I watch the snow blanket the trees. My phone buzzes. I look down. Jamie and I have been texting. I've said I'm bored. Jamie's been giving me movie recommendations. I see that he's sent a picture of the Christmas tree in his house, decked in lights, with his beagle leaping for an ornament, with a movie scene playing in the background. Home Alone 2. That's my rec. You can have my login.

I type back a smiley face and then put my phone facedown.

We go home, and Ba goes to sleep. I put on the movie that Jamie recommended. Professor Xu invites us out to a New

Year's party, hosted by another Chinese family, but the day of, Ba decides to stay in. We spend it watching dramas, and that's how the new year slips in.

A few days after New Year's, I run into Hana at the post office. I recognize her almost immediately, in her light puffer jacket, layered over another coat. Both practically swallow up her frame. Her hair is short, tucked under a beanie, the ends dyed blue. That's new. I stop right there in the post office, my textbook rental clutched under my arm. She's shipping off a flat box. I half consider ducking out of the store, when she turns from the register, and then she sees me.

I stand there.

Our eyes meet. Hers light up in recognition before cooling into a slight wariness. I need to do *something*. I smile on instinct. Someone is calling me up, and I turn and go through the motions of returning my textbook.

"Shipping slip?"

I hand the printout to them. They box it up. My palms are sweating. I pay and then turn. Hana isn't here. My heart drops. I head out of the post office.

"Hey."

Hana is there. I'm not watching her life through the screen of my phone. I'm not wondering about her. She's standing right here.

"Hi," I say. "How are you?"

God, it all sounds so stiff. I remember that I made it this way.

"Good. Was just shipping a holiday gift to a friend."

I tilt my head. "That's nice of you." Hana was always the gift giver. She was always so thoughtful about it. "I was . . . just shipping back a textbook rental."

"Nerd," she says softly. Her smile is like a flash of sun, and for a moment I feel almost sick for not having reached out to her all this time. We stand there. My mind is racing. People are walking by us. She's tan from the sun. There's a nose ring I haven't seen before. I can't bring myself to say something, but I also can't make myself walk away. "What are you up to?"

She tilts her head across the square. She says, tentatively, "I was thinking of getting some lunch." She pauses. "If you're hungry too . . . ?"

Without thinking, I nod. "Let's go."

Our boots crunch over slush as we walk across the parking lot. We get a small window-side table at the sandwich shop. I wonder what Hana will say. She doesn't accuse me of not texting her for the past two months. "I didn't know you were in town," I say, keeping my voice light.

"Oh, yeah, sorry. Should have texted." We both know why she didn't. After all, I left her last text on read. Many last texts, actually. The salt and vinegar kettle chips feel like shards in my mouth. We're awkward like this because of me. But we're here now, and I can pretend like it was in high school, like we're here for open lunch, and I do. Hana puts her chips in her sandwich. She always does that. I say, "So, tell me everything. How's California?"

She takes a long sip of her soda. "Oh. First thing, I'm such a *chicken* when it comes to weather now. Like, anything below fifty is freezing."

I raise an eyebrow. "I was wondering why you were wearing two winter coats."

She laughs. "Yeah, my brother was making fun of it earlier, too."

"You look good," I say. "At least one of us has seen sun in the past three months. What are you up to out there?" I gesture to her. "Other than experimenting with hair dye."

She laughs. She seems more sure of herself. More peaceful. She ticks off her fingers. "Hmm, okay, a short recap: got two tattoos, one of them on a dare, flunked a midterm, and then had a breakdown and changed my major twice, almost got trapped in the desert when someone's car broke down on a road trip."

I pause, my sandwich halfway to my mouth. "Oh my God, Hana. You *are* the main character."

"Yeah. There was lot of character development in that desert. I learned I couldn't change a car tire for shit." She glances at me. "What have you been up to?"

I go home every weekend. It seems like years have passed since we've last seen each other. I wonder if I should tell her about the Match-Up and the campus-wide fervor it caused, but it almost sounds weird, too out of context here. "Nothing much," I end up saying. "I like my classes. And I, uh, joined a ski team?"

She pauses. "Wait, *really?*"

I nod. "Signed up for it on a whim. Practices start after break."

"That's really cool. I wish our school had a ski team. I've been trying to plan a Big Bear trip with my friends for forever."

"Kinda easier to ski out here."

"Yeah." She glances out the window. "Remember when we used to ski?"

I remember us racing on the runs after dark, holding cups of hot chocolate with frigid fingers, and spending weekends sitting by the fireplace and defrosting our toes. "I do."

"We should go again. I'm here for one more weekend."

I nod.

"I do miss home," she says. "I missed fall. It's good to see snow."

"One of my roommates is from Texas. She was very excited about the snow."

"Ooh really?"

"Yeah. Ruhi. She does newspaper stuff and is in, like, IM volleyball and four other clubs. You two would like each other."

"She sounds great. You guys are friends?"

"Yeah. Me and Ruhi and this other friend, Ava. She's from California. But, like, super north, from a former mining city." Ava's *I'm from Nevada City, but it's in California, and I don't know why it's named Nevada City* sounds in my mind, and I smile a little. I miss them so much. "She's the theater kid. Oh, you'd love her." I feel a pang. I don't tell her that sometimes Ava's mannerisms remind me of Hana's. My roommates would love Hana, I think. She'd be the one planning the parties right with them. She wouldn't be ditching them every weekend to go home.

"That's cute that you guys are actually friends with each other. My roommate asked me if I wanted her leftover pizza and then Venmo requested me for it."

"Oh," I say. I ask, cautiously, "You do have friends, though?"

"Yeah, I do. I love them," she says. "We're all queer and half of us have a crush on each other at any given time. We're trying to figure out where to go for spring break and none of us can make a decision."

She sounds happy and bright. I feel this familiar twinge of envy, that she's out there, starting this life that doesn't quite include me, with a friend group and crushes that I don't know of. I know it's self-inflicted. I should have texted. I should have replied to her texts, but isn't this inevitable? Weren't we always going to grow apart? "You over Kristen?" I ask.

She nods. "That was ages ago. That's *such* a high school thing."

I chew on a stiff piece of bread and swallow, hard.

Her eyes flicker to me. "Any updates in the love life of Grace Tang?"

I clear my throat. "Well. I'm kind of dating this guy."

Hana's eyebrows shoot up and her phone clatters to the table.

"And you've just been sitting on that update all this time?" She leans forward. "Who is *this guy*? Can I see a picture? How'd you meet?"

Well, it's a funny story, actually. I invented this process that used a mathematical matching algorithm to tell us we were the perfect match—

"We take a class together. We're both math majors." I take out my phone, and I pull up his Instagram with three pictures, the most recent of which is with his club soccer team. "Oh, yeah. He plays soccer, too."

"Well, this is the cutest thing ever. Your kids will be geniuses who play soccer."

I laugh. "He's great. He's really sweet. His family seems wholesome. His parents met at our college, actually." Why I am saying so much I have no idea. It's almost like I'm trying to prove something to Hana. *Look at me, I'm doing okay. I have friends. I'm dating.*

"Good. He better be worthy of you." Hana holds my gaze for one second more, as if she's searching me, and I feel unnerved. Hana isn't Ava or Ruhi or Caroline or Danny. There are years of truths between us. Hana can unfurl the slightest uncertainty and press me on it.

"I should get going," Hana says. I catch a glimpse of my phone and an hour has passed. "But it was good to catch up."

"Yeah." I stand. Hana stacks her basket on the counter, and I toss mine on top of it, where it stacks neatly, just like we used to do when we came here for open lunch. I almost make it to my car before she asks.

"Grace?"

I turn.

"I've been meaning to ask you. What happened at the end of summer?"

I'm still. Icy air seeps into my lungs.

"I mean, did I do something? Was it that call?" She looks at me and I know she hasn't forgotten. I know she's hurt, that she's confused; that she's been wondering this and saving this question for the end.

How could I ever express something I couldn't make sense of?

"No," I say. "You didn't do anything. I was just busy."

It's not the truth, and she knows it. Before she can ask further, I turn and get into my car. I sit there for a moment. Things will never really be the same as last summer, I think. Or high school. Hana seems happier now that she is in college; different, like she is finally moving forward with the life that she wants to create. I am just the same as I always have been.

That is what I realized last summer: I will always be in her rearview mirror.

It isn't until hours later that I get a text from her: loved seeing you today. lmk if you want to hang out or ski or something.

That afternoon, I finally tell Ba about ski team.

"Oh," he says, looking up from his cup of coffee. "You joined a team for this?"

I nod. "It's just an alpine club ski team. It's not the varsity level or anything. Only some compete. If they want." I pause. "It starts in January. Practices are during the week. I'll still be home during weekends."

I wait for him to say something or prod me about it. Instead he just says, "Okay. As long as you're home over the weekends."

I relax. I help him clear away the plates. I settle in my room with a movie I find on YouTube, and in the distance I hear Ba play scales, over and over again, on the piano.

I look at Hana's text and I don't respond.

TWELVE

UPON CAROLINE'S REQUEST in the group chat, we meet the Sunday afternoon before spring semester starts. "So," Caroline says to me and Danny. She's pressing her lips tightly together, like she's barely holding in a smile. "We might have actually gone viral."

"*How?*" I ask at the same time that Danny says, "Us?"

"Well, I wrote a Medium article about the Match-Up," Caroline begins.

"You wrote Medium articles over your winter break?"

Caroline gives him a sharp look.

"Sorry. Continue."

"Basically it was on what we presented. How we put a spin on the stable match algorithm for campus dating. How you can be paired with your ideal match within certain parameters and dating pools. And then someone shared it and it got reposted hundreds of times, and then it made its way to other platforms, and then"—she leans forward excitedly—"after that a bunch of people commented and emailed me. The local radio station wants to interview us and"—she lowers her voice—"someone from the *New York Times* even reached out asking to chat."

"*Wow*," Danny says. "*The* New York Times?"

I'm feeling slightly dizzy. I thought this spreading around school was big. But now it's far, *far* beyond just this school. Part of me wishes she had consulted us before writing the piece, but I push that thought away. I'm being ridiculous. It *is* a group project, after all.

"Right?" Caroline looks smug. "Guys, this could be *big*. If the timing works out, we could publish our three-month follow-up to a huge audience."

Here I say something. "Wait, but that's the thing. We should make sure our algorithm holds up before we publish it to a wider audience. Like, if our matches are still together and happy around the three-month mark."

"About that," Danny says. "Remember the December follow-up survey we'd sent to the matches who had gone on at least one date, to see if they'd gone on more? Well, I took a random sample of the respondents. And out of the random sample of thirty, only about half said they want to go on additional dates."

I sit, stunned. Half? What *happened*? "Was it winter break? I guess people aren't hanging out with their matches much."

"But that's only three weeks," Danny says. "People go longer without seeing their significant others. Maybe it's just the course of this. There's an initial attraction. Intrigue, more like. Then it gets complicated."

"It shouldn't," I say. "We literally made it so you were matched up with the person it was the easiest to fall in love with. The algorithm did the hard work. That's the most complicated part. It should be smooth sailing from there."

"But stuff can come up over the course of a relationship," Danny says. "People change. Maybe it's something the survey couldn't capture. Maybe other things become important to them, more than they thought."

I think of the question that someone from our game theory class asked during our final presentation. *What if people change over time? What if their preferences change?*

Could it change this quickly? Or is something fundamentally wrong with—or missing from—the algorithm? Maybe we need to conduct another study. We could interview the people who have broken up and identify some common factors. Maybe it's lack of compatible communication styles. That wasn't in the survey. I make a mental note of it for the next version.

"Well, at least we still have some happy matches," Caroline says, trying to stay upbeat. "Grace, how's it going with Jamie?"

"It's good," I say. Stable, just like it should be. "There aren't any issues at all."

"Aw, see?" She turns to Danny. "It *can* work out, after all."

"And my roommate's still with her match," I say. "I'll ask her about it tonight."

Caroline smiles diplomatically. "It's all going to be fine, then. The algorithm still works."

Danny shrugs. "I guess so," he says. He glances at me and then gives me a reassuring smile. I force myself to nod. But none of this feels so sure anymore.

"What are the odds that your romantic preferences can change over a three-week period of time?"

I'm sitting on Jamie's bed later that afternoon, leaning against him, my knees scrunched to my chest as we watch an HBO show that he really likes. Something about a bunch of people trying to control a family media business in New York. Jamie glances over at me, an eyebrow raised. I really do like his eyes. They're deep brown and framed with dark lashes that catch the light. "Is that your way of asking me if I still have feelings for you?" He tips up my chin and presses a kiss to my forehead. "Because that should be pretty clear."

"Oh," I say softly. "I was just . . . thinking about the algorithm overall." I pause. "Half the couples stopped dating over winter break. Something had to have happened, right? How could they have been so happy before, only to suddenly end things?"

There's a pause.

"Maybe it wasn't sudden," Jamie says. "Maybe they tried to make it work and then it didn't. Maybe it wasn't necessarily attraction that brought people together at first, but maybe, I don't know, curiosity? And once that novelty fades, people realize there isn't really much holding them together."

"That's true," I say. "I was thinking that maybe there were things this version of the survey didn't account for. Like communication styles. They all fell apart over winter break when we were away from each other. But that doesn't mean they weren't compatible, right? The algorithm isn't a failure; it's just that we can make it better."

"I'm sure you can," Jamie says. "Although I do feel like this conversation's getting a little meta."

"Right." I jar out of my thoughts. I guess it is a bit strange to be discussing the potential failure of an algorithm with the person the algorithm matched you with. "Sorry."

"Oh, it's okay," Jamie says gently. "For what it's worth, I think your algorithm works. And *my* feelings didn't change over break."

I glance up at him and press my lips to his. He pulls me in closer, deepening the kiss. His fingers trail at the edge of my shirt, slipping under, and I suck in a breath.

When we finally break apart and I return to my position of snuggling against him, he says, "That reminds me. I was talking to my parents over break, and you came up, and—"

I sit up. "You and your parents were talking about me?"

"Yeah?" he says. "We're dating, Grace. Of course you'd come up."

I don't know why it feels so strange. We're together. Jamie talks to his mom every day. Of course she'd know about me. I haven't told Ba yet about Jamie. I'd thought about it, briefly, throughout break, when we were having dinner, or when we were on a walk, when I was in my room watching a movie and he was practicing the piano. There were so many times I could have mentioned it and yet I didn't. I don't quite know why I didn't end up telling Ba. Maybe I felt like I was waiting for something. A sign, a cue, an indication. Maybe I was feeling protective. Of Ba, or of Jamie. I don't know. "Yeah, of course."

"Well," he says, looking at me carefully. "I think my parents are making a trip up sometime later this month. They wanted to come to campus and see me. And maybe meet you, too."

The last part sounds like a question. I glance down at our linked fingers.

"If you want, of course," Jamie says. "I know I just put you on the spot here. No pressure. Just something to think about. We can grab dinner or something."

"Sounds good," I say. Jamie turns the show back on. We kiss for a while and talk about our classes this semester. I already know that Jamie's in my Real Analysis and Group Theory class this semester. I get a text in the roommate group chat, with Ava sending three broccoli emojis, and then, din? "All right. I have to go."

Outside I shrug my coat around me. My cheeks still feel warm. I brush my fingertips over my lips. I pull out my phone, checking for any texts. I pull up my latest text with Ba.

It would be so easy to tell him. I can call him right now, even. I think of bringing Jamie home on the weekends to meet him. I think of us eating dinner, quietly, as we find ways to talk. I don't know how to describe it. It's like I can't fathom it yet. Like I'm still waiting for something.

* * *

177

Applications to the summer math research program open up the first day of classes. I have about five weeks before they're due at the end of February. I scan the page.

The Summer Leighton Undergraduate Research Program will introduce undergraduate students to various topics and fields of study in mathematics. Students will, under the guidance of a faculty advisor, embark on a nine-week journey to cultivate and develop a research question, which they will then explore throughout the duration of the summer term. The program includes several department events such as roundtable discussions and panels with guest speakers to encourage and inspire students to explore careers in higher mathematics.

This program is quite literally made for me. Students come in with a blank slate; they either express a certain interest in a field, such as number theory, or real analysis, or discrete mathematics. I scan the examples of the research papers that students have come up with and also flip through requirements: résumé, a one-pager about describing why I wanted to participate, transcripts, and a reference letter from a faculty member. I get right to work. Within an hour I've drawn up a résumé. I'll work on the rest of the application later this week. I make a mental note to swing by one of Professor Rand's weekly office hours. Right now the Match-Up results might be a little shaky, but it's just because of winter break. They'll stabilize in the next few weeks, and we'll publish our follow-up results, and I can approach Professor Rand with the write-up. I'll appear the perfect, rigorous student. It'll all work out, and before I know it, my summer will be secured.

THIRTEEN

"YOU SAID YOU read romance books, right?" I ask Julia on Tuesday.

Julia glances at me. "Yeah. Why? You want book recommendations?"

I shrug. "I don't know. Maybe. I guess . . . in the books you read, at what point does someone realize they're in love?"

"Usually at the end," Julia says. "The whole plot has to happen first."

"What kind of plot?"

"All kinds of things. Misunderstandings, chance encounters, internal and external conflicts. Sometimes one character realizes they're in love with the other, but then the other doesn't realize it."

I think of Ruhi and Ava's favorite movie, *Love, Rosie*. They both adore the entire movie so much, but every time I watch it, I can't help but feel frustrated. It's so apparent to me, every time they miss each other yet again, every time they hold back words from each other, that they're right for each other. I almost want to shake the dusty monitor and tell them through the screen. "How do people not realize it? I feel like either you're in love or you're not, right? Wouldn't they know?"

She shrugs. "People don't always know themselves as well as they think they do."

"Imperfect information," I say. It keeps coming back. A crush is asymmetric information; you know how you feel, but you don't know how the other person feels. But what if you don't know how you feel?

What then?

How could I possibly account for that in our survey?

"Okay, yeah, make it all fancy and technical." Julia glances at me. "Why do you ask, anyway? Your algorithm giving you trouble?"

I pause. "No," I say defensively.

But Julia gives me a long and hard look. I can almost *hear* her say it: that she's right. That the algorithm can't do shit for love, after all. She doesn't say anything, which I actually do give her credit for. We're at the fountain, where we usually diverge toward our dorms. But Julia lingers, and so do I. "What *is* your deal with math, anyway?"

"Oh. I'm just terrible at it. I cried at the kitchen table doing my worksheets throughout my childhood only to get a two on my AP Calc test, much to my Asian parents' chagrin." She pulls out her phone. "Speaking of, my dad is calling me. See you

Thursday. Or tomorrow at practice, I guess. If you're going."

She turns and picks up her phone. "喂?" she says into the receiver. The wind picks up and carries her voice my way, so I can still overhear her talk, in Mandarin. "I already told you what Ma said. Okay? If she wants to move to California, then that's her decision. I can't change her mind."

I pause. It feels strange to hear Mandarin on this campus. It always feels too familiar that it's almost painful. I wonder what happened between her parents at Christmas. If they really did all argue at a Chinese restaurant. Julia gives me a sharp look, and I turn away.

"I've never really believed in New Year's resolutions," Ava says to me over dinner that night. It's just us. Ruhi's late. Ava's hair is cut even shorter and half-gathered up, but she's wearing the same oversized dark green Yosemite sweatshirt she always does. She spears a piece of potato and chews thoughtfully. "I feel like people set themselves up for disappointment. How do you ring in a new year by analyzing all your shortcomings from the previous year?"

"It's just an arbitrary day." I shrug. "Makes you feel like you have some kind reset button, I guess."

"I just think it adds more pressure, psychologically," Ava says. "I tried going vegetarian three New Year's in a row. Didn't even make it a week each time. And then I just quit meat one day in the middle of June, and, I dunno, it just stuck, I guess."

"Speaking of New Year's resolutions." Ruhi rushes to our

table with a plate piled high with chicken, rice, and salad. "We *are* doing an article on that, if anyone's interested in contributing." The chair scrapes as she hastily sits. "So sorry I'm late. The *Daily* meeting was a fucking nightmare."

I glance at her. "What happened?"

Ruhi rubs her palms over her cheeks. "Just . . . you know the editors that got together? The two news co-editors? Well, I think they're having a falling-out right now."

I stop eating.

"Oh." Ava leans forward. "Shit, really?"

Ruhi nods, her lips pressed in a line. "Yup. And of *course* they decided to take it out over article pitches because, *of course*, everyone must communally suffer. My friend Ari was legit in tears after that meeting and quit." She takes another forceful bite. "Which means that the editors have to take on some of the staff writer work."

"Wait," I jump in. "Did the editors say why? Or what happened between them?"

"Nope." Ruhi shakes her head, her mouth half-full. "But I think they had an actual fight." Ruhi's phone buzzes, and she flips it facedown. "They're just sending passive-aggressive messages now. Who the fuck fights over *Slack*?" She sighs.

They were *too* similar. Maybe that's an issue with the algorithm, too. Matching up people with similar interests and outlooks on life makes sense, but what if they're so similar they clash? I can barely swallow my bite of food. These are matches that *I* was responsible for. And now things have soured, and

183

Ruhi has more work, and she's more stressed, and it's all my fault. Ava must notice my silence, because she says, "It's okay, Grace. People break up. It happens."

"But it's happening more often than not," I say, and I can't keep an edge of panic from sliding into my voice. "The matches aren't turning out okay. I mean, what even is happening with you and Cameron right now? You haven't mentioned him at all."

Ava and Ruhi exchange a look.

"I . . ." Ava then plays with her fork, not quite meeting my eyes. I wait for her to respond.

"Ava?"

She drops her fork onto the plate. "There just . . . wasn't a spark."

My heart collides with my rib cage. "Why?"

Ava shrugs.

I need to get to the bottom of this. "Was it a lack of communication over break? Were *you* two too similar? Was he not responsive enough? Did you not go on enough dates? Did—"

"I don't *know*." Ava looks resigned. "It's not that deep. I tried. He did, too. He's *great*. I mean, nothing went wrong. I don't have feelings for him. He doesn't for me. It's mutual. And I appreciate you for setting us up, I really do, but it just . . . didn't work out."

We all sit at the table in silence.

Ava stands up. "I have rehearsal," she says abruptly. "I'll see you later."

"See you," I mumble.

"Show's next week, right?" Ruhi calls after her. She turns back. "Right. Okay."

I sullenly push around an overcooked piece of carrot. "I don't get it. She never had a bad date. What happened? Did her feelings for him go away? Did she ever like him in the first place?"

Ruhi eats her food quietly. It dawns on me that she knows something that I don't.

"What's going on?"

She sets her fork down. She looks at the table for a moment, as if she's debating on whether to tell me something. And then she meets my eyes. "Grace," she says slowly, and there's an edge to her voice. "She never developed feelings for Cameron in the first place because she likes someone else."

She clasps her hands. I pause. "Who?"

"Bryce Santoso."

Bryce. It dawns on me, slowly. Cameron wasn't at the holiday party. Bryce was. They were sitting next to each other in king's cup. They study together. They hang out in general all the time.

"She didn't tell me," I say. I look up. "And she told you?"

"The weekend before the holiday party," Ruhi says. She doesn't meet my eyes. "While you were gone."

They've known this since before winter break. They knew this *last year*.

Ruhi catches my expression. "She wasn't trying to keep it from you or anything. She just was trying to figure it out, and she was struggling between her feelings and, like, her thoughts about the algorithm, I guess. And you seemed so happy with

Jamie and she didn't want to throw a wrench into your class project or, like, disappoint you? So she talked it through with me."

"Right," I say. Of course they talk over the weekends. I miss out every time. This shouldn't surprise me by now. But still it stings. "Do you think something's wrong with my algorithm?"

Ruhi gives me a hard stare. Her lips press together. And then her phone starts buzzing. "Fuck. Now they're individually messaging me conflicting edits. I have to go."

I watch her gather up her plate and her cup of juice. I sit at the dining hall table all alone, listening to people talk and laugh around me.

The matches are falling apart. And not only that, it's causing a wider ripple effect, too. Ruhi's irritated and saddled with work. Ava's not quite confiding in me anymore.

I'd considered a possibility in which the algorithm wouldn't work. But what if it's worse than I thought? What if it's actually causing rifts? And even as I take the long way back from the dining hall tonight, through the dirty January slush, I still can't conjure an answer to those questions.

The next day, I text my project group chat about Ava and Cameron's match fizzling out, as well as the news editors'. Danny responds with a clenched teeth emoji. Caroline says we can include that in our three-month follow-up report. I stare at her text, with a strange feeling at the pit of my stomach. This isn't *data*, I think. These are the roommates I live with. I don't bring Cameron up to Ava again. I think Ruhi's told Ava that I know, because things all ease between us the next day.

Maybe the algorithm doesn't just need small tweaks. Maybe it needs a complete overhaul.

I go to my Wednesday morning class, which is Stochastic Modeling. I don't recognize anyone in my class, really, except for Bryce. He's some kind of engineering major, I think. He sits at the upper back of the lecture room, with a friend. I watch him lean in, as if to tell his friend a joke, his fingers deftly flipping his pen. He leans back and laughs a little bit. I turn back to lecture. The professor is young and fumbles through his notes. I go to Real Analysis after, which I'm in with Jamie.

I go get a late lunch with Jamie after class, and afterward I get out and get ready for ski team practice. I'd remembered to bring my skis and gear when I came back from break. The skis are still there, threaded through my car from the back seat. Practice starts at three, at the nearby mountain. It takes about twenty minutes to drive there. I ease my way through the snowy roads, hearing the salt crunch under my tires. I know the place we're about to practice at. This was the mountain Hana and I went to all the time, and so when I pull into the parking lot, I'm greeted with the familiar wooden sign with its peeling paint and the lodge that glows from within. I could have gone here with Hana over winter break. And yet I didn't.

I'm a few minutes late, and so I tuck my skis into the rack and head in, joining the crowd of people who have formed around a table. Johnny, one of the team captains, is standing on a chair, in a bright green patterned coat. "—free ski, anytime until six, for everyone," he's saying as I put on my boots. "If anyone wants to join the race team, come to me or Nicole. There's an invitational in two weekends, and we still have two spots to fill on the slalom team. All right, that's all. Let's send it."

The team cheers and disperses. I see Julia in a light blue coat, her long black hair done up in Dutch braids, leaning in to talk to Johnny. She looks up, and our eyes meet and she smiles before turning back to Johnny. I make my way past the tables that Hana and I used to sit at, near the fireplace, our feet propped up on the chairs and stretched toward the warmth to bring some feeling back into them, while Hana's dad makes a joke. I head out into the snow, and slowly, I gather my skis from the rack. I snap them on and clutch my poles.

I stand there for a second, aimlessly, and then I push off toward the direction of the lifts. People are grouping up. They must already know each other. Dimly, I remember Johnny hosting some kind of party at his off-campus apartment. I didn't go, of course. It was on a Saturday.

Why *am* I even here, anyway? The outline of the peaks is familiar to me, but I feel more lost than anything. What was the whole point of me joining ski team? Why had I signed up? Was it to prove a point? To myself? To Hana? That I, too, am thriving out here, doing something by myself that we used to do every weekend in middle school together? What am I proving to Hana, exactly, if I don't even have the guts to text her?

I can't think too hard about this. I'm here now, so I shuffle toward the lifts, catching one at the last second with two others.

I glance at the girl by my side, her cropped dyed hair peeking out of her helmet. "Dude, I can't tell which run to ski first," she says. "There are two blues coming up."

The guy with long hair shrugs. "We'll see when we get off. Game-time decision."

"Left one is steeper," I say, surprised at my own voice. "And has the obstacle course. Right levels out. It should be a green, really."

The girl turns. "Oh?" She brightens. "You're an upper-classman?"

"Oh, no. I used to ski here. I live nearby."

"A local." She pauses. "I'm Zoe, by the way. This is Sean. We went to the same high school in Wisconsin, and somehow both ended up here."

Sean pops his head out and waves. "Heyo."

"Oh, wow."

"I know, right?" Sean adjusts his goggles. "What are the odds?"

It's actually surprisingly high, the probability that two people from the same hometown end up at the same college. I remember calculating for me and Hana once.

I don't realize we're at the top of the slope until I feel the boards beneath my skis. I half stumble out, and Sean gives me a hand to steady myself. "Thanks."

"I gotchu," he says. "Lead the way."

I lead them down the easier run first, taking care to make extra-wide arcs. It's a little icy at this time of year. It feels so natural, skiing again, the wind whistling in my ears. At the bottom, I wait for them to catch up so we can all head to the lift together.

Zoe and Sean are fun to be around. They tell me stories about Johnny's ski mixer and how everyone got so drunk that he and Nicole ordered Ubers for everyone to go to a pancake diner at two in the morning. After we make it down a few blue runs without any mishaps, they egg each other on to do some tricks down the obstacle course. I stick with them, first out of obligation, and then because it feels natural, the three of us making our way down the mountains. *This* is why I joined ski team. To meet people.

The sun dips below the horizon, turning the hills a golden pink. Zoe and Sean leave early, saying that they need to make it back before they have class at six. I watch them head out, Zoe's laughs carrying across the snow.

I turn back toward the mountains. Out of the corner of my eye, I spy the hardest black diamond course, a notoriously icy run that Hana and I used to save until the end of the day. This time, I see a figure in a blue coat.

Julia.

She takes off, and by the time I can blink, she's a third of the way down the slope, gaining speed. But she doesn't wobble or veer out. She weaves down the mountain like she's taking flight, perfectly in control. She coasts to the bottom and brakes, hard, before high-fiving Nicole.

I take in a breath. And before I know it, I've dug my poles into the ground and I'm heading toward that lift. I make it just in time to catch the lift seat and nearly fall into it, knocking into the person next to me. I hurriedly straighten up.

"Hey," Julia says next to me. I can almost imagine her raised eyebrow behind her goggles. "You good? Almost took us both out with that one."

I straighten up. "Meant to catch it earlier. Sorry."

We sit in silence for a moment. And then Julia turns. "You know this lift is for the double black diamond course, right?"

"Well," I say evenly. "Good thing I grew up skiing it."

Her expression levels in awed surprise. "Right. You're a local." She nods toward the course. "Are you competing, then?"

"Probably not," I say. "You?"

"Yeah. I am. Fair warning, though. Nicole's ambushing everyone who makes it down this course with a competition invite."

And with that, our skis touch ground. Julia heads toward the edge. She adjusts her goggles and her poles. She gestures at me. "Go for it."

She's watching me. Daring me. I know it. I tip toward the edge, staring at the steep drop. The last time I did this run was two years ago. Hana was here. And then I push off.

I slowly edge my way down. I'm going faster than I have before, but instinct kicks in and I feel strangely light, like I've remembered this. It's way steeper than the runs I've done with Zoe and Sean, that's for sure. I carve extra wide, just barely hanging on to my speed, skidding past the ice patches. My heartbeat's loud in my ears. I brake at the bottom of the hill, so hard that I almost lose my balance.

But I make it. When I slowly straighten up, I see Nicole's red coat coming over to me.

"That was *stellar*," the co-captain says with a wide smile. "Hey, by the way, have you thought about competing? We have one spot left in the late-January invitational. It's just one extra practice during the week, and racing is *super* fun."

"Oh." I stop short. "It's over the weekend, right?"

"Yep, we leave Friday and come home Sunday morning. You barely even miss class, and it's really fun."

It's during weekends. I'm supposed to be home over the weekends. I can't do it.

But then I catch Julia's eye as she zips by us. Her goggles are pulled over her helmet. She gives me a discreet smile, as if to say, *Not bad, genius.*

I turn back to Nicole. "Maybe."

"Okay, well." She shrugs. "Just let me know. Think about it."

Nicole heads off to the lifts. When I look for Julia, she's gone, halfway up the mountain. It's getting dark out. The wind is picking up.

It's a weekend, I think, later, when I'm headed toward the cars. Once I'm in my car I take out my phone and already there's a text from Nicole in the ski team GroupMe.

great seeing you all out here today 😊 one more spot up
    for the invitational—inviting all new skiers trying out
    racing!

Of course I won't be able to go. I'm supposed to be home, doing classwork. Making dinner with my ba. I've said no to so many other things. It shouldn't be hard.

Yet I hover over the message. *What if I* want *to go?* I think. I realize as I warm up in front of my car that this is the first time I'm not stressing over the Match-Up. I think of Julia's impressed look, and my chest buzzes with a satisfactory warmth. I think of spending a weekend away, racing down the slopes. For a moment, I want that so badly it almost hurts.

Before I know it, I'm messaging Nicole.

Fourteen

That night, I show up five minutes before the Sunny Side Up improv team show with posters with large printouts of Ava's face that I'd surreptitiously printed in the library. I save a seat for Ruhi. She arrives two minutes late, which is uncharacteristic of her, breathlessly saying that she just got off FaceTime with Arjun.

The room is already packed. We fight to get two seats next to each other, relatively in the front. Someone blares out a kazoo, and the makeshift curtain drops and the show begins with each member introducing themselves by way of cooked egg preferences.

It makes me so happy to see Ava in her element during the show. *This* is the Ava I know—the tiny comedic powerhouse. Every single game they play, she is up on the stage—jumping in front of people, drawing laughs out of them, and cheering her teammates on. She and Bryce get paired together for their third game. And that is when I finally *see* it.

How could I have not noticed before? The way they always seem to gravitate back toward each other in a crowd? Cameron's impressions are great, he's quick on his feet, and he has a deep, dramatic voice that makes his monologues somehow funnier. But he's not the one that Ava searches for. At some point in their third game, she imitates a fire-breathing dragon and Bryce mimics the firefighter called to the scene, and they give such dramatic impressions that my stomach hurts from laughing. At the end of their bit, Ava's dragon and Bryce's firefighter hold hands, and the cheer from the crowd seems to shake the walls.

The Sunny Side Up show ends, and they all come onstage in their green T-shirts and take a large bow. Half our row gives her a standing ovation. Ava looks ecstatic and her cheeks are flushed, her frizzy hair coming out of its bun. She says something to Bryce, who is next to her, and his eyes crinkle in a laugh.

I turn and meet Ruhi's gaze. Our eyes lock behind the Ava posters we made. Ruhi smiles, imperceptibly, as if to say, *You see it, right?*

She's right. *I'm* the one who's missed it, all along.

The show ends, and we run up to Ava and wrap her up in a big hug. She nearly falls over herself laughing when we pose with her face cutouts, and she takes a picture to send to her family group chat. We give her a bouquet of flowers, and she positively beams. "You guys!" And then she peers in and her face goes deadpan. "You have *got* to be kidding me."

Inside the bouquet is a small bottle of Smirnoff Ice.

"You just got iced!" Ruhi bursts out. "Drink, drink!"

Ava laughs. "I am *not* taking a knee and chugging this right now." She cradles it to her chest. "But I *will* save this for the after-party." She throws her arms around us, me and Ruhi and the cutouts, and presses our cheeks to hers. "Thank you for coming."

We let Ava meet up with the rest of her improv teammates. She shows Bryce the bouquet of flowers and the hidden bottle of Smirnoff ice, and he laughs and glances back at us. I give her a big grin and a thumbs-up, swallowing the sourness.

He lets her take a sip from his water bottle. With the stage light haloed around them, it is so clear that I was wrong.

It's not just a matter of small fixes. My algorithm's been fundamentally wrong all along.

Ruhi and I lug our Ava face cutouts home and do our homework. Ava has her after-party with her improv team members, so she doesn't come home right away. In fact, it's almost two in the morning when she finally returns.

And when she does show up, she stands in the open doorway, beaming, her cheeks flushed, her mouth open.

I push myself up from bed. Ruhi swivels around, looking up from furiously writing another feature. I glimpse her browser riddled with tabs. Her desk is cluttered with cans of cold brew. "What?"

Ava looks at me, her eyebrows raised, her grin hidden behind her hands. "So. Um. Bryce and I just—"

"Talked?"

"Kissed."

I straighten up in my chair. A mini shriek escapes from Ruhi, and she launches herself from the desk. Ava hurriedly closes the door. She sheds her coat and then peels off her outer sweatshirt. "So we were at the after-party, right? We were on the balcony of one of the off-campus houses. I think by that point the party was winding down and it was just the two of us out there. The lights were all pretty and everything and it felt like—a *moment*, you know? So I, well. Told him that I really liked him."

"And what did he say?"

Ava's smile confirms it all.

"So he had feelings for you," Ruhi says softly. "Of course he did. We could all see it."

Ava smiles down at her feet. "Yeah. I thought so, too. He'd said that he'd been feeling that way for a long time, but he was too scared to act on it because, well, he'd never been in a relationship before. And we were best friends already and everything, so there's a lot at stake. But we had a long, long talk about it on that balcony. *Long*. And I *think* we want to make this happen."

"Wow," Ruhi says. "You went for it."

There is a small, tight bitterness in my chest. My phone lights up, and I see the screen light up with Jamie's latest text. I glance away from it.

Ava is buzzing with energy. "I had to work myself up to it." She laughs. "Getting iced definitely helped. I mean, we're simply two anxiety-ridden beans who prefer to joke about everything. But yeah. I thought, why not?" She glances up, and her brown eyes shine with her smile.

"Look at you," Ruhi says, in admiration. "You and Bryce manifested that friends-to-lovers arc."

Ava covers her face with her hands and peeks through her fingers at me.

I smile. There is a strange, sweet ache in me. She's so happy. She's bouncing, beaming from within. "This is wonderful, Ava."

Ava relaxes. She hugs her arms to herself. "So," she says, "is all of 302 in love?"

"Seems like it," I say, although the words clang a little hollow in me.

"Y'all better not take turns sexiling me," Ruhi says. "Or at least if you do, wait until my production meeting nights."

Ava's cheeks redden. "Okay, I wasn't even going there for now. I was thinking more, like, double dates?"

"Or Coffee House triple dates?" Ruhi asks us, with an arched eyebrow. "Arjun's planning on visiting in a month. For Valentine's Day, maybe."

"Oh!" Ava bounces on her toes. "Wait, we would actually form a full Thursday-night trivia team!"

"That is possibly the best triple-date proposition I've ever heard. Although I don't know how I feel about going against the *Daily* team in trivia."

"Look at her. She's too popular for our trivia team."

"Leagues above us," I say.

Ava suddenly checks her phone, reading a text that has just come in. She turns away from us, slightly.

"Ooooh," Ruhi says. "Is that a text from your *boyfriend*?"

Ava scrunches up her face and throws her phone on the beanbag. "You guys are unbelievable."

"We're just happy for you," I say. I can feel Jamie's text settling into my pocket; I know that it is looming, that he wants to know if I can meet his parents next week, anytime Tuesday or Wednesday as they pop into town to celebrate one of their friends' birthdays. I pull up the text. I picture the thought of the triple date: me and Ava and Ruhi, with our boyfriends, laughing around one of the wooden Coffee House tables.

And that is a wonderful image.

The next morning, I wake up late to notifications from Caroline in the project group chat.

Caroline: guess WHAT GUESS WHAT

Caroline: . . . hello is anybody out there

Danny: good morning to u too

Danny: what's up

Caroline: WE GOT THE NEW YORK MOTHERFUCKING TIMES, BABEYYYYYY

Caroline: Scheduled an interview for Feb 25th! Hopefully we have our follow-up results compiled by then

Danny: HUGE

Caroline: !!!!

I watch the conversation happen. My thumbs hesitate over the screen. This again. Caroline didn't even *ask* before she'd scheduled us an interview with a national newspaper. How can this move forward when there are so many uncertainties? When it seems like the algorithm is falling apart in front of our eyes?

I'm thinking of Jamie's text again. I chew on the inside of my cheek. If I meet his parents, that means we're at *that* stage of dating. It's pretty much as official as anything. And if I meet his parents, he'll have to meet Ba.

And I don't know why, but the thought of that makes me nervous.

I go put the electric kettle on and put my phone away. I should prepare for lecture.

FIFTEEN

I CATCH A glimpse of Ava when I'm picking up my pepper-mint tea latte from Coffee House the following Monday. I order a plain coffee for Jamie and put in just a little bit of milk, but no sugar, just how he likes it. He's supposed to meet me here in an hour. I catch her bright red curls peeking over the top of a sofa. Her back is to me, her backpack leaning against the side of the couch. I'm about to walk over to her and say hi when a head of dark curly hair peeks over the top of the sofa.

I stand there for a moment, clutching my latte, registering only too late that the tea is scalding me through the thin paper cup.

Bryce and Ava stand and head for the door. Their heads are tipped toward one another. They don't notice me and I don't stop them, or wave to them. I wonder about the precise factors that brought them together, or the things that they connected over, and I chase away that thought. I won't know. I just know that it's a wonder. Her hand brushes his. Even from across the room I can see it, the way her expression blooms, the way he reacts and laughs at whatever she's saying. It is as if I am watching them through a movie screen.

This is how I know they are perfect for each other. Not because of thirty questions or an algorithm. Because in the most crowded place on campus it is so clear, so earnestly apparent, that they are all the other sees.

Jamie comes to my table at Coffee House and slips into the chair across from me. "Hey."

"Hey," I say. I close my notebook. I realize I've been just listlessly staring at the notes I've taken during Real Analysis. I'm still thinking about Ava and Bryce. How perfect they were.

And how wrong my algorithm was.

"How was class on Thursday?" he asks. Jamie's taking an insane amount of classes this semester, like, six, to fulfill his film minor, so he can't make some of his Thursday classes because of section.

I shrug. "You didn't miss much. I can give you my notes, though."

"Yes, *please*." He shrugs off his coat. "You're carrying us, class attendance—wise."

Us digs into me, just a bit. "I try," I manage. "You might have to cover for me next Friday."

"Right. Ski trip?"

I nod.

"Ooooh. Excited?"

I find myself smiling a bit in spite of myself. "Yeah."

"Nice." He grins. "Okay, so. I know meeting parents in general can be scary. But they booked a nice dinner on Wednesday, and they're so excited to meet you. They'll love you."

There's this hopeful smile that brightens his brown eyes, his eyebrows quirking up a little. Something in me quietly splinters.

I'd once wondered, back before winter break, sitting in the library study room with Jamie, if love would appear the way an answer falls in your head during a test. I thought that it was just a matter of waiting, a slow, unfurling revelation. And yet that never came.

This visceral certainty finally comes now. And it is that I am not in love with Jamie Anton. I don't have with him what Ava and Bryce have with each other.

And I won't.

How could it *not* work? Here is someone who thinks the way I do, who laughs at my half-hearted jokes, whose eyes always search for mine in a crowd, whose hand slots with mine even despite our long coat sleeves. Here is someone who wants to bring me to dinner, who wants to show me his parents so badly. He likes me: I should like him. What is causing this to not work?

I'm meeting his parents. I think of Ba in that moment, and I am frozen, overwhelmed to the point where I'm slightly dizzy. Ba would like him. Of course he would, in his own way, but I know I can't make this happen. I can't put all of us through this when I know this to be true: that I like Jamie Anton, that I like him and admire him and think he's funny and cute and attractive and brilliant and even in spite of all those things I am not even remotely in the ballpark of being in love with him.

"I . . . I don't think I can," I finally force myself to say. And then I meet his eyes.

His expression caves just a little, but he straightens. "Oh? You sure? I mean, if it makes you feel any better, they're not going to, like, interrogate you or anything. But it doesn't have to be a dinner. It can be a coffee or a walk or something. They'll be nice."

"I'm sure they will," I say. "But it's not them, really. It's—"

Please, Grace, for the love of the God you used to believe in, please come up with something better than "It's not you, it's me"—

"I . . . uh. Can't," I manage to say. I take a breath. "Do . . . us. Anymore."

It's not better, that's for sure.

I say the last part quietly, as if I am trying to swallow the words down before they come out, before the decision is set and I can't turn back anymore. The table next to us is quiet, and I wonder if they've heard. I wonder how many breakups have occurred here. I feel like absolute shit for diverting even a bit of my focus to think about the statistical frequency of breakups.

I force myself to meet Jamie's eyes.

He is quiet, his lips parted slightly. The expression in his eyes has cooled. I know I have hurt him. I hate myself for it. "*What?*"

"I'm sorry," I whisper. It feels weird, somehow, that all my life things have been happening to me, and now I am here, initiating a breakup. "I don't know how to do this. I don't know how to be a good girlfriend or a girlfriend or—anything like that. I'm sorry." I scour my mind for any memory of the movies I used to watch with Hana. "You're wonderful, Jamie. It isn't you. It really isn't."

"You know that doesn't make it better, right?"

My cheeks burn. "Yeah."

"I guess I saw it coming," he says.

"You did?"

He glances down and fiddles with his sleeve. "I always wonder what you're thinking, you know. How you were feeling about us. I thought that you were just hard to read. But I think it wasn't really that. It was just me losing you a little bit." He clears his throat. "Did you really even have feelings for me?"

"I mean, I was attracted to you, and I admired you, and I thought you were really cool, but . . ." But that is not what he is asking me. "I don't know," I say, and this honesty kills me. I drink my tea quickly. It scalds me as it goes down and my mouth is on fire, but even that is better than having to talk. "I wanted to. I wanted this to work out."

When he meets my gaze next, his expression is unreadable. "Of course you did." He pauses. "You had something to prove."

"What?"

"Your algorithm." He runs a hand through his hair, and he exhales through his teeth. I sit there, too stunned to say anything. "That's all you talk about. I mean, here I am, literally ready to introduce you to my family. But you were just testing a hypothesis. Weren't you?"

My heart turns to ice. He shakes his head. "Never mind. I don't know if I want to hear the answer." He stands. "Thanks for the coffee," he says coolly.

I have lost him. Fuck, I've lost him like this, and I scramble for something to say. "Do you still want my notes?"

It's like I have a knack for being terrible at this.

He gives me a bewildered look of disbelief, and I want to chomp straight through my tongue. He shrugs his coat over his shoulders. He pushes the chair in with a scrape and walks out.

I sit there. I meet eyes with the people studying at the next table, and their looks tell me that they've heard this entire breakup. I rub my eyes with my cold fingertips. I stare at my computer for a while. I gather up my things, and I throw my notebook into my backpack and shrug it over my shoulder. I walk out of Coffee House and through the slush back home.

You were just testing a hypothesis.

I spend the rest of the evening curled up in a study room in the library, trying to get warm again. I usually spend so much time at the library for my job that I don't want to spend any additional time there. But I don't want to come back to my room, because my roommates will see me and know something

206

is wrong. I run Jamie's words over and over again, and I feel sick to the point where my stomach hurts. *So this is what he thinks of me.* It's cruel and sharp, and I'm scared he is right.

God, Grace, I think in that stuffy library room. *You don't deserve him.*

But I wasn't just using him. *It wasn't like that. It really wasn't.* I wish that he could reach into my mind somehow and read my thoughts. I wished I could tell him that this wasn't just an experiment. That this was more real than anything, that the moment he approached me in the classroom and made that first joke, I wanted it to work because I wanted to be the person that is capable of love. I was into him. I thought I was. I want to step out of my body for a moment and just lay everything out in front of me, analyze every moment, and then I put my head in my hands and want to laugh at even thinking of that.

What was I thinking? Whatever algorithm I've created doesn't work. I'm not the mathematician I thought I was; I made a flop of an equation with all the wrong variables and dragged everyone into this with me. Maybe he's right. Maybe this is the person I am, and I've fucked up. Maybe I wasn't in love with Jamie, but I still cared about him.

And I hurt him.

WINTER OF SENIOR YEAR

MID-DECEMBER CAME. AFTER school, I got a notification for an email from my MIT portal and didn't look at it. I went to my shift at the rec center. I texted Ba to see if I should pick up any groceries on the way home. My coworker Miles told me stories about one of his bandmates recently adopting a bearded dragon after months of a dedicated dinner table campaign. Five o'clock came by, and then six.

"How are you doing these days, by the way?" Miles asked during a quieter moment. "How's . . . ?"

I knew he was asking about my mom. "Not . . . great. Just finished another round of chemo this weekend. She's holding up, though."

He lowered his eyes. "I see."

"She'll be fine," I said. That was the prayer I decided to grip onto. A simple assurance. She'd be fine. She'd survived this once. The odds were good for her. She'd get through this again.

But it seemed harder this time. I found clumps of hair knotted in the broom in the kitchen. She wasn't eating much, not even soups that Ba made for her. If she got them down, she'd puke them back up. She curled up on the couch during the day, with the low hum of dramas on in front of her. I still drove her to church every Sunday. She'd sit in the back pew. After each service, people would come up to her and talk to her. A small crowd would form. She missed this past Sunday because she was at the hospital with Ba. But when she came home that night, she said, "I prayed for you, Xiǎoyàn. I know MIT results are coming out soon."

I'd turned away then. My mom was puking all the time and could barely sleep. How was she still thinking about *me*?

I shifted restlessly in my chair at the rec center front desk, checking people in for the basketball courts and signing people up for parties at the multipurpose room. I tried not to think about that email sitting in my inbox.

I clocked out at ten. Miles didn't ask if I wanted to stay behind and play a game of pool. I think he could tell I was being off today. I put on my coat and went to the parking lot, hunkered down in the car, and glanced at my phone. There was a text from Hana at five, telling me good luck. There was a text from Ba, telling me that he'd brought home takeout for dinner and that I didn't have to worry about it.

I paused over my phone screen.

I had to get in. I wanted to be here with her. MIT was her dream. Hers and now mine again.

I tried to log into the portal. I had to restart several times because I kept missing keys. And finally I got it, and with shaking fingers I clicked on the decision.

I stared at the screen.

I dropped my phone into my lap.

I stared out the windshield.

And suddenly I was hunched over the steering wheel, the heels of my hands pressed to my eyes as tears spurted out. I rocked back and forth, my chest heaving. I tore my hands away and pounded the dashboard.

I don't know how long I stayed in that car. All I know was that I sat in the parking lot, staring out the windshield. And then I rubbed my eyes until they were raw, and I drove home.

I opened the door and heard shuffling. The takeout was on the table, my half congealed. Ba walked in from the office and glanced at me. Ma shifted up from her position on the couch, her eyes meeting mine, glittering with hope.

"I got deferred," I said.

I saw my mother visibly shrink. And then in that moment she steeled herself. "There's still a chance. You still have a chance, Xiǎoyàn. Just wait until March comes. You'll get in."

"Yeah," I said. "There is." I didn't meet her eyes. I went to set the table for dinner.

SIXTEEN

"YOU GOOD?"

Julia glances over at me as I smooth down the piece of tape at the circulation desk. It's the day after my breakup. Someone gives me a funny look when I ask for their student ID card and I discover I'm holding it in my hand. Roberta's thankfully occupied with unboxing new books in the back room.

I nod listlessly. "Yeah," I say a full ninety seconds after Julia's question. "I'm good."

Is it really that obvious? Ava gave me a funny look while we were eating breakfast. Today Jamie sat on the opposite side of the lecture hall in our Group Theory class, the other class we share. I could barely take in what the professor was saying. I wonder when the news will break, when the word of mouth through friends of friends will reach me, or my roommates.

Julia doesn't say anything else. She checks back in books that have been dropped off. A gust of cold air sweeps past us. I glance up. Someone has just entered this library. She's wrapped up in a long coat, and she unravels her scarf as she wanders toward us. She's a visitor, I think. She has a name tag tucked under her scarf. She looks older than a student.

"Hi," Julia says. "Can I help you?"

"Oh, I just wanted to get out of the cold. I'll just wait around here if you don't mind."

"Not at all," Julia says, perfectly pleasant.

The woman cranes her neck up. "This library's really changed since my time. The staircases are all glass now."

"You went here?" Julia asks.

The woman laughs. "Yeah. My husband and I met here actually." She tilts her chin up. "In the stacks of the second floor. We found out we were trying to check out the same books for the same Classics research paper topic about the *Aeneid*."

"That's such a lovely meet-cute." Julia grins. She's loading books onto the carts to be reshelved.

That sounds familiar somehow. The woman glances at me. I smile at her, which she returns. And then her expression stills at the exact moment I catch her visitor name tag.

I freeze. She has his same strong jaw and dark eyes, and it all becomes so clear to me.

This is Jamie's mom. Jamie's mom is right here.

Does she know it's me? She's still looking at me. Her expression has changed, ever so slightly, her eyes widening.

And I practically throw myself at the reshelving cart. "I'm taking this."

Julia frowns. She gestures to the rest of the books to be checked in. "But—"

I grab the cart and lurch away. I feel Jamie's mom's gaze on me as I head toward the elevators. I shut myself in there and emerge on the third floor. I don't even know where these books are supposed to go. I just can't be down there.

I can't be freaking out right now, of all places, at work. I enter the maze of the second-floor nonfiction stacks, where I can be alone and walled in by books on all sides. I feel my cheeks getting hot and tears prick the corners of my eyes. I lean against the bookshelves, with their damp, mildewy smell, and I try to calm down.

I hear bootsteps. Someone turns the corner, and I grab the book cart.

Julia stares at me with a quizzical look. "Hey."

I jumped. "How'd you even *find* me here?"

Julia tilts her head. "It's not a big library."

"The reference desk—"

"Roberta's got it," Julia says. "Seriously. What's going on?"

"I'm fine," I say in a thick whisper. I turn to shove a book onto the shelf. "I'm just reshelving."

She intercepts my book. "First of all, you're putting Nora Roberts in the architecture section." She raises an eyebrow and lowers her voice. "So I don't buy that for a second."

"Okay! Fine. You're right." New tears spurt through, and I furiously swipe at my cheeks. "About this and"—I fling out my arm—"everything."

"Wait," Julia says. She tosses her hair over her shoulder, and her eyebrows knit together. "What are you talking about?"

"Your *op-ed*," I whisper, and I am hyperventilating in lung-fuls of library dust. "You were right in the end, all right? It's just all absolute algorithmic bullshit. I mean, I don't know the first thing about love, and if I do, it's that I'm bad at it, because I just broke up with Jamie for no reason and he was literally about to *introduce me to his parents* and now his mom is downstairs."

The words just rush out. There is dead silence between the two of us. "Yeah," I mumble. "Go on and say it. I know what you're thinking. And you're right. I'm just this heartless, unfeel-ing, analytical, I don't know. Machine."

Her expression softens. "Grace," she says. "You really believe that's what I still think of you?"

I peek through my fingers. "I mean, you weren't wrong at the Halloween party. It's what I kind of think of myself."

"Okay." Julia leans forward. "First off, I was totally, abso-lutely, one hundred percent wrong. Everything I said—I mean, that op-ed was bullshit, all right? I love writing for the news-paper, but to be honest I don't even know what I'm writing half the time. And sure, maybe I thought the algorithm was kind of ridiculous at first. But who am I to say? Who really understands how love works? I sure as fuck don't. And I had no place putting you down for trying to figure it out in your own way."

"But you do," I say. "You read all those books."

"You can stare at paintings all day and still not know how to create art," Julia says. "I'm only going to say this once. But I was kind of rooting for you. I really thought you'd figured it all out."

I shake my head and laugh. My cheeks feel raw. "Imagine. Eighteen-year-old math major cracking the code."

"I would have believed it," Julia says. "You're smart, Grace."

"But it didn't work."

"Well, I know at least ten people who went on first dates because of this. And my friends who started dating because of this."

"But it could be a correlation thing. It's, like, they started dating *and* they happen to be matched up. I don't know if it's directly causational—"

"You're going to ruin this moment with a math lecture."

I pause. "Sorry."

We look at each other. It's only just now occurred to me that Julia is the first person I've officially told about my breakup. It's the first time I've told Julia something personal, even. I observe her dark eyes, her sharp, curious expression. "I still feel like shit. I mean, I broke up with him at Coffee House, of all places."

"That's not that bad. I once broke up with a girl at a Denny's. And then stayed and ate breakfast after."

I glance over at her. I realize I truly have no idea what Julia's romantic history has been, and now we're sharing stories in the dead-end library stacks among books about brutalist architecture. "You *stayed*?"

"What? Not my best moment, but I was hungry. I like breakfast food."

"You know what? I do feel slightly less bad about myself."

"That's what I'm here for." And then she straightens up. "Okay. I should get back. She's gone now, by the way. Your ex's mom."

"Okay." I take a deep breath and tuck my hair behind my ears and press the backs of my hands against my cheeks. I still feel like some kind of mess, but there is a small bit of peace. I can finish work. "Yeah. I should actually reshelve these books in the right section."

Julia turns to leave. Before she disappears she turns and, so fleeting I almost miss it, she gives me a smile.

I smile back.

The next day, I go down to the parking lot before ski practice and find my car unable to start.

Seriously? I stare at my skis in there. I could skip out on ski practice. But I still need to jump-start my car, eventually, before I go home. And a part of me *does* want to go to ski practice. I scour my mind for people I know who have a car. I swallow my pride and reach out to the only person I really know, and text Julia's number that I pull from the group chat.

She pulls up ten minutes later in her SUV. She eases into the parking spot next to mine and rolls down her window. "Car's out?"

"Yeah."

She hops out. I pop open the trunk and stare at the jump-start cables. I look at Julia. "I'm gonna be honest," she says. "I've never jump-started a car."

"Me neither," I admit. I feel bad for looping her into this when I'm probably making us both late for ski practice. I try to look up a YouTube video with my cold, fumbling fingers. After a full two minutes of me trying to buffer the video, Julia says, "You know, I have an idea. What if you carpool with me to practice today, and we can jump your car after?"

I pause. "You sure?"

"Yeah, of course. I'm getting cold waiting for you to figure it out. Heads up, though, my car is a mess."

It is the better idea. Gingerly, I extract my skis through the trunk, de-snagging one from where it has somehow tangled with the seat belt in the passenger's side. Julia's trunk has much more space, although there's also more stuff there: receipts, bags of gear, a pile of books tucked in the corner. I neatly slot my skis and gear in among her piles of stuff and then climb in.

She drives out of the slushy parking lot and onto the road. "So. How'd your car go out on you?"

I shrug. "No clue."

"Huh. Shit luck, then."

I shrug. "Breakup and a car that won't start. It's almost funny."

"Symbolism," Julia says. "The car breakdown was a sign."

"Great. I like being the main character of a failed rom-com."

"Oh, it's only the second act. You'll have your happy ending soon enough."

"Yeah?" I look out toward the snowy road. Out of the formality of the library job, it's actually surprisingly easy to talk. "Please tell me more about this happy ending. It sounds nice."

"No spoilers," Julia says. She turns the music louder.

"You say this as if you know."

"I really don't. I just believe in you."

"Julia Zhang thinks I have game." I nod. "Nice."

She shakes her head and laughs as she pulls into the parking lot. "I should have left you behind."

We head to the lodge together and then go our separate ways. I strap my boots on and do a couple of practice runs before I join up with Sean and Zoe, deciding that I'll warm up with them first and then start skiing the harder routes when they leave for class. We do some runs together down the mountain. It's all coming back to me, the weekends I'd spent with Hana. I'm no longer as stiff. I'm much more used to the icy runs. I spend a little longer with them than I intended, because it's fun, just skiing like this. I teach Sean some tricks and how to ski backward. We hang out, and by the time we're sore and our cheeks are raw with the wind and our toes ache with the cold, we find time to goof off and do a couple of tricks on the way down. "You know how people play Ultimate Frisbee on skis?" Sean says as we head back into the lodge. "Johnny was talking about that. We should try that out."

"That would be chaos," Zoe says. "Someone's ankles would get taken out."

"I'm drafting Grace for my team," Sean says. "She's the best skier out of us."

"As if," I laugh. "I'm trying to make it through my first race in one piece."

"You're going to ace it," Sean says confidently.

"I'm going to wipe out on the course, and then I'm never getting put on the competition roster again."

Zoe laughs. "I don't believe that for a second."

As we go up on the next lift, I catch a glimpse of Julia's blue coat and helmet as she weaves fluidly down the slopes. She has crossed the corner of my vision several times at practice, but now I let myself watch her. She skids to a stop, sending up a spray of snow.

Zoe follows my line of sight. "She's incredible."

"Way too good for a club ski team," Sean adds.

"She could have gone pro for sure." Zoe glances at us. "I think she almost was. I heard Nicole and Johnny talking about it. She could have gone D1."

Julia, pro skier? It makes sense to me actually. She's not the sardonic person who works by my side in the library. Out here, she moves with silent power.

But then why did she come to Leighton, a small liberal arts college tucked away in the corner of Vermont, with nothing but a club ski team? She could have skied for Dartmouth or UVM or something. And yet she's here.

I wonder this when Sean and Zoe leave and I head up the harder runs. I make it down a black diamond run before Nicole catches me and teaches me how to go down a slalom course. "It's just tighter, faster turns," she says, pointing me down. "You have to make it around each gate. If you don't, you're disqualified. So make sure you control your speed, all right?"

I nod.

219

"Cool. Give it a try and come back up."

I stare down the poles dotting the course. I ease myself down, taking care to go around each pole. They're set closer together than I realized, once my speed picks up. I miss the last three gates on the bottom. I brake, my face burning, and trudge toward the lifts.

"That's great!" Nicole says, her voice bright. "You've got the basics down. The more you practice, the closer you can make your turns."

I flail my way down the next few runs. I try making my turns tighter, but then I miss a couple of gates. Then I arc wide and go slow. When I've gotten to the bottom of my fifth or so run, I see a bright flash of blue and spot Julia making her way down, passing the gates so cleanly it's like she's nudging them gently with her ski pole.

"I don't know if I'm cut out for this," I admit to Nicole at the top. I nod my head toward Julia. "I'm not like *that*."

"Well," Nicole says. "You've already made really good progress just in the last thirty minutes. Don't worry about it, Grace. Keep at it." And then she takes off, leaving me alone at the top of the mountain. Why *am* I doing this? Why bother competing at all? I stare at the way Julia makes her runs, with this swell of admiration and envy. I want that for myself. The way she's so easily, effortlessly in motion.

It's dark when Julia drives us back to campus. She shakes her hair out of the two braids and blasts the heater. She chugs water from her bottle and catches my glance. "How was practice?"

I shrug. "Could have been better."

"It's your first time training with slalom gates, right?"

I shrug. "I guess."

"Your form looked pretty good actually."

My cheeks warm. I glance at her doubtfully. "Really?"

"Really."

"I don't believe you. You're trying to make me feel better."

"Since when do I give out easy compliments?"

She's right. Come to think of it, maybe this is her first compliment to me, ever. Or maybe second, given when she said to me in the bookstore storeroom the other day when I was losing it about breaking up with Jamie. Maybe Julia *is* capable of kindness.

"You can come to the optional open ski on the weekend, if you want to feel more confident about it," Julia says. "I'm going Sunday afternoon. Want to come with?"

I only pause for a moment. Sunday afternoon works. "Yeah. Sure."

She pulls into the dorm parking lot. We pore over a few articles in the warmth of the car, and then we climb out. Under mine and Julia's combined phone flashlights, I dutifully clip the wires to various parts of car machinery.

And miraculously, it starts.

"Thank *God*." Julia rubs her fingers together to warm them up.

"Sorry!"

Julia laughs. "Don't worry, I was already pretty frozen from practice."

I reach for my skis. "Wait," she says. "Should we just carpool to the mountain on Sunday?"

I glance up. "You sure?"

She shrugs. "It's easier that way. Right?"

"Okay. If my skis don't take up too much space."

"My books probably take up more space," Julia says. "Really. It's fine. See you Sunday, then?"

I nod. "Thanks for reviving my car."

Julia flashes me a smile. *Another one.* I'm starting to get used to these rare bits of sun in her demeanor. Her SUV rattles to life, and she drives away.

That evening, I settle into the swivel chair at my desk and curl my knees to my chest. My nerves feel jangly. I go in the search bar and look up: *julia zhang ski.*

Results pop up; dozens of them. Competition results, first in junior world championships, a profile in the local newspaper. In each of these pictures, she's younger, pink-cheeked, with sun-streaked hair with blond highlights peeking out from her helmet. *Huh.* She used to have blond highlights. She still has those same dark eyes lined with eyeliner that stare out defiantly; the raised eyebrow, the corner of her lips curved in that telltale Julia smile, as if she knows a secret that you don't. Except it was more prominent here; maybe it was the way she posed, facing the camera head on, her shoulders set. There wasn't necessarily an arrogant air about her, but something more like—

Confidence.

I glance through the other pictures in the newspaper. There

is an action shot of her airborne, practically levitating, with powder spraying all around her. Just before I hit the article pay-wall, my eyes skim across words: *originally from Michigan, a junior slalom sensation, medal in Worlds, sights set on the Olympics.* There is a picture of her surrounded by her parents, flowers and a medal slung around her neck, her eyes flashing and her cheeks red, her expression triumphant. Her dad embraces her, smiling, small wire-rimmed glasses perched on his nose, just like my dad and every other Asian dad has. Her mother is tall like she is and has short, cropped black hair and a large down jacket, and grins for the cameras.

She wasn't just any skier; she was a *famous* skier. She was going for the Olympics three years ago. But all the articles and competition results stopped just short of two years ago.

And since then, nothing.

I hear footsteps shuffle to the door. The lock clicks, and I frantically close out of my tab. Ruhi shrugs off her hat and head-phones, and her wavy hair tumbles out. "Hey, Grace. Whatcha up to?"

"Oh, I'm"—I glance at my screen—"checking my email."

"You seem stressed by your email. Which, my God, what a mood." Ruhi clicks the hot water kettle on, shrugs her coat off, and flops onto the beanbag with a sigh.

I turn and relax. There has been a strange tension in me. "What have you been up to?"

"Class. I have to write a whole Comp Lit paper."

"Have you eaten?"

She shakes her head.

"Wanna get a late dinner with me?"

"Oh." Ruhi turns. "Uh. I have a *Daily* article to edit. One of the managing editors asked for a rewrite on one of my news articles, and then another keeps scrapping ideas from all the staff writers. They need to go to group therapy, I swear. Our meetings are getting toxic."

She seems resentful. *I did this*, I think. This activity she loves has become a source of stress. She's staring at her phone and chewing on her lip. I ask, "Do you want me to bring something back from the dining hall?"

There's a silence. And then she glances up apologetically. "Sorry. I'm good. Yeah. I'm just supposed to call Arjun because he's keeps changing his visiting dates on me. Sorry."

"Oh, right." I gather up my coat. "Everything okay with you two?"

"Yeah." She takes a hurried gulp of tea before practically dropping the mug. "Fuck, ow, hot. Yeah. We're fine. We'll figure it out. I'm sure." She picks up her mug again but then has second thoughts. "Maybe Ava will be down for dinner?"

"I'll text her." She's having dinner with Bryce probably. I leave the room and head down the staircase, my steps echoing. My limbs feel tense. My roommates and I aren't having dinner all the time anymore. This semester we're scattered and pulled in different directions.

Which is partially my fault.

Caroline texts me and Danny about our interview with the local radio station next Wednesday. It'll be great practice for the *New York Times*, she says. She asks when we can meet to put together the three-month follow-up report on the Match-Up to prepare for the *New York Times*. I don't respond.

My mind floats back to earlier. As I open the door and brace myself for the cold, I wonder what has brought Julia here, of all places. I wonder why I'm wondering at all.

SEVENTEEN

THE SKY IS overcast on Sunday. I've just gotten back from home and from my lunch with Ba when Julia drives by to pick me up. I climb in. "Hi."

She nods a hello. "Welcome back to my messy car."

I laugh and toe away a stray receipt that has fluttered to the ground, as well as a Nutri-Grain wrapper. "The mess has expanded in my absence."

"It never gets neater, that's for sure."

"Second law of thermodynamics. Things always move from order to chaos."

"If I get yet another math lecture from you within the walls of my own Subaru, you're getting ejected."

"Noted," I say. "It's technically physics."

"Tomato, tomahto. Besides, this car is an old piece of work from the early 2000s and it isn't perfect, but it got me through the whole drive up to college."

I glance at her. "Really?"

"Halfway across the country." Julia taps the steering wheel affectionately. "She's tough."

You were a professional skier, I think. I know this about her. She doesn't know I know. It feels strange. Julia's in a good mood. She hums along the way to the mountain, and I lean back and glance out the window.

I hop out at the parking lot and hear Julia calling my name from the behind the car. I walk around. She gestures me closer and opens the trunk, and there's another pair of skis lying next to mine. "Got race skis for you to practice in."

I glance at them. They're thinner, the middles curved in just a bit. "You sure? Where'd these come from?"

"Asked Nicole for a spare pair from the storeroom."

"Thanks," I say. "That's really nice of you."

She shrugs stiffly. "Can't believe she'd forgotten to give them to you." In a fluid motion, she picks up her skis and heads toward the lodge. I follow her, shrugging my new skis over my shoulders. They're lighter. It's just the two of us. It's overcast, and even the runs don't look like they're that busy at all. And Julia and I are just becoming friends. Or are we? We've spent hours together, that's for sure. But we've always been doing our job. We've never really hung out just because.

We finally get to the top of the run. And before I can say even a word, she's launched herself from the lip of the slope and she's a quarter of the way down, curving her body around the gates, tapping the gates easily with her pole, as if she's dancing across the snow.

I wait until she's halfway down and nearly out of sight before I take a deep, cold sigh, and ease myself down with my poles. The skiing part is second nature. I feel my heart drop a little and hear the wind whistle in my ears. But racing is a new concept. I feel light on my skis, but still, I turn awkwardly, curving wide arcs around the gates. I quickly skid around one, and then by the time I'm righting myself, I'm already almost at the next gate and practically fall over to tap it with my pole. By the time I'm at the bottom, I've completely missed the last gate. I flub to a stop.

When I glance up, Julia's out of sight. She's just training alone, as she always does. This is better for me, too. If I tumble headfirst down the slope, at least it's not in front of her.

I haul myself to the ski lifts, passing a child clutching onto her dad's ski pull as he happily slings her along. I pick my way carefully down the slope. The second time's not better. I'm still turning too wide, my movements too clunky. Julia's blue coat flashes in and out of view. There's no way I'm even remotely like her. I try to keep my head down.

There is flurry of powder as Julia zips right up to me. "Hey."

"What—" The lift chair knocks into the backs of our knees, sweeping us both into the air. I nearly careen into her before righting myself. "You literally just appeared out of thin air."

"Boo," she says, in a deadpan voice. And then, "Your turns are a little wide."

Heat floods my cheeks. So she *was* watching me. "Yeah. I know," I mutter.

"What?" She glances at me through her goggles.

"I think at this rate I'm beyond help," I groan. "I don't think I'm cut out for racing."

Julia laughs. "Don't be so dramatic. Like I said, your basics are good. You're a quick learner. Your turns just need work."

"I was falling over the gates. And my turns were a mess. Like you said."

"Everyone has problems with turn technique."

"Not you."

"Oh, trust me," she says. "I definitely did."

We get off the lift. I half expect Julia to take off, but she stays by my side. "Your timing is just slightly off," she says. "If you turn when you pass the gate, it's too late. You start turning just before you think you do." She pauses. "And you're not committing to it." She puts her hands on my waist and nudges me to rotate. "You've got to make sure you're pretty much perpendicular to the slope at the peak of the turn."

I feel the pressure of her hands on my waist. I lean and turn, slowly, and peer up at her, at her set expression, her slightly pursed lips. She steps away and her eyes meet mine. "Perfect."

I hold the position for a moment and straighten out, feeling lightheaded.

"So, are we getting down this mountain, or?"

I snap forward. "Right." I dig my poles into the snow and push off. Julia's right. Now that I've fixed my timing, I feel lighter on my skis. I twist, and I can almost feel the pressure of Julia's hands, like a reminder. It's still not easy, not yet. But the gates are closer when I tap them. By the time I arrive at the bottom, I don't feel off-balance.

"See? You're a natural." Julia flashes a jubilant grin as she pulls up next to me. "That feel better?"

"Yeah," I say. I find myself smiling. "It does."

Julia doesn't take off. Instead, we settle into an easy rhythm. The rest of the afternoon, we ride the lift together. I make my way down, and then she does, sometimes throwing small bits of feedback at me. I pitch my poles into the snow and watch her arc gracefully down the slope, her twin braids flying behind her. Someone even turns to watch. I don't blame them. I saw it in the newspaper articles and the highlight reels on the internet, and now I've seen it in person. She is a marvel to witness.

"What?" she says as she skids to a stop.

"That was really good."

"Yeah. I've been doing this for a while."

That's all she says? The wind picks up, and I wiggle my toes. I've gotten to the point in time where I can't feel them, and my face feels chapped, but I still want to keep going.

I lose track of how many more runs we go on before we call it quits. My last three times, I clear each and every gate, and Julia cheers. We get in the car. I kick aside some more receipts. The heater blasts, and I stretch my toes. I'll be sore, I'm sure, by tomorrow. But now I feel just warm.

"So," Julia says, shaking her hair out of her braids. It crests around her shoulders. "How are we feeling?"

I nod and ease a breath out. "Better."

"Told you." She gives me a confident grin. "You just had to get a couple of runs in you." She leans back and sighs, checking her phone. "Wow, it's later than I thought. Shit, the dining hall just closed."

I shrug. "It's okay. We can just grab some food at Coffee House."

"*Or,*" Julia says. She glances over at me. "Any objections to breakfast for dinner?"

I shrug. It's dark out. It is dinnertime, or close to it, and I do feel slight hunger gnawing at the pit of my stomach. "None."

"Great. We're going to Ellen's."

"What?"

"A diner. You'll love it."

"You sure?"

"Without a doubt. You'll see."

Instead of taking the main road back to campus, Julia turns at the intersection and continues for a while. We turn into the small parking lot of a small diner against the thick backdrop of trees, with a thatched roof and a green door. The warm light from inside spills out.

I read the sign next to the door. "Ellen's Diner."

"You ever been here before?"

I shake my head.

"Yeah. I think it's kind of a well-kept secret among

upperclassmen because they don't want freshmen flooding the place. Which makes sense, because the pancakes are so good it's criminal, and there's hot chocolate on tap."

The snow is falling, lightly, as we crunch in from the parking lot. I brush the snow from my eyelashes. Julia's phone buzzes in her hand, and she gives me a quick look. "Hold on, let me take this." She says into the phone, in Mandarin, "Ma, what's going on?"

I stand there awkwardly while Julia takes the call outside. I glance at her through the doorway. She's pacing in the snow, her expression knotted together. I turn back. The diner's half-full. There are college students all around us. The a cappella group. A group of friends who clearly had walked out of a hotboxed car, so much so that I can tell from across the place.

"Sorry," Julia says. She walks back in. Her cheeks are flushed, and there are snowflakes in her eyelashes. "It was my mom."

I nod. "I know."

"Oh, right. Your last name is Tang."

"How is she?" I ask carefully.

Julia exhales through her teeth. "She's . . . whatever. Let's get food."

Julia's frown fades as she orders chocolate chip pancakes and I order strawberry. I take a bite. Paired with the whipped cream, the pancakes are hot and light and fall apart immediately in my mouth with the burst of strawberries. "Oh, these are wonderful."

Julia gives me a smug look, her cheeks full. "See? I'm never wrong."

"Okay, calm down."

For a moment, we do nothing but eat. I'm famished, I discover, and these pancakes are truly the most delicious things I have ever consumed. Julia sips on her hot chocolate.

"So," I say. Julia glances back at me. "You're really good at skiing. How long have you been doing it for?"

She pauses. "A while."

That answer again. "You ever thought about going pro or something?"

Suddenly, her demeanor changes.

Her expression shuts down. She sets down the mug. There's a long silence before she says curtly, "Yeah. I have."

Oh. "I'm sorry. I didn't . . . it's just that I'd heard something—"

She sets down her fork and glances up. "The ski team is talking about me?"

"No! It's not like that. I don't think people were meaning to talk about you. They said you're just really good. Like, too good for a club ski team. It was a compliment."

"Well, fuck," she says softly.

I've ruined something.

"I'm sorry," I say again.

She doesn't respond. We eat in silence for a while. The hot-boxed students in the back are watching a video on YouTube with the volume dialed up, and they're laughing so hard they're losing their minds over it. I stare down at my plate, and the pancakes feel like mush in my mouth. I set my fork down. I'm no longer hungry.

"Yeah. They're right," Julia says finally, and her voice is quiet. "Skiing used to be my whole life."

I look up.

She shrugs. "Like. My *entire* life. My parents and grandmother moved from Michigan to Colorado. They left their entire community behind to settle down in Vail so I could train. So I could have some kind of a—a shot at worlds. And the Olympics, of course. I spent all my weekends and afternoons after school training. And summers I was doing conditioning. And it was all working, for a while. I was *good*."

"You still are," I say softly. "You're amazing, Julia. You should see yourself."

She takes a sip. Her lips set in a bitter line. "No, you don't get it. I was the top of the *fucking* game in slalom. It's like if I went to a tournament and didn't place, it would be disappointing. I was . . ." She stares at a nondescript spot on the table. "I don't really know how to describe the headspace I was in. Nothing else mattered. School was a blip. I barely made friends because I felt like everyone else kind of grew up together and I felt out of place." She gives me a glassy look. "So. It was just me and my parents and my wai-po and skiing. Which, there weren't that many Chinese kids in skiing, either. But I was going to be the one. The first."

There is a long pause.

"And then what?" My words barely come out.

"And then my parents started fighting," Julia says. "It shouldn't have been a big deal, right? Everyone's parents fight. But mine just turned on each other. The smallest things would blow up into these big arguments. It was clear they weren't happy. I couldn't tell if they were unhappy with each other or with where we'd moved to. But they came together for me. When I was competing, it got better. When I placed, they were happy."

"So you kept competing," I say.

She nods. "Yeah. So I was coming out of Junior Worlds and Junior Olympics. Olympic year was when I'd be sixteen. That was my window. And then the winter before, my wai-po had a heart attack in the middle of a snowstorm. I was the one who made the 911 call. It took over two hours to get her to a hospital. So she didn't make it."

I look up. Julia's not quite meeting my eyes. "I'm sorry," I say hollowly.

"It didn't hurt that much in the beginning," Julia says, still staring at a spot on the table. Her voice is soft. "But I think I just pushed it down. My wai-po was the one who always told me not to be hard on myself. And to eat. And now she was gone and it was just me and my parents who hated each other. So I developed, like . . . a weird thing around eating. I made myself work out even more instead of sleeping. It was all for Olympic year. I thought that if I . . . It sounds so messed up to say now, but I thought that if I . . . *placed*, it would fix my family." She sets her jaw. "So then came Olympic year. Nothing felt right during training. It felt like I was pushing myself, more than ever. I think my body started to break down. And then, during nationals, I lost control during a run." She closes her eyes for a long moment. "And I tore everything in my left knee. My ACL, meniscus, everything. So. That was that. My body gave out."

That was what had happened, then. She sighs and runs her fingers through her hair.

"I got surgery, and did physical therapy for a year, and I thought I could get back to it. But I tried and I couldn't. The first time I skied, I got a panic attack." She seems calm but I hear the slight tremble in her voice. She laughs bitterly. "I mean, how fucking ridiculous is that? Athletes come back all the time. I didn't understand why I couldn't and I felt like I had lost so much time. I missed the college recruitment window. It was just . . . a terrible year. My parents didn't know what to do with me. They were dealing with their own issues and also with a depressed kid."

There is a silence. She gives me a look, as if challenging me to say something. "You asked me a simple question, and I gave you my whole therapy consultation speech."

I swallow. I am just barely aware that this is the girl I have been working beside for months, someone I've seen nearly every day; this girl who I thought was an unreadable vault. And she has been holding this in all this time. I search for words. "No, this is . . . I want to hear this. About you."

Her dark eyes soften.

"I'm sorry." I shake my head. "About everything. I knew your parents weren't doing great, but I didn't know it was over this."

She shrugs. "I mean, I feel for them. All of us were in a bad place that year. They gave up so much, you know?" She twirls her fork. "I wanted to make it worth something. For all their sacrifices to have been a means to an end. I wanted to be their American dream, and I couldn't. So here I am, doing a club ski team because I still love the sport, and I *want* to love skiing again, but can't really go anywhere with it."

I glance down at my pancakes, at the congealed strawberry jam. I nod. "My mom's dream was for me to go to MIT. She wanted me to become a famous mathematician." I swallow, hard. "I didn't get in. Obviously."

I have said it. I brace myself. Julia tilts her head. "How'd she react?"

"I don't know." I pause. "She died last February."

Julia stills. "God, Grace. I am so sorry."

I hold her gaze and wait for her to avert it. I wait for her to quickly change the subject, or for the frequently asked questions; I have been answering them for ages. *How?* has a definitive answer. *How are you?* is something I still do not quite know how to answer, at least not honestly. I'd once described to Hana that it all felt like I was realizing suddenly that I'm in a frozen, icy lake, and I'm treading water. I'm not quite sinking and sometimes my limbs are numb and I forget for a moment that I'm out there, but the shock and pain always return.

"What was she like?" Julia asks.

My shoulders loosen. My throat gets tight. "Um," I say. "She was . . ." I let out a breath. What could I say? I think of her bringing me milk in the middle of the night. Her rattling off names of my peers at math competitions and telling me, sharply, that I'd never be better than them. Her making me an entire workbook on the library printer one summer. "Focused. And strict. And no one believed in me more than she did." I swallow. "I wanted that to all have been for something, too." There is a long, long silence. Julia doesn't avert her eyes. "But here I am." I hold up my fork. "Eating pancakes, I guess. A consolation prize for disappointing our parents."

Julia sighs. "At least these are decent pancakes."

"Fantastic pancakes, in fact."

By the time we get back to Julia's car, it's been dark for hours and a light dust of snow has settled on her car roof. We were in the diner for two hours. It's not like we haven't spent time together—we literally work five-hour shifts all the time. But somehow, it feels like we're only just getting to know each other. It feels different, talking about Ma's dreams for me with Julia. She's endured loss in her own way. Before Julia starts the car, she reaches over and gives my hand a long squeeze. I glance over. She doesn't say anything, just grips my hand tightly. And then our eyes meet, and she starts the car again.

"You know," Julia says as we head back, her headlights illuminating the flurry of snow, "you kind of are a famous mathematician, if you think about it. Your algorithm did shake up the whole school."

"I mean, it's hardly a new theory. Just a twist on an existing one."

"But it was a new take on something. And it was brilliant. Especially for a college freshman. Believe me, everyone was talking about you." Julia looks at me. "When I call you a genius, I mean it."

"So it's not ironic?"

"Half the time it is," Julia says. "But you're really smart. I knew from when I met you."

"Really? That was your first impression of me?"

She's driving on familiar campus roads now, and she pulls up to a stop sign. She glances over at me. "Yeah. You were a big nerd. I could tell."

I laugh. Of course she still has to humble me. "I'm personally taking it as a compliment."

My dorm building looms up. She pulls in the parking lot. I've spent a whole day with Julia now. The soreness has set into my legs; I know they're going to ache the next morning. Yet I linger in the car. Julia's eyes meet mine. I think she's going to rush me out, but then she says, "And what about me? What was your first impression of me?"

I take in a breath. "I thought—" What *did* I think? When was my first impression of her? When I saw her in the library? When I saw her name in the newspaper? When I saw her at the ski team meeting or the Halloween party? It feels like each time I run into her it is a surprise, a gut reaction, like *oh*, here we are again, in the same place. "I thought . . . you were kind of . . . hard to read. Sort of. And I thought I wasn't going to get to know you."

Her eyes meet mine. Her lips part, as if she's about to say something, but they curve into a small smile instead. "And yet you have."

SPRING OF SENIOR YEAR

MY MOTHER DRIFTED into the new year. In January, the doctors said that she wasn't responding well to chemo, not this time. The cancer had reached her liver at this point. It wasn't until I saw the doctors pull Ba aside and talk about making Ma comfortable that it hit me, finally, that they weren't trying to save her anymore.

The Takamuras brought us dinner most days. They visited the hospital, and Ma had a sleepy conversation with Hana's mom while Hana and I sat outside. She tipped my head onto her shoulder, and we sat like that, for minutes or hours, I don't remember, listening to the hum of the voices and watching the nurses walk around. But mostly I remembered Ba sitting there, talking to Ma softly. I would leave the room for water and come back to his hand curled around her, his other arm propping his head up on the edge of the bed, his eyes drifting closed. I went to the empty bathroom to cry and pace around. I had never really had a concrete plan for my life. My mother had always done it for me. In every permutation of every universe, I had expected my mother to be here. And now she wasn't going to even be at my high school graduation.

In the end, Ma made it to the sixteenth of February. Ma's father, my wai-gong, flew in. People from the church poured into the funeral service and filled the seats. The pastor himself gave a long speech and talked about my mother and how devoted she was and how she sang in the choir, how he heard God in her voice, how abundantly she blessed us all, how that blessing would continue forever now that she was in eternal heaven. Ba was still the whole time; my grandfather nodded along, not understanding a single word of the service. Ba and I and my grandfather came home after the service and had dinner. "You should visit her on Qingming day this year," my grandfather said quietly over his bowl of rice. "That's what we would have done back in Hangzhou." He was shrunken in and small. He had Ma's sharp nose.

Ba said, "I'm planning to."

"She should have stayed back," my grandfather said. "Why she left to come here is beyond me."

Ba didn't say anything to that.

The next morning, I drove to Hana's house. I lay on her floor in her bedroom and she stroked my hair. She put on one movie after another and the sound went in my ears and I didn't remember any of it. It was a Sunday. I didn't go to church. The next day, I woke up and went to school and continued with the rest of my life.

Senior year came to an end. Days brushed past me. The occasional baked goods and dinners showed up at my doorstep, less frequently now. There were assemblies and our school's Springfest, where everyone wore dresses and set up school club stands in the gym because it was still snowing out. I kept thinking about the days she wouldn't witness: She wouldn't see March 11, the day the snow finally melted. She wouldn't see the tulips bloom at the end of April.

Ba and I didn't talk about MIT. I finally told him the day the regular results came out, the rejection that I'd been carrying around this whole time. On a bus to the regional math competition, people opened their emails and yelled and hugged each other on the bus. Someone from our school had gotten into MIT. I congratulated him, my heart clenched in my chest.

As light crept back into the day and the winter months eased up, I tried to keep myself busy. I'd attended every single math team practice. I spent endless hours on the websites for the colleges I'd gotten into. Weighed one financial package against another. Did loan calculations. I still went to my job, because even if I didn't know where I was going for school yet, I still needed to save up for it. I did all kinds of mental math with my fifteen-an-hour minimum wage. Miles was there, too, saving up money. He wanted to take time off before college, he said. Work on music with his band. He thought about going to New York.

I started driving Ma's car. I looked in the glove box for the owner's manual, and I found a CD of Chinese songs, the same songs we'd play on road trips, the songs my parents once sang in that karaoke bar when they met. I tucked it back into the glove box. I found quarters in that glove box and a take-out receipt.

Hana texted me one afternoon. I got into the car and drove to her house, where she threw herself in my arms, squeezing me tightly, whispering, "I got in, oh my God, I got into USC."

I squeezed her tightly, holding her to me. "You did it," I said. "Congrats."

She glanced at me. *You?*

I knew she was asking about UCLA.

I shook my head and smiled. "Didn't get in. I'm going to Leighton. They're giving me a ton of financial aid." I'd made that decision alone, days ago. And then I hugged her again, just so we could move on.

"You're going to come see me all the time," Hana said. "Promise?"

I nodded and smiled. And from that point on, every second Hana was farther and farther away from me.

Her mind was already there. I knew it. I knew it in the way I saw her shopping online for summer clothes in AP Psych, the way I helped her frantically post and talk to potential roommates. I helped her draft introductions, and I grinned as she gushed about meeting the girl from Chicago who would become her roommate. "She also loves reading Jesmyn Ward and Celeste Ng!" I glanced at pictures of a girl who looked absolutely ethereal. "And she started her own sustainable business. She is so unbelievably cool." I knew it in the way she was already browsing for her classes when she hadn't even taken her APs yet.

"You think they all surf there?" Hana asked.

I glanced at her during lunch. "What?"

"Do you think they're gonna make fun of me in Cali if I don't surf?" She took a big bite of her panini.

I rolled my eyes and turned to the window. "They're not going to bar you from entering the state."

It wasn't that she was intentional about it. Hana was moving on with her life, after all. I was the one standing still. I didn't want this spring to pass. Time moving meant I had to move on without my mom, and I couldn't bear to imagine it.

Here was the other thing: I'd lied to Hana. Because I *had* gotten into UCLA. I never stopped thinking about California, not since the day I opened my email on my phone and felt a strange joy and guilt wash over me. I kept it like a tiny flame in my chest, a secret that would keep me warm. And as long as I didn't speak it, as long as I didn't tell my father, that flame wouldn't leave me. I checked the mailbox every day until I found a thick blue and gold packet and hid it in my room, underneath all my textbooks. I looked up beaches in Southern California and in the freezing April rain I dreamed of the endless sun and the wind in my hair. I thought of the promises Hana and I had made. I thought of her close to me. I thought of us on the beach. Lying on the sand, the sun burning our cheeks and shoulders.

I didn't tell Hana, not yet. Because once I told her, I knew that it would all be in motion. That she'd want me to come with her. Because until I told her, California was still this safe dream inside me.

I still had time.

I thought about California until the day that I calculated how much out-of-state tuition would be for UCLA, even with loans. I thought, for a moment, about taking a plane across the country. I thought about telling Ba. Coming up with a plan. Scrounging together savings and summers working at the rec center and paying student loans every month until I turned fifty. I thought about California up until mid-April, when I went into the kitchen for water and found my dad sitting at the dinner table. He looked at me with puffy eyes. I had never seen him cry since the funeral. And that was the moment I knew I would stay.

I guess I'd always known in my heart of hearts that going to California was never going to happen. I couldn't bear the thought of him being alone, of both of us being alone. He couldn't lose the two people he loved most in the same year. I had nursed that ridiculous hope up until then. But then, the following Monday, I logged into the acceptance portal and I turned UCLA down.

And by the time the summer rolled around, it was so, so easy to keep the lie. As if I was always destined to stay. As if California had never been a possibility at all.

* * *

The first of May came. Hana sported her USC sweatshirt, and I taped a piece of paper that said Leighton College over my shirt. I committed later that night and printed out the financial aid package to show Ba. With that and work-study, I wouldn't have to take much out in terms of loans. Hana and I went shopping for prom dresses, and I got a navy blue dress for thirty-five dollars from the back of a sales rack. We did each other's makeup at her house, and her parents took pictures of us, our arms wrapped around Momo, her husky. I went to prom with her and her group of theater friends, and we danced to the shitty DJ music. I dropped her off at the after-party. As she got out of the car, she glanced back at me, once. I smiled to spare her the question, and she knew that I wouldn't go with her. She shut the door, and I drove home and went to bed.

Then it was graduation. We filed into the school gym, and the air smelled like paint and hot grass. The valedictorian gave a speech, and the principal spoke after her. "This is only the beginning of your journey," he said. "This is the time of your life where you figure out what you want to do and pursue it fearlessly. We are with you every step of the way."

I took pictures with a bunch of people after. I think it sunk in there somewhere during the repetitions of "Pomp and Circumstance" that this was the last time any of us would all be together in one place, and even among the loosest of acquaintances, it was an occasion worth acknowledging. I took pictures with half the math team, with people from my AP Psychology class, with people from my English class whom I'd joked about how tedious the *Twelfth Night* readings were. Ba brought me flowers from the nearest mart and wore his blue bow tie to match my grad gown. I took pictures with Hana and we clutched onto each other and she hugged me tightly to her.

It was a bright, brilliant June day, my shoulders chafing under the dense, itchy fabric of our gowns. We went to lunch together, Hana's family and me and my ba, our grad caps folded in our laps. Hana's grandparents had even driven up from Virginia for the occasion. They'd picked a Japanese restaurant that had good soba. Hana's siblings play-fought with their chopsticks and made us laugh. On the way home, Ba's flowers sat in my lap. We were quiet. I rolled down the windows in the passenger's seat and let the hot breeze in. I finally let myself think, *I cannot fathom a beginning without you.*

EIGHTEEN

THE WEEK BEFORE the invitational tournament feels different. My roommates seem busier. Ava spends all her time with Bryce and working on a class presentation. When she comes back, she offloads her textbooks and heads right back out. Ruhi seems to be going through it. I wonder if it's because of the extra work from the *Daily*, or from issues with Arjun, or both. The other day, I saw her pacing in the stairwell, having what seemed to be a tense phone conversation. "So there's no weekend that works, and I'm out here busting my ass and half running this dysfunctional student publication on top of all my classes and trying to plan this, but *you* can't bother to text me within the same day," she says before our eyes met. That night she goes to a production meeting that doesn't end for hours. I feel awful and partially responsible.

Class isn't much better. I glance across to the other end of the lecture hall, where Jamie has moved to, and I feel like my stomach is sinking all over again. I still haven't told my room-mates about the breakup, which happened a week ago. The right moment hasn't come up. I know I have to, soon. You can't really keep secrets at a campus this size.

The only thing that hasn't changed much is work. We keep busy at the library as we help students check out textbooks for their new classes. Roberta has even started including me in con-versations, giving me book recommendations that I take down on my phone. I tell her I'm not much of a reader, and she recom-mends me audiobooks. "I listen to them when I drive," she says. It's sweet that she remembers that I commute back and forth.

Even talking with Julia feels different. Sometimes our eyes meet and I wonder what she is thinking. For the first time, I feel obligated to fill the silences. We talk now. I tell her about my classes. She tells me about this story she's trying to write for her creative writing workshop.

"Is it hard, coming up with things from your own imagina-tion?" I ask.

She pauses for a moment and swivels in her chair, tapping her pen against her leg. "It's fun for me," she says, like she's half admitting it to herself. "If I could have any dream job, really, it would be to do exactly that."

"You want to be a writer?"

"Sure," she says softly. Her earrings clink as she shrugs. She meets my eyes. "I— Yes. I do. It sounds weird to say out loud."

"Why?"

"I mean, it shouldn't. I don't know why I'm so self-conscious about saying it. It's part of the reason I wanted to come here."

That does make sense, why she came to Leighton, with its full alumni list of renowned poets and writers. "That's really cool. Being an author."

"Trading one lofty goal for another," she says. She shoulders her backpack. "I feel like in an ideal world, I could be a ski instructor in the winter and write in the summers or something."

"Wow," I say.

"What?" She gives me a guarded look.

I smile. "That sounds really nice. Peaceful, actually."

She gives me a half smile.

Caroline texts us Wednesday morning to be at the radio station twenty minutes before seven, which is when we're supposed to be on air. I just give her text a thumbs-up. Julia drives us over to practice. It's the practice before our invitational, so just the competition team is there. I feel lighter on my feet, more nimble. My thighs still ache like hell, but turns are closer, my times faster. Nicole gives me a gloved fist pump after she sees my slalom runs. "You're gonna absolutely *crush* it this weekend." And when Nicole's back is turned, Julia gives me a covert gloved thumbs-up.

After it's gotten dark out, Julia and I load our stuff in her trunk. I turn on my phone to see the notifications. The math group chat pops up, and I sigh and flop my phone down against my lap, facedown.

"What's up?"

"Oh, nothing," I say. "Just . . . I don't know if I should stay in this class group chat. It's all Jamie and his friends."

She takes her gloves off. "What, is Jamie bothering you about your breakup?"

I shake my head. "No, not at all. I mean, he doesn't really talk to me anymore, which makes sense. I just feel bad."

"I feel like you think breaking up with someone is like this great moral failure," Julia says. "And it's not. It just didn't work out."

I think about what Jamie has said, that I used our relationship to test out a hypothesis. *I didn't*, I think. I didn't mean to. "I did want it to work," I say, half for myself and half in response to her. I chew on the inside of my cheek.

"Like I said, it's not an inherently bad thing to realize you're not in love with someone," Julia says. "It happens. And you were honest about it. And all you owe them is your honesty."

She's right. Or at least, it makes sense, and I feel slightly better. I glance at her. "Have you ever been in love?"

Julia raises an eyebrow. "We're really unpacking romantic histories?"

"Sorry. That was personal."

"Well, I guess we *are* friends now," Julia says. "I mean, the long story short with my romantic history is that I don't have much of one."

"Really?"

"You sound doubtful." She eyes me warily.

"Well, you're—" My words pause in my throat. *Pretty* is the first word that I'd thought of, but I scramble to fill in something else. "You tell me a lot of stories. Like the story about you breaking up with someone in a diner. I'd assumed you were in a couple of relationships."

"Oh, sure, I guess I'm a flirt. I like having fun. I don't like when feelings get involved and things get emotionally complicated. So no relationships for me."

I sense that there *is* some history here. I remember what one of Julia's friends told me, at the holiday party; that she was emotionally closed off. "So you've never had feelings for someone."

She stares out the windshield. "Just once." She bites her thumbnail. "I was fifteen, and she was my best friend at the time. The person who made me realize I liked girls, actually."

I lean forward. "Really? What happened?"

"We trained a bunch. We were each other's biggest competitors. Somewhere along there we had a thing. It didn't work out well. The end."

"Oh," I say. I should stop here. But I want to know everything. "Why didn't it work out? Was it your parents or something?"

She shakes her head. "No, my parents didn't know at the time. I mean, I eventually did come out to them, and they were too mired in their own shit to care or take me seriously, but in this case it was just . . ." She shrugs. "Emily kept moving ahead. And I didn't. And she didn't look back." She smiles ruefully. "She made the Olympics, you know. Got bronze. I texted her congrats, and she never responded."

"God," I say. "I'm sorry she dumped you like that."

"It was never officially a *thing* to begin with." Julia looks forward, out the windshield. We've been sitting in this parking lot for a long time, but she doesn't make a move to start the car. Her jaw trembles slightly as she purses her lips. "So I guess there wasn't a true breakup. But whatever it was, it felt real enough to just get, like, emotionally eviscerated over. So I call it love. It hurt like it."

"Sounds like love," I say faintly. I feel like I am almost far away, like I'm in this car and watching myself from outside at the same time. "I think. I don't think I know it that well."

"Me neither," Julia says. "And I read about it all the time."

"You really like your romances."

She shrugs. "Yeah. The saving grace of my recovery year. Never stopped reading them."

"Really?"

"Oh, yeah. I listened to audiobooks on my drive out here. Not all romances. But those were definitely my favorite. I like it when people get happy endings."

"What about yours?"

Julia gives me a long look. "I don't know." She pauses. "Okay, I've overshared, and I'm freezing in this car. Let's drive back."

I lean my head on the cold window and listen to her muted, crackly car sound system on the way back.

I've lost track of time, so much so that when Julia drops me off at the dorm my phone blows up with texts.

Fuck. I'm supposed to be on air at the local radio station in five minutes. The map app says it takes seven to get there. I throw myself in my car and accelerate as much as I can without skidding on the ice-covered roads and pull up to a little green house.

This is the radio studio? It looks a little like the *Daily Leighton* house, with its shingled roofs and everything. One of the rooms is lit up, and I can *see* my project mates in it, sitting in front of their mics. I race up to the house and the door opens. By the time I burst into the studio room, both Danny and Caroline swivel to look at me, along with a long-haired guy wearing a flannel, who pretty much looks like a college kid himself. Matty Sorkin, I remember from Caroline's texts. Every time I've turned on the radio, this guy's trying to play some electronic indie music.

Caroline's expression freezes. Danny shoots me a wide smile.

"And . . . it appears that the group's third member has arrived," the radio host says.

"Hi," I say breathlessly. "Sorry, ski practice ran long and . . ." I trail off as Caroline stares daggers at me, swipes a hand across her neck. She mouths, "You're on air."

I clear my throat. "Hi. I'm Grace Tang."

"It's chill. So you're a competitive skier and the creator of an algorithm," Matty says, with an eyebrow tilt. "Anything you can't do, out of curiosity?"

I rack my brain to say quite literally anything. My throat is dry. "Well. I probably can't . . . juggle."

A feeble, forced laugh emerges from the host. "Can't have

'em all." Matty gives me a smile and then turns back to Danny and Caroline. "Now that everyone's here, let's talk about it. I mean, your whole campus went nuts over this algorithm. Why do you think so?"

"Love *is* a universal topic," Caroline says, polished and poised as ever. "We wanted to take something that was pretty academic and technical, and apply it to something that everyone's thought about at one point or another."

"And if they weren't thinking about it before, now they are," Danny quips.

"Clearly," Matty says. He turns to me. "How does it hold up, three months later? What was your thought process behind this?"

"It really was . . . just a project," I say. "I think we were all trying to get an A in the class. But when we were brainstorming, we were thinking about ways in which matching algorithms applied to our daily lives."

"Right, in so many ways," Caroline says smoothly. "It works really well in situations with a lot of preferences and a lot of moving parts. And so inevitably, I think we were thinking of matching people up with friends or study partners or something. And then we started talking about love. Specifically, about the subject of the person on your campus, or in your grade, rather, that was the most perfect for you."

"Right," Danny says. "*Your* person."

"And is that true?" Matty asks. "Can an algorithm predict love?"

Their heads turn to me. Caroline looks at me expectantly. And I realize, in that moment, that I never told them that I broke up with Jamie.

More than a week has passed and I haven't told them. And now I am sitting here, live on campus radio. And I have to say something.

"I . . ." My voice croaks and falters. "I don't think so."

Caroline gives me a bewildered look. Even Danny leans forward.

We're going wildly off script. I try desperately to salvage it. "I've . . . I mean, people have gone on dates. Like, my friends have. A lot of people I know on campus have. But at the end of the day, it's mostly a hypothetical. I don't really know how well it holds up in real life, in the long term."

"Right," Caroline says. Her green eyes narrow, like, *What the hell is going on?* "But there *are* real-life applications of this algorithm, right?"

"I *did* hear that there were real-life romances as a result of the algorithm among one of us in the room," Matty says. His tone is light, but I can tell from his expression that he's straining.

"Grace might have a story," Caroline says, probing me.

It comes out before I can stop myself.

"Well, we broke up, okay?"

My breakup announcement hangs in the air. The very live, being-broadcast-across-all-surrounding-areas air.

Danny looks at me, mouth agape. Caroline's eyes widen. Even the radio host does not know what to do with this response.

"He was great. But I didn't . . . I don't . . ." My cheeks are becoming hot. In here, there's no respite from the heater, and I realize I'm still wearing my ski jacket. I frantically shrug it off and press the back of my hand against my forehead. My sweater feels itchy. My *neck* is sweating. "My algorithm was to pair up people who had traits and an outlook that were compatible with each other. But there are still unknown variables, right? Tons of them. What about accounting for not only if you're right for someone, but how you feel about them? Like, no matter how right a person can be for you, maybe you just don't feel for them. *Real* feelings. Like you want to spend all your time together with them and you want to know all about them and think about them all the time. And that's not something you can determine through a math equation. Not to mention all the other unknowns. I mean, the more I think about it, the more ridiculous it seems for someone to capture it all in an equation. It's—impossible."

And with that, my words drop away. Everyone has heard. Not only the three stunned people in front of me. But every single person who has tuned in to this radio show to listen to Matty Sorkin's radio picks has heard me—me, of all people—publicly melt down about the algorithm.

What if Jamie heard? Or one of his friends?

"No, yeah, for sure," Matty says, to fill the ocean of silence that has now stretched between us. He clears his throat. "That was . . . really philosophical."

"Yeah," Danny says. "Wow."

"Lots to think about," Matty says, but he's not quite looking at me. Unfortunately, Caroline very much is. I can feel her gaze practically skewer me.

"Well, again, folks, you're listening to WBEK.1 FM. Thank you so much to our friends Caroline Babson, Danny Abrams, and Grace Tang, and now, for anyone who's a fan of the Animal Collective, I think you'll like this next song, from an up-and-coming electronic indie folk band . . ."

"My dudes," Danny says when we're standing and shivering on the front porch of the radio studio house. "Not gonna lie, that was kinda painful."

I wince. "Sorry," I whisper. It's swallowed immediately by the night. Danny gives me a sympathetic look, which makes me feel slightly better.

Caroline, on the other hand, doesn't say anything, which makes me more nervous. She's turned away from me, facing the parking lot, her arms crossed. When she finally says something, her voice is quiet. "Why didn't you *tell* us that you broke up with him?"

I swallow. "It was kind of recent."

"You broke up right before this?"

"No." I wrap my arms tight around my ski jacket. Icy air rushes into my lungs. "About a week ago."

"And you didn't think to tell us?"

I try to make myself as small as possible.

"I *know* it's personal, but you had to know that it would come up in this interview. It's literally related to the *entire* premise of our project. I feel like it's not unreasonable to expect some kind of update?"

Danny reaches out. "Caroline—"

"Any text to the group chat could have sufficed! 'Just so you guys know, Jamie and I are no longer a thing.' Cool! Great! That's all we needed. No further details. I don't know, I thought you guys were still happy. Now I look like an absolute *dick* prodding you about it on live radio." She throws her hands up. "Do we cancel all our interviews? What are we even going to say for the *New York Times*? Which, by the way, we need to prep for because people will actually read that. And I refuse to embarrass ourselves in national news."

I stand there for a second.

"It's not all about you, you know." My teeth are chattering. Before I can help myself, the words pour out of me. "I'm sorry I wasn't as prepared as I could be, okay? I didn't want it to go like that, either. But this isn't something you can just *project manage* your way through."

Caroline whirls around, her eyes flashing.

"Did you even *ask* us if we wanted to go on these interviews before you booked all of them? I wanted to make sure this was all proven before you put us on national *fucking* news. Because this is about actual people and these are real feelings that I'm working through right now. And if that embarrasses you so much, then I'm out." I pause. "Just admit that you like the attention of it. Go talk to the *New York Times* about my algorithm without me and get that shiny thing to put on your résumé because clearly that's all you care about."

"Hey, hey, hey," Danny says. "Grace, what the hell?"

I turn to him. He has his palms spread out, an incredulous look on his face. "Don't come for Caroline like that," he says. "It's *our* project. What happened to believing in it?"

The window to our side opens. Our radio host leans out. "Uh, so sorry to do this, guys. But can you take this discussion somewhere else?"

Silence hangs in the air. I pivot to walk to the parking lot, but Caroline doesn't let me off easy.

"It didn't work out for me," Caroline says, marching beside me. "It never did from the beginning. But I still believed in it. Because it could work for *someone*. Remember?"

I think of all the pairs this put together. Ava and Cameron. Ruhi's editors. Me and Jamie. Every single one of these has fallen apart, disastrously. Almost every single pairing has hurt someone in the process. I thought we could tweak it, make a better iteration of it, but it's fundamentally unfixable. "Well, I don't. I should have never suggested it in the first place."

Caroline stops. I don't. I run to my car and throw myself in. I start the engine and turn on my headlights. I immediately back out of the parking lot.

What *was* that?

What made me tell Caroline off? What made me go on that whole tangent, on live radio, no less? What had compelled me to say any of that?

In the rearview mirror, I see Danny walk out with Caroline, putting a comforting arm around her. Half-heartedly, I think to myself that they look nice together, there, under the moonlight. The algorithm should have paired them up.

Then I jolt back.

Fuck this, I think. I'm done pairing people together. I drive back to campus.

NINETEEN

I RUN UP the stairs of Spiegel and into my room, desperately hoping that my roommates are home so that we can talk, about literally anything, about Ruhi's Comp Lit essay or about Ava's improv practice or about a funny meme she found on Insta. But when I come into the room, Ava has her over-the-ear head-phones on and is working furiously on what I assume is an essay. Ruhi is curled up in bed, texting. She unfurls her hand and waves hi to me as I walk in. "How was practice?"

"Good. Did you guys listen to the radio?"

Ava turns and takes off her headphones. Ruhi's eyes widen and she sits up. "Oh, shit. I'm so sorry, Grace, we were totally going to tune in, but—"

"Oh, no. That's good."

Ava's brow furrows. "Wait, why?"

"It was the biggest mess ever. I didn't tell any of my group members that I'd ended things with Jamie, and then I—I went on this whole weird speech, and then . . ."

And then I had a whole internal crisis on air. And then—

"*Hold on.*" Ava stands up. "*You broke up with Jamie?*"

I stand still. I look at Ruhi, who has stopped texting. "Oh. I didn't tell you."

My roommates look at each other and then back at me. Ruhi asks, in a calm voice, "When did this happen?"

"Um." I clear my throat. "Super recently. The other day. I just—" I drop my backpack. "I don't know. Things didn't work out."

"But you're— You two—?" Ava stops.

"Were paired together, yeah," I say dully. "Well, it didn't work out. Turns out I didn't have the feelings for him I'd thought I'd have and I didn't realize it until recently." I take a deep breath. "So I broke up with him at Coffee House and bashed my own algorithm on the radio."

My roommates are silent.

"Well," Ava says finally. "As a theater kid, I do admire the flair for drama."

I flop down onto the beanbag, next to Ava. "I've ruined everything," I mumble. "On air."

Ava gives me a consolation pat. "If it makes you feel better, I feel like Matty Sorkin's sad indie music scene would be pretty sympathetic."

I unknot my shoulders. "Yeah. Okay. I don't want to think about this anymore. I'm going to do work."

Ruhi gives me a long, sympathetic look before she turns back to her phone. She opens her mouth, and then shuts it. Ava gives my shoulder a squeeze. I make a cup of mint tea and sit at my desk. I'm supposed to be doing my homework right now. And studying for a midterm next week, since there's no way I could even think of getting any studying done this weekend. I should be panicked over this. Last semester, I'd have the homework done the Friday before and I had time to do three practice midterms. I force myself to read through a chapter of my textbook, even though my eyes glaze over at every third word and I leave more questions blank on my problem set than I answer. I end up staring at the steam rising from my cup in the lamplight.

A text from Julia pops in. I take a breath and open it.

Weather forecast; snowfall and decent powder for this
    weekend

I wrap my hands around the still-scalding mug.

I don't reply to Julia's text for a long time, not until I'm in bed that night and staring at it. And right before I plug my phone in to charge, I swallow and text back: love to see it.

I look over that text exchange again when I plug my phone in to charge that night. I scroll through our previous texts, even though it's barely anything, even though there's only a handful of greetings and two-word responses to hold on to. In that moment, I am back in Julia's messy car, listening to her music. Wanting to stay in that diner with her for hours. Hearing her tell the story about her former best friend and feeling a hollow knocking in my chest somewhere, like a peculiar sense of familiarity. Being so solidly aware of her presence and of our closeness.

Real feelings. Like you want to spend all your time together with them and you want to know all about them and think about them all the time.

Suddenly I feel it all rush into my head and come into focus. My heartbeat quickens. It wasn't an abstract thought. I realize, without a doubt, who I was thinking of when I said those words.

I was thinking of Julia Zhang.

I don't even begin to process that thought. I wake up the next day and go to class and then to my library shift with Julia. I keep busy. I check in returned books. I catch two unsuspecting students trying to sneak in food from Coffee House. "You're really laying down the law today," Roberta comments.

I shrug weakly. "Can't have people bringing in chicken dinners again." She laughs. I avoid looking at Julia.

I go reshelve all the returned books. I lose myself in the stacks and take my time.

"You ready for the invitational?" Julia asks when we head out after our shift. I finally make eye contact. What does it *mean*? Is it possible that I can have feelings for girls? That I could feel something for Julia? Is it this same stirring feeling, the thoughts that settle into your consciousness? I think about the way I felt about my coworker back at the rec center, how one day he was just someone I chucked pens into cups with and then suddenly I was noticing his eyes, the freckles smattered across his cheeks, the way he'd laugh with his entire upper body.

Can I feel that about girls, too?

Have I?

"Uh," I say. "I don't know."

"You're nervous," Julia says, laughing. "It's written all over your face. Don't stress. You're going to be great."

"Yeah," I finally say. "I guess so."

We head out late Friday afternoon, after everyone's classes are out. I text Ba on the way to the parking lot; I told him last weekend that I'd be going to the invitational, but that I'll come back for dinner on Sunday. He didn't really react much to it. Maybe I can start competing more if this goes well.

Julia meets me in the parking lot with my skis and my bag of gear, and we load them onto the bus together. The competition team is smaller than I think it is; it's just fourteen of us. About three or four in each event. I sit by the window, and Julia slides next to me, casually. My train of thought accelerates into high-speed rail and I must be looking at her funny because Julia raises an eyebrow. "What?"

"Nothing," I say. I shake my head. *Grace, please get your shit together.*

As the sun dips below the horizon and we rumble along the highway on the six-hour drive to Maine, the rest of the team talks or sleeps or frantically does their homework. Nicole and Johnny toss peanut butter pretzels across the aisle into each other's mouths and chat about this new TV show they've started watching. Julia reads a book. I want to ask her what it's about, but I think better of it. I start to play music.

You're just friends.

My old playlists cycle through mindless indie pop songs from years ago. Suddenly, I hear Gregory Alan Isakov's soft voice sing the lyrics of "San Luis," and my heart stutters.

I had listened to this song on repeat last year. San Luis Obispo was a place I'd found on a pixelated map of California on my laptop, a name, a series of abstract pictures of sun-touched mountains that stretched on to the sea. Back when we were deciding on colleges together.

Hana. I sit up, and an ache permeates my chest, so sharp it hurts to inhale.

She's the one who I can talk to about this. About anything. I pull up my phone and scroll through our texts, and I look at the latest text I didn't reply to, back over winter break.

loved seeing you today. lmk if you want to hang out or ski or something.

What is wrong with me? Why can't I listen to a song from last year without it hurting? Why can't I even admit that my former best friend is out of my life because I was the one who stopped texting her?

And why did I even do that in the first place? Why do I keep doing that?

I frantically click out of the playlist. But it's no use; ever since yesterday's radio interview, it's like everything is now coming to the surface. The questions have started and they don't stop. Why do I take the same path to school every morning? Is it just a matter of habit? Is it because of a random series of decisions I made back on the first day of the semester? Is there any way I could have revised the algorithm to account for how well people know themselves and their own feelings? Should I have even done the algorithm in the first place? Did we all take it too seriously? Am I personally responsible for the decisions people make based on this?

Did I not know myself all this time? Can I actually, really, truly have feelings for Julia?

I can't circle within my own thoughts anymore; I yank out my headphones and surface for recycled bus air. But the bus is now quiet, the snowy roads illuminated by headlights. Julia has nodded off to sleep, her hand slotted between the pages of her book as a temporary bookmark. In front of me, I listen to Nicole and Johnny murmur what I think is a series of hypothetical questions.

"Would you rather get to relive years of your life or live life in reverse?"

There is a pause. "Living life in reverse is weird if you think about it," Nicole says quietly.

"You know people less and less the more you progress through life. You watch people become strangers."

No one speaks for a second. Then Nicole says, "That's deep.

I've never even thought of that before."

"Breakups wouldn't be that bad, though," Johnny counters. "I mean, you get the worst of it over with, and then it just keeps getting better and better."

I think of what would happen if I lived life in reverse. At some point, my mother would return and get healthier. We would end up with me in the back seat, following her into church on Sundays. In that moment, I want it to be a possibility more than anything.

What would she think about this?

And that's the question that finally snags me.

In junior year, after homecoming weekend, Hana told me that she'd kissed Kristen Levy, the lead of last year's spring musical, at the after-party. Weeks later, she argued with the leader of our youth group over marriage equality. She didn't come to church the following week. She'd stopped coming to youth group. That Sunday, Ma sat in the pew, the Takamura family space next to her empty, her fingers clasped tightly. In the parking lot, she didn't start the car. She turned to me.

"Hana told her family she was gay," Ma said, her voice flat and clipped. "The whole family's not coming to church anymore. I prayed for them."

I nodded. This was something I'd already known.

"She used to be such a good girl," Ma had said, starting the car. "Now look at the trouble she's caused."

I swallowed. "At least she won't get a boyfriend," I said lightly. "Isn't that what you always said not to do?"

Ma gave me a look, like she was disgusted with me. "Don't even joke about this, Xiǎoyàn."

She was silent on the car ride back home.

The ski team eats at a roadside fast-food place and pulls into our hotel late at night. It's a lodge-looking thing, with stone floors and an actual fire going on in the fireplace and what I hope is a fake deer head peeking out of the wall. I pull my phone out and check my texts; Ruhi and Ava have both texted me good luck, along with lots of their respective heart emojis (Ava the purple, Ruhi the pink). I grin at my phone screen.

Suddenly I hear my name and I raise my head, and Julia is glancing at me, waving a pair of hotel keys.

"We're roommates," she says, nodding toward the elevator. "Come on."

Roommates?

Roommates, on this weekend, of all times?

I stand there for a moment, frozen. Nicole gives me an inquisitive look. Julia glances back. I sprint to catch up with her and with our other teammates. We all ride the elevator up in silence, stretching our necks out from the long bus trip.

She's my friend. She's my teammate. We work together. Don't complicate this.

We enter the room.

There are no twin beds. I'm staring at one whole queen bed in this godforsaken room.

Oh, this universe just loves to mess with me.

"I call left side," Julia says breezily. "If that's cool."

"Sure, have at it." I don't really care which side I sleep on. If I can sleep much, even. My thoughts are still circling each other, like crows.

"Grace, you good?"

I turn. She's in a sports bra and leggings, her hair free of its braid, her makeup slightly smudged, tilting her water bottle up to drink from it. My gaze settles on her bare shoulders and her toned stomach. I meet her eyes. "I . . . I don't know," I finally admit.

"I know you're anxious," Julia says. "But don't think. Just go for it. Focus on the turns like we practiced."

I nod and run my hands through my hair. "Right. The turns."

"You know what you're doing," Julia says, and this time, she smiles. I give her a casual smile back, pretending that her gaze is doing nothing to me, pretending that she's just a friend, just a coworker, that I am not being unstitched from the inside and all my thoughts are slowly unraveling, that I am not at all affected by the presence of her. That night, I curl up at the very edge of the bed, the starched blankets tucked under my arms. I can smell a hint of her coconut shampoo. I reply to Zoe's and Sean's good-luck texts, to Ba's message. Sometime in the night, I fall asleep before I can fully realize the thought that has slowly been dawning on me, and that I have been scared to tell myself.

The next morning passes by in a blur. We wake up to my alarm before light seeps through the curtains. Sleepily, I fumble on my race gear and shrug on my ski jacket, and we head down to breakfast. My thoughts, which had quieted over the course of the night, come surging back.

I have to focus on my race today; I can't think about anything else. And somehow, that does occupy my mind. I feel the familiar jangle of nerves at the pit of my stomach. Competition nerves. I almost welcome it.

We scarf down some hotel breakfast; then we're on the bus, pulling up to the invitational. The slopes have been closed down to the public for that day, and everywhere we're surrounded by buses and cars unloading their stuff. Registration is quick; the roster comes before us, and before long, everyone's lining up. I'm one of the very first to compete. I scan the gates on my way up. Before I know it, I am at the top of the slope, glancing down. My heart picks up, like it always does when I'm poised before a run.

Slalom consists of two runs. I am alone up here for my first, at the edge of the slope. I dig my ski poles in and hover my weight forward, toward my toes. Very briefly I catch the sight of the flag; in a moment, it will lower. Right now I am balanced, right over the edge.

The trees are so small at the base; the people mill around, their ski jackets like brightly colored dots. The clouds have cleared the sun, and the sky through my goggles is that rarified blue, the hills dusted with a layer of the new snow. Julia is right; the conditions *are* perfect.

Julia.

Is there any point in denying it, now that I am all alone on the top of this ski slope? Here, I could shout and the wind would carry it away. And finally, I let myself think it.

I like Julia.

There.

The flag lowers.

I launch myself forward.

The ground is fresh and soft from the recent snowfall. I hurtle toward the gates, but practiced instinct and adrenaline kicks in and I am surprisingly in control. I don't go too fast. I cut around the gates, close enough, already beginning to turn for the next. The gates clear in front of me, one by one, until it is a smooth, clear sailing through to the end. I don't realize how fast I'm going until I brake, hard, sending snow spraying.

I glance at the clock and stop.

Because I had beaten my best time. Not by a few seconds. By seven seconds.

It's not anywhere near enough to place me. Everyone else is too good. But I didn't miss a gate. I pulled my personal best time. I remember now, the snowy afternoons, the cold noons, the twilight hours racing with Hana on the slopes. The thrill that runs through me when we course down the hill, her in my sight. It is this again but tenfold.

Someone shouts my name, and I ski toward the small crowd in deep green jackets. Nicole and Johnny and the members practically fold me in with them. "That was— Oh my *God*, Grace. Unbelievable," Nicole says, her voice muffled against my jacket hood. "You *did that*."

"Where's Julia?" I ask breathlessly.

"She's on her way up," Johnny says. "Oh, wait. There she is!"

I turn, and I can spot her goggles, bright blue against the muted shades of her race jacket and helmet. My heartbeat still thuds. Her tiny figure perches on the lip of the slip. She pauses for a moment in anticipation. And then the next moment she's off. It is like she has been holding back in practice; here, she explodes with power, carving down the slope with a ferocious, almost weightless speed, tapping the gates with her ski poles. She makes it look so, so easy.

I know at least a fraction of the joy she feels right now, the rush of soaring down the hill, balanced on the thin planes of two skis. As I watch her, my heart is light in my chest. It almost feels like how things were last weekend when it was just the two of us, before we laid our pasts in front of each other. It feels like I'm up there with her. As if I'm somehow still in motion.

TWENTY

JULIA PLACES FIRST in the slalom on her first run. Of course she does. I don't place—I didn't expect to—but Julia still gives me a grin and a thumbs-up. "Crushed it. Cleanest run I've ever seen."

Her smile makes my heart thrill. But now that she's back on the ground, the words disappear from my lips again.

She's your friend. Don't complicate it.

I clear my second run. I'm one of the first to go, Julia the last. She holds on to her place and beats everyone out easily. Johnny places fifth in the giant slalom and Nicole tenth. According to her, it's the strongest seasonal start our team has ever had. We pile into a place Nicole knows that serves breakfast all day, and one of the other members of the team leans in and tells me, in a hushed voice like they're telling me trade secrets, about the diner near Leighton called Ellen's. I laugh and tell him that I know about it. There's something about this ski team with breakfast food, I swear. Julia gives me a knowing look. She's surprisingly stoic about winning her event, even though the rest of the team is entirely ecstatic. On the bus ride back from dinner, I catch her profile in the light of the diner lights, the way the dark strands of her hair are illuminated, her softened expression. And then I realize, with a start, that's she's glancing at me, too.

"What?" I ask.

She turns away and shrugs. "Thought you were going to say something."

After that, we head back to the hotel and pile into Nicole's room in our sweatpants. Johnny plays music on a speaker while she hauls up a whole duffel bag of drink mixers and hard seltzers. We click cups of prosecco together, paper on paper, and the bubbles settle on my tongue. A junior on the team named Chase does a whole impromptu lecture on IPAs, and Julia looks unimpressed. "Look, I'm from Colorado and even I think that shit's nasty." And then she refills all our prosecco cups.

After we've all taken sufficient shots, Johnny pulls out a deck of cards and we attempt to play a fourteen-person card game before it descends into chaos. We then play Cheers to the Governor, a game in which we count from one to fourteen around the circle, ending each round with "Cheers to the governor." It becomes increasingly more complicated the more rounds we finish and the more rules we make. The rules, which I easily keep up with during the first half, start melding together in my head. I mess up halfway through the sequence, and we all practically fall apart, drunk and laughing. "We got the math major,"

Julia says. She sways and leans on me a little, her loose long hair falling in my lap.

After the last, long round, we all raise up our drinks and cheer, relieved. "All right, all right," Johnny says. "I wanted to make a toast, not only to this hypothetical governor, but also to this team. Incredible, as always." He turns. "And a special shout-out to the frosh who crushed it today. To Grace, who competed in her first race ever, and . . . to Julia, who placed the highest Leighton's ever placed."

The whole room shakes with our cheers. I tip back my drink. The room seems softer now, like how it was during my holiday party with my roommates. *This* is what it's like to be in college, to be fully *in*, to get to spend weekends like this, at a party, competing, being with my friends and team. I turn to grin at Julia, but her expression seems to be frozen into a stiff smile. She's looking down at something on her phone and clutching her can of seltzer tightly. Her expression doesn't change when Nicole shouts out other members of our team. And when we turn back to start another game, I see that Julia's gone.

I push myself up and set my cup down. I'm definitely drunk, at least slightly. I tiptoe out of the room and into the hallway. It's empty. On instinct, I head three doors down. Her stuff is still sprawled there across her half of the bed, but she's nowhere to be seen.

I wander down into the lobby. There she is, pacing in front of the fireplace, speaking Mandarin into the phone.

"I—I've been trying, Ba. I just— It's a Saturday night. I can't be your messenger all the time. Fine, what if she's saying those things about you? You need to be able to talk to each other. I'm—" She pauses. "No. I'm not *taking her side*. Fine. Sell the house." Another pause. "Fine. What if I am? I'm a college student, aren't I? I'm skiing right now . . . No, I'm not training, it's just for fun. I'm sorry. I'm *sorry*, I have to go." She shuts her phone, her shoulders heaving.

I move to tiptoe away, but suddenly she turns and her gaze latches onto mine.

After a moment, she says, "You heard all that."

I'm silent.

I eavesdropped, and she knows that I have understood it all. I freeze in place, but instead she simply sighs and sits onto an armchair, sitting forward, her head in her hands. She's going to tell me to leave, and I will. She drains the cup in front of her. I glance at it.

"Thought I'd have some stale lobby coffee to sound more sober to my dad," Julia says. "Didn't work." She laughs bitterly; her shoulders shake with it. When she speaks, her words drag on a little bit. "My parents seem to not have better plans on Saturday nights than talk about each other to me."

I walk forward and settle in the armchair across from her.

"I don't know," she sighs, laying her palms in her lap. "It feels weird, being the de facto therapist for them."

I lean forward. "You don't have to be," I say gently.

Julia stares at me. "But I feel like I should," she says. "I'm the reason they moved out there. They put their entire lives on hold

279

for me when everyone said they were ridiculous for it. And I *left* them, to come all the way out here, to be an English major of all things, to get drunk on the weekends and to join a ski team for fun. They say I'm selfish and I don't even blame them. What the fuck am I doing out here?" She looks lost, totally lost. And then her shoulders deflate. "Sorry. I'm venting again."

I shake my head. "I think I know what it's like," I say. "To be trapped under your own expectations." To be pinned under the leaden weight of the dreams that have been set for you, because your parents gave up everything for it. "Even if I'm not the skiing expert."

Julia rests her cheek on her knees. "I wish I skied like you."

"You have got to be joking."

She shakes her head, except her knees are still hugged to her chest, so her entire body sways a little, just a bit. "I'm not. It's just . . . you look so happy when you ski. I wish you could see yourself."

I pause. "Really?"

"Normally I can't really tell what you're thinking," she says. She smiles with half-lidded eyes. "But when you ski, it's just pure joy."

"You really watch me ski that carefully?"

"I do," she says, and she's completely serious.

Her answer stills me, for a moment. The flames flicker. They're stronger, now, or maybe my cheeks have just warmed to the heat. She holds my gaze. I don't look away. I wonder what to say next.

"I don't really want to go back to the party," Julia says, her voice soft.

"Don't have to." The prosecco's *really* getting to me. The room glitters, bright in firelight. "What do you want to do?"

She pauses for a moment and then raises an eyebrow. "There's a game room. Wanna play pool?"

I laugh. "Oh, *do* I?" I grin. If there's any way all those errant after-hour games working at the rec center paid off, it's now. "Come on," I say. I'm determined to cheer her up. "Let's go."

"Are you any good?"

I rack up the cues, even though the room is still kind of sparkly around the edges and I can't tell if I'm racking them up neatly. "Why don't you find out?"

She takes the lone cue stick and grins at me. "I'll break." She leans over. In one sure, precise motion, she knocks the cue into the triangle. The cue scatters, sinking one ball. She attempts another shot and misses.

Julia glances at me. "I'm solids."

I lean over the table. *You're on.* Like I have so many times under the harsh lights of the rec center game room—it's like I can almost still smell the artificial padded floors, even now—I drape my index finger over my cue stick. I take a deep breath. Quickly, I knock the green stripe into the corner pocket.

I aim for the other corner. Aim, then strike. I shoot forward, halting at the last second. The cue delicately taps into the red stripe, and it rolls, just ever so slightly tipping into the pocket.

Right before I take my next shot, I make the mistake of looking up.

Julia tilts her head at me, a smile on her lips. I overshoot, and the orange stripe slams into the wall, inches away from the center pocket.

"Okay," Julia says. "I see what I'm working with." She hoists the cue stick up, scrutinizing the table for a moment. And then she leans over and sinks two at the same time in the corner and center pockets. She sinks another, and then misses the fourth.

"Trick shot," Julia says, passing me the cue stick. Our fingers brush, and my heart jolts in my chest. "You should learn sometime."

"Who says I haven't?" I lean forward, tapping the cue so it ricochets from the side and strikes the blue stripe. It sinks. *Okay*, I think. Now purple stripe. It's a long shot. I'm not good at long shots; I never got them when I played with Miles. I was good at angles and short shots. But I'm feeling bold tonight. I strike the cue ball, and it rolls forward, knocking the purple into the corner pocket. Then I get the green.

Success.

I'm in a tough spot. The cue's wedged in the corner. I don't have many shots left. I aim for the maroon, hoping that the angles match up.

Thunk.

Now there are *actually* no shots left. As a last-ditch effort, I attempt another trick shot. It careens into a pocket. Scratch. "Fuck."

"Had it going well for a while there," Julia says. She leans down and sinks two shots, one after another. Finally, she leans over the eight ball. Misses. "Fuck me."

"Allow me," I say. Now I have an excellent angle. I sink the final orange stripe and then shoot for the eight ball. It bounces off the wall, inches away from the pocket.

"No, allow *me*," Julia says. She walks right up to me and takes the cue stick, her face inches away from mine. I freeze. She smiles. And then she leans over, to the side, so close she is almost on top of me, so close I can smell the coconut of her shampoo, feel her body against mine. My breath catches. And before I even blink, she sinks the eight ball and straightens up.

"Touché," I say softly.

She tosses the pool cue onto the table and glances at me. "You put up a good fight. Almost had me for a moment there."

"That was just lucky. I set you up."

"Then we make a good team, don't we, Grace?" A smile plays on the corner of her lips. She's drunk, too, more smiley. Her voice is low as she says my name.

"Rematch."

Julia shrugs. "Sure."

I win the next one, and Julia beats me at the next two in a row. The last game goes by quickly, and when she sinks the eight ball, I press against the wall, holding my palms against my flushed cheeks. I lean against the door, opening it just a fraction. Cool air laps against my forehead. It is bitterly cold outside, but for once it doesn't dig into me. I don't know if it's because I'm drunk or because I've just played four heated games of pool in row. Julia gingerly steps outside and looks up. "Oh, look at that moon."

I peek up. Stars blanket the sky. The moon is full, brighter than I have ever seen it, the soft light framing the forest and the mountaintops, its silvery sheen tracing her features.

She looks beautiful, I think. I tip forward, just slightly, and my foot slips from the door. It shuts behind us and locks.

I glance back.

Julia laughs. "I got the keys. We can just go around the front."

It is so perfectly still out here. There is no wind, just a frozen chill that settles over everything. It dawns on me, gradually, that we are out here, in this hotel by the mountains, states away from anywhere I know as home. I feel strangely untethered, like I am floating, somehow, an unmoored version of Grace Tang. As if my path finally stretches in front of me and frays into possibilities.

"You think you'd get tired of looking up," Julia says, her voice small in wonder. "But I could do this every night."

The bitter chill has finally reached me now. Instinctively, I lean toward Julia for warmth. She glances at me.

The moonlight settles across her features, the slight breeze ruffling her hair just a bit. For a moment, we are frozen, inches away from each other. Her dark eyes search mine.

And something very fundamentally shifts in that moment, an awareness that dawns across the both of us. We're no longer playing games with each other, because she is looking at me, *really* looking, as if she is trying to read me.

I am so still.

Her gaze flickers down and settles on my lips.

Don't think. Just go for it.

When Julia speaks again, it's barely above a whisper. "You cold, Grace?"

In response, I lean forward and press my lips against hers.

The night shrinks, contracts around us.

She leans in, her lips soft and yielding, her fingers reaching for my hips. My heart thuds in my chest, heat blossoming through my limbs. And as her cold fingertips touch the bare skin of my waist, I gasp, just slightly, and she pulls back, her eyes bright and hungry and uncertain. "Yeah?" she asks. *You sure?*

I nod and pull her to me.

She pushes me against the doorframe, her hand slipping under my shirt and settling on the small of my back, pulling me to her. And as the chill seeps in, I push myself closer into her, savoring her warmth.

I'm kissing her.

I'm kissing Julia.

She shivers, slightly. "Hold on."

I pull away. "Are you—"

"That was nice," she says, and then pauses.

"Oh." My hands drop. I wait. For the *but*. It's over, I think. "Sorry," I say, my words tumbling out. "We can stop."

Her eyes meet mine. "Who says I want to stop?"

My heart stutters in my chest.

"I'm just freezing." She exhales in a laugh. "Wanna do this in our room?"

I nod. She links her fingers around mine. She's *holding my hand*. We run down the snowy sidewalk and burst into the hotel through the front doors. She doesn't let go: not as we run down the hallway, up the elevator, past the closed door to the room where Nicole and half the ski team are, their voices rising from within. Her key clicks in the lock and we're inside, in our room.

And I reach for her.

We stumble against the wall, and she's kissing me again, more fiercely than ever. The room is dark; I'm only aware of her solid presence, her lips hot against my skin, her breath in my ears. I reached for her shirt, and she reaches up and shrugs out of it. She tugs my shirt off, our lips breaking apart for that split second and crashing back onto each other again. We kick off our shoes and half stumble across the room, tipping backward onto the bed, Julia on top of me. I murmur, "All these damn pillows," and she laughs. I reach up and meet her laugh with my lips, threading my fingers through her hair. Her fingers trail down, before they pause at the waistband of my sweatpants. "Okay?"

I pause for a moment. "It's my first . . . I've never . . ."

"Okay," she said. Her hand travels back up.

"No," I say. This has been real all along. But my heart kicks in my chest; *this* is what I've been wanting all this time, aching for, almost. "I want to."

"Okay," she whispers again. And as her fingers slip under my waistband, my thoughts jumble into fragments, and then nothing.

Julia.

Her lips, tracing down my neck.

Her fingertips, grabbing on to my hips, as if to never let me go.

Her heat on me.

I've never wanted it more.

TWENTY-ONE

WHEN I WAKE, it's still early. Gray light slats through the window. I blink a little, and then my eyes fly open. Gone is the champagne buzz and the way that it blurred the lights together. It's the morning, and Julia's arm is around me.

My head spins. I can feel her fingers curled around my stomach, hear the slow steady rhythm of her breathing. And I remember everything.

The chill of the cold night melting away with her mouth on mine, with us stumbling back into the warmth of the lodge not long before we came back to *this* room. With furtive kisses in the dark and her eyes glancing up at me. With her lips on mine, on my collarbone, on my stomach, on my—

It thrills me now, even thinking about it.

It *happened*.

But now it's the next morning and I'm awake, and thoughts are racing through my head. Would it end with awkward stares and hands scrambling to pull on shirts? Would I still be able to look her in the eye again?

I'd done this.

I'd kissed her first. Pulled her to me.

What have you done?

What if I ruined everything?

I grab for my phone, which is mired somewhere in pile of clothes on the floor. It's 7:43 a.m.

Beside me, Julia stirs, her hand trailing off me. Her hair tumbles over her bare shoulders. Her eyes flutter open, and she blinks. "Hmm," she says sleepily. She doesn't look away. She doesn't bolt, or scramble for her clothes. I freeze in place.

Instead she nods at the phone and mumbles something.

"What?"

"Time?"

"Oh. Seven forty-five."

"*Fuck.* We have to be on that bus by eight thirty, don't we?"

"I—I think that's what Nicole said?"

She slowly rolls over and runs her hand through her hair. "The stellar idea of giving a bunch of hungover college kids an eight-thirty departure time."

I don't say anything. My nerves feel jangly, exposed. We're in bed. *Together.* She finally glances up at me. "You good?"

"Oh, yeah," I say. My words come out clipped. "I'm. You know. Good. Great. I mean—" Heat rises to my cheeks with a vengeance. Why can't I form complete sentences? I've never *spent* a night with anyone, and I'm increasingly aware of how

I must look; my lips dry, my hair all over the place. "I hope it was good for you, too? I mean, are you good? With. You know. Like. What we did? I've never done it with a girl so I, uh. Don't know if I didn't do anything right or—"

My words cut off as she presses her lips against mine, gently. She pulls away and glances at me. "That was really your first time with a girl?"

I nod.

"Had me fooled," she says. She tilts her head. "You had fun?"

I nod, my heartbeat still catching up to that kiss. "Yeah."

"Cool. Me too."

And that's that. She rolls out of bed and shrugs on her hoodie. I fumble for my clothes, too. Bra. Shirt, sweatpants. I feel sore, and I remember I competed yesterday. *Yesterday.* It feels like ages ago: the bus ride up, the competition, the team after-party. I glance over at Julia, at the way her hair in her messy bun falls down to her shoulders, at her pursed lips. A part of me wishes that it was still Saturday night. That we're still alone, outside, under the stars, so I could still be kissing her. I glance at my phone. It's 7:58. We're going to get on the bus and go back to campus. And then—what?

She's your friend.

You work together.

I clear my throat. "Things won't . . . be weird between us, will they? Or, like . . . different?"

Julia looks up. It's not the teasing look that she usually gives me. She gives me a long, searching gaze. I feel vulnerable, exposed. "I don't think so," she says, calmly, and then the corner of her mouth tilts up and she gives me a cavalier smile. "Don't worry. Things don't have to be different at all."

Of course I tell myself that it doesn't have to be different. But on the bus ride back everything is different; the way the honey-peach morning light streams through the windows that are lined with snow streaks, the crisp morning air, the music in my headphones. Julia has the window seat this time, and she leans against the nook of the seat and the windowpane as she sleeps, her earbuds tucked in, the ends of her hair peeking out from her sweatshirt hood. She's stretched out, just a little, her knees resting against mine, bumping into me every once in a while. Every time there's a small jolt from that point of contact.

I didn't bring any homework or reading with me since I usually get carsick, so I listen to my shuffled playlists on my phone and look out the window as the highway crosses into Vermont again. The bus heater clatters in the background. I look at the snowcapped mountains in the distance, the stark, cut outlines against the sky, the trees clustered and bare. I wonder if I will ever leave this state for more than a weekend, or if I'll grow up and get a job and traverse these same highways every day on my way to work.

Our bus rolls in during the early afternoon. I lug all my ski stuff to the car and sit in it to get out of the cold. I eat dinner with Ba, and he asks me how the invitational was. I say that I skied well and that one of my friends got first. I try to gauge

291

his tone to see if he's resentful that I spent most of the weekend away. But Ba doesn't say anything, really. He watches TV after dinner, and then I pull up my homework.

I actually haven't done an iota of studying for my Group Theory midterm the following week, and I'm starting to panic. Maybe I'll stay up with Ruhi tonight and hit her up for a cold brew can.

Then I get a text from Caroline. It's not to the group chat. She's texted me directly.

> Hey I just wanted to clear the air about things the other night with the radio show and everything
> I didn't mean to push you on a sensitive subject
> I don't think we have to write a follow-up report. But I still think we should do the NYT interview together. It's still a cool concept and worth covering
> Lmk what you think, happy to discuss. I'm going to include you unless you say otherwise.

I lay my phone facedown on my stomach and sink into my seat, leaning my cheek against the headrest. Well, she's kind of being nice, even after everything we said to each other. But at the same time I know she's probably trying to get us all to do the interview together.

Can I? All this time I'd been doing what a true mathematician does; turning over different theories in my head, thinking of different algorithms, different ways to put the puzzle pieces together. That's what I'd been working along in my head ever since that first afternoon, when I was searching out the patterns that made the Disney prince quiz tick. Once I'd figured out a pattern, it all fell into place so easily.

I'd been thinking about the *how* all this time. But I never stopped to think if I should have created this in the first place.

I don't want to think about it anymore.

I don't reply to Caroline's text.

And will things just return to normal? I wonder this as I park my car and walk back across campus to Spiegel. My heartbeat jolts every time I think of her lips on mine. I'm going to see her at work this week. At practice. I wonder if she's going to look at me differently.

Things don't have to be different at all, Julia had said. Do I want them to be?

I return to a full room. Ruhi is perched on her bed, hunched over her laptop, her wireless earbuds in. Ava and Bryce are cuddling on the beanbag, Bryce trying to absentmindedly solve a Rubik's cube with one hand. Ava brightens when I come in. "Our student athlete!"

I laugh. "Hardly."

"How was it?" Bryce asks. "Ava tells me it was your first ski race ever."

"Made it down without wiping out, so I consider it a solid success."

"Love to see it." Ava rolls off the beanbag and glances closely at me. "Did you get sunburned? Your cheeks are red."

"Oh. Yeah, probably windburn or something." *Keep cool*, I think to myself. *They don't know about you and Julia.* I place the back of my hand against my cheek. It's warmer than usual. I scramble for an excuse, but Ava's already turned away. "Anyway. Now that we're all here, how do we feel about hitting up the Pollack dessert bar?"

Ruhi straightens up and sighs. "Sure. I'm in."

I follow them to the dining hall. Ava and Bryce lead the way, their fingers threaded through each other's. Ruhi's staring at something on her phone. The Sunday-night special is an ice cream bar, which Ava and I (and half of campus, it seems) take liberal advantage of. Bryce shakes his head at us. "Why people like having ice cream when it's cold out, I can never fathom."

"Welcome to Vermont," I say. "If people only had ice cream when it was warm out, it would be an eight-week window."

Ava glances at Bryce and brushes his jaw affectionately. "You're the one who chose to come all the way up from Florida for college."

"A decision I question every day," Bryce says. He catches Ava's deadpan look. "Kidding, kidding." He presses a light kiss to her forehead.

Ruhi's quieter tonight. She peeks at her phone. Ava glances at her. "You okay?"

Ruhi sits up and wrings out her shoulders. "Yeah. Just . . . trying to coordinate stuff with Arjun for next weekend."

"Ooooh, he's finally coming?"

"If he ever books his flights." There's an edge to her voice. "He was just telling me that the following weekend would work better, and I'm just like, *please*, dude, make up your mind." She runs her fingers through her hair and exhales. Her expression cools. "Anyway. If things do work out by then, what do y'all think we should do while he's here?"

Ava and Bryce jump to offer date ideas. My phone lights up with a text from Nicole saying that she'd love for me to sign up for the next invitational. It's in two weekends, during Lunar New Year, I remember. I flick through my messages. Caroline's text is still there among the others, waiting for me, unanswered. The *NYT* Valentine's interview, I think ironically. How nice that article would have sounded.

College economics group cracks the code for love.

It sounds ridiculous to me, now. I know nothing. Furtively, I check if Julia's texted me. She hasn't. I go over our last texts from before the ski tournament. Then a text comes in from Ba, asking me if I'm willing to pass on my AP study books to one of Professor Xu's kids. I say of course and tell him they're in my room somewhere.

I put away my phone and return to the conversation at hand.

TWENTY-TWO

I BRACE MYSELF for the next time I see Julia. I go to work on Tuesday, and Julia's there, talking to Roberta about a book they'd recently read together. When I come in, Julia turns to me, as if she's going to say something—*about us*, I think frantically. Instead she gives me a nonchalant smile. "Roberta has made the most ambitious Goodreads challenge for the year."

I pause. "O . . . kay?" I say. "That's great?"

"It's this website for tracking books," Roberta explains. "My challenge is two hundred a year."

I blink. "Books? A *year*?"

"Sure," she says. "What else does someone do in their free time?"

During my shift, I help Roberta put up seasonal decorations around the circulation counter. There's pink tinsel everywhere, and Roberta puts up little heart figures she'd crocheted, with faces and little cute legs and everything. I can't help but glance over at Julia, who's checking out someone's books and talking to the student about it. When the person leaves, she turns, letting her hair fall in a curtain over her shoulder. Her earrings glint in the light. I try to adjust the tinsel just right. Valentine's Day is around the corner. We were supposed to have finished our three-month follow-up by the end of January. Danny sent out an email with the survey weeks ago. The old me would have been diligently checking the monthly survey results and looking to see if people had submitted any success stories to the form, but ever since my breakup with Jamie, I haven't even bothered to look into it. Caroline has set up a Google Calendar invite for the *New York Times* interview. It won't matter. We won't have anything to talk about. I still haven't made up my mind about whether I'll do it yet.

The application for the summer math research program sits on my desktop, unfinished. It's due in three weeks. The last step is to request a letter of recommendation from a faculty member. I'm dreading the thought of facing Professor Rand. He's going to ask about the follow-up, too, and I'll have to say that there is none. And I'll look like a fraud.

Julia meets my eyes. I'm losing my mind in the campus library, of all places. God, it's bad for me. I almost can't bear to be in her cool, unflappable presence. When our shift's over, I grab my backpack and quickly grab a study room upstairs, where I determine that I am, indeed, quite fucked for this upcoming Group Theory midterm. I glance at the group chat that I barely check anymore. I can't ask Jamie for help. There are office hours tomorrow, but they directly conflict with ski practice, and I want to go.

Julia still comes to pick me up the next day. "Hey, genius. You get aux today."

"Big responsibility."

"Choose wisely."

I play some songs off Ava's public Spotify. We're quiet on the way to practice. I form and swallow words. We head toward the ski lodge and do our runs. Julia turns to me, as if she's going to say something, but before she can Zoe and Sean come practically out of nowhere to ambush me. "How's our slalom champ?" Zoe says, tucking her dyed hair in her beanie.

I laugh. "That would be Julia." I feel electric every time I mention her name. "And she was great."

"Really?" Sean's eyes widen. "And is she as good as everyone says?"

I glance toward Julia, who has caught up with Johnny and a couple of others. "Yeah. Her technique is incredible. She easily beat out everyone's time on the first run and held it for the second."

"Okay, we need *details*," Sean presses. "What happened? Was there an after-party? Was there a chocolate fountain? Anything wild happen this weekend?"

I do all I can to keep a straight face. "Nothing much, really. We drank and played games after Saturday. Wasn't up too late." That, at least, wasn't a lie. I turn. "Trick slope today?"

I *have* gotten better, it seems. I coast ahead of Zoe and Sean today. While they ease their way up the trick ramps, I'm far ahead of them. While I wait at the bottom of the slope, I glance up, trying to see where Julia is. What was she going to say to me today? Did she want to train together?

Or am I reading too much into things?

The sky is clear today, the snow just melting into ice a bit. It feels good to be back with Zoe and Sean and joke around with them. I don't even know them that much—I know that Zoe does architecture, Sean product design. We don't ask questions, get into serious conversations. We just goof off on the slopes, and it feels freeing.

I end practice exhausted and wait at the lodge for Julia to finish up, peeling my sweaty hair from my bun. I see her helmet come into view. She comes into the lodge, her cheeks pink and her hair just slipping out of her Dutch braids. "Ready?"

I follow her to the car and load our stuff in. We get in, and Julia turns on the heater, pressing her fingers to the vents. She passes her phone to me. "Aux," she says. I reach for it, but the phone slips from her fingers and into the crack between my seat and the gear.

"Oh, shit, sorry," I say, reaching for it.

"I got it." She leans down. Our fingers brush each other's reaching for the phone, and we lean up, our faces inches from each other, my fingers laced around hers, holding the phone.

She doesn't move.

Neither do I.

And when we meet each other's eyes, it's like her calm

exterior falls away under the dim light, slowly. The tip of her nose is pink. Her lips part, her gaze unveiled into something sharper.

I hold it.

A long moment passes.

And then she says, in a low voice, "Grace, if I kissed you right now, would it be ridiculous?"

My heartbeat rushes into my ears. I shake my head, just slightly.

Her lips crush into mine. My hands reach for her. Heat rushes from my cheeks to the tips of my fingers. I feel her trace my jaw and I shiver, leaning into her. The car is silent, the sky darkening between us. When we finally pull away, just slightly, she whispers against my lips, "I think my roommate is out. Do you want to go back to my room?"

It is as if some strange spell is broken. I follow Julia to her dorm in the other building. Saunders. I see the gray staircase and remember the familiar hallway from Halloween this past year.

Once Julia's door is closed behind us, she pulls me to her and we collide. Heat rushes to my cheeks; my sense of everything around me dissolves into fragments. Julia's dark eyes are warm in the glow of the string lights. Her long hair fans around her as her deft fingers curl under my shirt. The passage of time slows; I mark it with her kisses, with the different places her touch lingers.

After, we lie on her futon. She puts a Hulu show on her projector but neither one of us is really watching it. She gets up after a while and starts lighting her scented candles around her side of the room, one by one. The faint scent of vanilla and jasmine drift around the room.

"Careful with that one there," I say, pointing to one precariously teetering on the edge of the table, near her bookshelf. She shifts it slightly. "I'm surprised they let you keep candles in this dorm."

"Oh, they most definitely do not," Julia says. "But if anyone is going to burn this dorm down, it's the party boys next door with their apple bong." She pauses. "Although, speaking of parties, my roommate and I are throwing one this weekend. A fun little Valentine's gathering, but with friends. You should come."

She settles back down on the futon. Her fingertips settle on my knee. I look down. I tip her jaw to mine and kiss her slowly. She pulls me closer to her. I don't think about what this is. What this means for me, to want this, to want her as badly as I do. I don't think at all.

"You've been staring at your phone for nearly half an hour," Ava says that Friday.

I glance up. I've been staring at Julia's last text, sent an hour ago:

see u tonight, hopefully

"Julia's throwing a party," I say finally. "Should I go?"

"Oooh." She leans over the railing of her lofted bed, an eyebrow raised. "Yeah, why not?"

"It's Friday night."

"And that's *fine*," Ava says. "Just tell your dad you'll see him later this weekend. Like you did last week. You're an adult, Grace."

And yet I still hesitate. It feels strange, to make a habit out of this. "But it's not, like, a big thing. It's just a party."

"Live a little," Ava says. "Come on. Julia's party sounds fun. And you went home last weekend on a Sunday. I'm sure he'll be okay with you staying tonight."

I shrug. I text, I have something tonight with a friend. Can I come home tomorrow?

And not thirty seconds later, my phone rings. It's Ba.

It's strange. He's never called me before.

"Hello?"

"What do you have tonight?"

"I—" I glance up at Ava. "It's just something with my friends. From ski team. I just thought . . ."

"You should come home. I've already started dinner."

"But—"

"Xiǎoyàn. Come home."

I stare at the phone. "Guess I'm going home."

"Grace," Ava starts to say something, and then falters and shrugs. I pick up my keys, gather up my backpack, and slowly head down the Spiegel stairs. I still haven't replied to Julia's text; I'll do it later. I clench my fingers around the wheel on the way home. *Why* do I always have to come home? Why did I never say anything, in the early days of the year, so much so that now it has become a habit, that my roommates have given up, and now I barely get a say in this? I take the exit I have so many times before and pass through the roads. Every weekend I relive the roads I drove through in high school. I can never leave.

I sling my bag over my shoulder and walk in. "Ba," I say. I drop my bag to the floor. The house is clean for once, with things put away. My dad is sitting in his chair at the dinner table. There's a bowl of rice in my place, with dishes of mushrooms and bok choy in the center. He's looking straight at me with a strange, tense expression I've never seen before.

"Ba? Everything okay?"

He gestures to the food. "Eat."

I settle in my seat. I take mouthfuls of rice and vegetables. I eat a piece of braised pork. But Ba's not talking. He, too, is taking measured, careful bites of his food. Finally I set my chopsticks down. "What's going on?"

Finally he straightens up. "Why did you never tell me you had a boyfriend?"

I become very still.

"*What?*"

He looks at me, frankly, through his glasses. "I listened to a recording of your radio interview."

I shrink into myself. I'm withering under his gaze. How can I even begin to explain any of this? I can't come up with any cover stories on the spot. So I just sit there and ask numbly, "How did you hear that?"

"One of Professor Xu's friends sent it to me." He sets down his chopsticks. "But how I got it isn't important. You didn't tell me about this. Any of this. I had to hear about it from a stranger. About how you invented this—this algorithm to find yourself a *boyfriend*."

I wince at how it sounds. "It's not like that," I say weakly. "It was for a class. And we're not together anymore, so it doesn't matter. It really doesn't."

Please, Ba. Drop it.

He doesn't move. I face his stark, angry glare. "Why do you always keep things from me, Xiǎoyàn?"

I swallow. "What do you mean, always? I tell you everything."

He points to a stack of papers on the counter, the ones I'd missed on the way in. The papers are rimmed blue and yellow.

And my heart drops.

"I was looking for your AP books and I found these." He pauses. "You hid this from us, too."

My name is on those letters. Those acceptance letters from California schools that I stupidly, sentimentally didn't throw away. I try to scrounge up words to say, but not a single sound comes out.

"Why did you apply?"

I know what I should do. I should take the folders and tell him that it was a mistake and that I never meant any of this. But I look at him instead and lift my chin. "I wanted to go to California," I whisper.

"But you wanted to go to MIT," he says.

I swallow. "MIT was *her* dream. Not mine."

He stiffens at the mention of Ma.

"How were you going to pay for a school out there?"

"How was I going to pay for MIT?" I snap out. My limbs feel leaden.

"We would have figured it out."

"Why couldn't we have figured it out for Berkeley? For UCLA?"

My father sets his jaw. "You wanted to spend hundreds of thousands of dollars to go out, to go across the country, to leave your own mother—"

"I didn't *know!*" I dig my nails into my palms. "I applied before—before she got sick again." My shoulders go limp.

"And what if she wasn't sick?" Ba says softly. "Would you have left us behind without a second thought?"

I don't answer.

"After all she did for you."

Tears prick the corner of my eyes. "All her rules?" I blink my hands out. "All the things she told me I couldn't do? Wanting to keep me close by so she could keep an eye on me so I could never live life on my own?"

"She wanted the best for you."

"What part of that is wanting what was good for me?" I swallow. "I love and miss Ma, but all that—it wasn't what I wanted, Ba. It was what she wanted. Any kid should be allowed to choose where they apply for college, but I wasn't. It was all decided for me." I pause. I'm shaking. All this time we've been silent, and now our voices fill the dining room. "It doesn't matter anymore," I say, my voice bitter. "I didn't end up going anywhere. I stayed. I come home every weekend for dinner and barely feel like I've left. Happy?"

Ba's jaw locks. "You *want* to be there on the weekends?"

"I—"

"I'm a college professor. I hear what happens on the weekends on campus. At least at home you can study. You came home last weekend, and I *knew* you'd been drinking. You want to do that every weekend? Go to parties? Run around getting boyfriends—"

A brittle laugh escapes me, so sharp Ba comes to a startled stop.

Our gazes lock onto each other.

"You used to be so sweet, Xiǎoyàn," he says. He stares at me in fury. "Now you're like this. You're dishonest. And you're disrespectful. You think this is the kind of daughter we wanted you to become?"

His words hang in the air. I take a step back. Something in me snaps cleanly.

"I will *never* be that daughter," I say. I take in a ragged breath, my lungs raw. "Fine. I'm dishonest and I'm a liar. I always have been. I lied about applying to California and I lied about studying during senior year and I—" My voice breaks. "I even lied about MIT. I never got deferred, Ba. I got rejected in December and I couldn't bring myself to tell her, so I lied about that, too, okay?"

This time, everything pours out of me, every shrapnel of

truth, every piece of deceit, because there can't be a second time I do this. I can't break my father twice. I can no longer meet Ba's eyes. I've started, and I can't bear to stop, and I can't bear to witness the aftermath.

"I never turned out the way she wanted. I'm not obedient or a genius or *anything*, really; I'm just a liar and a failure of a kid who never achieved any of her dreams, and I think about it all the time, how much it breaks her heart because it breaks mine, too." I'm panting now. "I'm sorry that she had all her dreams for me and I couldn't achieve any of them. All her years of taking me to math competitions and taking me to church were for nothing because I didn't get into MIT and I never made anything of myself." I start laughing, in shock. "You know what? I—I don't even *know* if I'd get another boyfriend someday, because I like girls, too. Just like Hana does. I'm a big—fucking—*disappointment* to everyone."

Ba flinches. There is a silence. Finally, I have said it.

Everything.

I let my words linger in the air. Long minutes pass. I finally look up.

Ba isn't looking at me. He's turned away, staring at the floor, as if he cannot even bring himself to look at me.

Now you know.

"*You . . .*" His voice is thin. He can't even complete his sentence.

"I do," I say, my voice trembling, my throat tight. "So, I'm sorry, Ba, if you and Ma came all the way to this place to hope for something else. Because this is what I am."

This house has seemed too big, too empty for the two of us. But for the first time, the walls seem to close in. I can't be here for another second.

"I'm going back to campus." My voice is small. I go to the counter to pick up my keys. I pick up the admissions folders, too, and I tear them in two. I shove it all into the recycling bin. I haul my coat over my shoulders and I leave.

I throw my backpack into the car. I jam my keys into the ignition and start it. I look to the glow in the door. For a moment, I wonder if he's going to come out and run onto the driveway, and tell me to come in. But he doesn't appear.

He can't bear to face me, I think. What parent could?

So I back out of the driveway, and I drive.

What else can I do? I don't want to head back to campus, not yet. I know that once I go on the highway I don't know if I can come back. And so I wander. I drive down one road, and then another. I emerge into the main part and see the lone flicker of the sandwich shop. I see the ice cream store where we got the frozen lemonades, summers ago, ages ago. Someone is mopping up the floors inside.

I pass by the church.

I pass by the rec center.

I pass by the school.

And after a while, I pull a U-turn and then drive into the parking lot of my high school.

There is no one else here. There is only me. Everyone else has moved on, gone out of state, gone somewhere else, but I am still here, alone, this person who cannot leave her hometown and now cannot bring herself to be home.

I'm sorry, I say in my mind. I don't know who I'm saying it to; whether it's to my mom, or to my dad, who for all I know is still standing in the kitchen, still in shock. Or to God, whom I haven't spoken to in a year. Maybe it's just an errant thought in the empty vacuum space of my own thoughts, reaching no one.

I lean back against my seat. I feel hollow inside. I just stare at the blinking traffic lights in the distance, in the lone streetlights that hover over the parking lot, at the dark windows of the school. After a while, I realize there is not much else I can do here, so I turn my car on, and I drive again. I go back to the main road. Past the school. Past the rec center. Past the church.

I think about how easy it would be to take the on-ramp west. How far could I drive, before the highway ends? If I didn't stop, would it take me all the way to California?

I never find out.

I pull onto the highway and head north, my headlights beaming in the darkness. I pass the trees and the winding roads. I change lanes to avoid the pothole before Exit 18, and slow before my hairpin exit. It has been baked into my memory, this weekly voyage across this highway, this tethered cord stretching across central Vermont and pulled tight around my chest, this space I know better than anywhere else. I have long memorized this back-and-forth, from the first time I plugged in the college's address to the GPS to when I went home. It hasn't changed.

And yet this drive feels different. It dawns on me, slowly, that I have, in fact, told my dad *everything*.

About my college applications.

About MIT.

About how I wasn't straight.

I can't take any of it back.

The first two confessions I have been chewing on all this time; I have thought about them, turned sick in guilt over them. But the last part gives me a terrifying, weightless feeling at the pit of my stomach. I am in free fall. What do I do now, with the rest of my night, now that I've fucked everything up beyond repair?

I pull into the parking lot. I turn my car off and get out. I walk across campus aimlessly, going in circles around the admin buildings and around the math building. I hear laughter stream across from campus.

I don't want to go back to my dorm. Maybe my roommates are out right now. But they might be staying in, and I don't want to face them, or tell them why I came home hours after I left.

While I try to think of something else to do, I clutch my coat closed with my left hand while my right pulls out my phone.

I check my texts.

My dad has said nothing. The last text is still from Julia.

I pause. I'm in the middle of campus now, by the frozen fountain. I glance up, where the path in front of me leads to

Julia's dorm. I can *see* her room, with its string lights, and hear the music pouring out. And I throw caution to the wind.

Fuck it, I think.

I break into a sprint.

TWENTY-THREE

THEY WERE *right*, I think. People *can* have imperfect information about their preferences. How did I not know this all along? This time, as I run toward Julia's party, it is so immediately apparent how I feel about her. I grab the door from a couple of people dressed in flannels who are heading out, and rush up the stairs two at a time. I hear the heels of my boots stomp up the echoing stairwell. And now a wave of emotion swells in me; how could I have been keeping this from myself all this time?

I like her, I think. I want to be with her. I finally allow myself to feel the truth of it.

I burst into the hallway. Julia's room is at the end of the hallway. Music floats out. The door's open and people run out, giggling, making a beeline for the water fountain.

She's in there. She must be.

My heart soars. I slip into the room, push against the group

312

of people crowded around the beer pong table. Voices rise over one another.

I see her in the corner, her cup in her hand, wearing a black tank top, her long, straight hair falling over her shoulder. She leans against the dresser that's been converted into a makeshift bar. She's done her makeup, her eyes lined, her lips dark red and curved up in that small smile. In this moment she is so beautiful. She's with another person, someone I vaguely recognize, whose light brown curls frame her face, with chipped pink nail polish and glitter on her cheeks.

I head straight for her. My pulse begins drumming in my ears. A rush of adrenaline surges through me, waiting for the moment her eyes find mine, until—

Until the girl beside her leans in and whispers something in Julia's ear, her fingertips curling around Julia's arm. Julia leans in to listen. The distance closes between them. She then laughs, stumbles against the girl, and steadies herself.

I come to a stop.

Someone bumps into me with their Solo cup, sloshing a mixed drink all over the back of my hoodie. "Shit! I'm so sorry."

Julia turns, and her eyes lock onto mine.

I freeze in place.

She and the girl break apart.

"Hey!" Julia heads over, giving me a wide smile, looping her arm around my shoulders. She's slightly drunk, I can tell. "You came."

"I—" All words dissipate from the tip of my tongue. Suddenly

I feel overdressed in my worn hoodie and leggings. This room is *hot*. I glance past Julia's shoulder, and the other girl is staring straight through at me, her jaw set, her lips pressed in a thin line as she cradles her cup.

All my thoughts flood me at once. What *do* I say to her? I should have prepared something to say. Julia's in front of me, and her dark brown eyes are on mine. She tilts her head. "Everything good? Want something to drink?"

I open my mouth. "I—" I shake my head. "Can we—talk?"

She raises an eyebrow. "Yeah, of course. Come on." She links her arm through mine, and I follow her out.

She leans against the wall, a casual smile curving up. "What's up?"

My mind scrambles. What do I say?

"I, uh," I say, "just came out. To my dad."

She straightens. Her eyes grow wide. "Really? Oh my God, Grace." She holds me by my shoulders and folds me into a sloppy hug. Euphoria blooms in my chest. I smell her perfume, her coconut shampoo, and she is so close I want to pull her in to kiss. "How did it go?"

I suppress the wave of shame that comes to me. "It was— It happened," I say. "But that's not the point. I—" I take a deep breath. I remember her words, just last week, and yet it seems so long ago. *Don't think. Just go for it.*

I like you.

"Julia," I say. "I—"

"Hey, Julia," someone calls out from the doorway.

She turns. It's the girl from inside, the one with the chipped pink nails. "We're starting another round of king's cup. You in?" Her gaze lands on me pointedly, as if to say, *Who the fuck is she?*

"We'll be in in a bit." Julia pauses. "I'm just talking to a friend. By the way, Eliza, have you met Grace? We're on ski team together."

I snap still.

Friend.

And then suddenly it becomes so very painfully clear.

"Oh, right," Eliza says. "That algorithm girl, right?" She gives me a long look. "I've heard a lot about you."

"El," Julia says, admonishing her, but she's laughing. *Laughing.* Eliza gives me a half-hearted wave and goes back in. Julia turns to me. "Don't mind her. You were saying?"

Heat rises to my cheeks. The hallway is suddenly too bright. I think of this past week, our fingers threaded through each other's hair, her lips on mine. I think of the silences in the car, of us huddled under the stars, leaning against each other to keep warm. I think of running up the stairs and down the hall that led to this very room, thinking that it all had amounted to something; thinking I had finally, finally gotten it right; that all this meant we are right for each other; that she felt about me how I'd felt about her.

And I couldn't have been more wrong.

I whisper, "Is that what we are? Friends?"

Julia's eyes widen. The smile drops. She says, her voice quiet, "Aren't we?"

"That's all it's meant to you?" My voice trembles. "Nothing more?"

"Grace. . . *You* were the one who didn't want things to be different."

She's right. *Things won't be different, will they?* I'd asked, back when I'd kept the fact that I'd liked girls folded up tightly in me, back when I was scared to let any of this be out in the open. I whisper, "But what if I want it to be more?"

"You're saying . . ." Julia opens her mouth, as if to say something. She's beautiful, standing here, her lips parted, looking at me. A shred of hope claws through my chest. "You'd want us to . . . be together? To date? You know I don't do relationships or anything like that, right?"

I stand still.

She pushes air from her lips and runs her hands through her hair, like she's trying to get her head straight. She blinks, hard. "God. Sorry. This is a lot to process right now. I just . . . I don't know what to say, Grace. I thought we wanted the same thing."

What exactly did I truly want all this time? Was I asking her out to be in a relationship? In the blur of that moment, I'm not sure. But what I do know is that I came to confess my feelings for her. To get some kind of confirmation that we both felt the same way about each other. And now I know my answer. She never felt the same way I'd felt about her. All along she'd just wanted something casual. To be with one person, and then move on to the next.

How could I have assumed any different? Her friend Eliza

appears at the door, and I realize where I recognize her from; she was the person that was flirting with Julia the night of the holiday party. How could we be right for each other, in any universe?

"Right," I whisper. I've misconstrued everything. A chorus of cheers breaks out from inside her room. I've come back all the way for this. To take Julia away from her party. I don't belong here. "Shit. I'm sorry. I'm just going to—"

"Wait," she says. "I— Can we talk about this? When I'm not drunk?"

I don't answer. I don't meet her eyes. I duck into the room and yank my coat out of the pile. I push past everyone.

I run out.

I pace around campus. I pass people on their way to parties, laughing and practically falling over each other, their breaths frosty in the air. I burst into my dorm building and climb the stairs to the third floor. I want to bury myself in my blankets and hide. I dart into my room, hoping desperately that it's late enough on a Friday night that Ruhi is out at a party, and that Ava is on a date with Bryce.

But no such luck. My roommates glance up when I come in.

"Grace?" Ava pauses, halfway through scrubbing her makeup. Ruhi glances up from the beanbag, where she's reading something. "I thought you were home?"

"Why are you still *here*?" I burst out. "And not *out*?"

Ava startles. She exchanges a bewildered glance with Ruhi.

"I—I just came back from my date."

"And I needed to finish up some CE," Ruhi says. Her eyebrows knit together. "What's going on?"

Normally I'd sink into the beanbag and tell them. But I can't bear to look at anyone right now. I head straight for my bed.

"Grace," Ruhi says insistently. "*Talk* to us. What happened?"

"I—" I whirl around. *I just had the worst fight of my life. My dad won't look me in the eye. And Julia—*

I realize that my roommates know nothing about Julia. All this time and I've kept Julia close to my chest, like a secret. And that's the way it'll stay: my own awful secret.

"Did you go home?" Ruhi presses.

"Yeah," I say dully. "I went home." I lift my eyes. "My dad and I had a fight. And everything imploded, and then I came out to him."

Both my roommates' eyes widen. Ruhi whispers, "You—came out? As in, you're . . . ?"

I throw my hands up. "Queer, I guess." I jolt at the word. "I don't fucking know. Not straight." What *am I?* I don't know. It had all just come out. I didn't even have time to figure out the technicalities of my identity. It wasn't like I could google it in the middle of fighting with my dad.

Ava's mouth drops. For something that seems to be a bombshell of information, Ruhi is still calm about it. She pauses and straightens up. She and Ava share a look. "*Oh.* I see."

"Yeah," I say, barely able to meet their eyes. "And everything went about as badly as it possibly could. And now I'm here."

"Wait," Ava says sharply. "Your dad kicked you out?"

I shake my head. "I left. Maybe I should have stayed. Maybe I should have never said anything in the first place."

"You know what? That is no way to treat your kid, and your dad should know that. After all the rules he put on you and all the controlling—"

I jerk up. "You don't know anything about my family."

"Well, I'm getting a good idea of what it's like," Ava says, her eyes flashing. Now her voice is getting louder. "And after all you've been through he should have never shut you out. He should know better."

I flinch at Ava's sharp words. It doesn't feel right. I think of my father, graying, his knuckles tight. I shake my head in my hands. "Ava. Stop."

But she doesn't stop. "You have to stand your ground, Grace. I mean, this is so shitty of him. If I were you I'd just—"

"Well, you're not me and this isn't your perfect fucking family, okay?"

Ava recoils. Her eyes widen, and her expression crumbles. I sink back against my bed. Ruhi just stares at me, her mouth open.

What am I doing? Ava is standing up for me, or she's trying to. But in that moment, all that I have left is this stale anger that has simmered for months. Ava, with her happy family that has beach photo shoots and FaceTimes together and goes to therapy and spends the holidays playing board games, whose mom gave us all gifts on the day of move-in. Here is Ava, with her brilliant smile and her bright voice and her strong opinions, who laughs often and gives and gives because she can, because she has the capacity to, because she doesn't screw things up tightly inside of her, because she hasn't fucked up everything like I have.

And right now I resent her so deeply for it.

"Grace," Ruhi says in a low, warning voice. Of course she's taking her side. "What the fuck?"

"My dad and I are messed up, all right?" I say, my voice shaking. Ava shrinks. "But guess what? That's all I have left! My dad! Without him, it's just me. You know this. You've known this since move-in."

Ruhi reaches out for my hand.

"Grace," Ava says softly. "I was just trying to help—"

I look her in the eye. "No." My voice starts shaking uncontrollably. I yank my hand from Ruhi's. *They pity me*, I think with a sick feeling. "I don't need anyone's help at all. I just want to be alone, okay?"

Ava and Ruhi exchange a look. They both get up and put their coats on. And they head for the door.

It's always been the two of them. They are the two rays of sun in the room. For months I've let them carry me on their loud voices. I sang along to their playlists and curled up with them during movies and kept them company on the floors of the dorm bathrooms after parties and shared popcorn with them. I basked in their warmth. In their sunlight. And with them, I could pretend that I, too, was like them. That I had groups of friends back home and family traditions. I could pretend that I didn't go home just to sit in silence. They were the roommates to thank my lucky stars for. The roommates I thought were too good for me.

And they are.

And now they see the truth of who I am.

It was never meant to last, anyway. As they close the door behind them, I think of Hana. I think of how I always imploded every single thing I loved.

Julia texts me Saturday morning:

hey
everything good between us?
lmk if you want to talk about it

I don't respond. I think about skipping class that week, and then I end up feeling so guilty that I go anyway. It doesn't matter. It's the class before the midterm in Group Theory, and I watch the professor write things out on the squeaky chalkboard, and for the first time, I realize that I don't understand half of it. This semester has caught up with me, and I didn't even realize it.

So I don't go back to the dorm immediately after class. I don't want to, anyway. I linger in empty math basement classrooms and try to go over lecture notes, and then get distracted and end up watching a bunch of YouTube videos. A deep dive into outer space hypotheticals. An instructional video on my lecture topic that I think will help but doesn't. A video on adults talking about coming out to their families. I sit in the far corner of the dining hall and eat meals alone, and when I go back to my dorm, my room is thankfully empty.

Ba doesn't text me at all.

Julia intercepts me as I'm going into work on Tuesday. She catches me in front of the doorway. "Grace."

I turn. I meet Julia's eyes. My heart leaps, out of instinct, and then staggers.

"Can we talk about Friday night? Is everything okay?"

I glance away. "Yeah."

"Come *on,*" she says. "You're doing it again."

"*What?*"

"The thing where you're thinking something and you don't say it. You're being avoidant."

I gesture to the door. "We literally have work right now."

"Roberta will be okay. She can see us through the door."

I look straight at her. "Did you mean what you said on Friday?"

"I—" Julia pauses. "You caught me off guard, Grace. I mean, I was at a party with my friends and then you just came and"— her voice lowers—"I don't know, confessed your feelings for me?" She's not quite meeting my eyes. I flinch at the phrase. "And I didn't know how to respond in that moment on the spot. I guess I just need to know where it all came from for you, and—" She catches my expression and turns. "Shoot. We need more time for this. I think we should talk through it after."

"We don't have to." I turn away. I don't want to think about it at all. I don't want to talk. "It really is nothing, Julia. I misread things between us. That's all. I'm sorry for interrupting your party."

"Grace. Come on. That's not it."

"We're going to be late for our shift."

She doesn't say anything else. We walk into the library, silently, together.

TWENTY-FOUR

I FAIL THE midterm on Wednesday. Or I'm pretty sure I do, at least. I leave a third of the questions blank, and for the first time in my college life, I fervently hope for a curve before I turn the test in. I think about calling in sick to my work shift tomorrow because I can't bear the thought of facing Julia again. I actually do feel a little ill. Maybe it's just me feeling awful about everything. I go back to the dorm and curl up in bed.

At some point, Ruhi creeps into the room. "Hey."

I don't respond.

"I know you're awake, Grace."

Her voice sounds thick. I bury my face in the pillow. "If this is about trying to get me to apologize to Ava—"

"Arjun just broke up with me, and I want to go on a walk."

I sit up.

Ruhi looks at me and shrugs, deadpan. "I wanted you to come with. We both look like we could use one."

"Shit," I say. I clamber down from my bed and wordlessly fold Ruhi into a hug before I remember that I probably smell like Easy Mac and two-day-old pajamas. I step away gingerly. "I'm so sorry." I look around for tissues. "Do you need— Can I—"

"Just a walk." Ruhi's eyes are red and puffy. She's already cried it out. And I wasn't there.

"Where's Ava?"

"With Bryce," Ruhi says. "I haven't told her yet. I just got off a call with him. Besides, telling both of you would make it more real. I just wanted it to stay quiet for . . . a moment, I guess."

I know what Ruhi means. Ava would gather a box of cookies and a blanket within a moment, complete with an entire speech. It would become a whole thing. And here I am, just standing here. But maybe that is what Ruhi wants right now. "Okay," I say. "Let's walk."

I change into a clean shirt and shrug my coat over my shoulders while Ruhi puts on three layers of hoodies and two socks before she puts her coats and boots on. I grab a couple of tissues and stuff them in my pocket, just in case, and we head out.

Our boots crunch softly in the snow. There is a fresh layer from last night, and it hasn't been cleared yet. It's icy out, bitingly so. The sun is out, in theory, but I can't feel it. "Thanks for coming," Ruhi says. She clears her throat.

"Of course," I say. "What happened?"

"It just . . ." Ruhi shakes her head. "There wasn't *anything*, really. It just didn't work out. And I tried, I really did."

"Yes," I said. "You tried more than anyone else would have."

"Right. And I thought it was a point of pride. I mean, *I* was going to make it work. I was always looking up the cheapest flights and trying to arrange it all and I was like—I didn't *mind* doing it at the time, you know? It was fun for me. And I know long distance from Vermont to Seattle is no fun. But then we started texting less, and he started responding less and he wasn't all that much there for me anymore and I just—I guess I realized I was doing all this emotional labor for the both of us. My heart was in it, but his wasn't."

Her voice wobbles a little, and she presses her palms to her eyes before continuing. "So it just . . . fucking . . . ended."

"God, Ruhi," I say. "I'm sorry. That's awful."

"But the thing was, it *wasn't* awful. And there were such lovely parts of our relationship. The summer before college we hung out every day and grabbed breakfast on the weekends with our families. And that was *good*. When it was easy, it was good. But when it was hard—"

"He didn't fight for you," I whisper. "And that's reason enough. You deserve so much more."

She looks at me, tears stuck to her long lashes. "You think so?"

We're sitting on the lip of the empty fountain now, the stone digging into our butts. I lean close to her. "You deserve the entire world. You deserve someone who texts you *good morning* and initiates the calls with you. You deserve someone who plans out twenty things for your birthday like you do for others and leaves you little gifts or notes all the time and takes you out for dates all the time and listens to you and listens to your podcasts and your EDM and loves you and your full GCal with their entire soul." I exhale.

Ruhi's laughing and kind of crying again now. "Grace, no one listens to my weird podcasts."

"Well, they would, just so they could hang out with you."

"I can't even imagine that. But that does sound really nice." She hugs her arms around herself and leans her head against my shoulder.

"I don't think I know a lot about love at all, but that much I know. You deserve that much." I pause. "Ruhi, I had no idea this was all happening. I'm so sorry."

"No, don't be. You were dealing with your own shit. I think I just always . . . I don't know. I've always managed crises on my own, you know? I thought I had a grip on this one."

"But you don't have to," I say. "I'm here. So is Ava. So are your other friends."

She nods and shivers a little.

"Wanna go back in?"

"Yes, please. I'm pretty much covered in half-frozen snot." Her phone buzzes, and she checks it and lets out a sigh. "Ugh, not this. I forgot I have to go in for a production meeting, and I'm a whole mess." She stares at her phone for a second. "Fuck it." She puts it on silent. "I'm not going in today. I'm going to let them fight it out. I'm going to go home and watch a movie."

"Can I join?"

Ruhi puts down her phone. "What? Don't you have ski team?"

I shook my head. "I'm not going."

"But—"

"Let's hang out at the dorm today," I say. "We can order in dinner."

"Ooooh. Yes. I could eat five Crunchwraps right now."

I stop. "Seriously, you want Taco Bell?"

"Am I being *judged* for my breakup food?"

"Not judging," I say, laughing. "Fine, only slightly. But I'll order it with you. Come on. I'll make you hot chocolate, too."

"I'm sorry about the mess with the newspaper," I say when we finally trudge into our room and take our boots off. "I feel like I'm partially responsible for all the drama."

"Oh, Grace." Ruhi looks over and gives a teary smile. "It wasn't you. Everybody was just sorting their shit out. If anything, I'm sorry for being in such a bad mood lately. I didn't realize how stressed my relationship made me."

We order a colossal amount of Taco Bell, enough to feed an entire dorm floor. Ava texts the group chat to say that she's at Bryce's place and probably is going to come home late. A tiny part of me wonders if Ava is just happy and spending time with her new boyfriend, or if she also kind of wants to avoid me as well. But I try to put those thoughts aside. I still want to talk to her.

So it's just the two of us when the food arrives. Ruhi puts

on the movie *Clueless*. I turn off the dorm lights and plug in the Christmas lights, which we've still left up. We settle on the floor against the beanbag with a pile of Crunchwraps and bean burritos between us.

I have forgotten how easy it is to be with her. Everything is always so loud and exciting with Ava. But with Ruhi we are able to sit together, in a quiet, comfortable silence, with occasional commentary on the outfits and young Paul Rudd.

Halfway through the movie, she says between bites, "So, why are you not at ski team practice?"

The bean burrito turns to mush in my mouth. I shrug. "Didn't have time."

It's bullshit, and she knows it. "Grace."

I don't say anything.

"This is about Julia, isn't it?"

I look up. "How do you know?"

"Context clues. She's talked about you nonstop in *Daily* meetings. Brought up stories about you. I had a feeling there was something going on between you two."

"Well, there isn't anymore." I put down my food. "Also, I thought tonight was about making you feel better."

She holds up her food. "I do. And I promise you I already have all of Cher's lines memorized." She pauses. "I mean, if you don't want to talk about it, I won't. But I know you're hurting, too. I noticed how happy you were when you came back from ski practices with her. Both Ava and I did."

I screw my eyes shut. "I just. I know I snapped at Ava, and it wasn't cool of me. I know she was trying to stick up for me. But I can't hear another lecture about how I should have the guts to face my dad or whatever."

"I wasn't going to lecture you," Ruhi says gently. "I know how it's like with immigrant families. It's complicated. That's how it was for my sister, too."

I look up. "Your sister went through this?"

"I mean, she was the kid that we all looked up to. She was the kid that the aunties all talked about. She was good at everything. And it wasn't like she was an asshole about it or anything, she just had, like, super focus and work ethic. She worked her ass off and got into med school at Yale." Ruhi wrings her hands. "Anyway. She came out as bi in the first year of med school."

She doesn't whisper the word *bi*. She just says it. "My grandparents say she broke their hearts. They didn't talk to her at family events. My parents didn't comfort her or anything. They blamed her for making family events awkward. They refused to meet her girlfriend. And Janvi put up with it for two years until last winter break."

Ruhi shakes her head. "And she—she finally told my whole family *off*. She told my parents that what they did was no way to love their own kid. She told them that she deserved respect and understanding. She said that she deserved happiness. She was a force, Grace. I'd never seen anything like it. They had a whole big fight about it for weeks, and it went into months. But then my parents started asking questions. And they invited her girlfriend over for Thanksgiving last year. And they adore her.

330

It took time, but . . . Janvi got there."

I nod. I glance across the room, at one of the photos that Ruhi has with her sister at a wedding, at the tall, striking girl dressed in a bright peach lehenga. I feel a rush of admiration for someone I've never met. "I'm glad. I'm happy for Janvi. But I don't know about me."

Ruhi nods. "I get it. It takes time. I had a whole talk with her the night she came out. She told me that she wrestled with her sexuality for a long time. She told me that she'd known that she wasn't straight ever since her sophomore year of high school. That she just pushed it down throughout college because it was easier not to think about it. She couldn't imagine bringing a girl home until the first year of med school. She told me that she felt guilty because she loved our family so much and felt like she owed them so much and didn't want to let them down. And that's why it took her so long. Because it's complicated. And that's what you and your dad's conversation reminded me of."

I squeeze my eyes shut. The movie is still playing in the background. I remember what Ma said when Hana came out. *She used to be such a good girl. Now look at the trouble she's caused.* How Ma iced out Hana's parents because they supported her unconditionally and all left the church; to Ma, it was like they'd abandoned her.

There is a long silence. I want to talk about it, but I'm scared that if I do then I will cry and there will be no going back. Ruhi saves me. I feel a hand clasp my own. I open my eyes. She squeezes my fingers. "That's all I wanted to say. I'm not going

331

to pretend like I know how things are for you. I don't know everything about what's going on between you and Julia. But what I do know is that you deserve happiness. And it may take days or weeks or years, but I hope that someday, if and when you're ready, you find a way to ask for it."

I nod. I squeeze Ruhi's hand back. "You deserve this kind of happiness, too. You deserve the entire world. This infinite universe."

She laughs. "Thank you, my love. I'll settle for the Crunchwraps tonight."

The movie ends. Ruhi and I doze off for a bit, curled up on the beanbags and wrapped in blankets, and only wake up when Ava comes in around midnight. Her face is a momentary baffled picture of shock, seeing us in the sea of bean burrito wrappers and hot sauce packets, but then Ruhi tells her about the breakup with Arjun and Ava rushes to pull her into a hug. And from that point on, Ava and I become a semi-united front for Ruhi.

In the morning, Ava wakes up early before any of us to go to class. When Ruhi and I wake up, we see that there is a box of a dozen Coffee House doughnuts on Ruhi's desk and a sticky note with a heart drawn in highlighter. Even I soften at this.

Ruhi tucks a doughnut in a Kleenex and heads off to class, too. I'm left alone. I stare across the room, at the dates on Ruhi's large whiteboard calendar. I'm about to be late for class. I hurry out the door and suddenly realize halfway on the path to the math building that I don't want to go to class. I take the right fork that leads away from the math building, away from the campus library and the dorms, and toward the admin buildings.

Toward the chapel.

The doors are closed to keep in the heat, but I tug the heavy wrought-iron handles and manage to pry open the doors. I walk in. I have always known, in a dim sense, that there is a church on campus. I hear the carillon bells each day at noon and dinnertime. But I have never come close. Now I am here, in a chapel that is not the one I have known, standing with my school backpack at the edge of the pews.

The church is dimly, softly lit. There is no service. I take a seat at the second pew and look up. Light filters in through the stained-glass windows, in all kinds of brilliant shades. I think about how the glass had to be put together, carefully, piece by piece, in perfect geometric symmetry. How those windows and cathedrals took years and decades to build, how someone could devote their entire lifetime to just putting together glass. How they could steadfastly carry this belief that there is always something grander than them. In that way religion is beautiful to me. I think of picking out Ma's songbird voice in the choir and being filled with so much wonder and admiration I felt as if I could levitate.

But that's not all it is. I think of the Sundays I have spent looking up at the windows during services while the minister talked about temptation and sin. In Sunday school, they explained that we were all born wanting to make mistakes. That our lives are a terrain of errors that have already been absolved.

That our debt has been paid but we still owed everything.

"Why would God love us," Hana once asked the Sunday school teacher, "if all we do is make mistakes?"

"Because we are forgiven," he said. "We are loved, as His children, unconditionally, as we are. Even with our mistakes."

I think about that time, back when Hana was still a part of the church, back when I prayed, back when Ma was here and I thought there still was a God to believe in. And suddenly I'm crying in this chapel I've never stepped foot in before, my palms clapped to my eyes, my forehead on the back of the pew in front of me.

In that moment the door opens, and someone comes in with an armful of pamphlets.

I hiccup, so loudly it echoes.

"Oh." The woman looks slightly startled to see me here. Her brown hair is tucked up in a bun, and her dark eyes are warm. She peers closer, alarmed. "Oh, I'm so sorry, dear. What's going on? Are you all right?"

I quickly swipe at my cheeks. "Yes. Sorry. I was just . . . I don't know. I'm okay. I promise." I look around. "Am I interrupting something?"

"Oh, not at all," she says. "I'm Dr. Hamed. The interfaith group coordinator. I'm just setting up for an event we're having later tonight."

"Leighton has an interfaith group?"

"Yes, of course," she says gently. "It meets every week in the conference room above Coffee House." She looks at me over her glasses. "Would you like to join?"

I look at her, for a moment. And then I find my voice. "I'm sorry," I say. "I'm not that religious."

I wait for her to judge me. To ask me why I am here, then, sitting in the chapel, crying, even, in the heart of this building beneath the stained windows. But she doesn't. Her expression relaxes, and she gives me a kind smile. "I understand. Stay as long as you like. Don't mind me."

I sit there some more while she comes in and out with name tags. And then I stand and walk towards the chapel doors.

I have thought about forgiveness many times. When I chose Leighton and turned down the California schools, when I came home on the weekends, when I stopped talking to Hana, I wondered if I would then be forgiven. If Ma, wherever she was, would forgive me for lying to her. For dreaming about the sky and the ocean on the other side of the country at one point. If she would forgive me for going to the party with Hana that night, for getting drunk until the room spun, for ignoring her calls, for pulling my best friend to me and feeling my heart jump in my chest as I wondered about us being in California. Together. I wondered if she'd forgive me for what I'd done back then, and for what I have done now. For talking to Julia and kissing her and feeling that same flutter in my chest.

I realize, finally, that all this time I have been searching for that kind of forgiveness. From God or from my mother, or from my best friend, I don't know. Maybe all of them. My whole life I've searched for systems to believe, with intricate rules and sound logic. It's why I fell in love with math. It's why I believed in the church.

But where do I go from here? What do I do for the rest of my life? I squeeze my eyes tightly.

You deserve happiness, Ruhi had said.

There is something I need to do.

I pull out my phone. I take a deep breath. I exhale and hear my sigh rise up and echo.

My fingers hover over the phone.

Slowly, for the next twenty minutes, I draft the longest text I have ever written.

I send it to Hana.

And I wait.

SUMMER AFTER SENIOR YEAR

BY THE SUMMER, my best friend was all but physically across the country. We drove around like we always had. We got frozen lemonades and hiked to the waterfall. We lay on the rocks, listening to the rush of the water. I felt the sweat on my shoulders, trickling into my sports bra. Hana was going to leave for college, two weeks before I did.

"You gonna miss this place?" I asked softly.

Hana blew air up her bangs. "Of course I will, Grace. I'll miss you."

I looked away so she couldn't see my expression. She could say that, but she was leaving, anyway.

"Will you miss home?"

I laugh. "Leighton's only forty minutes away."

We listened to the sounds of the water rushing. And when we were done with our frozen lemonades, we headed back into the car. Hana was silent the whole ride home, as if she was trying to say something. We listened to her music, the Indie Pop Spotify mix. That night, I stayed at Hana's. Her parents were out on a date night. Her siblings were in their rooms. She and I sat in the backyard, passing back and forth the bottle of white wine that she'd snuck from her parents' pantry. We drank, and I grimaced at the sour taste. We talked, at first about school and what people were up to this summer, and then as we got drunker we started talking about other things: opinions on the movies we'd watched as kids, YouTube videos we watched, speculation on the kids in our school and where they'd end up in ten years, an unsolved proof that I'd seen somewhere about chromatic polynomials.

And then we fell silent.

There's an urgency, the summer before you go away for college, I came to learn. The days are longer, the sunsets fuller. The summer stretches wide before you, lulling you into a false sense of security before calcifying into the remaining days. The air is hot and sweet. The silences are full of ending promises and things unsaid.

"I wish you could come with me to California," Hana finally said softly, her dark eyes meeting mine.

I looked up, my chest caving in. "Hana."

"Do you remember that night when we went to Travis's party?"

"Please," I warned. I thought of the string lights and music, the taste of cold beer, the sweet citrus of Hana's perfume, and it was so visceral it pained me.

She knew, too, that there was something there.

"I just have to say it, okay?" Hana said, her voice sharp. "Just let me. I don't know what I'd do without you, Grace. I've always wanted to get out of this town. But I don't want to leave you."

"Don't fucking do this to me," I said, and Hana flinched. "It was never an option for me, okay? Don't act like it's so hard to leave. Because I don't get a choice."

Hana was quiet. "I'm sorry," she said. "I shouldn't have brought this up. I just wish . . . Sorry. I don't know."

My toes were cold. I stared ahead. "It's late. Let's go to bed."

We slept in Hana's queen bed, the way we always had, except this time I curled myself up as close to the edge as I could. In the morning, I drove home. And I didn't answer a single one of Hana's texts. Not even when she told me when she'd booked flight tickets. Not even when she apologized and said that she didn't know what she'd said that made me upset but she wanted to see me again before she left. I let the texts go unanswered. Because going to see her again meant again facing the fact that she was leaving.

I stared at my phone the day she had left. And when I looked up her Insta account and saw palm trees in her story, I grabbed my phone to my chest and curled up in my bed. *I'll respond to her in a week or two*, I thought. *I just need time to process it right now.* When I first met her in church, the new girl in school whose last name slotted next to mine, this transplant from upstate New York, she'd perched at the edge of her chair as if she was about to take off any minute. She was always destined to leave this place anyway. It was only a matter of time.

What do you do when your newly estranged friend settles into college? You keep yourself busy with work.

In the last two weeks before Leighton started, I hung around the rec center. The days were busier. The summer camps were coming to an end, and the fall sport season was beginning. We signed kids in for tryouts and open gyms. After hours, Miles and I played lots of pool. We'd started getting competitive. He lost a game and had to clean up the cake-smeared table left after a kid's party. He won the next and made me promise to come to his next band set on the Village Green.

"If you have time, that is."

I had nothing but time. Next Friday, I drove to the Village Green at sunset. The bands were setting up, playing under the shade of the gazebo. I watched the sky turn pink as music floated over us. When he tipped toward the mic and sang, his voice was softer than I'd imagined. His gaze swept over the crowd and settled on me. He grinned at me. They were pretty good, I had to admit. I congratulated him after his set and hugged him. He brightened and invited me to a party later that night at one of his bandmates' houses. I told him maybe.

I drove home. Ba was out of town to present his paper at a conference in Boston, and I had the silent house to myself. I sat outside for ten minutes, looking at the houses in the neighborhood, feeling unmoored. Then the mosquitos started eating me alive and I went back in. I tried to watch a movie on my phone because our larger TV only had Chinese cable.

Around midnight, I got a FaceTime from Hana. I stared at the phone buzzing in my hands, panicked. What would I say to her? Should I apologize for not texting her back? Was she okay?

This could be an emergency. I picked up.

"Hi!" someone yelled into the blurry phone. The room was dark, the phone screen blurry. "Helloooo."

"Hana?" I lurched forward. "Are you okay?"

"Oh, she's *fantastic*," the girl said, and laughter erupted in the background. "We're all just sliiiighty tipsy in someone's room, and she said I could randomly call anyone on her contact list so. How are you, Grace Tang?"

"Wait, you're calling *Grace*?" Hana's voice came on in the background. Her voice became insistent. "Give me my phone. Give it!"

The screen became blurry again. Hana's face appeared. "Listen. I'm so sorry. We were playing truth or dare. I didn't mean it."

I swallowed. "Oh," I said. Hana looked up and shushed her friends, who seemed to be giggling. At *me*. At this prank call. "Okay. Bye."

"Wait—" she said before I ended the call. I sat straight up on the couch, my heart pounding in my ears. I threw my phone to the couch. And then, after a moment, I picked it up and texted my coworker.

He responded within minutes with the address of the party.

I threw on a sundress I dug up from the back of my closet, the one I wore to my school's Springfest. I drove to the party and parked at the end of the block. I wove through all the cars parked on the driveway. I texted Miles, and he appeared at the doorway, a cup clutched in his hand. "You came!"

This party was larger than the Halloween one and flowed through several floors. There was an assortment of half-opened handles on the kitchen counter and I poured myself a cup of juice. I couldn't get drunk at a party again, especially not when I was driving home. Miles introduced me to his bandmates, and we all settled around the carpeted staircase. We joined some people I vaguely recognized, Ella and Vibha, as some of Hana's theater friends. Miles and his bandmates talked about their upcoming move. Two of his friends were starting at Middlebury during the February term. Miles was taking a gap year. They were all going to live in New York for a bit to try to play some gigs.

Everyone was leaving, I realized. I drank my juice and felt like I was floating out of my body. It felt strange not being at a party with Hana. Everyone was laughing and drunk, and I felt too nervous, too exposed. But slowly I settled in. We started playing a card game on the steps. Everyone smiled at me.

People ran up past us, giggling and whispering. I became aware of how I settled against Miles, of his sweet cologne. I didn't move. Neither did he. I won a game of cards, and everyone cheered for me. This is what I could have been doing all this time. High school could have been fun for me.

The two other bandmates left early. I stayed behind. So did Miles, and I offered to drive him home. Eventually the night wore on and our circle thinned. I checked my phone for the time and saw texts come in from Hana. It was one, then two in the morning. At a little past three, I finally stood and helped Miles up. We walked down the stairs and out of the party.

We were quiet as we walked across the lawn. "Thanks for inviting me," I finally said. "To this. And to your concert earlier."

"I'm glad you came," Miles said. He was slightly tipsy, I could tell. "You know, I was thinking of inviting you to my gigs for a while."

We were at my car now. I turned around. "Why didn't you?"

"Yeah, but . . ." Miles fidgeted with his hands. "I . . ." His words trailed off, for the first time. "Just never had the guts to, I guess."

"What do you mean?"

He tilted his head. He gave me a smile, his expression a little tentatively hopeful.

Oh. I think of Hana telling me last year that she could tell that Miles had a crush on me. Was that true? Had it been true all this time? Did I have feelings, too? I thought of the times I observed his drumming on the table and laughed at his jokes while we played pool.

This was the natural conclusion, wasn't it? What it had all been leading to?

My heartbeat rushed in my ears. All of a sudden there was a

curious urge to kiss him. I wanted to know what it was like to be kissed. Logically, I knew it was a bad idea. It was the last week of summer. He was leaving soon. *Fuck it*, I thought. I stood up on my tiptoes and tilted up, toward him.

And then we were kissing. He pressed me against my car, and I let him. I'd thought of it in the abstract, what it would be like to kiss someone and how it would work. But I didn't think much now: I just let him guide me. I unlocked my car's back door and pulled him in. He didn't let go of me. His fingers traced my knee and trailed up my thigh. My phone buzzed again, on my lap, lit up with a call from Hana. I didn't answer. She was living her life, and I mine. As Miles reached to slip off the straps of my sundress I pushed away all thoughts of my best friend.

TWENTY-FIVE

I'M SITTING IN a library study room the next day when Hana calls me. It's a FaceTime call. I take a deep breath, my fingers trembling, and I pick up.

"Hi," she says. We haven't spoken over the phone all this year, I realize. This was someone I saw every day in school. Had lunch with most days in the week. And this is the first time I'm talking to her through a screen.

"Hi," I say. "Thanks for calling."

She sits, her arms curled around her knees. She always sits like that. Light streams in from the window behind her. It's just past four in California. I've forgotten that.

"What's up?" she says warily, but it sounds hollow, as if we are acquaintances who encounter each other again, years later, in a department store. "Everything okay?"

My shoulders tense up. What do I say? All this time, and I've been living inside of my own head. Waiting for everything to fall into place, to follow some rational order, to align myself to the things I have always believed in. Theories and numbers. What I was taught in church. I have spent so long waiting for things to collect themselves into some sort of sense that I've disappeared inside myself.

I take a deep breath. "I need to tell you something." I pause. "About last summer."

Hana leans forward.

"I know things were weird between us. I made it weird and I just—" I falter. "I don't know. Stopped reaching out, I guess."

Hana's gaze flickers. There is real hurt there.

I continue. "Part of it was that I just didn't really know how to cope with . . . everything, I guess. With losing my mom. And with seeing my dad go through that. And high school was ending and you were about to leave for California. And . . . it was—inevitable, you know? Like no matter how much we hung out that summer, you were going to leave at the end of it. And I guess I realized that at one point and I couldn't bear it. So I shut you out. I thought that if I did it first, it wouldn't hurt as much. But I shouldn't have, because it ended up hurting the both of us. And I'm sorry for that. God, I'm so, so sorry I did that to you."

I close my eyes. "I guess it didn't help that I had feelings for you, too. At the time."

There it is, finally.

I, Grace Tang, was in love with my best friend. This is the truth of that summer. This is what I have been running from, trying to press down since that sleepover, since that night under the stars, since that time Hana held my hand and my heart rose in my chest, and then broke, when she said she wished I could come to California with her. That I loved her so much I couldn't bear the thought of her gone, so I cut it off myself and shut myself away from her.

"Oh, Grace," Hana says.

I open my eyes and meet hers.

There is a long silence.

"For how long?"

"Since Halloween that year, I think," I say. "Until you went to college."

Another silence.

"I think I did, too," she says. She meets my eyes. "For part of the summer, at least. Have feelings."

Ah.

"I . . . sensed something. But I didn't know you felt it, too. I thought I was just being my dumbass self, having a silly crush on who I thought was my straight best friend. I . . . I don't know. I thought I kind of ruined things. That you didn't want to even be my friend anymore."

"That's not true," I say. "Any of that." I shake my head. "I'm only now realizing it. I didn't recognize it at the time, because I didn't even know I could be into girls. I'd been raised all my life to not think like that, so I didn't even recognize when I did."

"Right," Hana says. "Because of the church."

I nod. Hana is perhaps the only person who understands.

347

After all it is the first place we met each other: first passing in the halls of the school, then in youth group, where we were put next to each other, the two Asian girls with the same first two letters of their surnames.

It was because of Ma, too. I remember her words: *Look at what Hana's done to her family. Look at the mess she's made. It's not normal, Xiǎoyàn.* She gave up a six-year friendship to stick to these beliefs of all beliefs, and that is still not something I understand.

It hurts me when I think of this. And I realize that this shame has been wedged in me so deeply I didn't even recognize how much it has affected me. "I finally realized it this year. That I could like girls. That I liked you, at one point." I take a deep breath.

"How'd you realize?"

"Well," I say. "I, uh, kind of did this thing where I invented a campus-wide algorithm to determine people's most compatible match. And then I got matched up with a guy who I'd calculated as my perfect match, but I fell for a girl on my ski team instead?"

Hana's mouth hangs wide open for a moment, speechless.

There is a long, long silence.

I've lost her, I think.

"I'm sorry, but that is the most Grace Tang coming-out story I've ever heard in my entire life."

And then we both burst out laughing at the same time, out of the sheer incredulity of it all. "I'm going to need the whole story."

So I tell her: about the algorithm, about how it got across the whole campus, about all the matches. I tell her about Jamie. I tell her about Julia and the op-ed and the ski team. She listens, through it all, her eyes wide. "So," I end, "that's how I know. I think I had this whole . . . idea, I guess, that I needed to have this system to figure out the concept of love. And I didn't really get it at the time, so I made up an algorithm thinking that it would explain everything. Except, as it turns out, the algorithm didn't account for everything about love. And I didn't really account for the fact that I was, you know. Not straight. Queer? Bi? Pan? I don't really know what to call myself yet. I'm still figuring that part out."

"And that's okay," Hana says. "It took me a long, long time to sort out my own identity as a lesbian. I mean, I remember talking about it with you in high school. And you're just beginning to figure that out."

"Yeah. I am." I take a breath. "I only just came out to my dad last weekend."

"You *did*?" Hana says. "How'd it go?"

I laugh. "Not great," I admit. "I'm still sorting that one through."

"God," Hana says. "I'm sorry. I wish it went better."

"Me too," I say. "I think I had to say it, though. I'm glad I did. Even though he's . . . not really talking to me right now."

"It was a process for my parents, too," Hana says. "I think it was a shock at first."

"But they ended up supporting you."

"They did," Hana says. "And I hope that's the case for you, too. At any rate, I'm here for you. Three thousand miles isn't going to stop me from supporting my best friend. I mean it. Websites, incredibly informative Google Docs, sapphic fan-fic, movie recs, advice on how to get this hot ski teammate of yours—"

I laugh. "Thanks," I say. "Don't think that crush is going to pan out. But I might take you up on the Google Doc." I shift in my seat. "Anyway, enough about me. How are you doing?"

We stay on FaceTime so long I witness the California sun set behind her, a beautiful gold that spreads like yolk. Hana tells me about her life in college, about the girl she likes, about life out there. For the first time, I don't see it as I did before: like a ticking clock, like some kind of twisted confirmation that she belonged out west all along. That her existence here was a temporal fluke that contained her; that I was just some holding space until she could start her life for real.

We talk, and I feel this rush of emotion for her, this swell of affection. And you know what, maybe part of it is love, a kind of love that I don't have a name for yet. Maybe parts of us have been in love with each other, a little bit, only as best friends growing up can love each other, platonic and a little bit roman-tic, all at once. Because there is this intimacy that comes with understanding every version of them. We grew from the same roots, from the same town, and there is no one else who knows me better. And now in this homecoming to each other we tell the secrets that have knotted up between us, and it is such a relief.

* * *

350

I feel a lightness after my conversation with Hana. We make a plan to FaceTime every other week, and when we get off the phone with each other, I send her a heart emoji. She replies immediately with one back; the beginning of a back-and-forth, a conversation, finally.

It's late and dark out; I've missed my office hours for Group Theory. I sigh. I can always go to next week's. Maybe I am becoming a real college student after all, hoping for some kind of miraculous curve to materialize.

It's Friday night again. Ba still hasn't texted me. Lunar New Year is this Sunday. I think about going to the dining hall, and then realize that I'm not very hungry. I go back to the dorm to make myself a pot of tea instead. Maybe I'll try to root for something in the fridge. I wonder if either of my roommates will be back.

The room is empty when I return. I see Ava's and Ruhi's backpacks. Ruhi's computer is just blinking off, the empty doughnut carton still precariously balanced on top of the books. Ava's desk is messy, with her sprawl of books. Bryce's hoodie is draped over the back of her chair. They've gone to dinner. I settle onto the beanbag and wait for the water kettle to brew. I make myself a cup of mint green tea and lean back.

Just then the door opens and Ruhi walks in. "And then I literally told him, 'No, you cannot cite the campus meme page—'"

She stops short, and Ava almost bumps into her. Without thinking, I abruptly rise to my toes.

"Hi," I say.

"Hey, Grace." Ava's voice is small. Her eyes don't quite meet mine.

"Um. Can we talk? Are you guys busy right now?"

Ava doesn't move. Ruhi sits in her seat. "What's up?"

"I just wanted to say . . ." I swallow. "I don't know. I'm really sorry for lashing out the other day."

Ava meets my eyes.

"I know you were trying to be helpful. But things in my family have always been complicated."

There's a pause.

"No, *I'm* the one who should be sorry," Ava says. "I overstepped my bounds. I didn't mean to assume things about you and your dad. It wasn't my place."

"Yeah, but . . ." I sigh. "I shouldn't have taken it out on you. I guess I'd been keeping a lot of things from my dad over the past year, and they all came out at once, and it was a lot for both of us to handle." I lift my head. "And I just kind of let that all implode. But I'm figuring that out. I just want things to be okay between us."

Ava nods. "Of course."

"Speaking of figuring things out. I know I already let this out the other day, but I guess I should, you know, come out to you guys. Officially. Uh. I don't know how these things go. Maybe I just say it? Anyway, I think I'm . . . not straight? Queer? I don't know. Point is, I just figured out I'm into girls. So. Yeah."

It feels strange saying it, but I've said it before and I can say it again. I can keep saying it. This is who I am. I barely have time to look up and gauge their reactions when Ruhi pulls me into a fierce hug and Ava piles on, and we all collectively topple backward, sinking into the big blue beanbag.

"I'm so fucking proud of you," Ruhi whispers.

"I love you, you know that?" Ava nudges closer to me. The beanbag sways, and in that moment, my heart swells, practically bursting with happiness. Ava shifts, and Ruhi's elbow ends up in my face and I laugh. "There has *got* to be a better hug configuration than this."

"It's the Spiegel 302 cuddle puddle," Ava says. "The machine-generated found family of it all."

"The best random roommates I could have ever had," Ruhi says.

"At least *that* algorithm worked for me."

"Oh, Grace," Ruhi says.

"I guess mine didn't account for the whole part about my sexuality. There *was* imperfect information, after all."

Ava shrugs. "To be fair, you just figured that out."

Ruhi glances at me. "Do you think you'd try again? With the algorithm?"

I shake my head. "I don't know. I don't really know how I feel about it. I mean, I almost feel like it created more drama on campus than it did solve anything about the subject of love."

"What makes you think that?" Ava asks.

"I don't know. It was working for a while. Like with you and Cameron. And Ruhi's editors. But I'm thinking about it now and the more I think about it, the more I realize that it really *was* telling people who to date. Which isn't right."

"I don't know," Ava says. "I don't think it was, like, telling me to date Cameron. And we are good friends now. It was just thought-provoking, if anything. Like, thinking about love and compatibility and what makes two people click. I think it was a good theory."

"Besides," Ruhi says, "who really knows anything definitive about love, anyway? We're all just walking around with our theories."

That's true. I don't have all the answers. Maybe I never will. I turn to Ruhi. "How are you holding up, by the way?"

She shrugs. "I mean, it fucking sucks. But I think part of me saw this coming for a while. Long distance is just hard. Especially as a freshman." She nudges me playfully. "Well, *I* hope this algorithm is run again next year. I want to meet the love of my life." At my incredulous look, she says, "Worth a shot. You never know."

Maybe it really is just a theory. A hypothesis. Maybe I didn't need to shoulder the task of figuring out how love works.

But that's for me to think about later. I glance at Ruhi, who had her own heartbreak so recently, and I pull her into another extra-tight hug. "What a week we've had," I say.

"Yeah. Tell me about it."

"We should do something." I sit up. "Go get cookies at Coffee House?"

"Even better," Ava says, eyeing the mini fridge. "We could

make cookies right here. I knew I stashed emergency cookie dough for a reason."

In this moment I love her so much.

Ava pulls a roll of cookie dough out of the fridge, and we head down to the tiny, questionably clean dorm kitchenette. She puts on ABBA, and Ruhi and I sing along to the lyrics. We scoop cookie dough onto the baking sheet with abandon, and by some careless error (of course), we end up eating more than half the cookie dough itself. We dance around in the kitchenette, and once the cookies are done, we pile them onto a plate and head back up to our room, shouting along to the lyrics of "Dancing Queen."

The cookies *do* get slightly burnt by the kitchenette oven, but it doesn't matter. These are the best cookies I've ever had. It's Friday night. I try to distract myself. We put *Love, Rosie* on and eat chocolate chip cookies until my stomach hurts. Ava mentions a party we can go to, but by the end of the movie, we're sleepy, lulled by our string lights. We stay in that room, curled around each other.

At about midnight, I check my phone to see the time. And I see a text from Ba.

I sit straight up, my heart thudding in my chest, my palms cold.

小燕，明天回家吧。我想跟你谈一谈。

If you can tomorrow, please come home. I'd like to talk to you.

TWENTY-SIX

PART OF ME doesn't want to go home. I can't relive Ba's anger again. What if I go home, only to face a stony silence? What if I am summoned home because it is an obligation, because I am, after all, an obedient daughter who comes home every weekend?

But I know that sooner or later, we will have to talk. And I have to go home to set things straight.

I want to talk to him.

And he wants to talk, too.

I remind myself of that over and over as I walk down to my car the next afternoon. I drive out of the campus roads and turn onto the highway. I know this highway by heart now, the bridge between my hometown and my college town, between who I was in high school and who I am becoming. Or trying to become. The closer I get to my town, the louder the residual shame wells up in me, the reminders of what he'd said to me last weekend. I grit my teeth and drive on, until I pull into the driveway of my house. Until I see the lights on in the doorway.

I open the door. I set my backpack on the floor.

My dad sits at the dinner table, on his phone. When he hears me come in, he straightens up.

"Ba," I say. I root myself firmly into the ground.

He stands. His eyes meet mine. "Here," he says. His voice is hesitant. It does not close upon itself. "Sit."

I sit at the dinner table. The afternoon light slats in through the windows. The table lays bare and vast between us.

"Are you cold?" he asks.

I shake my head. He stands anyway and pulls a cup from the cupboard. He shakes the loose-leaf oolong from the box and puts a spoonful in my cup. And he pours hot water over it and brings it over to me. He sits back down.

"Xiǎoyàn-ah," he says. *My little swallow bird.* I look past him, at the wall, at the twin brush paintings that stand on either side of the window. They are of mountains and clouds, and the small dips of paint in the corner form my namesake, soaring between the clouds.

What will he say next? I lay my fingertips on the scalding sides of the cup and keep them there. I brace myself. My limbs are tensed, ready to flee at any second.

"Let me tell you a story," he says. "When you were two years old, your ma drove to the mall with you."

He pauses. I did not expect this.

"It was the big mall, the one that was an hour away. And in

one of the stores, while she was looking at some pots and pans, you wandered off. 不见了。"

Ba looks at me. The light settles on his thinning hair, his heavy-lidded eyes that peer out from me. His voice is still soft.

"She was all alone, an hour away from home. She searched for you all around the store and throughout each level of the mall. She didn't have a phone on her, and so she couldn't call me. Two hours passed, and she was thinking about having someone at the store call security when they found you had somehow made your way outside, because you'd just wanted to play in the snow."

I've heard this story before. Ma told me it once accusingly. She said it was the worst day of her life. She'd looked pale, terrified, as if it was something that still haunted her. I didn't know how to apologize for something that I didn't even remember doing.

"吓坏了," my dad says. "You scared your mother halfway to death. And from that moment, she didn't let you out of her sight. When she dropped you off at school, she worried about you getting hurt at the playground or about an intruder. She worried about the ways you'd get sick each winter."

"I know that," I said. She packed soups in my thermos, bitter, pungent ones that I would dump out in the school bathroom.

"She had always been like that. She was afraid to let you go. Her only child. And so I became afraid with her," my father says softly. He pauses. "Even years later. Even when it was time to let you fly."

His words still me. I look up and he meets my eyes. The silence moves, expands between us.

"So when she . . . left, and we lost her, I just didn't know what to do. I wanted to take care of you the way she had taken care of you. But then I became afraid of losing you, too. You don't have to come home every weekend," Ba says.

I think of Ba, alone at home seven days a week, and my heart breaks all over again.

"Ba—"

"I know I asked you to come home this weekend. But that's only because I wanted to talk. I'm learning how to take care of you, still. And I realize that sometimes, it means letting you go." His shoulders rise as he sighs. "We shouldn't have held you back from making decisions about college, Xiǎoyàn. Nor should I hold you back from the rest of your life now. I don't want to make you come home when you don't want to."

My lip trembles. "But I do want to come home sometimes. I want to see you."

He gives me a small smile. "Give your lǎo ba some credit. I've survived thus far on my own cooking, haven't I?"

His words are light. I try to offer a smile. He relents. "Besides, I just started talking to someone. A counselor in the university office. And Xu a-yi and her friends have been kind to me. Don't worry about me. I'm not alone."

"Okay," I say. It's a relief. "Maybe every other week, then."

We sip our tea in silence for a while.

"There is one more thing I want to say."

I tense up in anticipation.

"I should have said this earlier. You are my daughter, no matter what you have done or accomplished." There is a long pause, as if he is thinking about his words carefully. "Or who you choose."

My stomach tightens into a hard, painful knot.

He's finally said it.

I whisper, "Do you think Ma would feel the same?"

"How can she not?"

How could she not? Bitterness floods my mouth. I think of what she said about Hana.

"She believed in God," I say, tears springing to my eyes. My voice catches. "And God hates that part of me. That's what the church said. That it's wrong to think . . . or to live like that."

There is a silence. I don't know why I'm talking about God with my dad, who believes in nothing but science, whose religion is empirical fact, who never once went to church with us all those years.

"My little swallow bird," he says slowly in Mandarin. "How could you ever hate something you created yourself?"

TWENTY-SEVEN

"HEY," JULIA SAYS, sliding into the table across from me on Monday afternoon. We're tucked into the corner of Coffee House. "You wanted to talk?"

I'd texted her from home on Sunday morning. Ba and I sat through that weekend. There were periods we talked and periods where we just quietly watched his shows. It wasn't something out of the ordinary, really. But something had shifted. I was ready to start to have all these conversations I'd been avoiding.

"Yeah. Thanks for coming." I slide a plate to her. "Doughnut?"

"I'd go for a doughnut." She takes a bite and leans forward, watching me carefully. "What's up?"

"You're right," I say. "I think we did need to talk." I clear my throat. My hands feel light. My nerves are buzzing through them like live wires. In the distance, I see someone setting a mic up. It's probably stand-up comedy night. I look Julia in the eye and take a deep breath. "I don't know where to start, really. You know how I made this whole algorithm thing?"

Julia smiles. "Might have heard of it."

"Yeah, well, I thought I could match people up with the love of their life, and it pretty much failed in epic proportions. And you called me on my shit. Of course you did, because I tried determining matches for other people and it just didn't work. *I* had this whole theory of the kind of person I would fall in love with, and it didn't even account for the fact that I liked girls because I, well. Took a while to realize that I could like girls." I look up. "And that made me realize something else." My breath catches. My heart kicks up on instinct. But when my voice comes out, it's soft but steady. "I liked you, Julia. I had feelings for you. Have, still. And I didn't mean to ambush you with that at your—your *Valentine's Day* party, of all times. But it was just that moment that I realized, and then I'd wanted to tell you."

That was the moment I'd seen her at the party, laughing with another girl. Realizing that she might not feel the same. I swallow. "I just feel like I should be honest from here on out. I know you don't feel the same way, Julia. And that's okay."

It's almost painful to look at her. I do it anyway. Even wrapped up in a sweater, her hair in a loose bun, she's a wonder to perceive.

She meets my eyes. I hold steady. "But that's the thing," Julia says softly. "That's . . . not entirely true."

Something stirs in my chest.

"I . . . I don't know. I'm still figuring it out. It's complicated. And I wished I'd phrased what I said in a gentler way, or kinder.

But I . . ." She takes a long breath. "I don't know. We had a good thing going, Grace. Can't we just continue that?"

She wants to keep things as they were: she wants us to kiss on ski tournaments, to reach for each other in the space of a car, to visit each other's rooms with no strings attached. She wants to stay casual. I almost consider it.

"I don't think I can," I say quietly. "Not when there's feelings involved."

"And I can't do that," Julia says. She's not quite looking me in the eye now.

"Why not?" It all goes back to this, the one thing that hasn't changed since the Halloween party. Why can't she commit to someone?

"I can't do . . . relationships," she says. "I mean, that's part of the reason why I never filled out the survey in the first place. I can't commit to someone. I don't want to find love. Because with love there's always collateral damage."

She meets my eyes.

"You can't possibly believe that," I say slowly. "That's not always true."

"That's just how it's always been. My parents used to be in love, and now they can't stand the sight of each other in the same room. I was in love with—with Emily, and now we don't even talk. If you love someone, odds are it'll hurt you."

"I wouldn't do that," I say. "I wouldn't do what Emily did."

"You can't guarantee that."

"You're right. There's no guarantee." I shake my head. "But

that doesn't mean you just shut everything down."

"I'm not."

"But you are," I press. "What about the books you talk about all the time? What about all the love stories you read?"

"They always end up happy," Julia says. "And they stay happy. It's fiction. It's intentional. It's different."

I can't believe what she's saying. That all this time, she doesn't actually believe in love. "True love doesn't work like that," I say. "There isn't a hundred percent chance you end up happy, or stay happy, or that it all goes well. And if there's anything that I've learned, it's one of the least predictable things. But that doesn't mean you shouldn't pursue it at all. It's still worth it."

There is a pause. Julia's eyes widen, for a moment, and I see her expression soften.

And then something seems to shutter, and her features cool into a smirk. "Come on, genius," she says in mocking tone. "Spare me this lecture, okay?"

And it's like I've been struck in the chest. I open my mouth, but no words emerge.

She doesn't meet my eyes. I realize now that I see myself in her. What I used to be, anyway. Someone who has withdrawn into herself. Someone who's locked her emotions into a vault of her own making.

But I am no longer that person. I can't be. I'm smarting, and I feel raw, but at last it is all out there. At least the truth is laid between us and that is all I can give: my honesty.

In the distant background, I hear someone attempt a joke

at the mic, only to be met with feeble laughter. "Okay," I say finally, in surrender. "I understand." I get up, and my chair scrapes. I turn and walk away.

To top it off, I can confirm that I did, in fact, flunk my midterm.

I didn't have a good feeling about it—nothing good comes out of leaving three entire questions blank—but seeing the numbers and the red slashes throughout my exam is like an extra gut punch. I still can do enough mental math to calculate my raw score of 62/100. And judging by the way everyone reacts to their papers being handed back, I'm not the only one.

"Tell you what," the Group Theory professor says. "I'm setting up extra office hours this week. Come find me after class if you have any quick questions. And the standard deviation on the curve is going to be pretty generous, too."

So after class, I end up in line to see my professor. Behind my ex-boyfriend. And a third of the class, it seems.

I clutch my midterm to my chest. In front of me, Jamie stares at his paper, running his fingers through hair like he always does. I remembered when I found it endearing. When I thought that love was something that could be predetermined; that since we were right for each other we would eventually fall into it, somehow. He's still cute, I'll admit. But my heart doesn't flip for him like it did for Julia.

Like it still does.

I must have been staring a little too long, because he looks up from his exam paper. At me.

"You waiting to talk about the midterm?"

I nod. "Yeah. You?"

"Oh, yeah. It was ass."

I laugh. "Glad I'm not alone."

"We're hoping for that large standard deviation for the curve," he says.

"Double digits, hopefully."

We're talking again. It's easy, or easier than I remember. If I hadn't made my algorithm, could we have been friends? Or would our paths never have crossed?

"You know," he says, "I am surprised to see you here. I feel like fall semester I always thought you knew everything."

I shake my head. First semester seems like years ago. I thought I'd known everything, too. I was so certain of the algorithm. I thought I was on the brink of figuring everything out. "Turns out, I don't know shit. I'm just another college freshman who pretty much failed her midterm."

He smiles. "Join the club."

"Speaking of," I say. "I . . . just wanted to say that . . . I never meant to hurt you, Jamie. It wasn't ever . . . It was all real. I wanted it to work out."

He sighs. "I know. I didn't mean to sound so harsh about it." He shrugs. "I guess part of me knew it wasn't working, either. I'd just broken up with my girlfriend from high school at the time. I just . . . wanted to be in a relationship. I wanted something to work out. Guess I should have processed it first." He pauses. "My mom says hi, by the way."

And then we're both laughing, out of sheer relief. The person in front of Jamie leaves. He turns to talk to the professor, but not before holding up his test and giving me a playful grimace. I clutch my exam paper to my chest. I still feel raw from my conversation with Julia.

But Jamie and I will be okay, I think. At least there's that.

Julia and I barely talk at work on Tuesday. Roberta asks me if things are okay between us, and I nod. I go home and see the *New York Times* interview is set for this Friday, on the calendar that Caroline has shared with me and Danny. She hasn't unshared it with me; I see the faint orange square over 2 p.m.

It's near the end of February. Professor Rand has office hours, from ten to eleven. The application for the summer math research program is due in a week.

It's pretty much my last chance to ask for his recommendation. I used to be the last person to fall behind on things. It feels shitty of me, to scramble at the last second like this, in asking for a letter of recommendation from the math department head. For so long I'd been waiting for the Match-Up to work itself out, or stabilize, or for me to think of different iterations that could course-correct the algorithm. And then I just didn't want to think about it; I'd wanted to focus on ski team, or my library job, anything but my failed mathematical endeavors. I almost think about not applying.

But I need to at least try, I think. I wasn't planning on

applying for anything else this summer. I need to at least plead my case.

I trudge slowly to the math department building. Instead of going to the lecture halls, I take the creaky wooden stairs up, toward the second landing, where the faculty offices are.

Professor Rand's door is open. I knock on the frosty glass and peer around.

He looks up from where he's scrolling something on his computer. Our eyes meet. He stands, and he puts on his glasses. He adjusts his wispy hair. "Oh. Hi. Grace Tang, right? Please, sit."

I slide onto the woolen chair. "You remember me?"

He crosses his arms. "Well, I try to make an effort to remember all the faces in my class. And your project was very memorable." He pauses and smiles. "I still remember you and your groupmates talking about a three-month follow-up. It was all very impressive. How did it all turn out, by the way?"

My shoulders slump. A hard knot forms in my stomach. "We're . . . Well. We were working on one. It just might not happen anymore."

Professor Rand tilts his head. "Oh."

"I thought . . ." I stop and start again. "It was all going really well into winter break, but then everyone and their matches started falling apart. And I thought it was just a winter-break thing, but then it turned out that some people weren't really into their matches in the first place, and some other matches started falling out, and fighting, and I realized I—" My voice falters. I can't subject the math department head to my freshman-year sexuality crisis. It hasn't even been six months since I sat in his lecture and worked on the idea of the Match-Up, and already it seems like that version of myself is so far from me now. "It didn't work," I finally say. The back of my neck gets hot. "It didn't work, and it failed, and the matches fell apart in the long run."

There is a long silence. His expression is unreadable.

I clear my throat. "And I realize this is probably not the strongest way to ask you for a faculty recommendation to the Summer Leighton Undergraduate Research Program."

Professor Rand peers at me for a while through his glasses. And then he glances at something on his computer. "Are you aware that applications are due in a week?"

I nod. I try to swallow, but my mouth is dry. The heater rattles.

"And I usually advise my students to request recommendations at least three weeks in advance."

"I know," I say quietly. "I'm sorry. I should have done it sooner. I was going to. But the results of the algorithm were starting to fall apart, and I really thought I could turn this around. I don't know. I thought—maybe if I could adjust the weighting of the system or something, then I could look at releasing a new iteration of the algorithm. But I think one fundamental underlying assumption of the algorithm was that when individuals used it, their knowledge about their romantic and personal preferences would be perfect and complete." I shake my head. "And in a lot of cases, it wasn't. And I don't know if that can ever be . . . fully true." It's all spilling out of me, but I've started talking. I can't stop. "And I know that doesn't excuse me coming to request a recommendation at the last minute, but I just didn't want to come to you with a failed project. But I have. And I've been wanting to apply to this summer program all year because I've wanted to do math all my life, but I don't think I'm a very good mathematician. Or a student. So. Um. I understand if you don't have the time to write me one. Or if you don't want to, I guess. I would get it."

My former professor doesn't say anything.

I've really, absolutely fucked it, I think. Between my family life, my romantic life, and now my academics, I've officially completed the trifecta of fuckups.

"Thank you for your time," I say, in an almost whisper. I turn to get my coat.

"Did you think you were going to solve for true love, Grace?"

I shift back. "What?"

Professor Rand gives me a small, curious smile. "Would you have only considered it a success if you matched up everyone on campus for perpetuity? Because that would have been an impossible metric of success."

"Not . . . all," I say. "But I didn't expect pretty much every match to fall apart, either."

Professor Rand nods. "I thought the project itself was incredible when your team presented it, Grace. Not because of the end result, or the follow-up. So many students turned in papers and presentations that I could tell were based on Google searches for applications of the stable match algorithm. But your team didn't." He pushes up his sleeves and leans forward. "You chose to explore a really complex question and commit to it, regardless of how the endeavor would materially turn out. The individuals I admire most in my field aren't the ones who solve problems perfectly. They cultivate their curiosity and creativity and take risks. So, by that definition, Grace, you are a very promising mathematician. And the project was far from a failure."

My heart rises.

He leans back. "And I would, of course, be happy to write you a letter of recommendation."

I emerge from the math building, dazed, with a lightness in my chest. I can apply to the program. I'm getting a letter of rec.

I go back to my dorm room and check my phone. I still have the calendar hold for the *New York Times* interview. Something has eased; I think I just might finally be able to face this project again. I go to the form spreadsheet that lists the responses from the qualitative survey that Danny sent. I checked them once months ago. Where we'd once been getting responses about how happy people were to be set up with each other, we were now getting stories about people who thought they'd found their perfect match, only for it to fizzle out. Or to realize that they'd built someone up as such an ideal match in their head and then were disappointed in real life.

There's one new reply in the response spreadsheet. I click over to it and brace myself for another breakup story.

Hi, I'm Rachel O'Connor, and I'm a freshman. We talked at your holiday party. I just wanted to thank you and the Match-Up for putting together me and my girlfriend. I never would have met her otherwise—I'm an English major and she's mechanical engineering, but thanks to participating in this survey on a whim, we've been dating for four months so far and it's the best relationship I've been in.

I sit up. I suck in a breath, my laptop balanced on the fulcrum of my knee, and read on.

I don't know what the exact mechanism behind this algorithm is (read: me being an English major and having failed the Calc AB AP test in high school, lmao) but whatever was in that mathematical formula that conspired to bring us together, I just wanted to say that it has changed my life. ☺

Also—I should have totally submitted this story earlier, but I'd always forgotten to. My friend told me she knew you and that you would want to hear this story, so, here it is.

I finish reading the response. My heart is racing in my chest. I go to Instagram and look up Rachel's name.

Her profile is public. It's *her*, the girl who was talking to me at the holiday party. The girl with the dark hair and hazel eyes and freckles. She was matched up with someone. She's *still dating* her. The most recent picture is of her kissing her girlfriend's cheek against a backdrop of trees and snow. They're both laughing, grinning at the camera. And then there is a light, hopeful flutter. Maybe the algorithm wasn't right for *everyone*. But it was right for someone in the end.

Who was the friend? It must be Ruhi, I think. They're both English majors. But wouldn't Ruhi have told me about this in person? I scroll down a little bit. She's posted pictures with her friends.

And then I come across the picture from Halloween.

I see them all there, dressed up in costumes, posing around the futon. I recognize the girl with the tarot cards. Claudia and Tashie.

And sitting at the end, her arms wrapped around Rachel, is Julia.

I zoom in on the photo in disbelief.

I make myself a cup of mint green tea and pace around the room.

And then I dial a number on my phone.

"Hey, Caroline," I say. "Can we talk?"

TWENTY-EIGHT

I DRIVE TO ski team practice the next day.

"Where were you last week?" Zoe asks as she throws her arms around me. "Sean and I missed you last week. I even did one of those ski jump tricks."

"It was a pretty sick run," Sean adds.

"Oh, I was . . ." I pause. "Busy, I guess. Was going through a lot. Glad to be here."

"You going to the ski invitational this weekend?"

I shake my head. "Not this one. Maybe I'll race again at some point, but I just, I don't know. I like skiing with you guys."

And so I do. It feels good to cram into the lifts together with Zoe and Sean. Between runs, Zoe catches us up on every single detail of this recent K-drama that she's starting to watch, with all the plot twists and almost confessions. Sean and I listen along, rapt.

I catch the sight of Julia's blue helmet over the tops of the slopes. She's training with Nicole today, probably for the next tournament. It feels strangely surreal, that weeks ago we were carpooling to practice together. That we spent a whole day together, just us, on the slopes.

"Still pining?" Sean asks me softly when Zoe sends her first run down.

I turn to him. "What?" I see that he's followed my gaze. "You knew?"

"I think the whole ski team kind of did," he says. "We were really rooting for you two. At least, Zoe and I were."

I smile. Even my ski teammates could see what I hadn't. "Well, it didn't work out, really. But it's okay."

Sean nods. He starts to push off, but before he does, he turns back to look at me. "Who knows? Maybe there'll be a Match-Up next year, too."

I start laughing, to no one, really. After all this time, people still believe in the idea of the algorithm.

Maybe it really is that small hope, that anything, even a mathematical matching algorithm, can change your life.

I push off to join them. We do runs until the stars are out and our cheeks have frozen over, until we can't feel our toes anymore. I bundle up and start to head back to my car when I see Julia by it.

It is her, cradling her blue helmet in her arm. She looks beautiful in this lamplight, so pretty that it hurts, and yet I force myself to look up and meet her eyes.

"Hey," she says softly.

I pause. I lower my skis to the ground. "Hi."

She shifts her weight from foot to foot. I know after all these months that she does this when she's nervous, or anxious.

"My friend sent in something for the Match-Up," she says. "Did you get it?"

I nod. "Were you . . . the one who told her to submit it?"

She nods. "Yeah. I was."

I whisper, "Why?"

She looks up.

"I mean, I'm glad you did. I just don't know why you did it. You don't even believe in it."

"I thought it was a story that you should read," she says. "I thought you'd like it."

"I did," I say softly. "You're right. Thank you."

Snow is starting to fall now, small flakes illuminated by the lamplight. I open my car trunk and load my skis in. I turn to go, but then Julia says, "Wait."

I turn.

"There's something else I wanted to talk about. Between us."

"Julia," I say. "Things will be okay between us. Don't worry about it."

"No, that's not . . ." She pauses. "I wanted to tell you that you're right."

Snow flecks my cheeks. I stand very still.

"I think ever since . . . my ski accident, I've just been shutting things down. After what happened with my parents, and with Emily, there was just . . . so much anger and sadness and grief and guilt around that time. I didn't really allow myself to *feel* it while it was happening. Or feel anything, for that matter."

She lifts up her head, her eyes meeting mine. "You asked me about my happy ending once."

I nod. I remember it so clearly: us in the space of her car, music playing, the feeling that anything and everything could transpire in that space.

"I didn't really think much of the question at the time. I remember thinking how ridiculous it was, because, well, I guess I always thought that it was something that just happened in stories." She pauses. "But then I went to Rachel's birthday brunch the other day, and her girlfriend was there, and they just looked . . . I don't know. Like there wasn't anyone else at Ellen's. Like the happy ending I'd always read about."

She takes a deep breath.

"And as we were in the far corner, I looked over at the table near the window where we sat that one time, and I almost felt a shock. Like—" She paused. "Like there was some moment of déjà vu, like there was something big that happened there, like I'd known that place my whole life, like it was the beginning of something and it was the happiest I ever was at college." Her eyes met mine as her words tumble out. "And in that moment, I realized exactly how I felt about you."

I whisper, "Which is . . . ?"

"Of course I fucking like you, Grace. I've liked you all this time."

I stand very, very still, my heartbeat soaring in my chest, rushing into my ears.

She shakes her head. "And I'm an absolute fool for not telling you sooner. Or not telling you that day. Of course I want to be with you. And I don't want to be in my own head anymore, or be cautious to the point where I shut my own feelings down. In any instance it would be worth it with you."

She pauses.

I reach forward and pull her to me.

She kisses me back fiercely, her fingers threading through my hair. She drops her helmet to the ground and pulls me up until I'm on the tip of my boots and we stumble backward, against my car. Her nose is cold, but her lips are warm and so soft that I could just spend hours kissing her.

We finally break apart.

"Um," she says breathlessly, her eyes bright, a real, true, genuine smile on her cheeks. "What now?"

I take her hand and thread my fingers through hers.

"I know it's late, but if I asked you out on a breakfast diner date to Ellen's right now, would you say no?"

"Are you kidding me?" She raises her eyebrows gleefully. "I'd never say no. I'd have breakfast for dinner every day if I could."

"Well," I say. "I guess we'll have diner dates every day."

She pulls me into another kiss. "Grace Tang, you're about to be *so* sick of me and pancakes."

I laugh. "That's a hypothesis I'm willing to disprove."

* * *

"You don't have to keep coming home, you know," Ba says. "Your lǎo ba is doing fine."

"Who says I'm here to see you?" I grin and hold up a spoonful of vinegar-pickled cucumbers. "I just miss the food at home."

Ba *has* gotten much better at his cooking. Although the vinegar-pickled cucumbers were always his strength. I lean forward. "How's your work?"

"Teaching's all right," Ba says. "I think I'm making a trip to Indiana next month."

"Indiana?"

"I'm collaborating with a few researchers at Purdue. We're attempting to update the database of discovered and unknown tree species across the globe. To track the forest biodiversity." He pauses. "And I'm working on the preliminary stages of a grant proposal to look at the resilience and thermal responses of seeds in Australia. If we get funding, we might be able to do some field research."

"*Australia*," I say. "That's amazing, Ba."

"I think I want to start traveling more," he says. He glances at me. "If it's fine by you."

We are still learning to be on our own, both of us. "Of course," I say. "Go for it."

His expression lights up. His eyes crinkle behind the wire-rimmed glasses, and this is the Ba who I grew up with, the one who collected helicopter seeds and pointed out all kinds of tree species on road trips. He stands and starts stacking the dishes. He presents a bowl of grapes. "How is school, Xiǎoyàn?"

I pop in a grape. "It's okay," I say. "Classes are good. I just submitted my application for the summer research program." And the Group Theory professor ended up giving us a generous curve, which currently nets me, out of all miracles, at a shaky A minus. I still love math, I think, in spite of everything. The other day I went to go see a guest speaker lecture. Turns out, he'd won the Fields Medal a few years ago for analytic number theory, and I came away with a whole page of notes. Maybe I'll just stick with pure numbers this time instead of involving people.

Truth be told, though, it isn't like the algorithm was a complete failure. Maybe at the end of the day things like this are always meant to happen, numbers or not; people meet. Sometimes it works out. Sometimes, even if the odds are good, they might not fall in love. Sometimes, you meet someone who doesn't even believe in those odds, and they're the person whose kisses make you lightheaded and giddy with joy.

"What about everything else?"

I take a deep breath. "I actually wanted to talk about that," I say.

Ba looks up, alarmed. "Is everything all right?"

"Oh, yeah. It's great. I—" I fold my hands in my lap. "I have a girlfriend, Ba. I wanted you to know."

I watch carefully for his reaction. But his expression doesn't change. He simply raises an eyebrow, slightly, as if I'm telling him about the weather. "Oh?"

"Yeah. Her name is Julia Zhang. We work together at the

library and compete together on ski team. She's an incredible skier and an English major, and she wants to be an author some-day." I pause, and my voice catches. "And she makes me really happy. And I want you to meet her sometime. If you want, that is. Maybe she can come over for lunch."

"She's Chinese?" Ba asks.

"Yeah." I nod. I go to her Instagram and pull up a picture of her, with her friends. "Here's a picture of her."

He leans forward. He scrutinizes the picture for a long while. My heartbeat knocks in my chest. I don't know what questions he's going to ask. I've never introduced anyone to my dad before. I brace myself.

Finally he leans back. "How many dumplings, do you think?"

I pause. "Hmm?"

"When she comes over for lunch, how many dumplings do you think she'd want?" Ba asks. "I want to make enough."

And before I can help it, the room in front of me is suddenly blurry with tears.

TWENTY-NINE

The New York Times

AT A VERMONT COLLEGE, STUDENTS CALCULATE THE ODDS OF TRUE LOVE

The scene seems like it's out of a wintry rom-com; snow falls as students crowd into Leighton College's lodge-like Packer Cafe, colloquially referred to as Coffee House by Leighton students. The scene indoors is cozy; from the doorway you can see students lounging on couches writing last-minute essays, friends meeting up, and—yes—people going on dates.

The Match-Up, which was created in October of last year by freshman Grace Tang (18) and seniors Caroline Babson (22) and Danny Abrams (21), began out of a Game Theory and Market Design class, taught by economics professor Charlie Rand. The aim was to create an original market design. Peers designed systems such as matching students to tutors, or jobs to prospective hires. But this group, in particular, aimed for something more theoretical: love itself.

"Dating apps today present so many options that individuals are often overwhelmed. We wanted to propose the idea of an ideal match on campus," Ms. Babson says over the phone. "So we designed a thirty-question survey that asked people all sorts of questions. The questions ranged from their dating preferences to their values, their outlook on life, their opinions on social issues, and what makes a meaningful partner to them."

Overnight, this survey went viral, racking up thousands of responses. At the end of the week-long survey window, sixty-eight percent of Leighton College's student body had signed up to find their ideal match. Says Mr. Abrams, "The biggest success is that everyone on campus got really into it. I mean, if you're presented with the opportunity to find your ideal match on campus, or in your year, specifically, would you? And for most of campus, that answer was yes."

What came of this survey? Did it, indeed, find love?

"That's the interesting part," Ms. Tang says. "The short answer is that it didn't find everyone's perfect match. I mean, the initial goal was certainly to pair everyone up." The algorithm worked according to plan:

it sought each survey responder the most compatible match out of the available population. "The goal was that if you got matched with compatible values and preferences, it would make it more likely for you to fall in love. But as we discovered, there were a lot of unknowns and things that were not quite factored into the algorithm. People might not have accurate information about themselves, so that affects how they answer the questions. And of course, the biggest thing is that compatibility does not necessarily equate to love."

But at the end of the day, the students don't consider the project a failure. The project members agree that the Match-Up has sparked thought-provoking conversations about the factors and predictability of love itself. "It was a great hypothesis to test out," Ms. Babson says. "And there have been some great relationships that have come out of this whole thing."

She says this last part with a laugh. She is in part referencing the relationships that flourished between individuals who were matched up. But the Match-Up has had a wider impact on love beyond the matches.

In fact, Ms. Babson and Mr. Abrams, who were initially matched with other people, are now happily in a relationship.

"The Match-Up certainly works in its own mysterious ways," he adds.

"That's the wonderful thing," Ms. Tang says. "Will this match guarantee love? Probably not. But it will certainly help you meet new people. And the more people you meet, the more likely you are to fall in love. And at the end of the day, that still holds true."

"My own girlfriend in the *New York Times*, before me," Julia says, bundled in her ski gear, sipping on her coffee and grinning at the two newspapers on Ruhi's desk: one a printout of the *NYT* article, and one of the *Daily Leighton* feature of the *New York Times* article. "I'm upstaged yet again."

"Rightfully so," Ruhi says from the beanbag. "Grace is a genius."

"That she is," Julia says. She grins at me teasingly and pulls me in for a kiss. I lace my fingers through her long hair and cup her cheek, kissing her back. She says against my lips, "The article was brilliant. Please upstage me all the time."

"I've impressed a *Daily* person?" I feign shock and look at Ruhi.

"It's not hard to," Julia says. "Especially if it's you." She sets the article down. "All right. Let's go."

As we walk out of the dorm, we spot Ava and Bryce, walking our way. They wave to us. "Trivia night tonight at Coffee House?" Ava calls over.

"You know it," Julia says. After all this time, we did make the trivia team happen after all; the *Daily Leighton* team has generously absorbed me, Ava, and Bryce into their ranks.

"Where *are* you taking me, by the way?" I ask, following her down to the parking lot. "Ski practice doesn't start until three." It's twelve forty-five."

"It may be a date-related activity," Julia says. "But the location is a secret."

"We're showing up to the pancake diner in full ski gear?"

"It's not Ellen's," Julia says. "All right. No more questions. You'll figure it out soon enough."

I hop into the car as she starts the engine and fiddles with the radio. I notice, for once, that it's *clean*. And then I look in the back, where our skis poke through and—

"We're going *sledding*?"

Julia glances at me and raises an eyebrow. "You down?"

She grins at me, and my heart leaps. She could suggest anywhere and I would be down. I can just be in this car with her, in this moment, with the radio humming and the light filtering through the windows, and I'd be happy.

"Of course," I say, laughing.

Julia drives out of campus. The roads look familiar for a while, before she abruptly turns and pulls onto a one-lane road, into a forest clearing. A wide expanse of snow stretches up above us. I look over at the pristine hills, fresh with snow.

"So I've got two," Julia says, unlocking the trunk. She hands one sled to me.

I hold the sides and glance over. "We're racing, by the way."

"I'm game," she says. She pulls her hair back and smirks at me, and in that moment, my heart tumbles out of my chest all over again. "As if you think you could beat me."

"Oh, you're on."

We trudge to the top of the hill, pulling our sleds behind us. The new snow feels fresh and light, the cold air nipping at my cheeks. We settle on our sleds.

"On a count of three, two—"

I push off.

"Hey!"

I hurtle down the hill, and there it is again—the weightless feeling, my heart rising, the wind racing through my hair, impossibly fast and free. I let out a wild joyful whoop, and I hear Julia laughing behind me, and it's the best thing I've ever heard.

I try to slow down and coast to a stop at the bottom, but I swerve too much to the right and, before I know it, I've tumbled face-first into the snow.

When I come up, I still hear Julia laughing as she trudges over to me.

"You should have seen yourself," she says. "This is what you get for trying to get a head start."

"You got me," I say, trying to brush the snow off my face. "I probably look ridiculous."

Julia comes over and kneels in front of me, her face inches from mine. She pauses, and with her glove, she brushes snow off my cheeks. "Oh, yes, this is the look." She laughs. I try to blink the snow out of my eyes. She leans down, and her lips gently brush the corner of my eyelid, her breath warm against my forehead. "There. Snow's gone. There's that girl I love."

I become still.

Did she—

"You said—"

"I did," she says. Her eyes soften.

I love you, I think. I've carried around those words for so long. I don't know when it came first to me, but I do remember when I first realized it; one day I was just working at the library with her and I glanced over and suddenly my heart swelled and that was it, that was all it took to find the answer I'd been looking for all along. Every time I wanted to tell her I held back.

But this time, I reach up and press my lips to hers. "I love you, too," I whisper. "I've loved you all this time."

Julia kisses me back deeply. She presses forward, and before I know it, I've toppled backward, into fresh snow, bringing Julia with me.

"Hey!" she says.

"Now we're both covered in snow," I say. "We're even."

She laughs and reaches for another kiss.

"Go again?" she says.

I nod.

We stand and brush snow off our coats. We pull our sleds up to the top of the hill again. I haven't gone sledding in years. The last time I remember was when I was ten, with Ma, on her day off from work. I remember her pulling the blue disc up onto the hill, me following in her footsteps, bundled in three layers. I remember hurtling down, my mother cheering behind me. I remember her loud laugh more than anything, ringing out clear over the hills.

This time, I follow Julia up the hills. We set down our sleds, but Julia abandons hers and comes over to mine. "Care to make room?"

"Of course," I say, my cheeks warm. She settles in behind me and pulls me to her. I feel her behind me, her arms around me, her hair tickling my cheeks, the cold air in my lungs, my heart soaring.

"I love you," I say again, and the words feel true and certain to me.

"I love you, too, Grace."

"You're going to get tired of me saying it."

She presses a kiss to my cheek. And she whispers, her voice low, "That's impossible."

"Just you wait."

"I said what I said."

I smile and face forward. "Ready?"

I feel her nod behind me.

She pulls me to her and we push off, over the hill, and at long last, it feels like taking flight.

ACKNOWLEDGMENTS

To MY AGENT, Jess Regel—thank you for believing in this book from the very start, for your excitement and enthusiasm, and for always being the champion of my stories.

To my editor, Alexandra Cooper—I thank my lucky stars all the time that I get to work with you. You are a genius and your brilliant notes always manage to capture and nurture the heart of my books; this one became its best self because of you. To my wonderful team at Quill Tree Books: Allison Weintraub, Rosemary Brosnan, Kelly Haberstroh, Alexandra Rakaczki, Sarah Strowbridge, Allison Brown, Lisa Calcasola, Audrey Diestelkamp, Patty Rosati, Mimi Rankin, and Kerry Moynagh, thank you so much for continuing to make a home for my books, and for your tireless advocacy.

Thank you to my wonderful and inimitable cover design team: Laura Mock for design and David Curtis for art direction. To Christina Chung, thank you for creating the gorgeous, detailed cover art that makes me emotional every time I look at it.

To my immediate and extended family: my parents, my

rock-star brother, Justin, my cousins and relatives who have shown me so much care and support in my career and in general: thank you.

To Katia, Dave, and Paula: thank you for being my family as well, for crossing the country to show up for me, for sending articles through email, and for being so supportive and accepting.

And to more dear friends—I am here and writing this book because of you. To Racquel, for holding this story idea in cupped palms when I first pitched it over text, for holding my hand every step of the way, and for trading revelations and song recommendations. To Joelle, for witnessing the daily trials and tribulations of writing, and for being a deep source of support and humor. To my beloved DACU, my found family—Chloe, Racquel (again), Tashie, Zoe—I love you all so sincerely and would be nowhere without you. To Jake, for being the icon you are. To Camryn, for ten (!!) years of friendship. To Andi, always, for everything. I owe you so much. To my dearest writing/publishing friends who have been there for me and cheered this book on: Grace, Maeeda, Michael, Kamilah, Jen, Page, Kei, Squish, Aamna, Kalie, Syd, Layla, Fari, Lin. Thank you.

To Gaby, Eghosa, Cate—so much love for my Squirrels and our legendary 304 parties. To Katherine, for such dear friendship and for being the biggest Simbaverse advocate. To Lauren, for being your brilliant, funny self. To Becca for being the first to read every book and text me about it. To Rachel and Pranavi, for being such sources of joy. To Lexi, for the texts and the mutual cheerleading. To Therese, for the heartfelt chats. To Fiona, for making New York home. Endless thanks also go to Jess, Abbie, Gracie, Marina, Maeve, Adna, Jordan, Lily, Julian, Audrey, Anna.

To the ski/ski team subject matter experts: Daniela, Adrian, Sophia: thank you.

To the Stanford Marriage Pact, for being such a fun tradition in my college years, and to Liam, for so generously sharing insights with me: thank you.

Thank you to the *Punisher* album, which was formative in the drafting of this book. I will be playing "Graceland Too" on repeat.

To librarians and teachers and educators: thank you for the work that you do to bring stories to the world. To everyone who has read and supported and reviewed and expressed excitement over my books: I can always try to find the words but somehow it will never be enough. You have my endless gratitude.